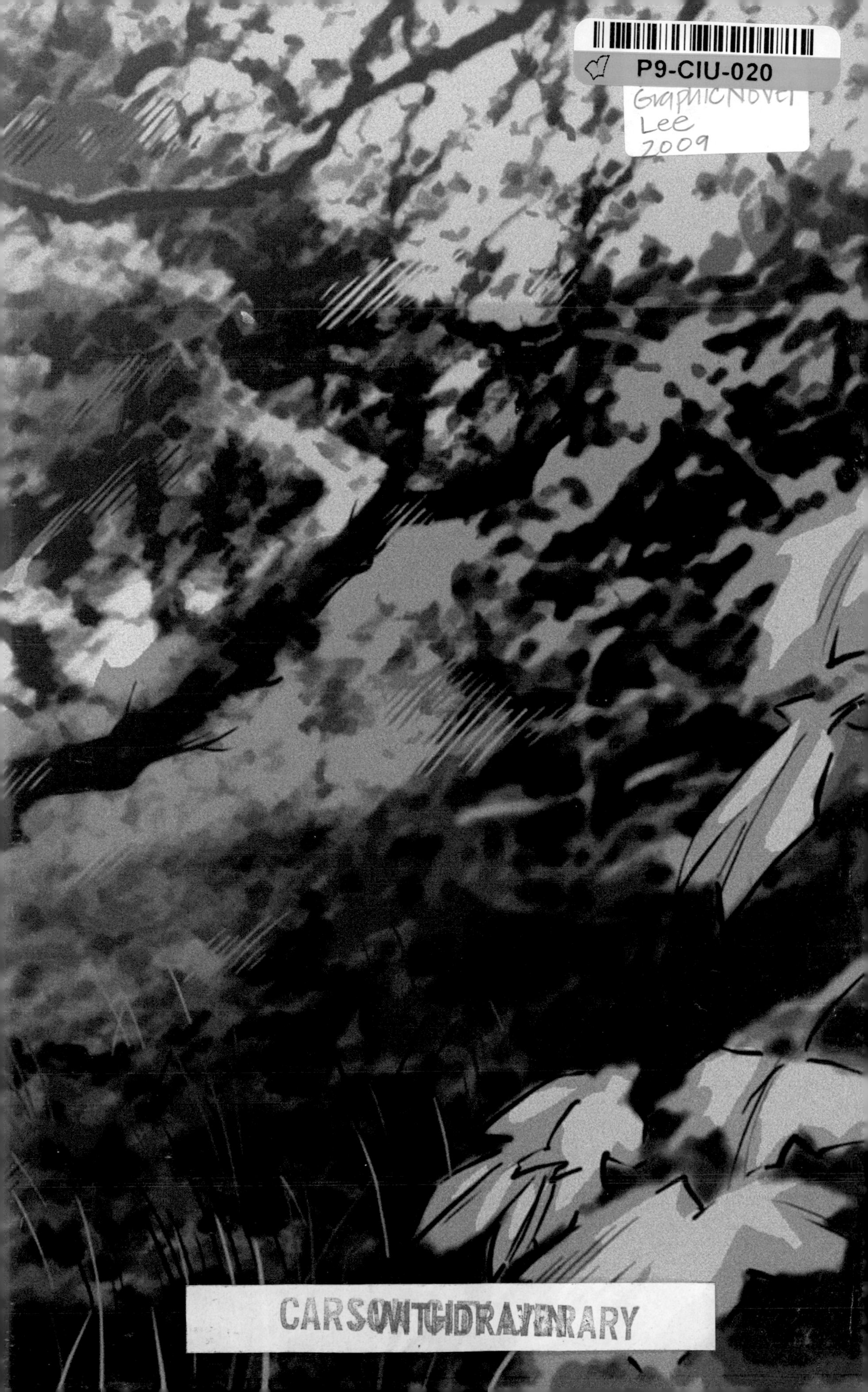

OUTLAW
THE LEGEND OF
ROBIN HOOD

OUTLAW
THE LEGEND OF
ROBIN HOOD
A GRAPHIC NOVEL

WRITTEN BY TONY LEE

ILLUSTRATED BY   COLORED BY
SAM HART   ARTUR FUJITA

CANDLEWICK PRESS

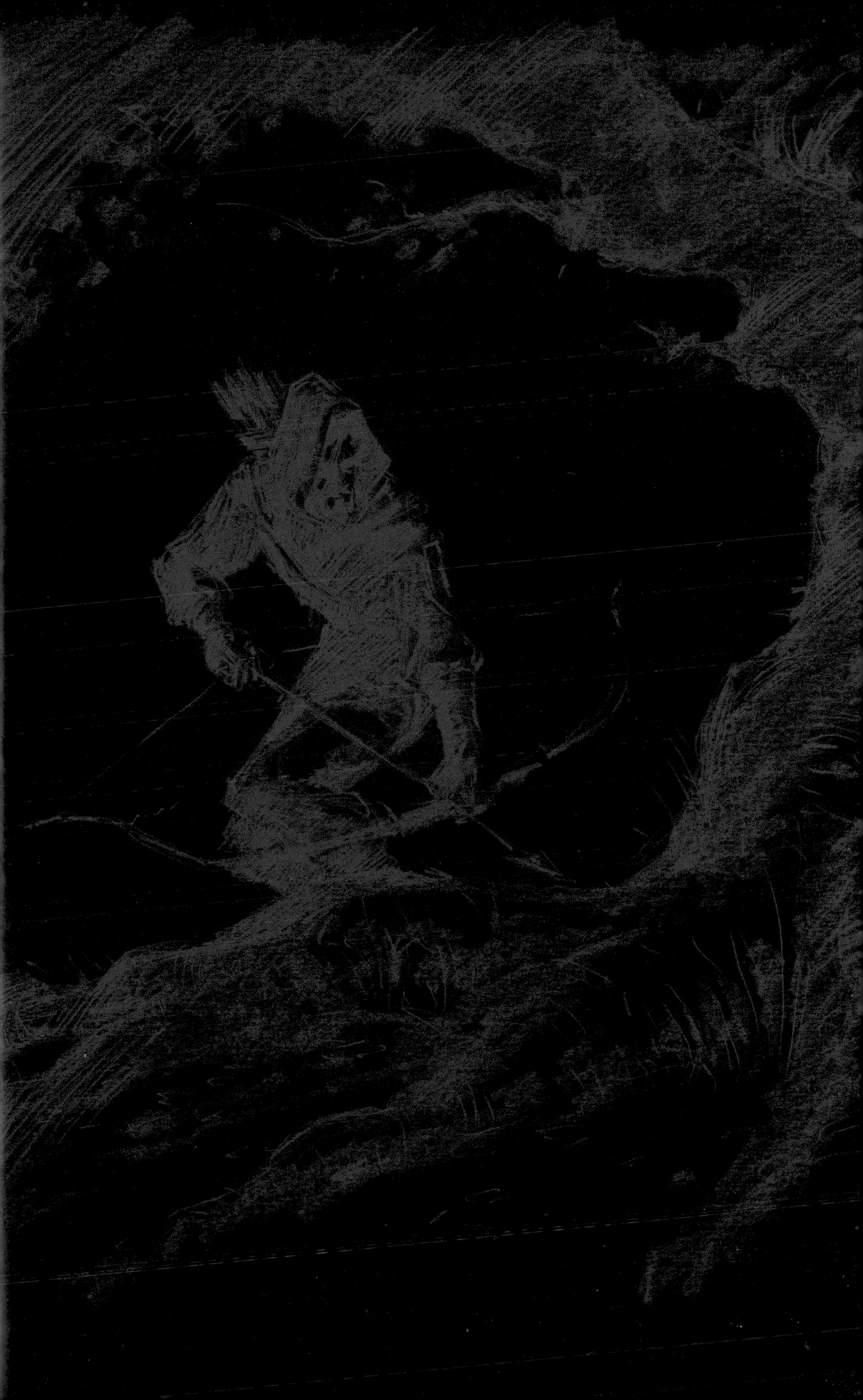

Wolfshead (Wulf's•hed)·(n)
Taken from the Latin phrase *Caput gerat lupinum,* meaning either "Let his be a wolf's head; let him wear the wolf's head" or "Treat him as you would a wild beast."

In Old English law, a person who was declared a wolfshead, more commonly known as an outlaw, could be hunted down and killed by anyone—just as if he were a wolf or wild animal.

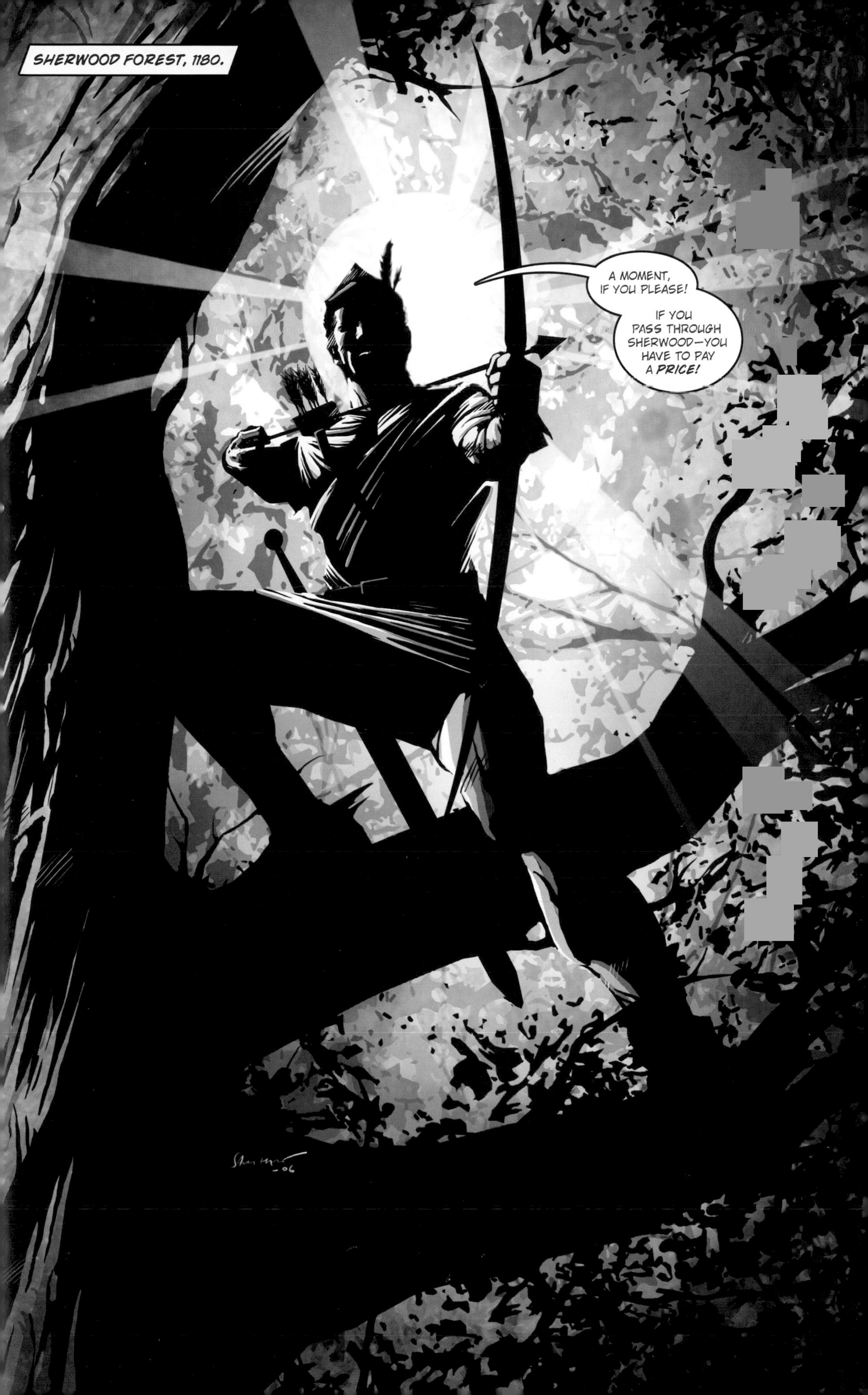
SHERWOOD FOREST, 1180.
A MOMENT, IF YOU PLEASE!
IF YOU PASS THROUGH SHERWOOD—YOU HAVE TO PAY A PRICE!

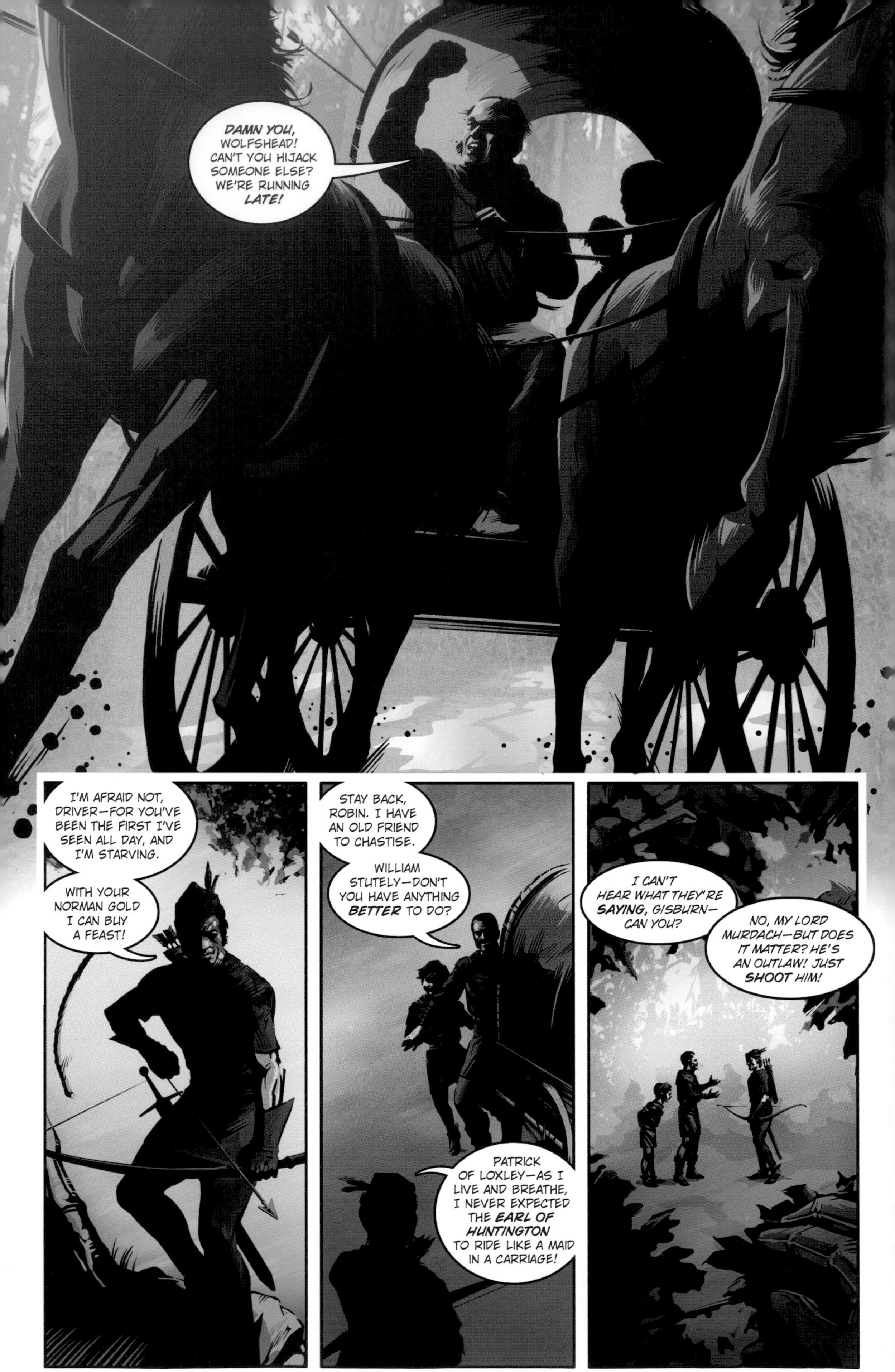
DAMN YOU, WOLFSHEAD! CAN'T YOU HIJACK SOMEONE ELSE? WE'RE RUNNING LATE!
I'M AFRAID NOT, DRIVER—FOR YOU'VE BEEN THE FIRST I'VE SEEN ALL DAY, AND I'M STARVING.
WITH YOUR NORMAN GOLD I CAN BUY A FEAST!
STAY BACK, ROBIN. I HAVE AN OLD FRIEND TO CHASTISE.
WILLIAM STUTELY—DON'T YOU HAVE ANYTHING BETTER TO DO?
PATRICK OF LOXLEY—AS I LIVE AND BREATHE, I NEVER EXPECTED THE EARL OF HUNTINGTON TO RIDE LIKE A MAID IN A CARRIAGE!
I CAN'T HEAR WHAT THEY'RE SAYING, GISBURN—CAN YOU?
NO, MY LORD MURDACH—BUT DOES IT MATTER? HE'S AN OUTLAW! JUST SHOOT HIM!

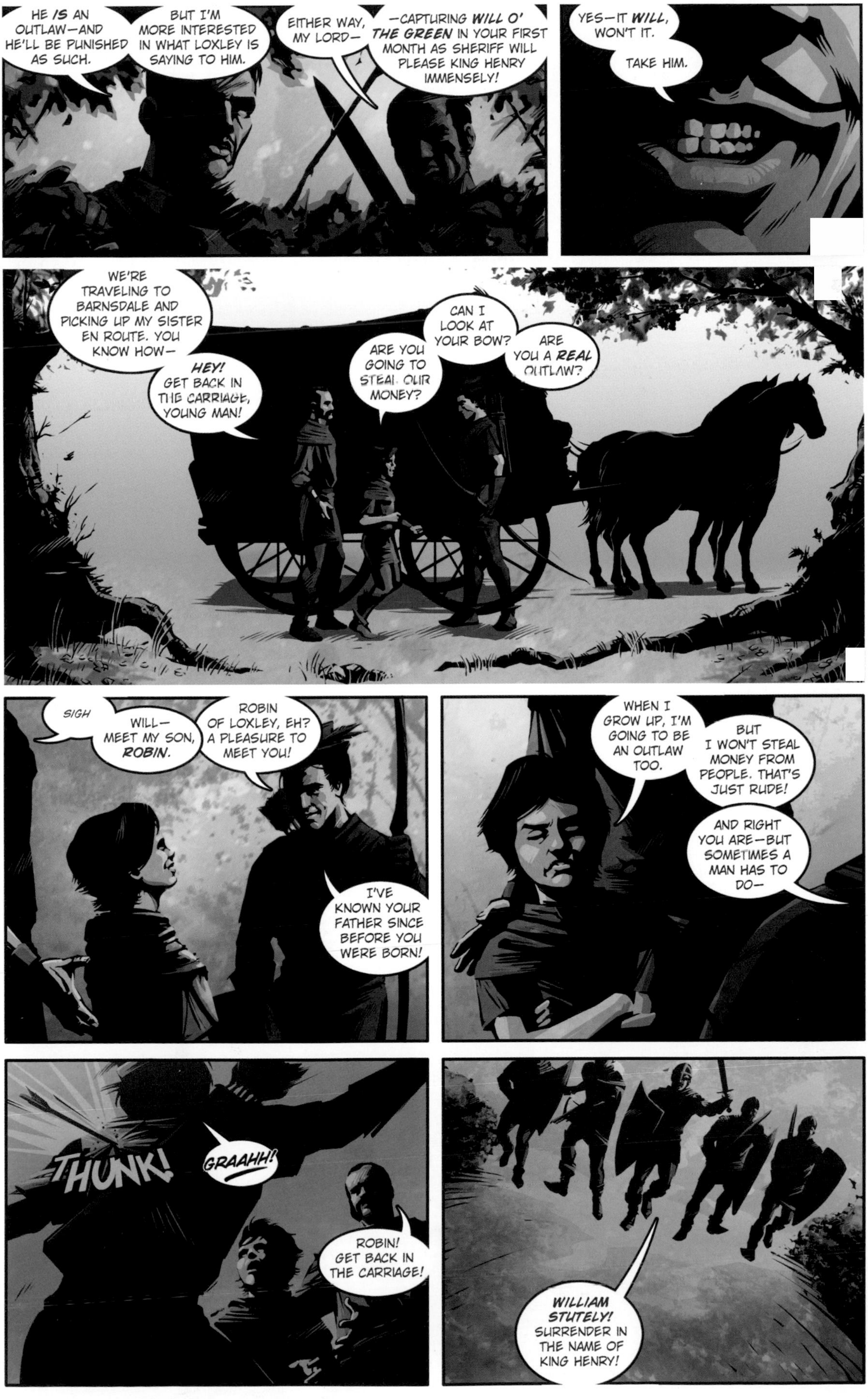
HE IS AN OUTLAW—AND HE'LL BE PUNISHED AS SUCH.
BUT I'M MORE INTERESTED IN WHAT LOXLEY IS SAYING TO HIM.
EITHER WAY, MY LORD—
—CAPTURING WILL O' THE GREEN IN YOUR FIRST MONTH AS SHERIFF WILL PLEASE KING HENRY IMMENSELY!
YES—IT WILL, WON'T IT.
TAKE HIM.
WE'RE TRAVELING TO BARNSDALE AND PICKING UP MY SISTER EN ROUTE. YOU KNOW HOW—
HEY! GET BACK IN THE CARRIAGE, YOUNG MAN!
ARE YOU GOING TO STEAL OUR MONEY?
CAN I LOOK AT YOUR BOW?
ARE YOU A REAL OUTLAW?
SIGH
WILL—MEET MY SON, ROBIN.
ROBIN OF LOXLEY, EH? A PLEASURE TO MEET YOU!
I'VE KNOWN YOUR FATHER SINCE BEFORE YOU WERE BORN!
WHEN I GROW UP, I'M GOING TO BE AN OUTLAW TOO.
BUT I WON'T STEAL MONEY FROM PEOPLE. THAT'S JUST RUDE!
AND RIGHT YOU ARE—BUT SOMETIMES A MAN HAS TO DO—
THUNK!
GRAAHH!
ROBIN! GET BACK IN THE CARRIAGE!
WILLIAM STUTELY! SURRENDER IN THE NAME OF KING HENRY!

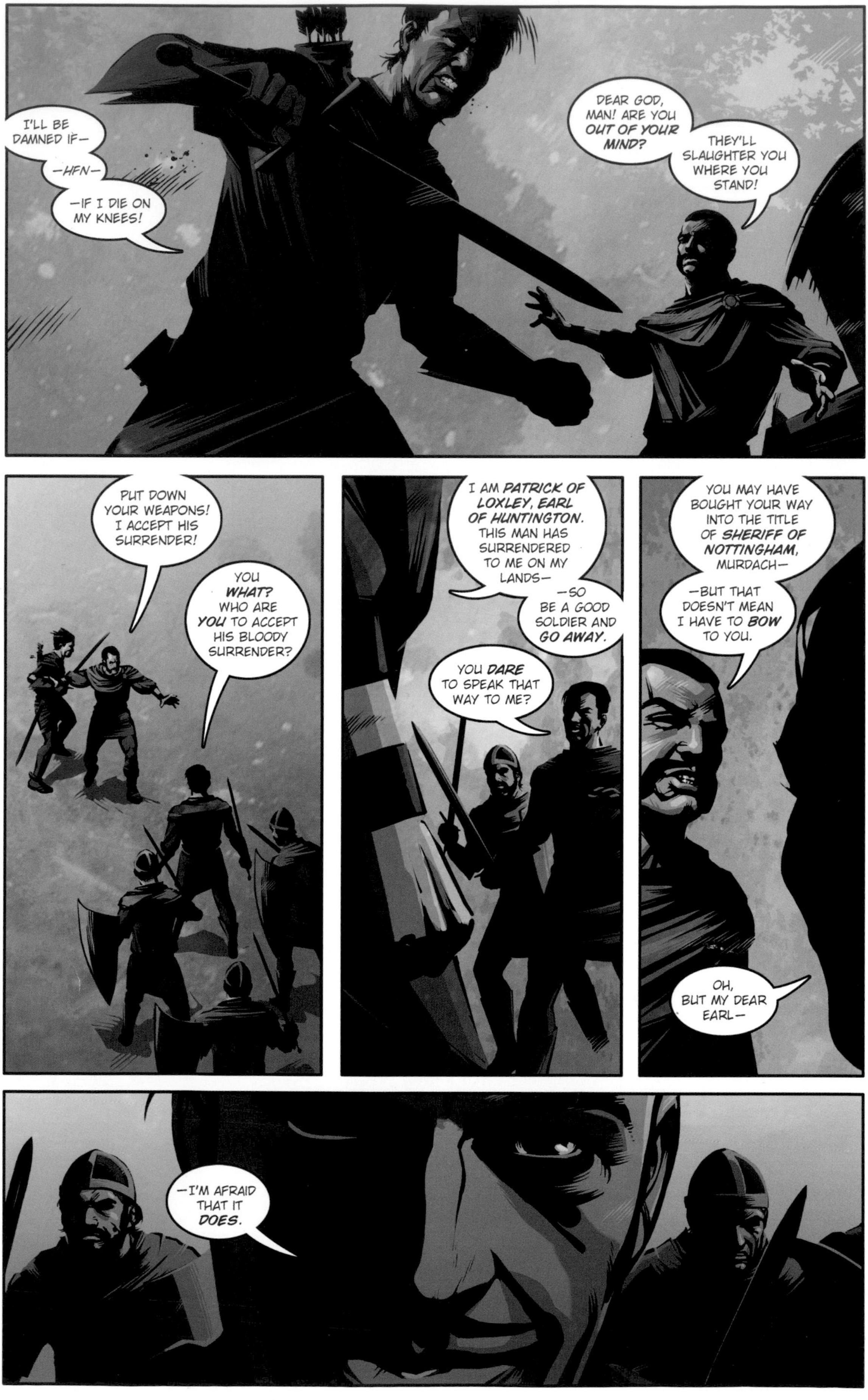
I'LL BE DAMNED IF—
—HFN—
—IF I DIE ON MY KNEES!
DEAR GOD, MAN! ARE YOU OUT OF YOUR MIND?
THEY'LL SLAUGHTER YOU WHERE YOU STAND!
PUT DOWN YOUR WEAPONS! I ACCEPT HIS SURRENDER!
YOU WHAT? WHO ARE YOU TO ACCEPT HIS BLOODY SURRENDER?
I AM PATRICK OF LOXLEY, EARL OF HUNTINGTON. THIS MAN HAS SURRENDERED TO ME ON MY LANDS—
—SO BE A GOOD SOLDIER AND GO AWAY.
YOU DARE TO SPEAK THAT WAY TO ME?
YOU MAY HAVE BOUGHT YOUR WAY INTO THE TITLE OF SHERIFF OF NOTTINGHAM, MURDACH—
—BUT THAT DOESN'T MEAN I HAVE TO BOW TO YOU.
OH, BUT MY DEAR EARL—
—I'M AFRAID THAT IT DOES.

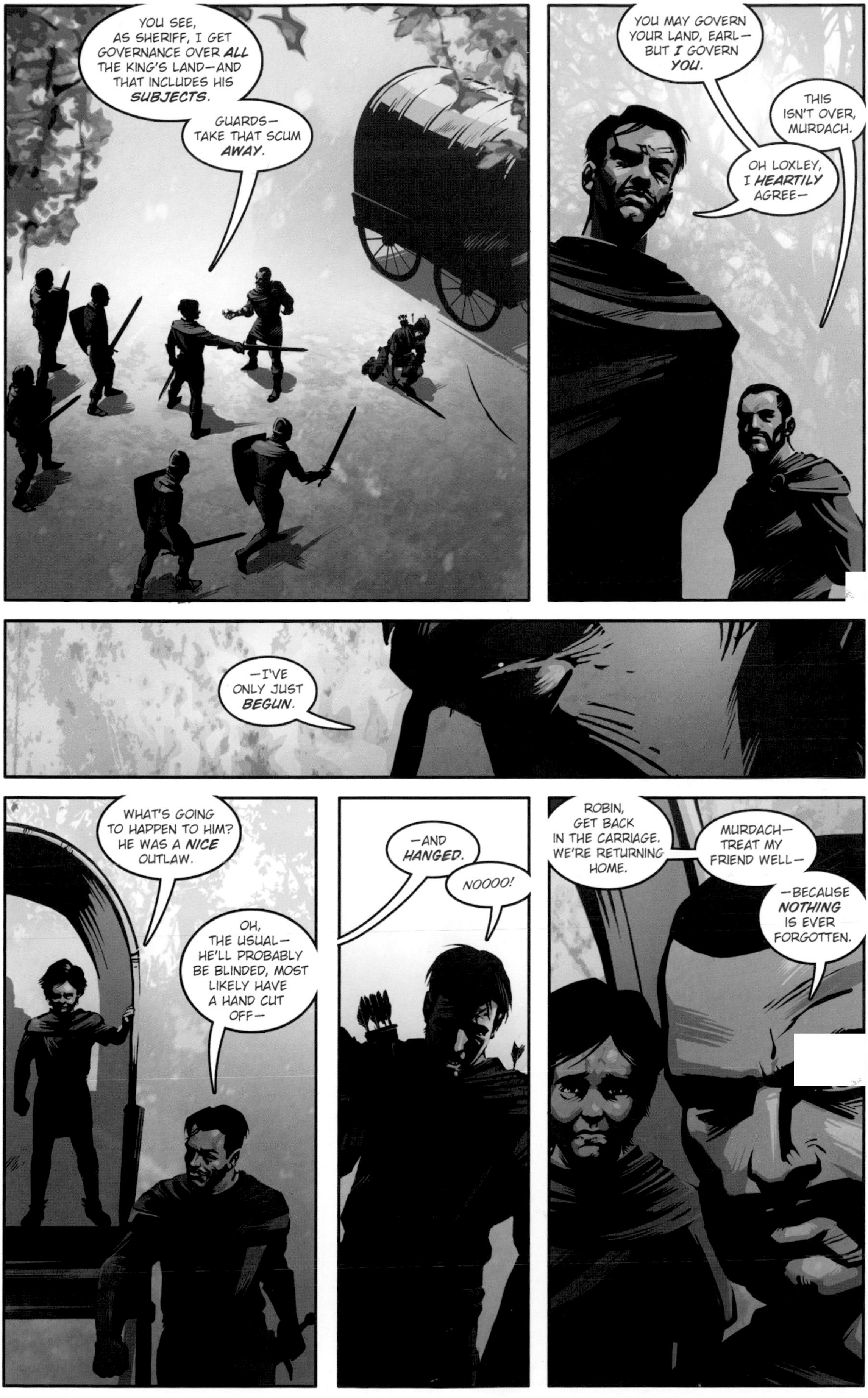
YOU SEE, AS SHERIFF, I GET GOVERNANCE OVER ALL THE KING'S LAND—AND THAT INCLUDES HIS SUBJECTS.
GUARDS— TAKE THAT SCUM AWAY.
YOU MAY GOVERN YOUR LAND, EARL— BUT I GOVERN YOU.
THIS ISN'T OVER, MURDACH.
OH LOXLEY, I HEARTILY AGREE—
—I'VE ONLY JUST BEGUN.
WHAT'S GOING TO HAPPEN TO HIM? HE WAS A NICE OUTLAW.
OH, THE USUAL— HE'LL PROBABLY BE BLINDED, MOST LIKELY HAVE A HAND CUT OFF—
—AND HANGED.
NOOOO!
ROBIN, GET BACK IN THE CARRIAGE. WE'RE RETURNING HOME.
MURDACH— TREAT MY FRIEND WELL—
—BECAUSE NOTHING IS EVER FORGOTTEN.

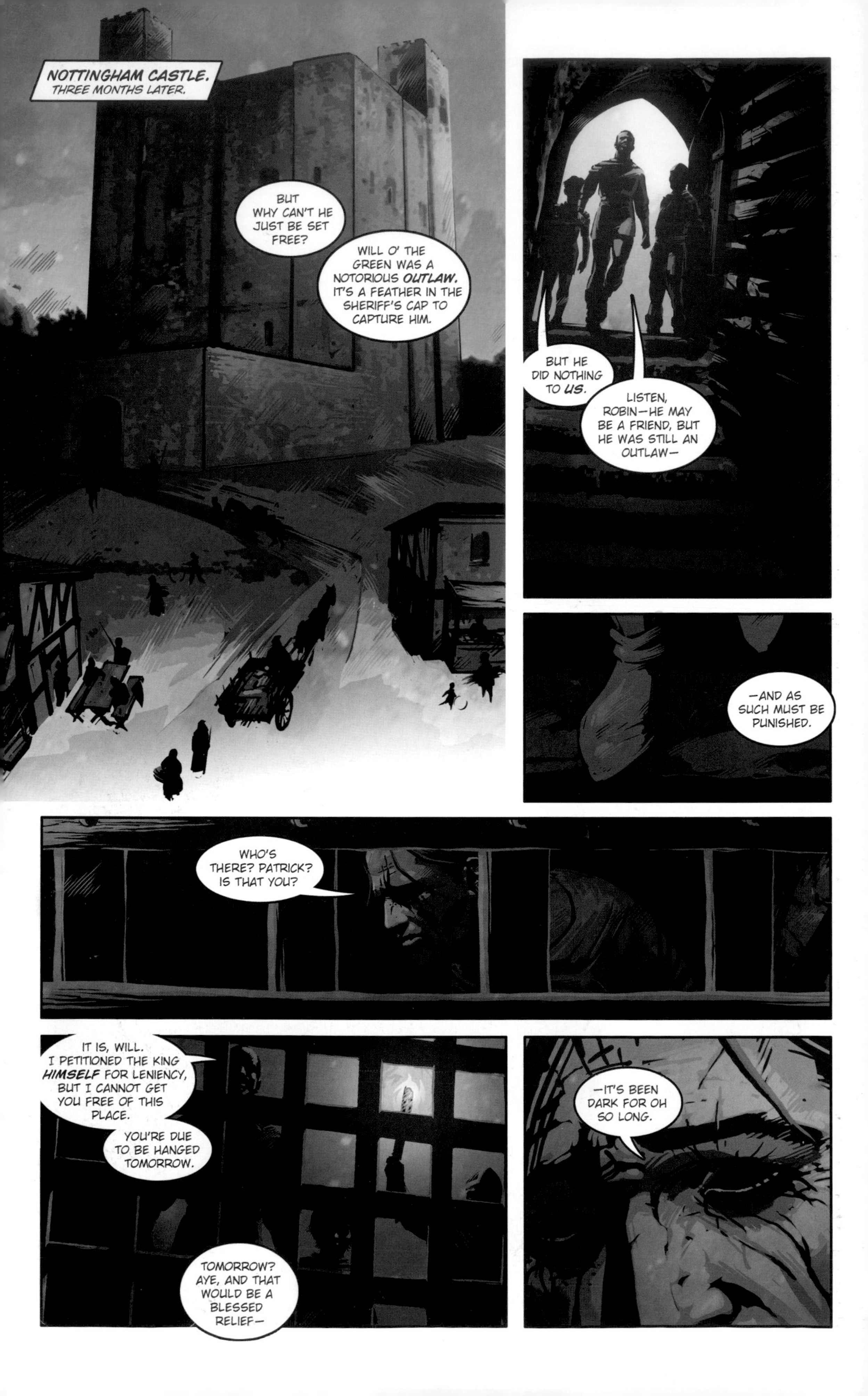
NOTTINGHAM CASTLE.
THREE MONTHS LATER.
BUT WHY CAN'T HE JUST BE SET FREE?
WILL O' THE GREEN WAS A NOTORIOUS OUTLAW. IT'S A FEATHER IN THE SHERIFF'S CAP TO CAPTURE HIM.
BUT HE DID NOTHING TO US.
LISTEN, ROBIN—HE MAY BE A FRIEND, BUT HE WAS STILL AN OUTLAW—
—AND AS SUCH MUST BE PUNISHED.
WHO'S THERE? PATRICK? IS THAT YOU?
IT IS, WILL. I PETITIONED THE KING HIMSELF FOR LENIENCY, BUT I CANNOT GET YOU FREE OF THIS PLACE.
YOU'RE DUE TO BE HANGED TOMORROW.
TOMORROW? AYE, AND THAT WOULD BE A BLESSED RELIEF—
—IT'S BEEN DARK FOR OH SO LONG.

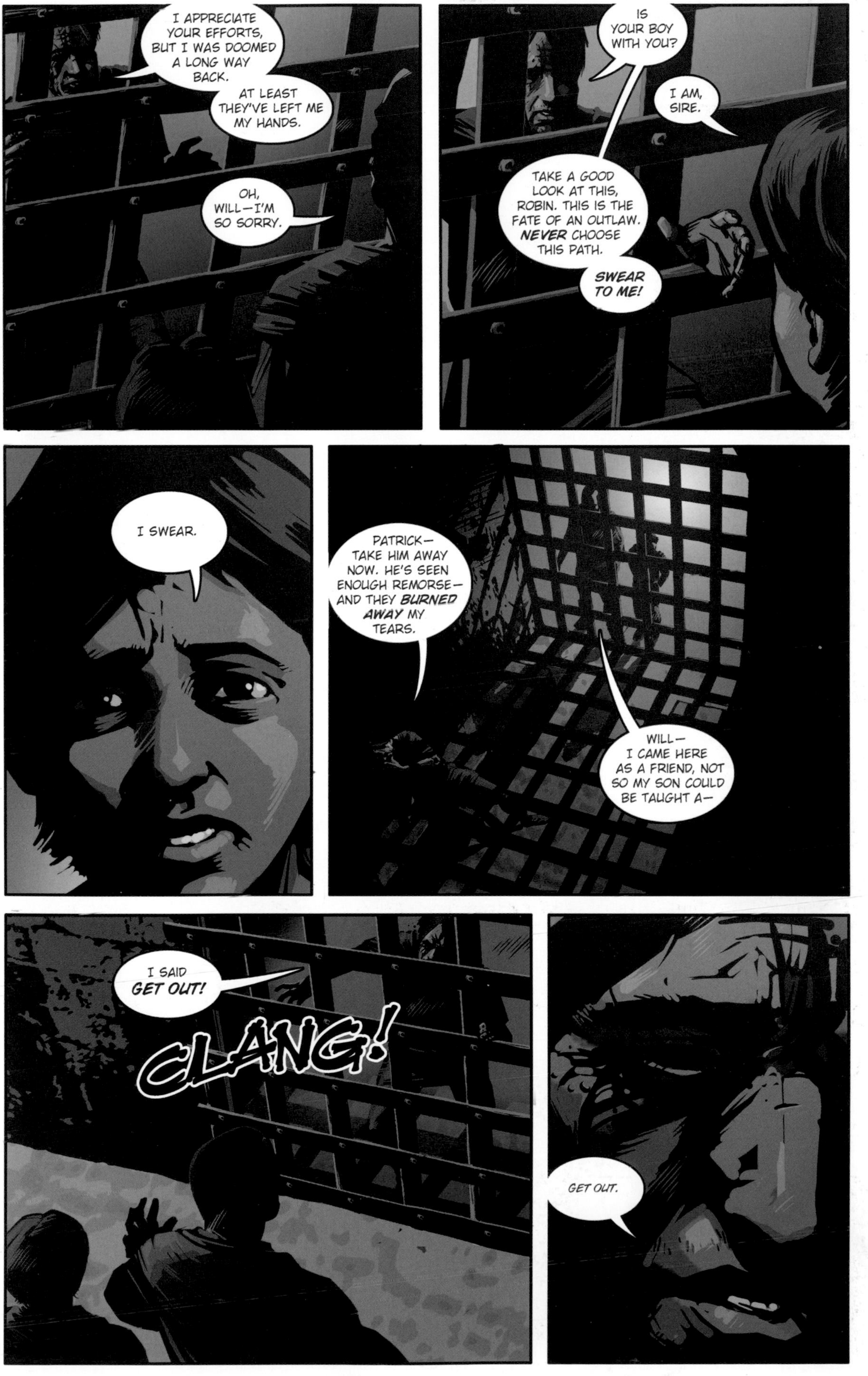
I APPRECIATE YOUR EFFORTS, BUT I WAS DOOMED A LONG WAY BACK.
AT LEAST THEY'VE LEFT ME MY HANDS.
OH, WILL—I'M SO SORRY.
IS YOUR BOY WITH YOU?
I AM, SIRE.
TAKE A GOOD LOOK AT THIS, ROBIN. THIS IS THE FATE OF AN OUTLAW. NEVER CHOOSE THIS PATH.
SWEAR TO ME!
I SWEAR.
PATRICK—TAKE HIM AWAY NOW. HE'S SEEN ENOUGH REMORSE—AND THEY BURNED AWAY MY TEARS.
WILL—I CAME HERE AS A FRIEND, NOT SO MY SON COULD BE TAUGHT A—
I SAID GET OUT!
CLANG!
GET OUT.

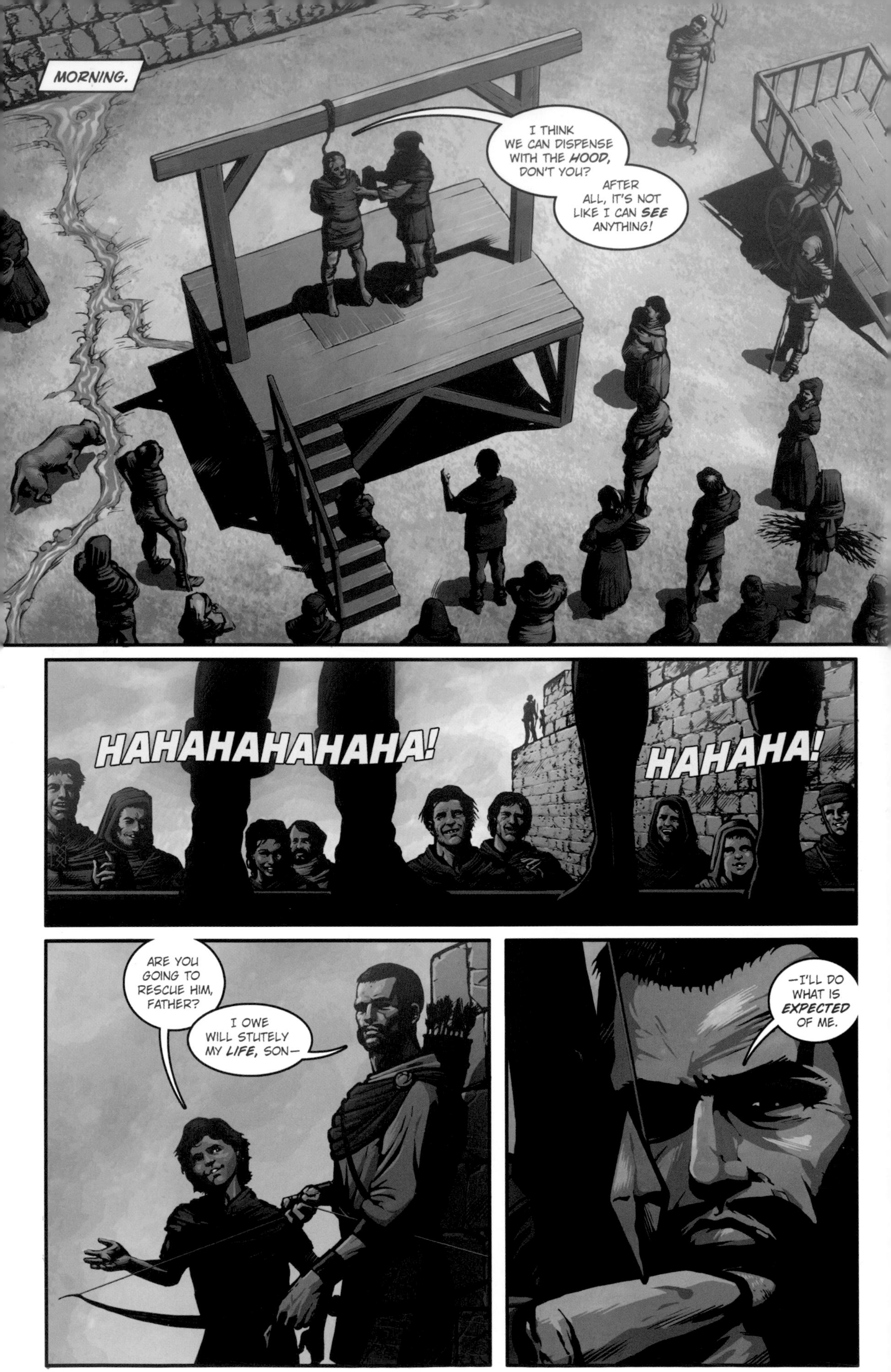

MORNING.
I THINK WE CAN DISPENSE WITH THE HOOD, DON'T YOU?
AFTER ALL, IT'S NOT LIKE I CAN SEE ANYTHING!
HAHAHAHAHAHAHA!
HAHAHA!
ARE YOU GOING TO RESCUE HIM, FATHER?
I OWE WILL STUTELY MY LIFE, SON—
—I'LL DO WHAT IS EXPECTED OF ME.

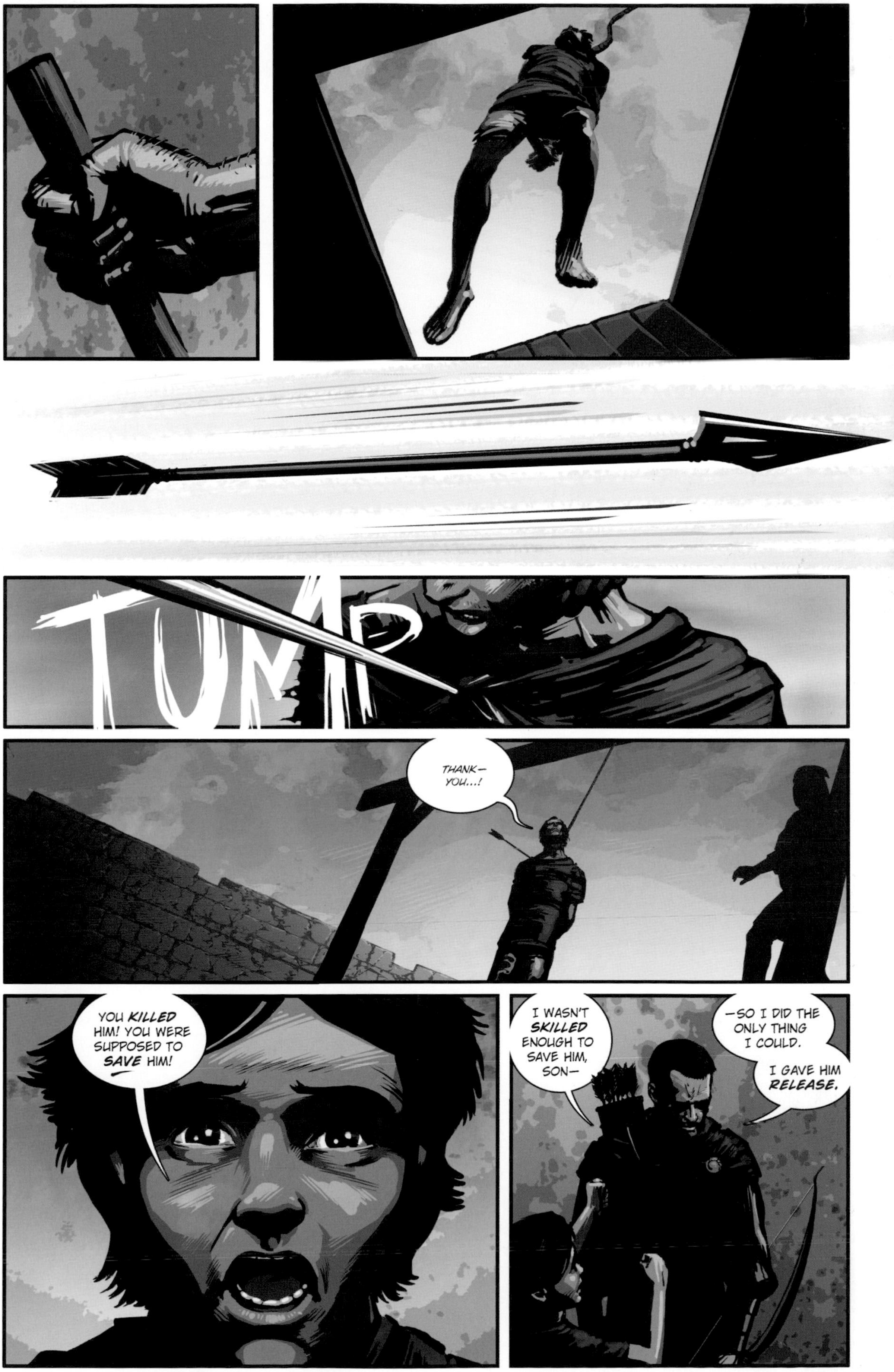
TUMP
THANK— YOU...!
YOU KILLED HIM! YOU WERE SUPPOSED TO SAVE HIM!
I WASN'T SKILLED ENOUGH TO SAVE HIM, SON—
—SO I DID THE ONLY THING I COULD.
I GAVE HIM RELEASE.

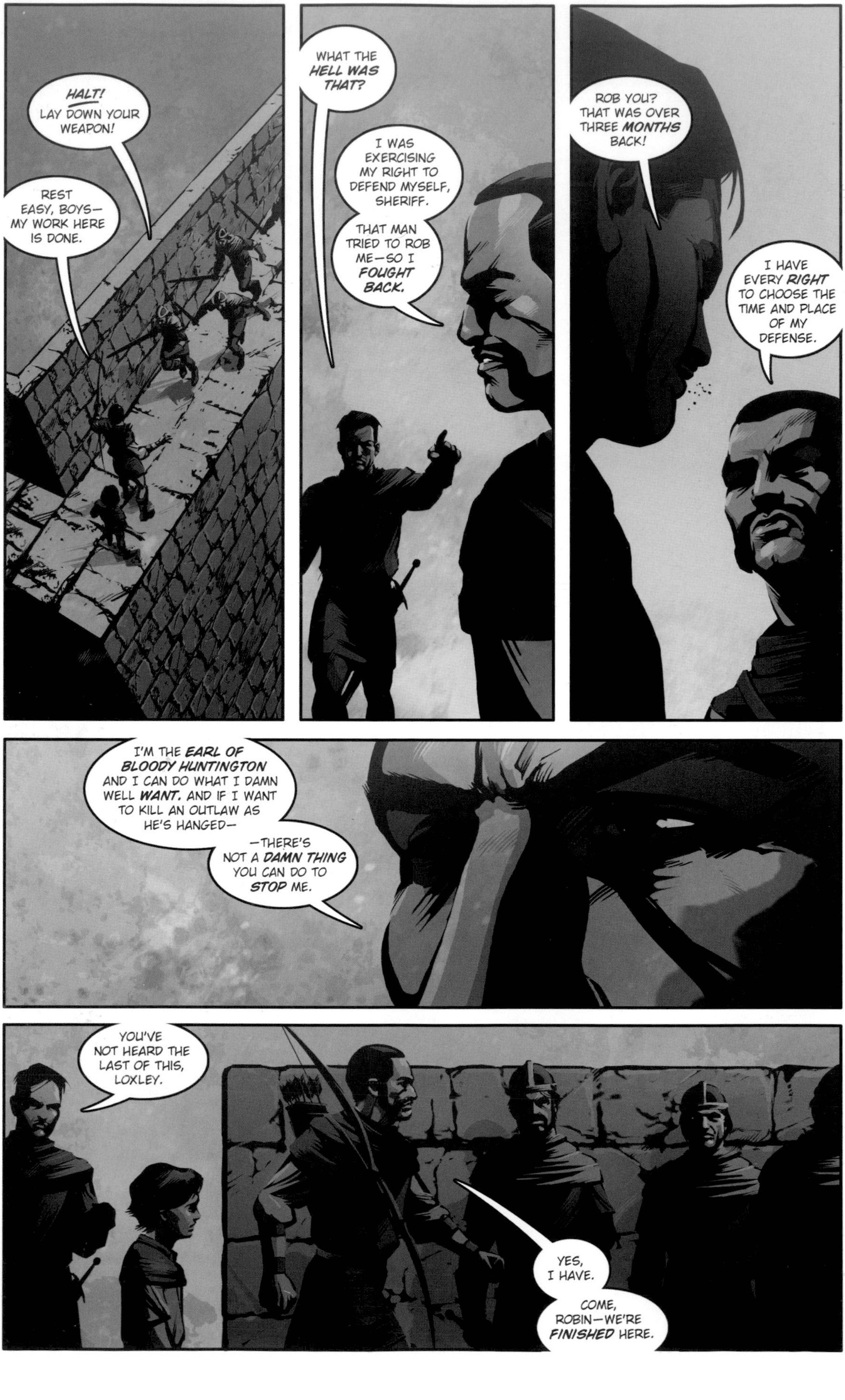
HALT! LAY DOWN YOUR WEAPON!
REST EASY, BOYS— MY WORK HERE IS DONE.
WHAT THE HELL WAS THAT?
I WAS EXERCISING MY RIGHT TO DEFEND MYSELF, SHERIFF.
THAT MAN TRIED TO ROB ME—SO I FOUGHT BACK.
ROB YOU? THAT WAS OVER THREE MONTHS BACK!
I HAVE EVERY RIGHT TO CHOOSE THE TIME AND PLACE OF MY DEFENSE.
I'M THE EARL OF BLOODY HUNTINGTON AND I CAN DO WHAT I DAMN WELL WANT. AND IF I WANT TO KILL AN OUTLAW AS HE'S HANGED—
—THERE'S NOT A DAMN THING YOU CAN DO TO STOP ME.
YOU'VE NOT HEARD THE LAST OF THIS, LOXLEY.
YES, I HAVE.
COME, ROBIN—WE'RE FINISHED HERE.

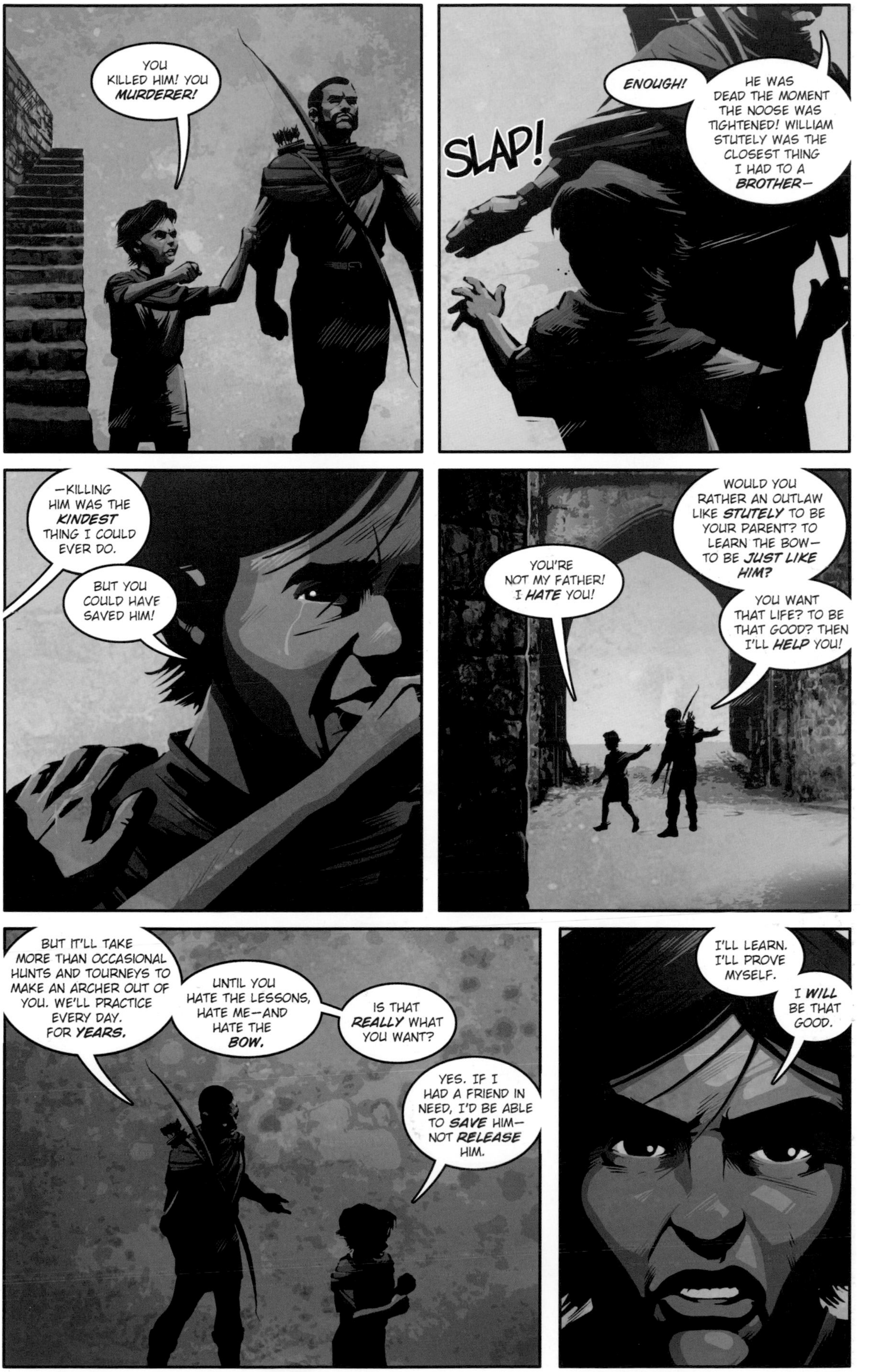

YOU KILLED HIM! YOU MURDERER!
SLAP!
ENOUGH!
HE WAS DEAD THE MOMENT THE NOOSE WAS TIGHTENED! WILLIAM STUTELY WAS THE CLOSEST THING I HAD TO A BROTHER—
—KILLING HIM WAS THE KINDEST THING I COULD EVER DO.
BUT YOU COULD HAVE SAVED HIM!
YOU'RE NOT MY FATHER! I HATE YOU!
WOULD YOU RATHER AN OUTLAW LIKE STUTELY TO BE YOUR PARENT? TO LEARN THE BOW— TO BE JUST LIKE HIM?
YOU WANT THAT LIFE? TO BE THAT GOOD? THEN I'LL HELP YOU!
BUT IT'LL TAKE MORE THAN OCCASIONAL HUNTS AND TOURNEYS TO MAKE AN ARCHER OUT OF YOU. WE'LL PRACTICE EVERY DAY. FOR YEARS.
UNTIL YOU HATE THE LESSONS, HATE ME—AND HATE THE BOW.
IS THAT REALLY WHAT YOU WANT?
YES. IF I HAD A FRIEND IN NEED, I'D BE ABLE TO SAVE HIM— NOT RELEASE HIM.
I'LL LEARN. I'LL PROVE MYSELF.
I WILL BE THAT GOOD.

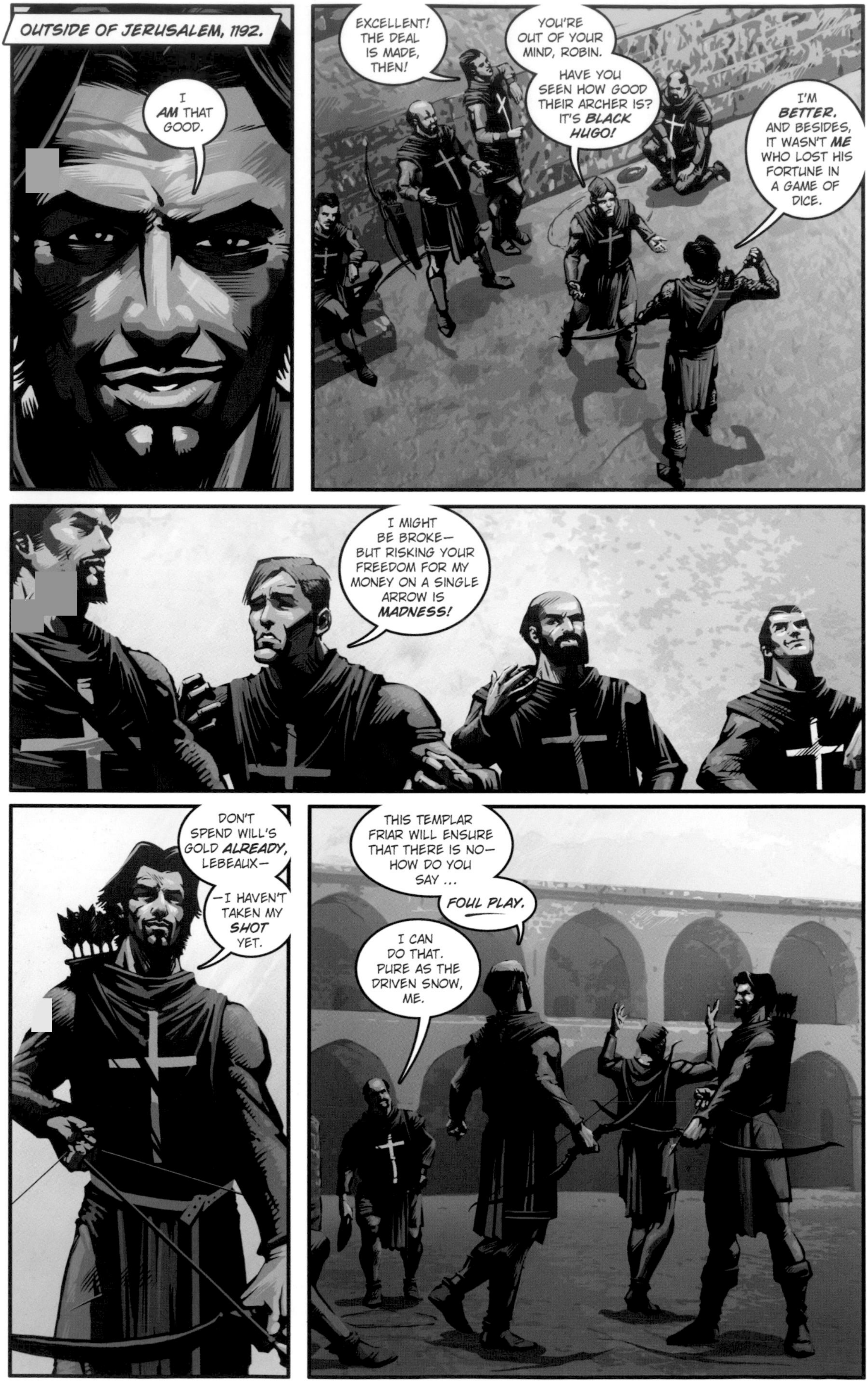
OUTSIDE OF JERUSALEM, 1192.
I AM THAT GOOD.
EXCELLENT! THE DEAL IS MADE, THEN!
YOU'RE OUT OF YOUR MIND, ROBIN.
HAVE YOU SEEN HOW GOOD THEIR ARCHER IS? IT'S BLACK HUGO!
I'M BETTER. AND BESIDES, IT WASN'T ME WHO LOST HIS FORTUNE IN A GAME OF DICE.
I MIGHT BE BROKE— BUT RISKING YOUR FREEDOM FOR MY MONEY ON A SINGLE ARROW IS MADNESS!
DON'T SPEND WILL'S GOLD ALREADY, LEBEAUX—
—I HAVEN'T TAKEN MY SHOT YET.
THIS TEMPLAR FRIAR WILL ENSURE THAT THERE IS NO— HOW DO YOU SAY ...
FOUL PLAY.
I CAN DO THAT. PURE AS THE DRIVEN SNOW, ME.

YOU WILL EACH WALK TEN PACES, AT WHICH POINT THIS WOODEN PLATE WILL BE THROWN INTO THE AIR. YOU THEN AIM AND FIRE.

THE CLOSEST ARROW TO THE *CENTER* WINS.

BEGIN!

DON'T ACCIDENTALLY SHOOT YOUR *FOOT* OR ANYTHING, HUGO.

WHOOSH

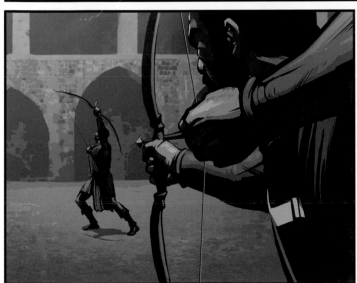

ROBIN!

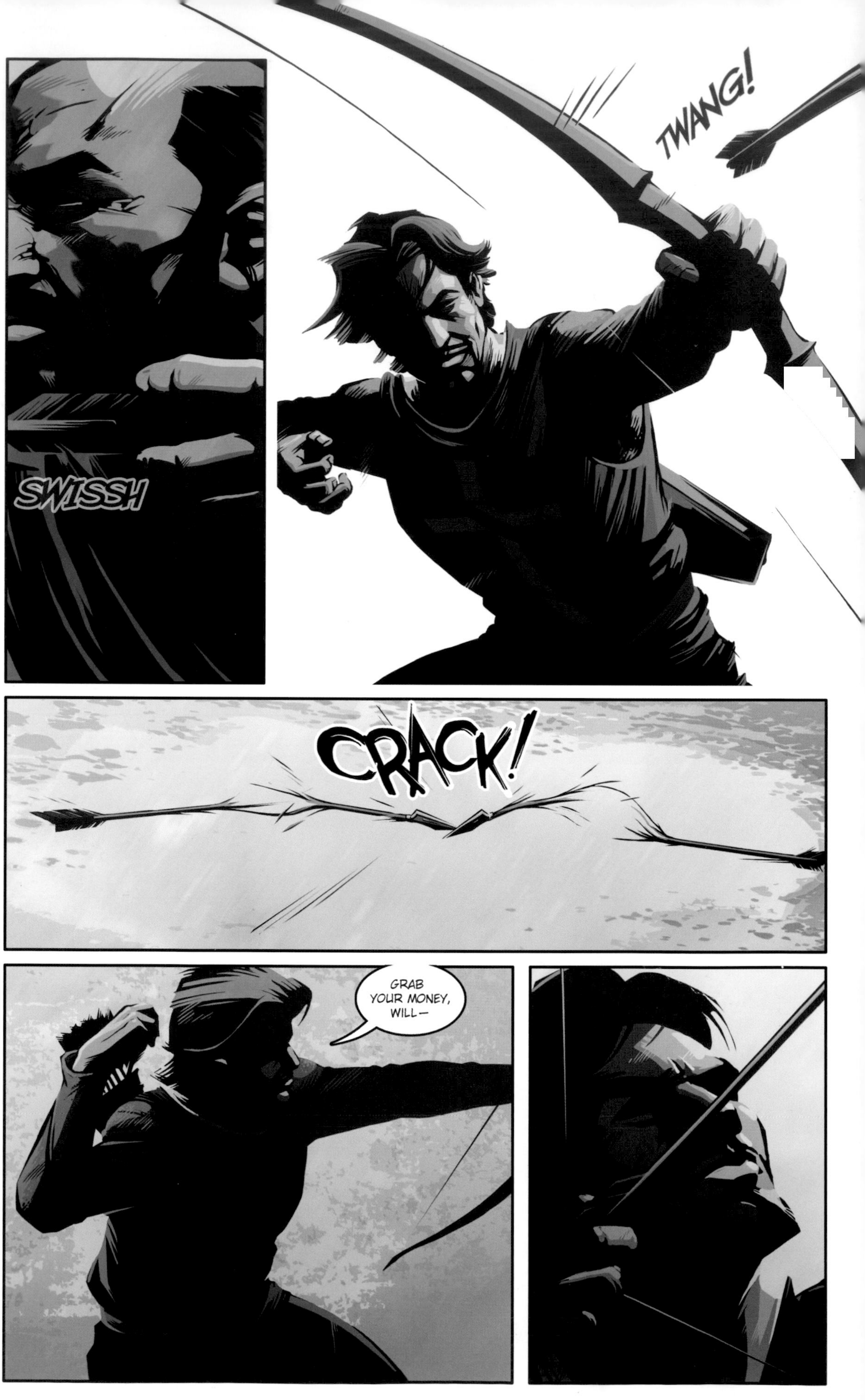
SWISSH
TWANG!
CRACK!
GRAB YOUR MONEY, WILL—

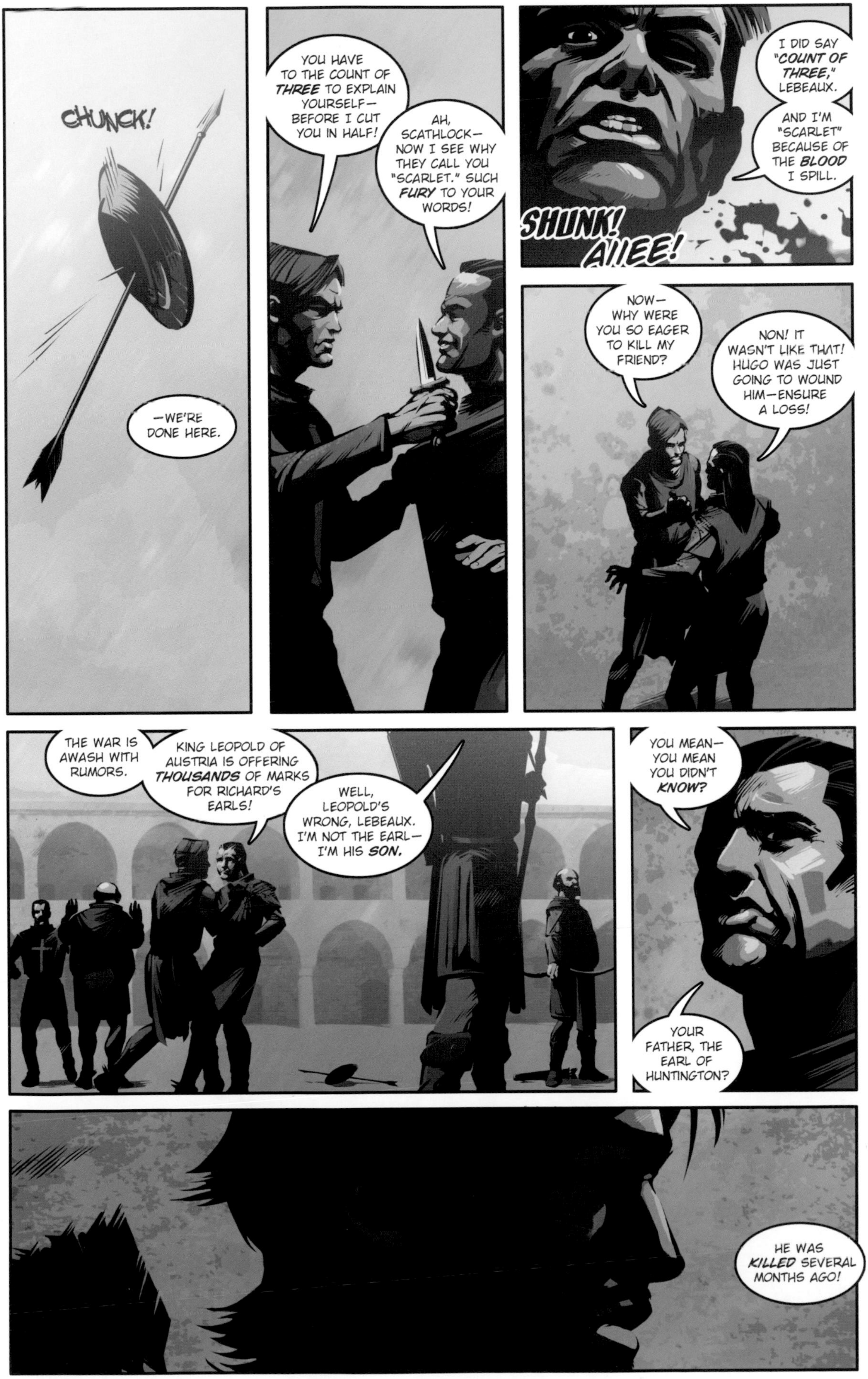
CHUNCK!
—WE'RE DONE HERE.
YOU HAVE TO THE COUNT OF *THREE* TO EXPLAIN YOURSELF— BEFORE I CUT YOU IN HALF!
AH, SCATHLOCK— NOW I SEE WHY THEY CALL YOU "SCARLET." SUCH *FURY* TO YOUR WORDS!
I DID SAY *"COUNT OF THREE,"* LEBEAUX.
AND I'M "SCARLET" BECAUSE OF THE *BLOOD* I SPILL.
SHUNK! AIIEE!
NOW— WHY WERE YOU SO EAGER TO KILL MY FRIEND?
NON! IT WASN'T LIKE THAT! HUGO WAS JUST GOING TO WOUND HIM—ENSURE A LOSS!
THE WAR IS AWASH WITH RUMORS.
KING LEOPOLD OF AUSTRIA IS OFFERING *THOUSANDS* OF MARKS FOR RICHARD'S EARLS!
WELL, LEOPOLD'S WRONG, LEBEAUX. I'M NOT THE EARL— I'M HIS *SON.*
YOU MEAN— YOU MEAN YOU DIDN'T *KNOW?*
YOUR FATHER, THE EARL OF HUNTINGTON?
HE WAS *KILLED* SEVERAL MONTHS AGO!

EVER SINCE RICHARD THREW DOWN THAT GERMAN BANNER AT *ACRE*, LEOPOLD'S WANTED REVENGE.

IT'S TRUE ABOUT YOUR FATHER, YOU KNOW. I HAVE A FRIEND IN THE NUNNERY AT KIRKLEES ABBEY.

EVERY NOW AND THEN SHE SENDS ME NEWS— YOUR FATHER'S *MURDER* WAS MENTIONED.

DID THEY SAY WHO DID IT?

NO. HE WAS OUT HAWKING WITH *JOHN OF LYE* ABOUT FIVE, SIX MONTHS BACK—THEIR BODIES WERE FOUND BY A PASSING MERCHANT.

PROBABLY THE WORK OF *BANDITS*.

ROBIN— I'M SORRY...

I NEED TO GET BACK HOME. DO WE KNOW ANYONE RETURNING TO ENGLAND?

THERE'S GATLAND. HE WAS TALKING ABOUT LEAVING THIS WEEK.

GODS, MAN— DO YOU NOT AT LEAST WANT TO *TALK* ABOUT THIS? HE WAS YOUR FATHER!

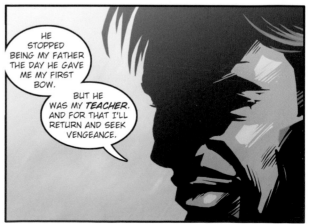

HE STOPPED BEING MY FATHER THE DAY HE GAVE ME MY FIRST BOW.

BUT HE WAS MY *TEACHER*. AND FOR THAT I'LL RETURN AND SEEK VENGEANCE.

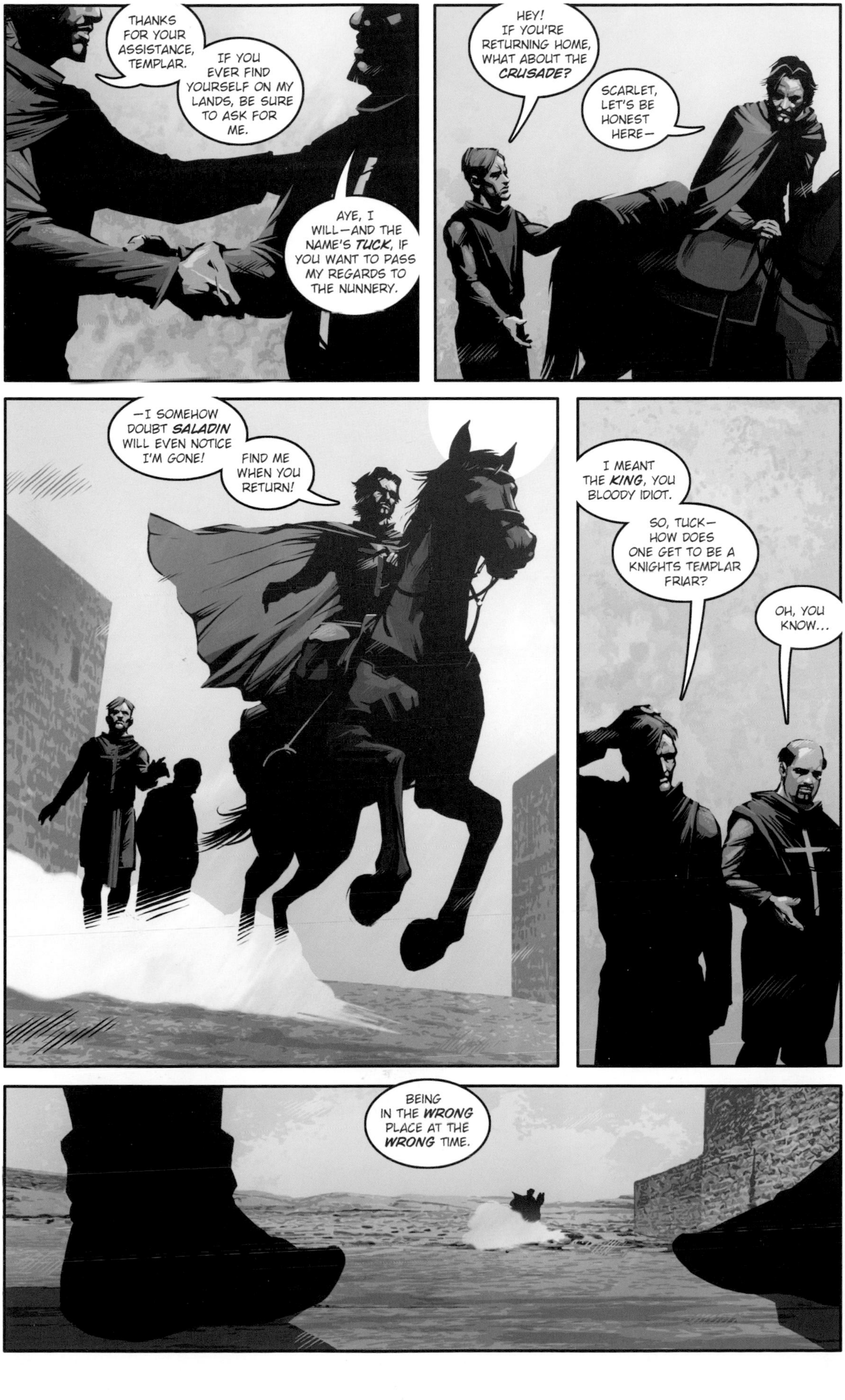
THANKS FOR YOUR ASSISTANCE, TEMPLAR.
IF YOU EVER FIND YOURSELF ON MY LANDS, BE SURE TO ASK FOR ME.
AYE, I WILL—AND THE NAME'S ***TUCK***, IF YOU WANT TO PASS MY REGARDS TO THE NUNNERY.
HEY! IF YOU'RE RETURNING HOME, WHAT ABOUT THE ***CRUSADE?***
SCARLET, LET'S BE HONEST HERE—
—I SOMEHOW DOUBT ***SALADIN*** WILL EVEN NOTICE I'M GONE!
FIND ME WHEN YOU RETURN!
I MEANT THE ***KING***, YOU BLOODY IDIOT.
SO, TUCK—HOW DOES ONE GET TO BE A KNIGHTS TEMPLAR FRIAR?
OH, YOU KNOW...
BEING IN THE ***WRONG*** PLACE AT THE ***WRONG*** TIME.

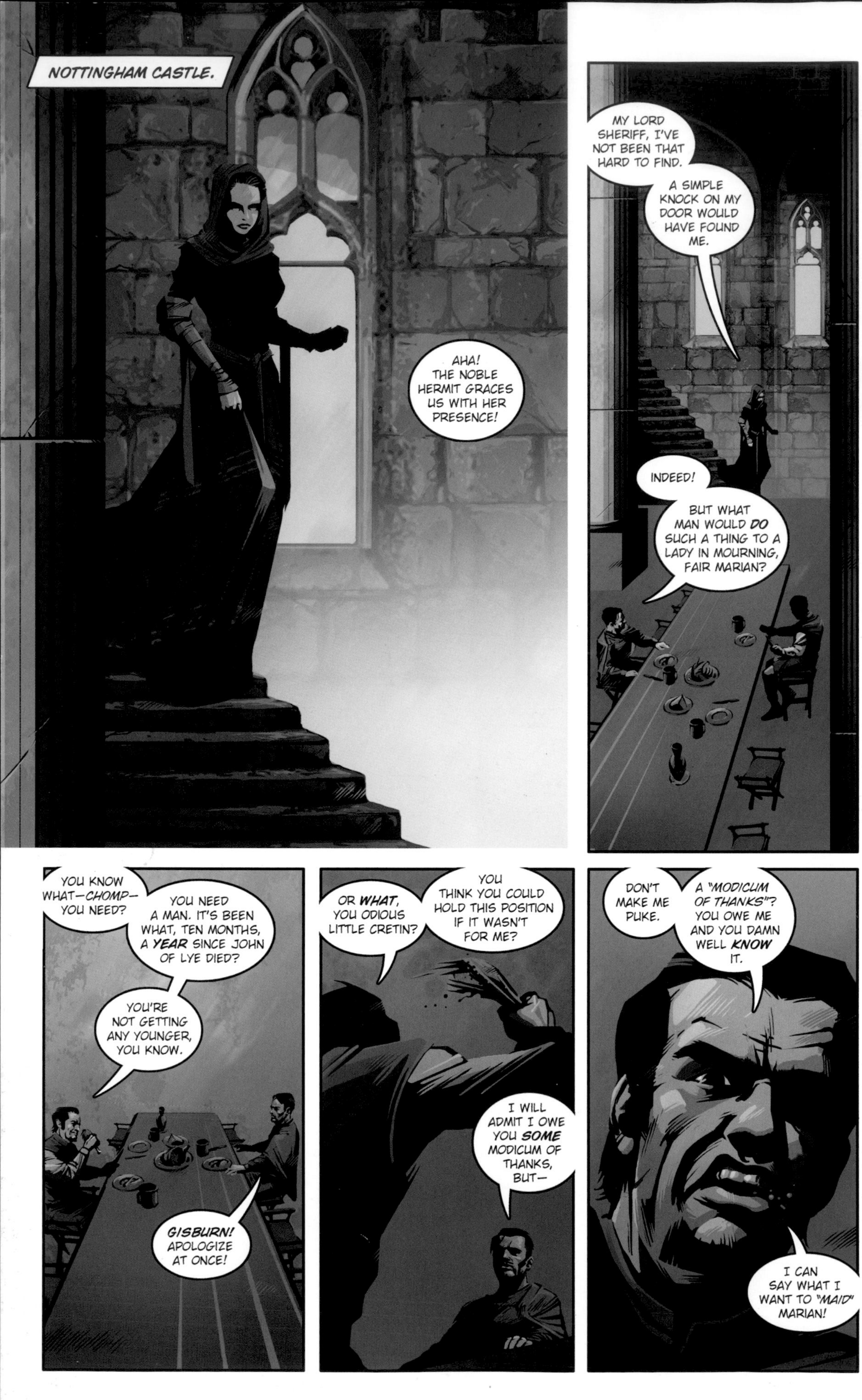
NOTTINGHAM CASTLE.
AHA! THE NOBLE HERMIT GRACES US WITH HER PRESENCE!
MY LORD SHERIFF, I'VE NOT BEEN THAT HARD TO FIND.
A SIMPLE KNOCK ON MY DOOR WOULD HAVE FOUND ME.
INDEED!
BUT WHAT MAN WOULD DO SUCH A THING TO A LADY IN MOURNING, FAIR MARIAN?
YOU KNOW WHAT—CHOMP—YOU NEED?
YOU NEED A MAN. IT'S BEEN WHAT, TEN MONTHS, A YEAR SINCE JOHN OF LYE DIED?
YOU'RE NOT GETTING ANY YOUNGER, YOU KNOW.
GISBURN! APOLOGIZE AT ONCE!
OR WHAT, YOU ODIOUS LITTLE CRETIN?
YOU THINK YOU COULD HOLD THIS POSITION IF IT WASN'T FOR ME?
I WILL ADMIT I OWE YOU SOME MODICUM OF THANKS, BUT—
DON'T MAKE ME PUKE.
A "MODICUM OF THANKS"? YOU OWE ME AND YOU DAMN WELL KNOW IT.
I CAN SAY WHAT I WANT TO "MAID" MARIAN!

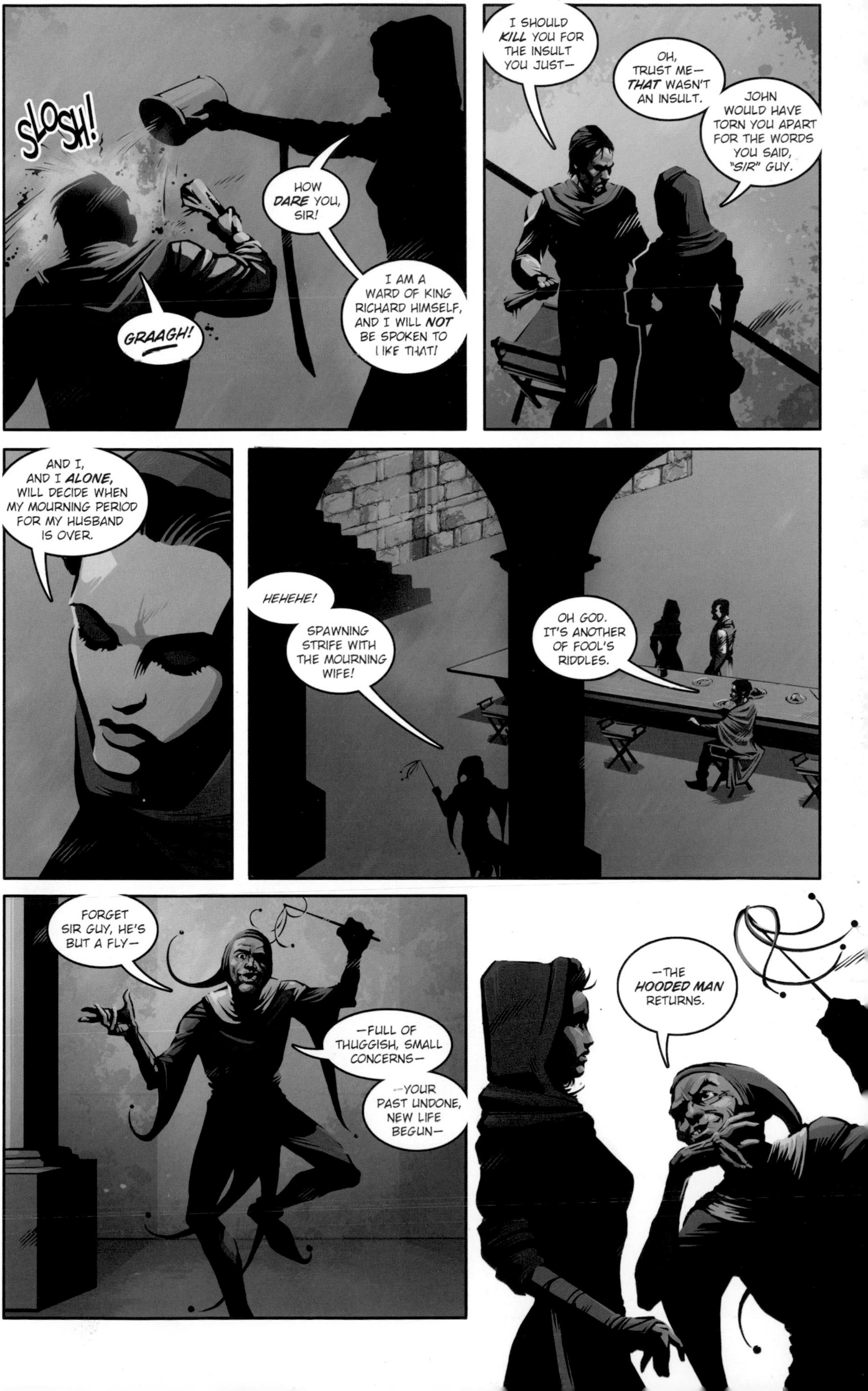
SLOSH!
GRAAGH!
HOW DARE YOU, SIR!
I AM A WARD OF KING RICHARD HIMSELF, AND I WILL NOT BE SPOKEN TO LIKE THAT!
I SHOULD KILL YOU FOR THE INSULT YOU JUST—
OH, TRUST ME— THAT WASN'T AN INSULT.
JOHN WOULD HAVE TORN YOU APART FOR THE WORDS YOU SAID, "SIR" GUY.
AND I, AND I ALONE, WILL DECIDE WHEN MY MOURNING PERIOD FOR MY HUSBAND IS OVER.
HEHEHE!
SPAWNING STRIFE WITH THE MOURNING WIFE!
OH GOD. IT'S ANOTHER OF FOOL'S RIDDLES.
FORGET SIR GUY, HE'S BUT A FLY—
—FULL OF THUGGISH, SMALL CONCERNS—
—YOUR PAST UNDONE, NEW LIFE BEGUN—
—THE HOODED MAN RETURNS.

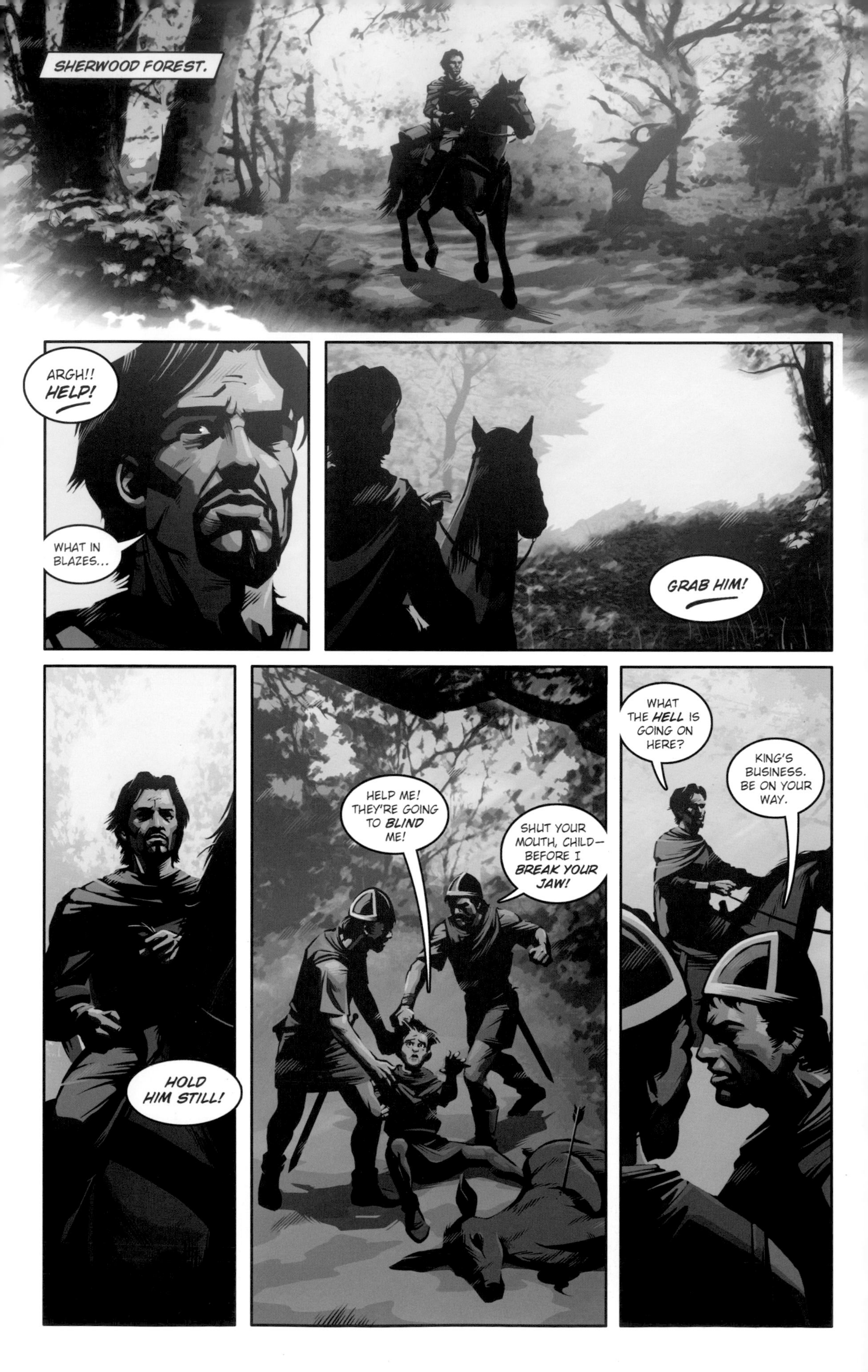
SHERWOOD FOREST.
ARGH!! HELP!
WHAT IN BLAZES...
GRAB HIM!
HOLD HIM STILL!
HELP ME! THEY'RE GOING TO BLIND ME!
SHUT YOUR MOUTH, CHILD— BEFORE I BREAK YOUR JAW!
WHAT THE HELL IS GOING ON HERE?
KING'S BUSINESS. BE ON YOUR WAY.

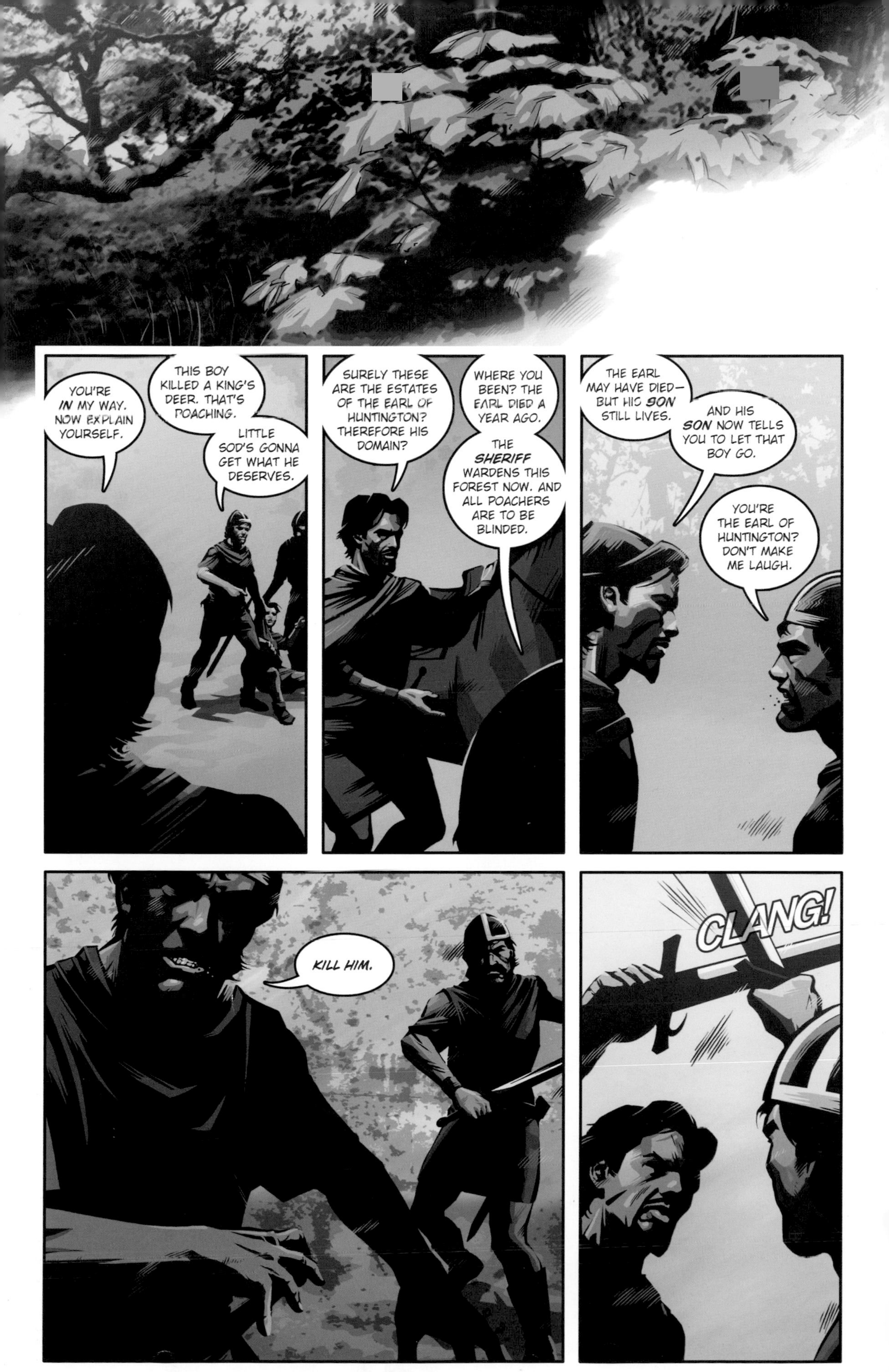
YOU'RE IN MY WAY. NOW EXPLAIN YOURSELF.
THIS BOY KILLED A KING'S DEER. THAT'S POACHING.
LITTLE SOD'S GONNA GET WHAT HE DESERVES.
SURELY THESE ARE THE ESTATES OF THE EARL OF HUNTINGTON? THEREFORE HIS DOMAIN?
WHERE YOU BEEN? THE EARL DIED A YEAR AGO.
THE SHERIFF WARDENS THIS FOREST NOW. AND ALL POACHERS ARE TO BE BLINDED.
THE EARL MAY HAVE DIED— BUT HIS SON STILL LIVES.
AND HIS SON NOW TELLS YOU TO LET THAT BOY GO.
YOU'RE THE EARL OF HUNTINGTON? DON'T MAKE ME LAUGH.
KILL HIM.
CLANG!

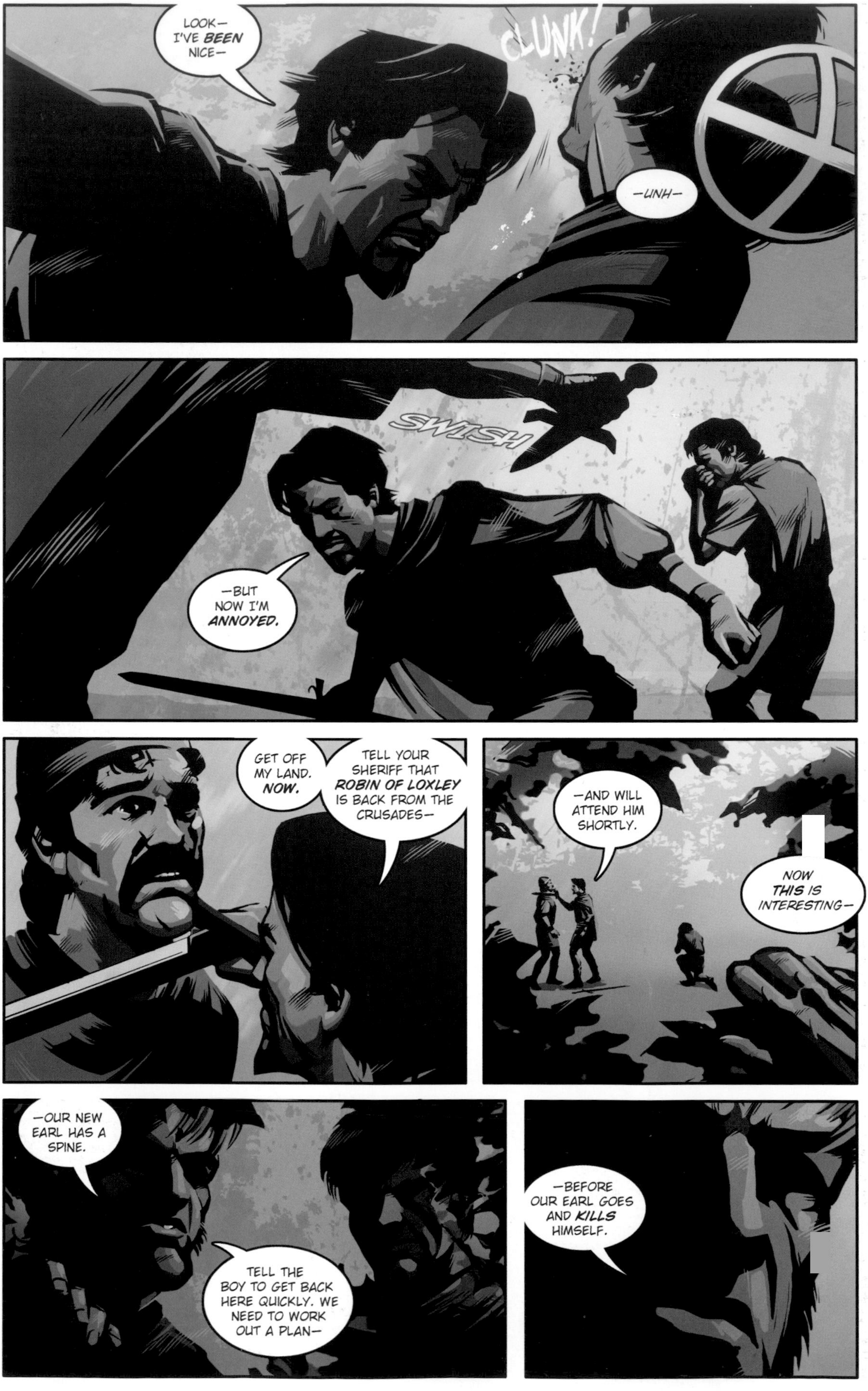
LOOK— I'VE BEEN NICE—
CLUNK!
—UNH—
SWISH
—BUT NOW I'M ANNOYED.
GET OFF MY LAND. NOW.
TELL YOUR SHERIFF THAT ROBIN OF LOXLEY IS BACK FROM THE CRUSADES—
—AND WILL ATTEND HIM SHORTLY.
NOW THIS IS INTERESTING—
—OUR NEW EARL HAS A SPINE.
TELL THE BOY TO GET BACK HERE QUICKLY. WE NEED TO WORK OUT A PLAN—
—BEFORE OUR EARL GOES AND KILLS HIMSELF.

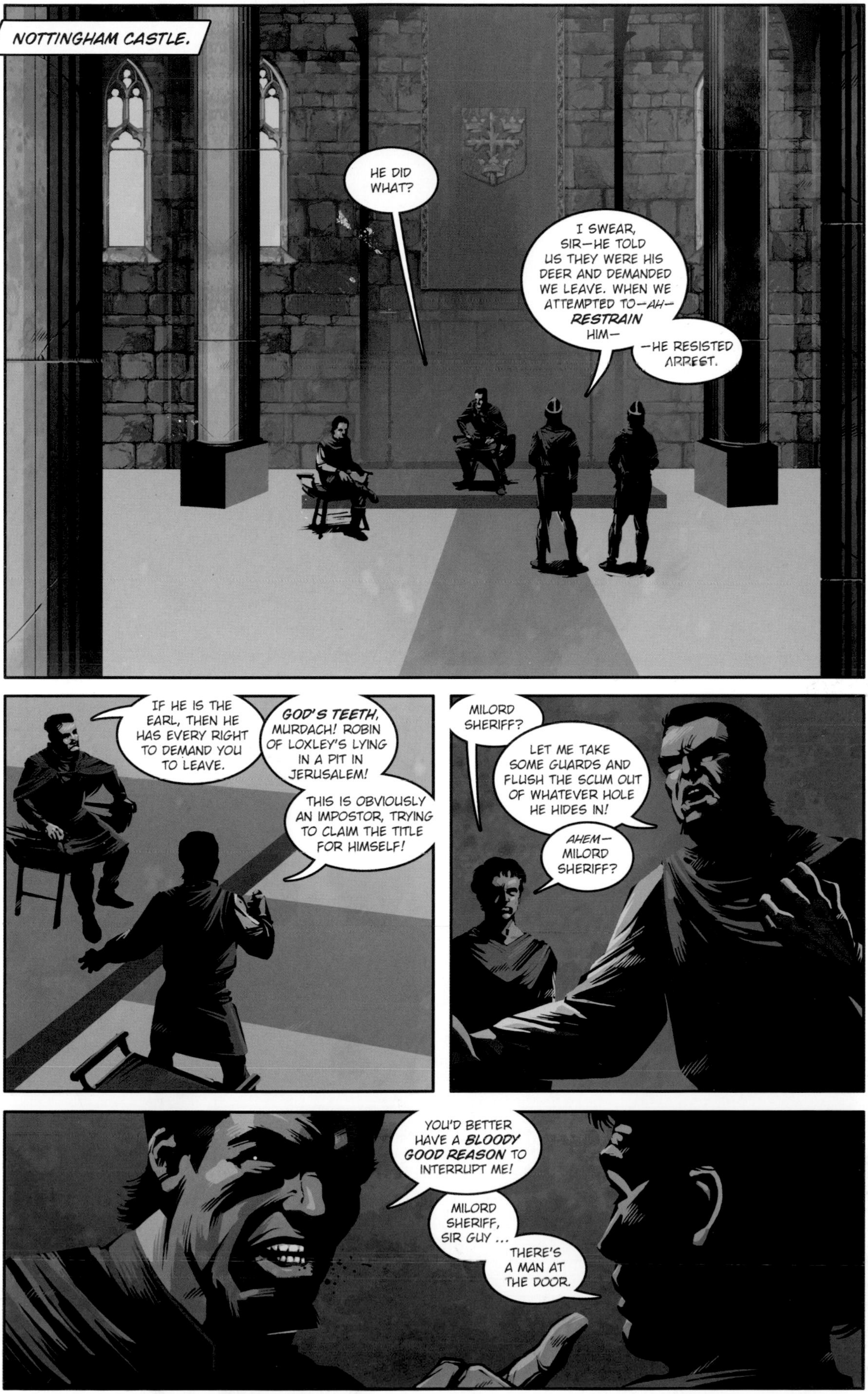
NOTTINGHAM CASTLE.
HE DID WHAT?
I SWEAR, SIR—HE TOLD US THEY WERE HIS DEER AND DEMANDED WE LEAVE. WHEN WE ATTEMPTED TO—AH—RESTRAIN HIM—
—HE RESISTED ARREST.
IF HE IS THE EARL, THEN HE HAS EVERY RIGHT TO DEMAND YOU TO LEAVE.
GOD'S TEETH, MURDACH! ROBIN OF LOXLEY'S LYING IN A PIT IN JERUSALEM!
THIS IS OBVIOUSLY AN IMPOSTOR, TRYING TO CLAIM THE TITLE FOR HIMSELF!
MILORD SHERIFF?
LET ME TAKE SOME GUARDS AND FLUSH THE SCUM OUT OF WHATEVER HOLE HE HIDES IN!
AHEM— MILORD SHERIFF?
YOU'D BETTER HAVE A BLOODY GOOD REASON TO INTERRUPT ME!
MILORD SHERIFF, SIR GUY ...
THERE'S A MAN AT THE DOOR.

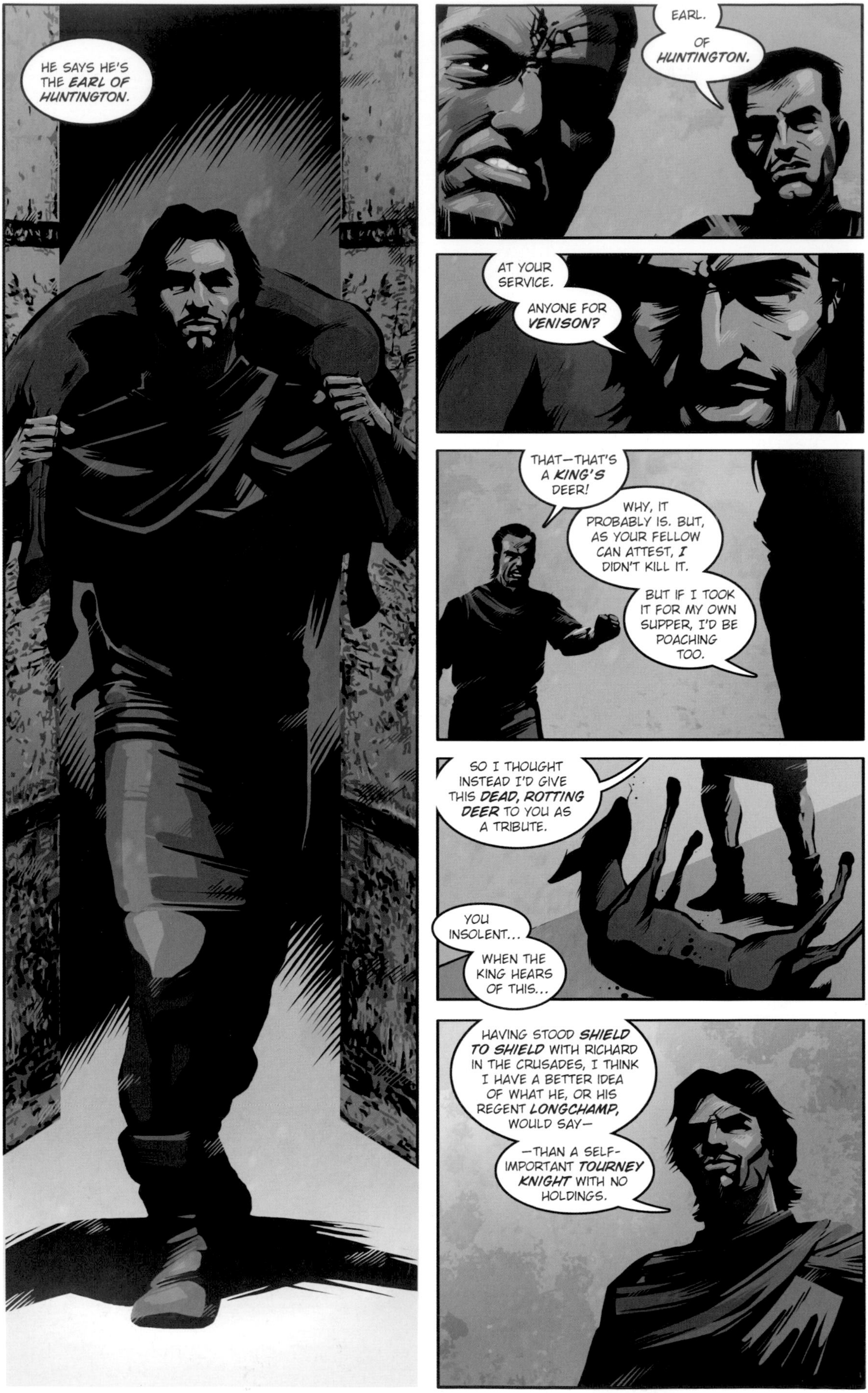
HE SAYS HE'S THE EARL OF HUNTINGTON.
EARL.
OF HUNTINGTON.
AT YOUR SERVICE.
ANYONE FOR VENISON?
THAT—THAT'S A KING'S DEER!
WHY, IT PROBABLY IS. BUT, AS YOUR FELLOW CAN ATTEST, I DIDN'T KILL IT.
BUT IF I TOOK IT FOR MY OWN SUPPER, I'D BE POACHING TOO.
SO I THOUGHT INSTEAD I'D GIVE THIS DEAD, ROTTING DEER TO YOU AS A TRIBUTE.
YOU INSOLENT...
WHEN THE KING HEARS OF THIS...
HAVING STOOD SHIELD TO SHIELD WITH RICHARD IN THE CRUSADES, I THINK I HAVE A BETTER IDEA OF WHAT HE, OR HIS REGENT LONGCHAMP, WOULD SAY—
—THAN A SELF-IMPORTANT TOURNEY KNIGHT WITH NO HOLDINGS.

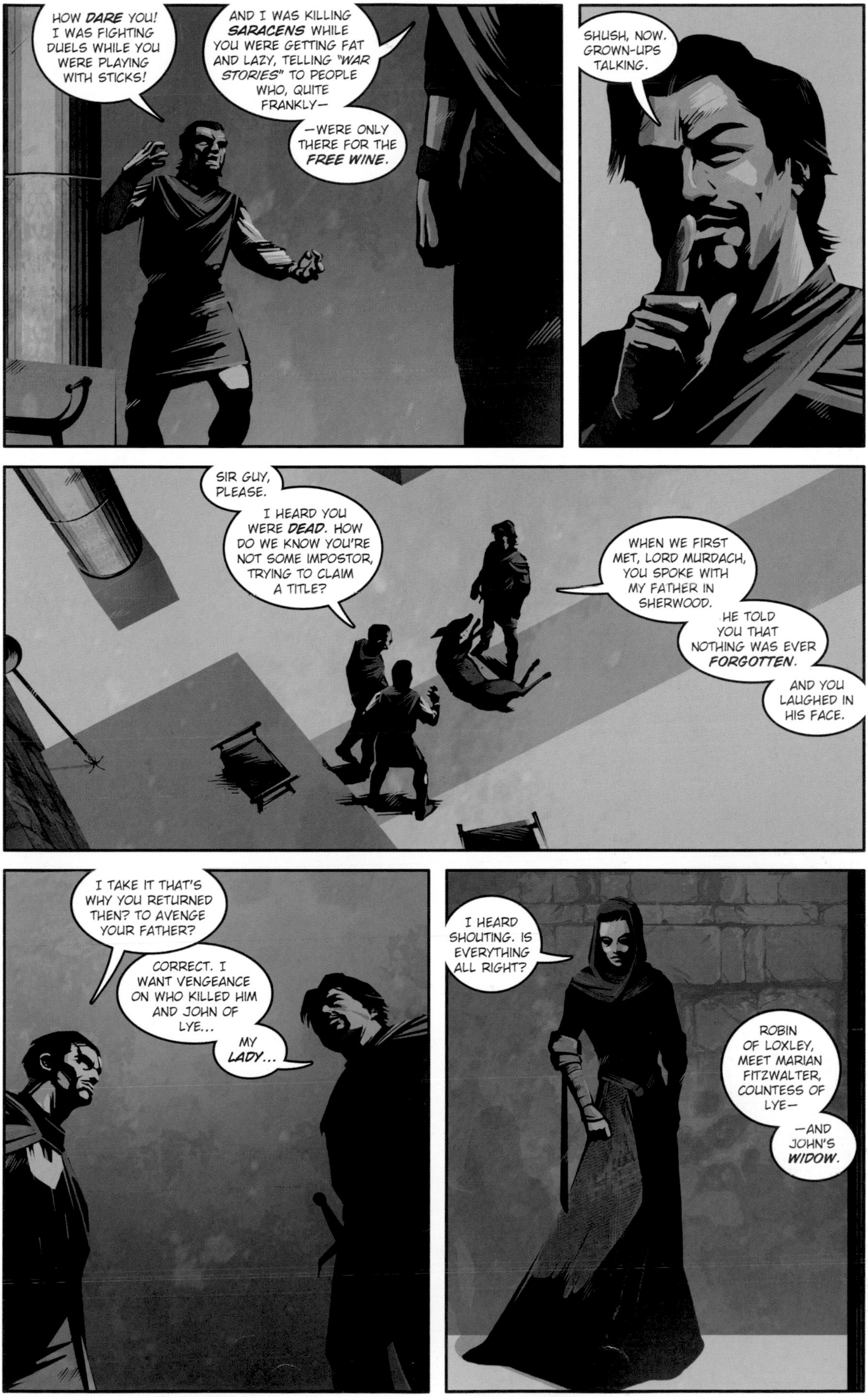
HOW DARE YOU! I WAS FIGHTING DUELS WHILE YOU WERE PLAYING WITH STICKS!
AND I WAS KILLING SARACENS WHILE YOU WERE GETTING FAT AND LAZY, TELLING "WAR STORIES" TO PEOPLE WHO, QUITE FRANKLY—
—WERE ONLY THERE FOR THE FREE WINE.
SHUSH, NOW. GROWN-UPS TALKING.
SIR GUY, PLEASE.
I HEARD YOU WERE DEAD. HOW DO WE KNOW YOU'RE NOT SOME IMPOSTOR, TRYING TO CLAIM A TITLE?
WHEN WE FIRST MET, LORD MURDACH, YOU SPOKE WITH MY FATHER IN SHERWOOD.
HE TOLD YOU THAT NOTHING WAS EVER FORGOTTEN.
AND YOU LAUGHED IN HIS FACE.
I TAKE IT THAT'S WHY YOU RETURNED THEN? TO AVENGE YOUR FATHER?
CORRECT. I WANT VENGEANCE ON WHO KILLED HIM AND JOHN OF LYE...
MY LADY...
I HEARD SHOUTING. IS EVERYTHING ALL RIGHT?
ROBIN OF LOXLEY, MEET MARIAN FITZWALTER, COUNTESS OF LYE—
—AND JOHN'S WIDOW.

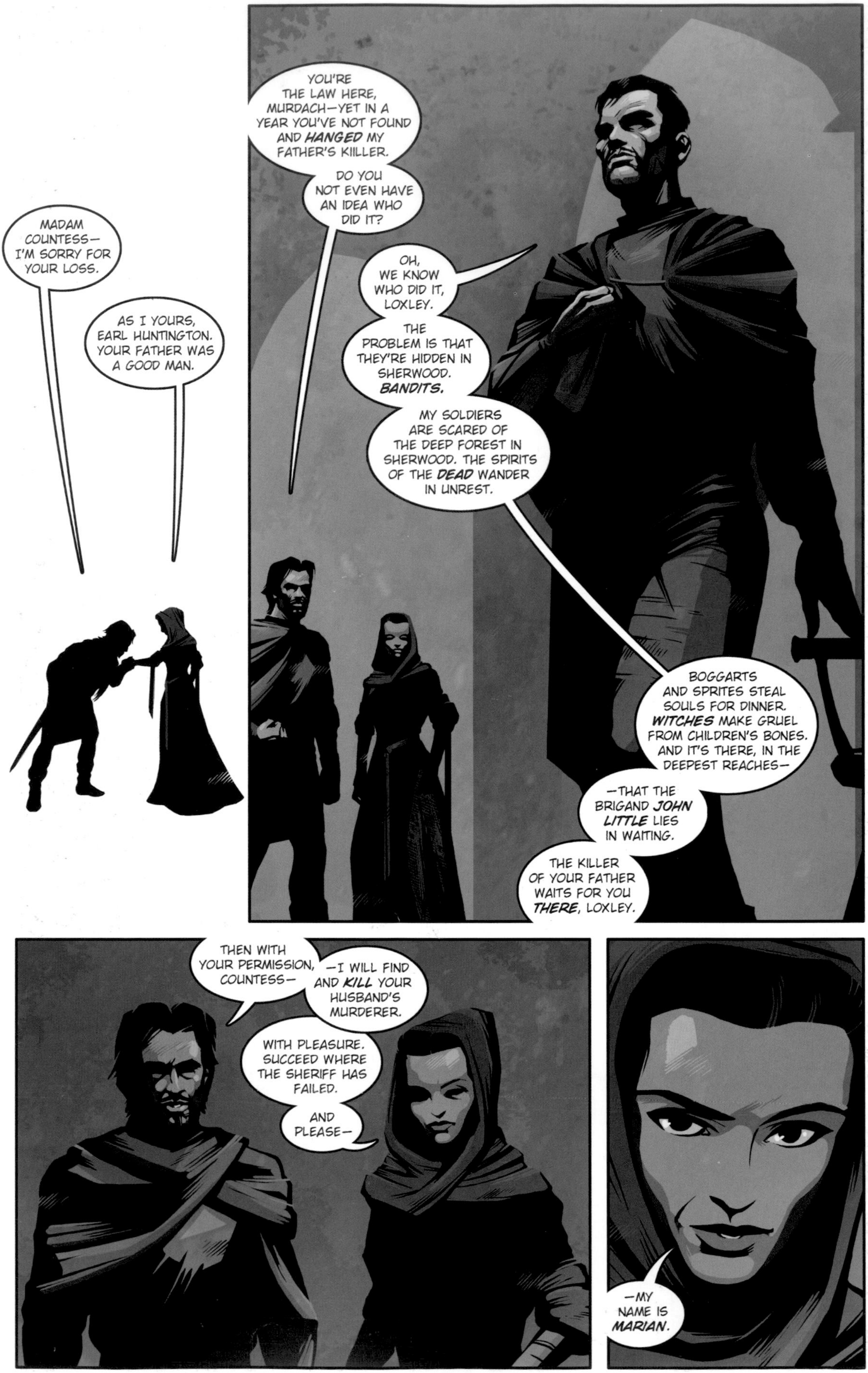
MADAM COUNTESS— I'M SORRY FOR YOUR LOSS.
AS I YOURS, EARL HUNTINGTON. YOUR FATHER WAS A GOOD MAN.
YOU'RE THE LAW HERE, MURDACH—YET IN A YEAR YOU'VE NOT FOUND AND HANGED MY FATHER'S KIILLER.
DO YOU NOT EVEN HAVE AN IDEA WHO DID IT?
OH, WE KNOW WHO DID IT, LOXLEY.
THE PROBLEM IS THAT THEY'RE HIDDEN IN SHERWOOD. BANDITS.
MY SOLDIERS ARE SCARED OF THE DEEP FOREST IN SHERWOOD. THE SPIRITS OF THE DEAD WANDER IN UNREST.
BOGGARTS AND SPRITES STEAL SOULS FOR DINNER. WITCHES MAKE GRUEL FROM CHILDREN'S BONES. AND IT'S THERE, IN THE DEEPEST REACHES—
—THAT THE BRIGAND JOHN LITTLE LIES IN WAITING.
THE KILLER OF YOUR FATHER WAITS FOR YOU THERE, LOXLEY.
THEN WITH YOUR PERMISSION, COUNTESS—
—I WILL FIND AND KILL YOUR HUSBAND'S MURDERER.
WITH PLEASURE. SUCCEED WHERE THE SHERIFF HAS FAILED.
AND PLEASE—
—MY NAME IS MARIAN.

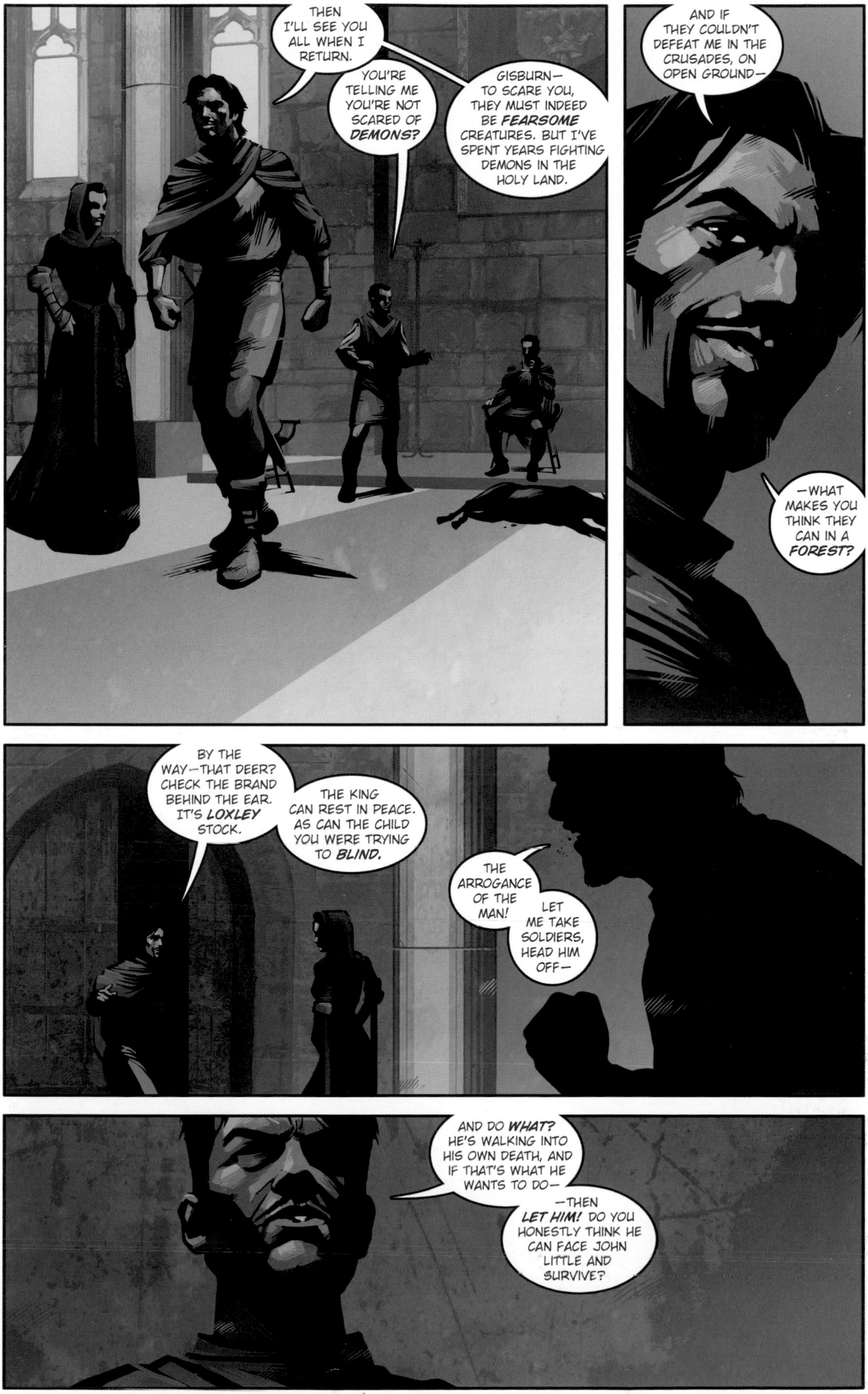
THEN I'LL SEE YOU ALL WHEN I RETURN.
YOU'RE TELLING ME YOU'RE NOT SCARED OF **DEMONS?**
GISBURN— TO SCARE YOU, THEY MUST INDEED BE **FEARSOME** CREATURES. BUT I'VE SPENT YEARS FIGHTING DEMONS IN THE HOLY LAND.
AND IF THEY COULDN'T DEFEAT ME IN THE CRUSADES, ON OPEN GROUND—
—WHAT MAKES YOU THINK THEY CAN IN A **FOREST?**
BY THE WAY—THAT DEER? CHECK THE BRAND BEHIND THE EAR. IT'S **LOXLEY** STOCK.
THE KING CAN REST IN PEACE. AS CAN THE CHILD YOU WERE TRYING TO **BLIND.**
THE ARROGANCE OF THE MAN!
LET ME TAKE SOLDIERS, HEAD HIM OFF—
AND DO **WHAT?** HE'S WALKING INTO HIS OWN DEATH, AND IF THAT'S WHAT HE WANTS TO DO—
—THEN **LET HIM!** DO YOU HONESTLY THINK HE CAN FACE JOHN LITTLE AND SURVIVE?

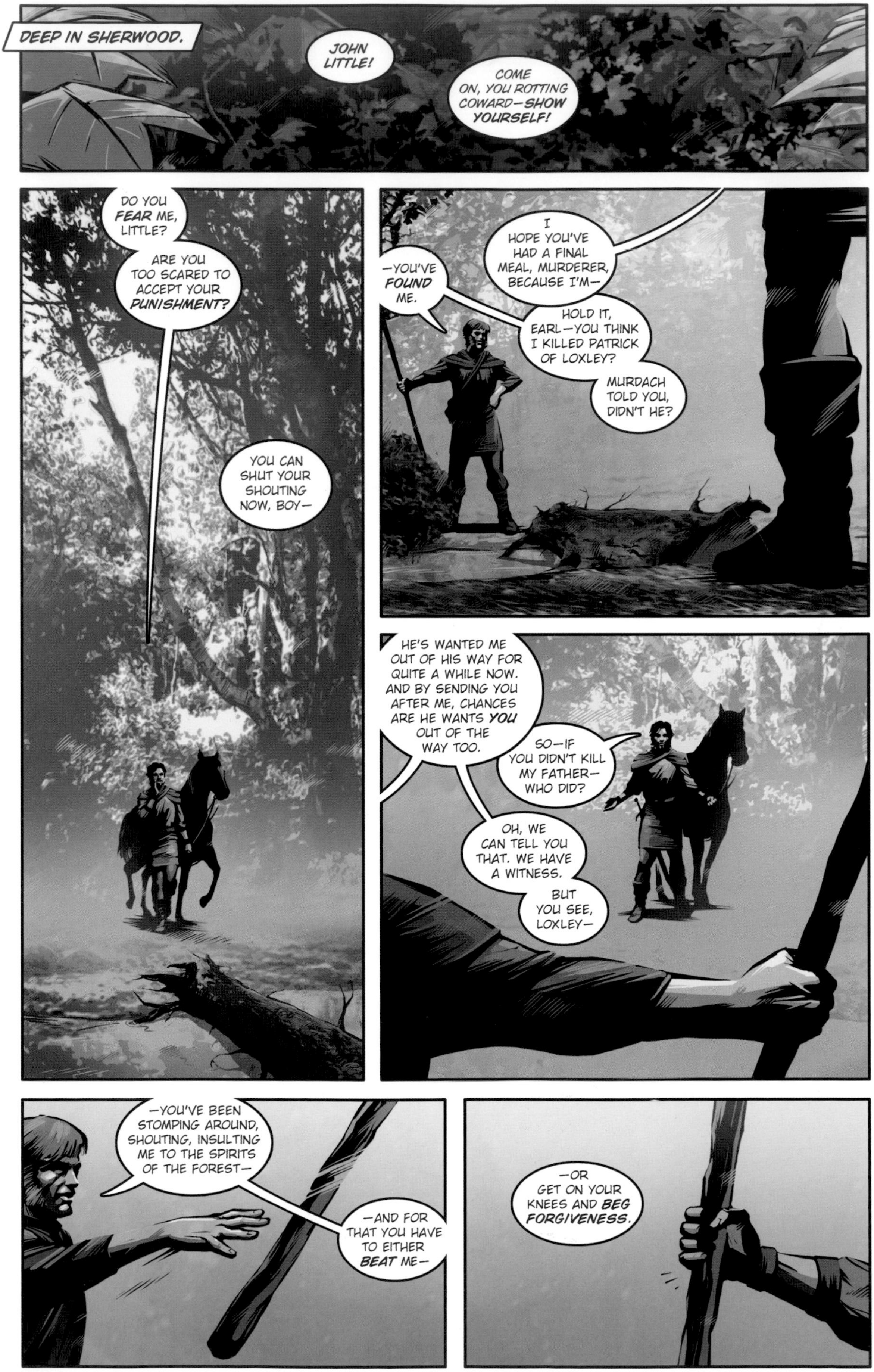
DEEP IN SHERWOOD.
JOHN LITTLE!
COME ON, YOU ROTTING COWARD—SHOW YOURSELF!
DO YOU FEAR ME, LITTLE?
ARE YOU TOO SCARED TO ACCEPT YOUR PUNISHMENT?
YOU CAN SHUT YOUR SHOUTING NOW, BOY—
I HOPE YOU'VE HAD A FINAL MEAL, MURDERER, BECAUSE I'M—
—YOU'VE FOUND ME.
HOLD IT, EARL—YOU THINK I KILLED PATRICK OF LOXLEY?
MURDACH TOLD YOU, DIDN'T HE?
HE'S WANTED ME OUT OF HIS WAY FOR QUITE A WHILE NOW. AND BY SENDING YOU AFTER ME, CHANCES ARE HE WANTS YOU OUT OF THE WAY TOO.
SO—IF YOU DIDN'T KILL MY FATHER—WHO DID?
OH, WE CAN TELL YOU THAT. WE HAVE A WITNESS.
BUT YOU SEE, LOXLEY—
—YOU'VE BEEN STOMPING AROUND, SHOUTING, INSULTING ME TO THE SPIRITS OF THE FOREST—
—AND FOR THAT YOU HAVE TO EITHER BEAT ME—
—OR GET ON YOUR KNEES AND BEG FORGIVENESS.

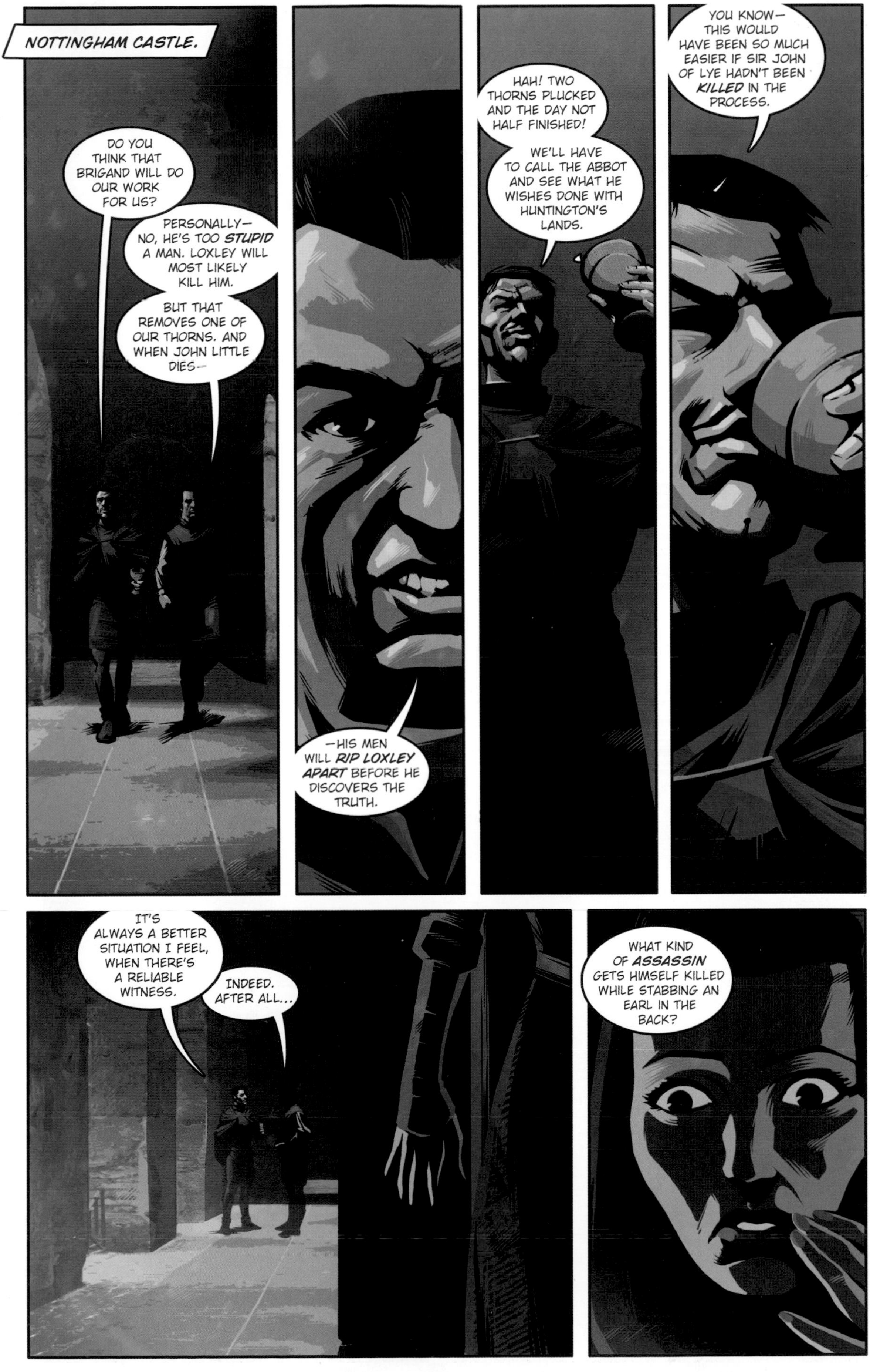
NOTTINGHAM CASTLE.
DO YOU THINK THAT BRIGAND WILL DO OUR WORK FOR US?
PERSONALLY— NO, HE'S TOO STUPID A MAN. LOXLEY WILL MOST LIKELY KILL HIM.
BUT THAT REMOVES ONE OF OUR THORNS. AND WHEN JOHN LITTLE DIES—
—HIS MEN WILL RIP LOXLEY APART BEFORE HE DISCOVERS THE TRUTH.
HAH! TWO THORNS PLUCKED AND THE DAY NOT HALF FINISHED!
WE'LL HAVE TO CALL THE ABBOT AND SEE WHAT HE WISHES DONE WITH HUNTINGTON'S LANDS.
YOU KNOW— THIS WOULD HAVE BEEN SO MUCH EASIER IF SIR JOHN OF LYE HADN'T BEEN KILLED IN THE PROCESS.
IT'S ALWAYS A BETTER SITUATION I FEEL, WHEN THERE'S A RELIABLE WITNESS.
INDEED. AFTER ALL...
WHAT KIND OF ASSASSIN GETS HIMSELF KILLED WHILE STABBING AN EARL IN THE BACK?

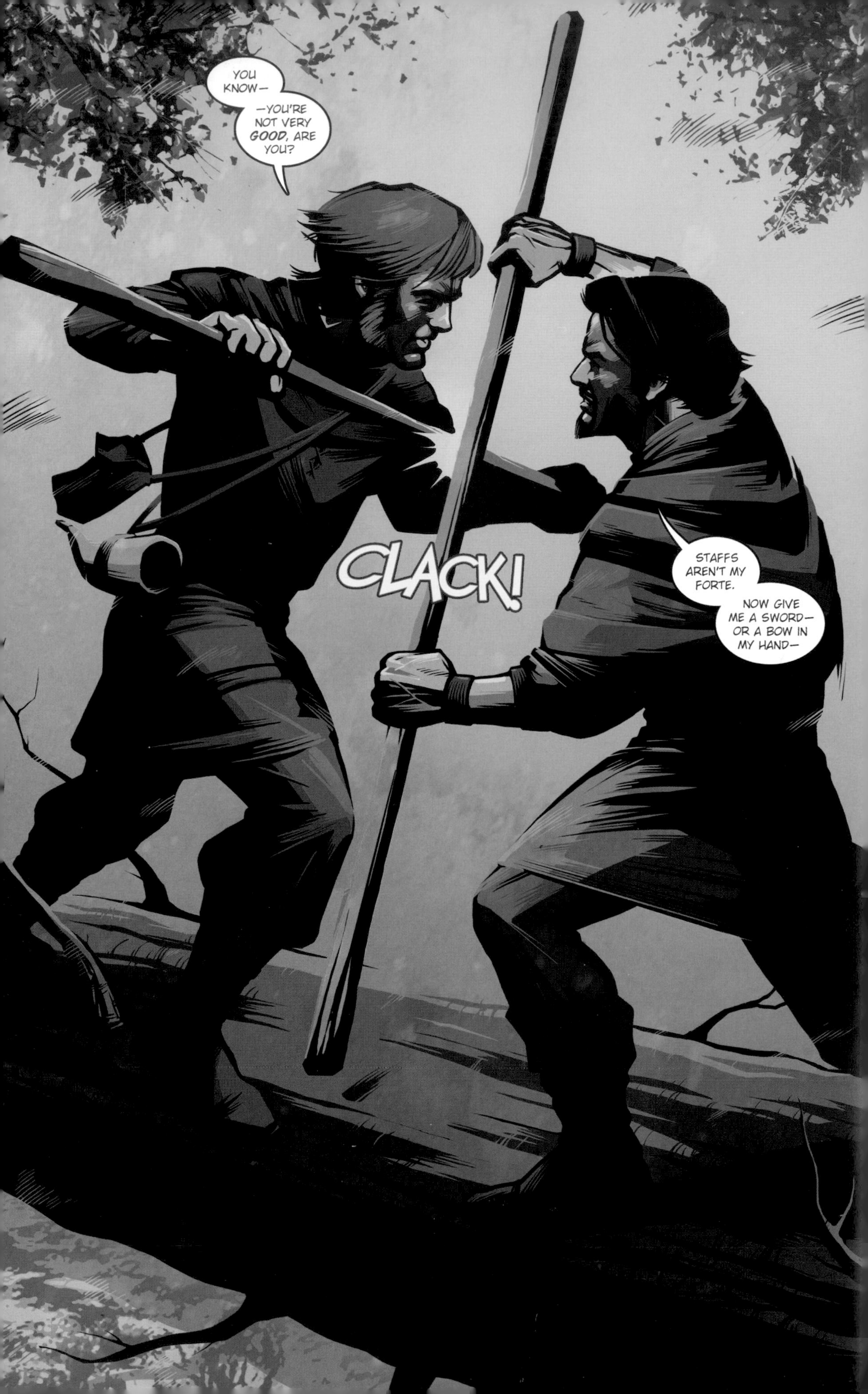
YOU KNOW—
—YOU'RE NOT VERY **GOOD**, ARE YOU?
CLACK!
STAFFS AREN'T MY FORTE.
NOW GIVE ME A SWORD— OR A BOW IN MY HAND—

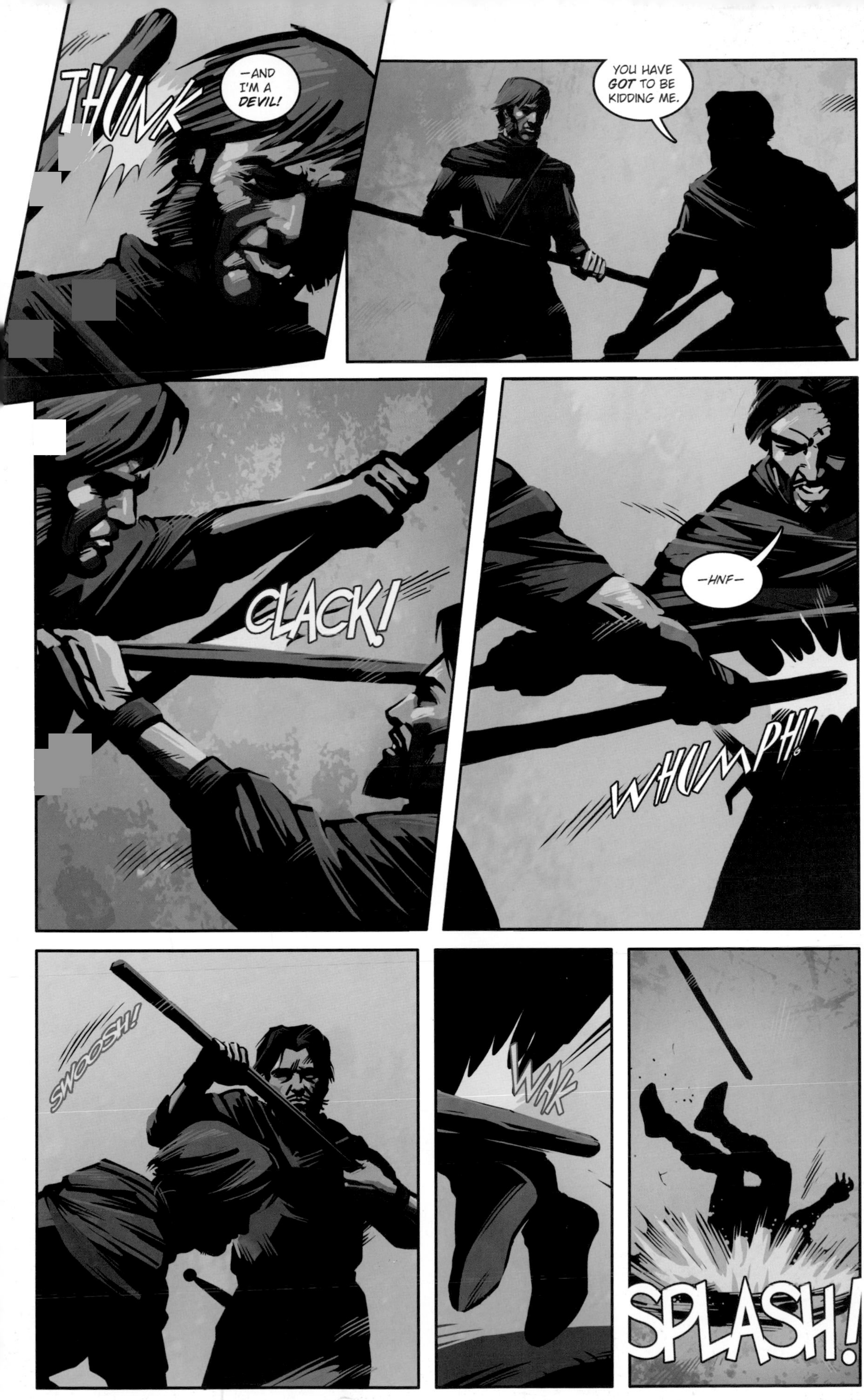
THUNK
—AND I'M A DEVIL!
YOU HAVE GOT TO BE KIDDING ME.
CLACK!
—HNF—
WHUMPH!
SWOOSH!
WAK
SPLASH!

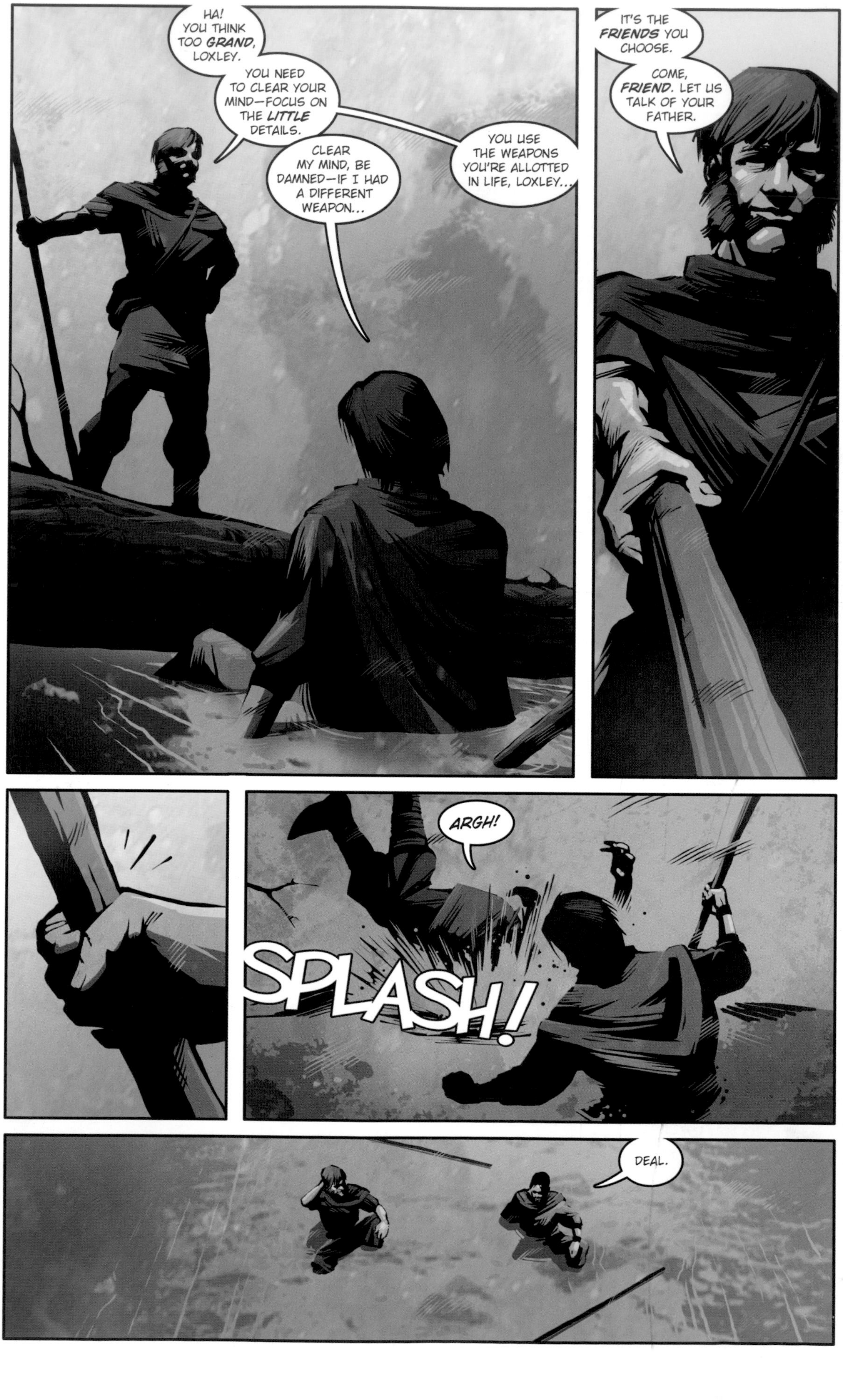
HA! YOU THINK TOO GRAND, LOXLEY.
YOU NEED TO CLEAR YOUR MIND—FOCUS ON THE LITTLE DETAILS.
CLEAR MY MIND, BE DAMNED—IF I HAD A DIFFERENT WEAPON...
YOU USE THE WEAPONS YOU'RE ALLOTTED IN LIFE, LOXLEY...
IT'S THE FRIENDS YOU CHOOSE.
COME, FRIEND. LET US TALK OF YOUR FATHER.
ARGH!
SPLASH!
DEAL.

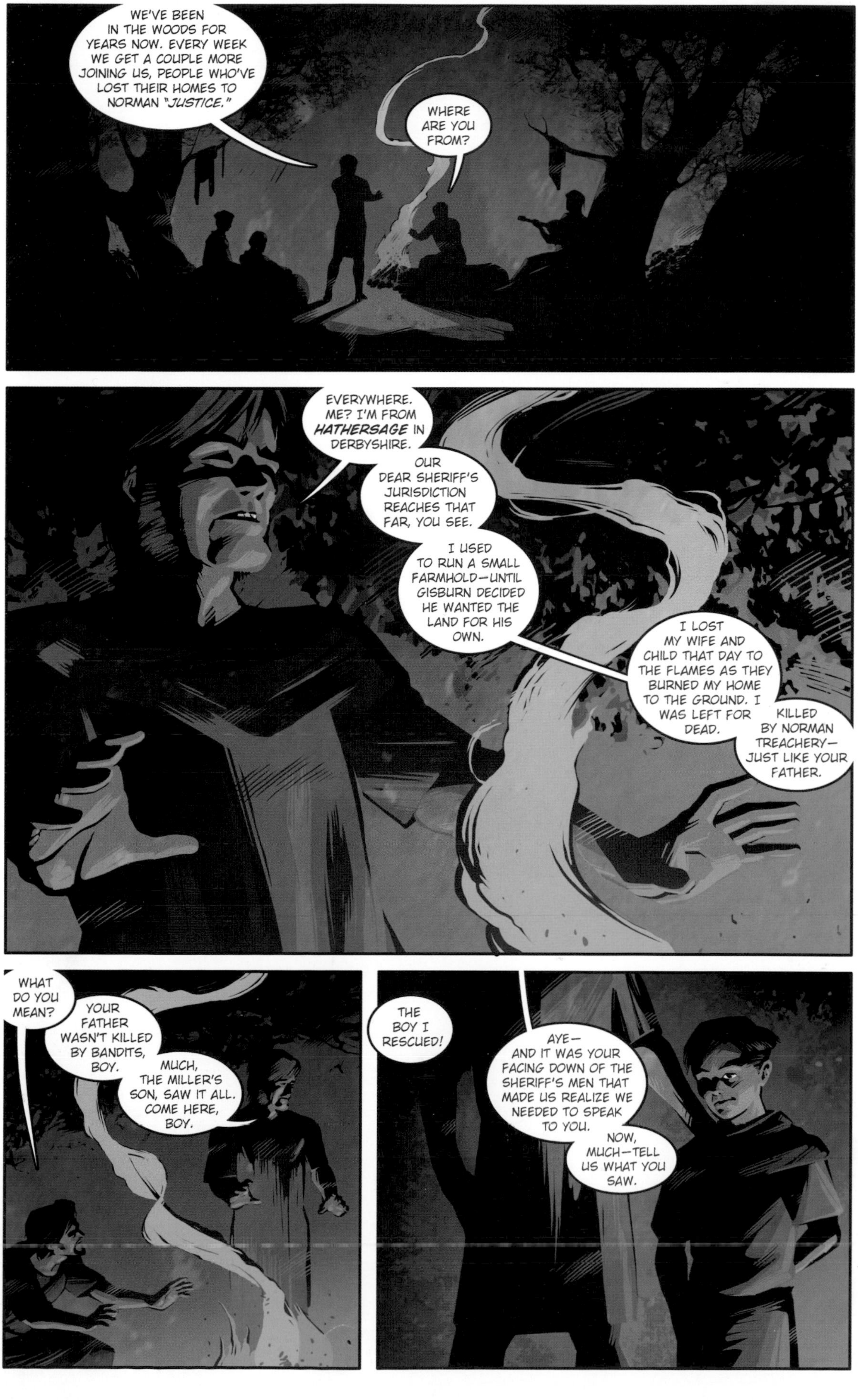
WE'VE BEEN IN THE WOODS FOR YEARS NOW. EVERY WEEK WE GET A COUPLE MORE JOINING US, PEOPLE WHO'VE LOST THEIR HOMES TO NORMAN "JUSTICE."
WHERE ARE YOU FROM?
EVERYWHERE. ME? I'M FROM HATHERSAGE IN DERBYSHIRE.
OUR DEAR SHERIFF'S JURISDICTION REACHES THAT FAR, YOU SEE.
I USED TO RUN A SMALL FARMHOLD—UNTIL GISBURN DECIDED HE WANTED THE LAND FOR HIS OWN.
I LOST MY WIFE AND CHILD THAT DAY TO THE FLAMES AS THEY BURNED MY HOME TO THE GROUND. I WAS LEFT FOR DEAD.
KILLED BY NORMAN TREACHERY—JUST LIKE YOUR FATHER.
WHAT DO YOU MEAN?
YOUR FATHER WASN'T KILLED BY BANDITS, BOY.
MUCH, THE MILLER'S SON, SAW IT ALL. COME HERE, BOY.
THE BOY I RESCUED!
AYE—AND IT WAS YOUR FACING DOWN OF THE SHERIFF'S MEN THAT MADE US REALIZE WE NEEDED TO SPEAK TO YOU.
NOW, MUCH—TELL US WHAT YOU SAW.

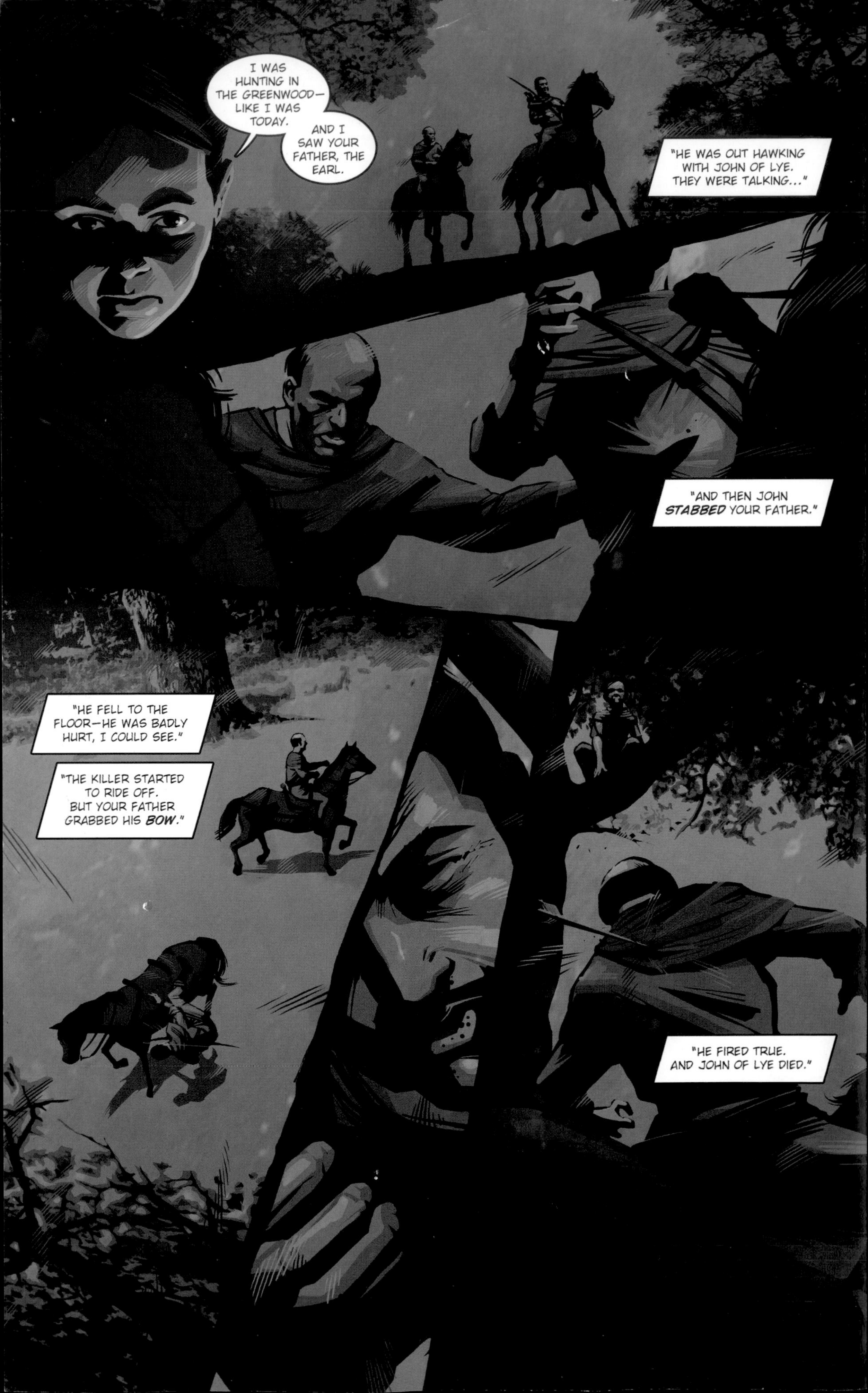
I WAS HUNTING IN THE GREENWOOD— LIKE I WAS TODAY.
AND I SAW YOUR FATHER, THE EARL.
"HE WAS OUT HAWKING WITH JOHN OF LYE. THEY WERE TALKING..."
"AND THEN JOHN STABBED YOUR FATHER."
"HE FELL TO THE FLOOR—HE WAS BADLY HURT, I COULD SEE."
"THE KILLER STARTED TO RIDE OFF. BUT YOUR FATHER GRABBED HIS BOW."
"HE FIRED TRUE. AND JOHN OF LYE DIED."

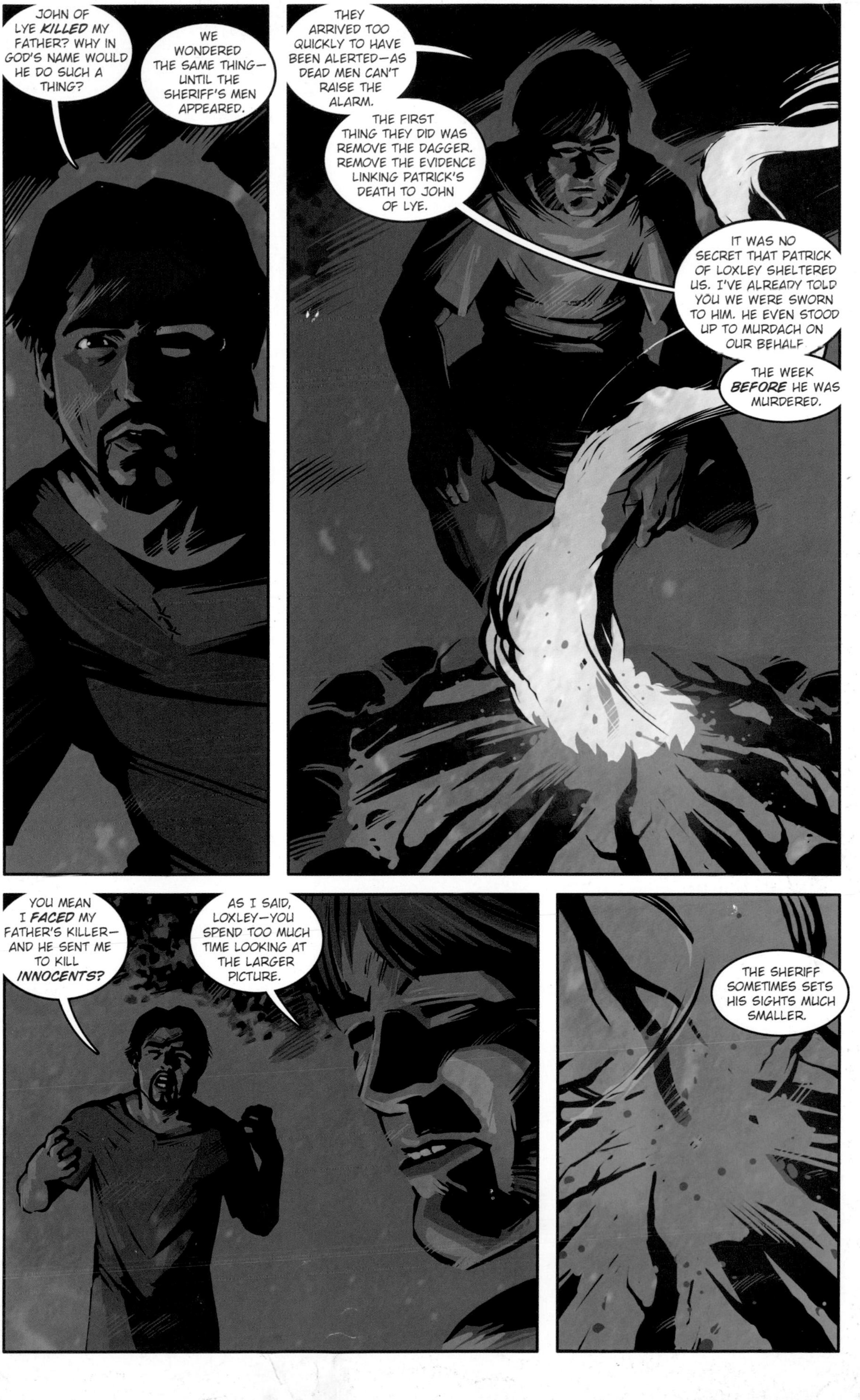
JOHN OF LYE KILLED MY FATHER? WHY IN GOD'S NAME WOULD HE DO SUCH A THING?
WE WONDERED THE SAME THING— UNTIL THE SHERIFF'S MEN APPEARED.
THEY ARRIVED TOO QUICKLY TO HAVE BEEN ALERTED—AS DEAD MEN CAN'T RAISE THE ALARM.
THE FIRST THING THEY DID WAS REMOVE THE DAGGER. REMOVE THE EVIDENCE LINKING PATRICK'S DEATH TO JOHN OF LYE.
IT WAS NO SECRET THAT PATRICK OF LOXLEY SHELTERED US. I'VE ALREADY TOLD YOU WE WERE SWORN TO HIM. HE EVEN STOOD UP TO MURDACH ON OUR BEHALF.
THE WEEK BEFORE HE WAS MURDERED.
YOU MEAN I FACED MY FATHER'S KILLER— AND HE SENT ME TO KILL INNOCENTS?
AS I SAID, LOXLEY—YOU SPEND TOO MUCH TIME LOOKING AT THE LARGER PICTURE.
THE SHERIFF SOMETIMES SETS HIS SIGHTS MUCH SMALLER.

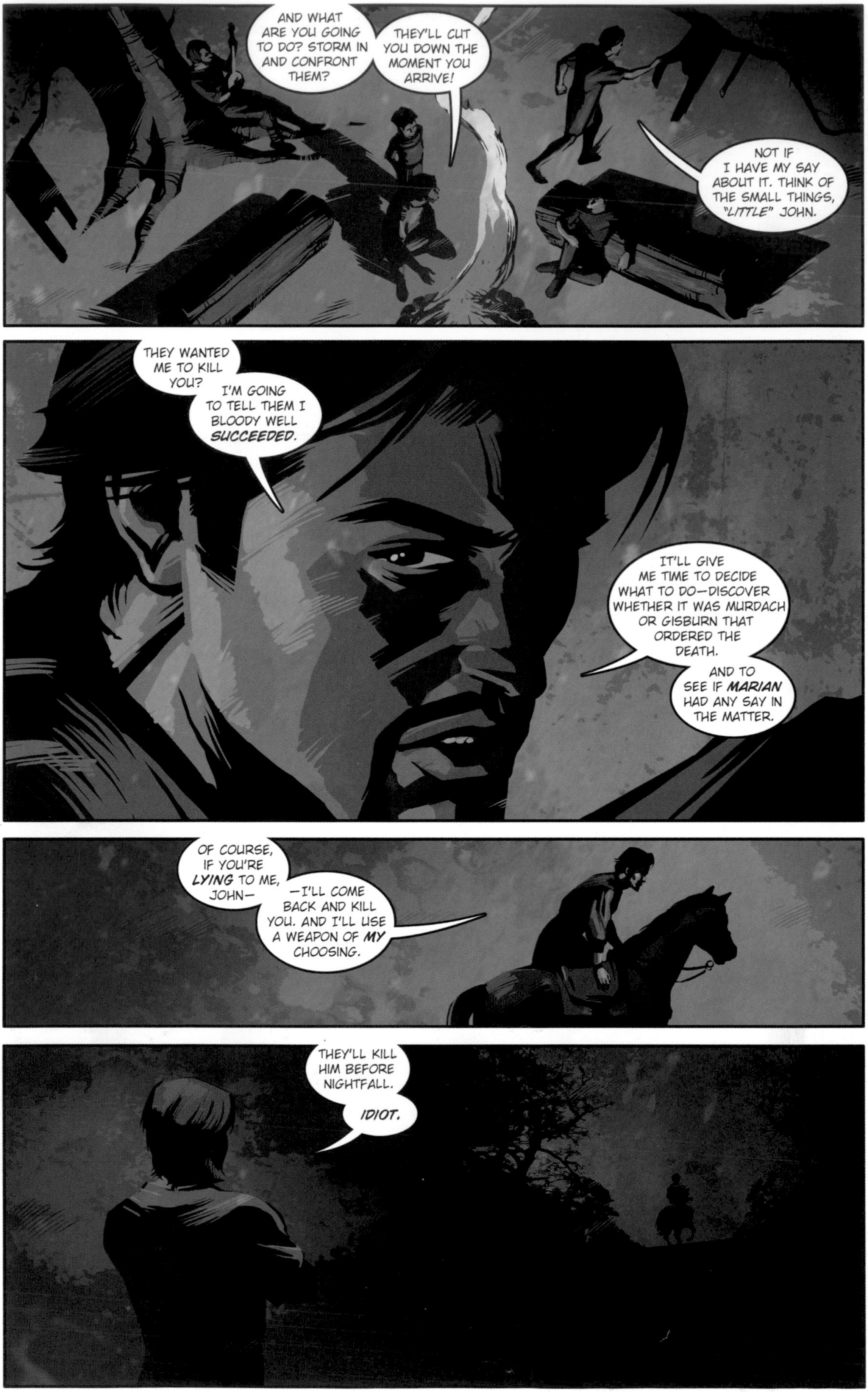
AND WHAT ARE YOU GOING TO DO? STORM IN AND CONFRONT THEM?
THEY'LL CUT YOU DOWN THE MOMENT YOU ARRIVE!
NOT IF I HAVE MY SAY ABOUT IT. THINK OF THE SMALL THINGS, *"LITTLE"* JOHN.
THEY WANTED ME TO KILL YOU?
I'M GOING TO TELL THEM I BLOODY WELL ***SUCCEEDED***.
IT'LL GIVE ME TIME TO DECIDE WHAT TO DO—DISCOVER WHETHER IT WAS MURDACH OR GISBURN THAT ORDERED THE DEATH.
AND TO SEE IF ***MARIAN*** HAD ANY SAY IN THE MATTER.
OF COURSE, IF YOU'RE ***LYING*** TO ME, JOHN—
—I'LL COME BACK AND KILL YOU. AND I'LL USE A WEAPON OF ***MY*** CHOOSING.
THEY'LL KILL HIM BEFORE NIGHTFALL.
IDIOT.

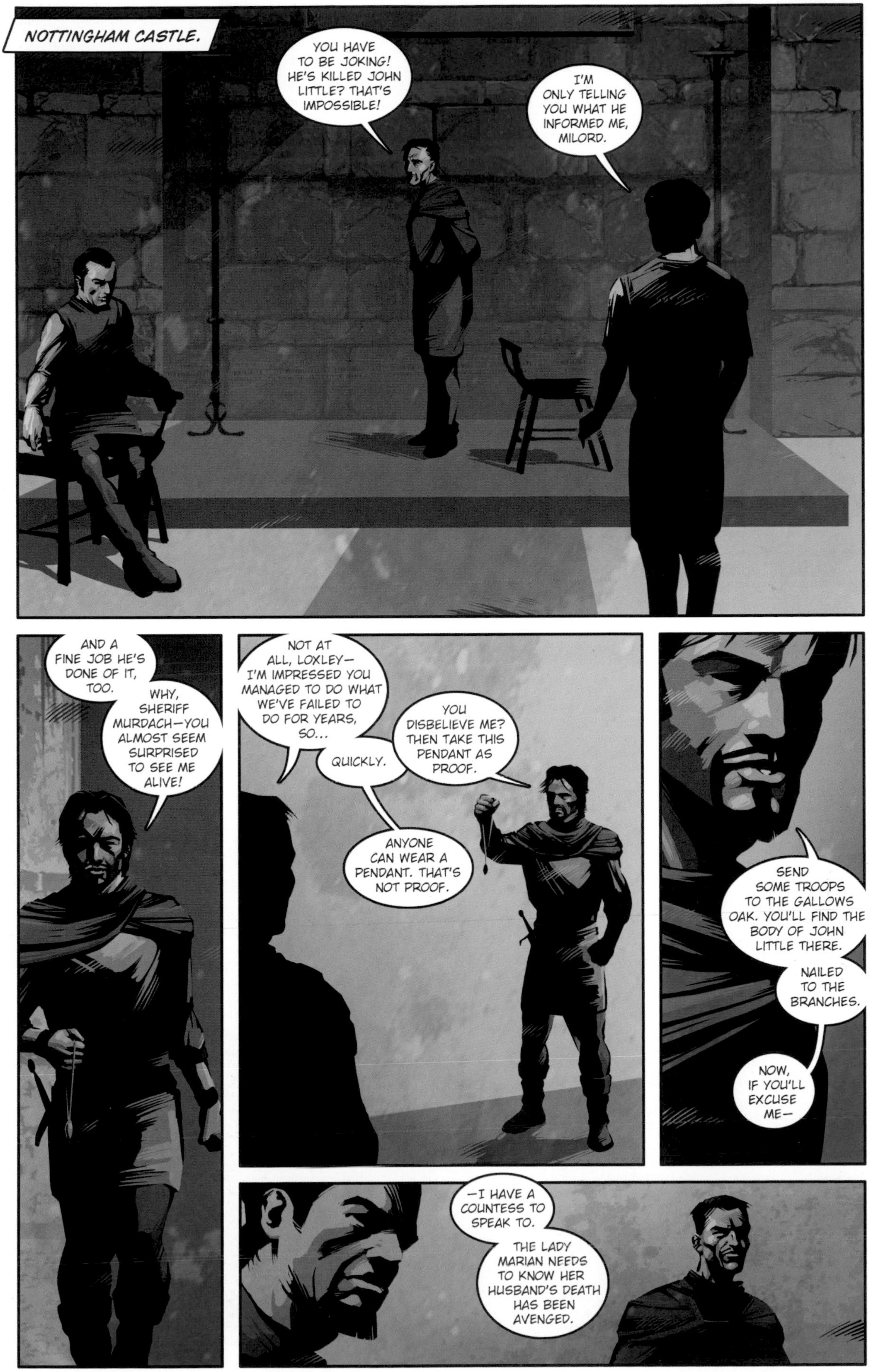
NOTTINGHAM CASTLE.
YOU HAVE TO BE JOKING! HE'S KILLED JOHN LITTLE? THAT'S IMPOSSIBLE!
I'M ONLY TELLING YOU WHAT HE INFORMED ME, MILORD.
AND A FINE JOB HE'S DONE OF IT, TOO.
WHY, SHERIFF MURDACH—YOU ALMOST SEEM SURPRISED TO SEE ME ALIVE!
NOT AT ALL, LOXLEY—I'M IMPRESSED YOU MANAGED TO DO WHAT WE'VE FAILED TO DO FOR YEARS, SO...
QUICKLY.
YOU DISBELIEVE ME? THEN TAKE THIS PENDANT AS PROOF.
ANYONE CAN WEAR A PENDANT. THAT'S NOT PROOF.
SEND SOME TROOPS TO THE GALLOWS OAK. YOU'LL FIND THE BODY OF JOHN LITTLE THERE.
NAILED TO THE BRANCHES.
NOW, IF YOU'LL EXCUSE ME—
—I HAVE A COUNTESS TO SPEAK TO.
THE LADY MARIAN NEEDS TO KNOW HER HUSBAND'S DEATH HAS BEEN AVENGED.

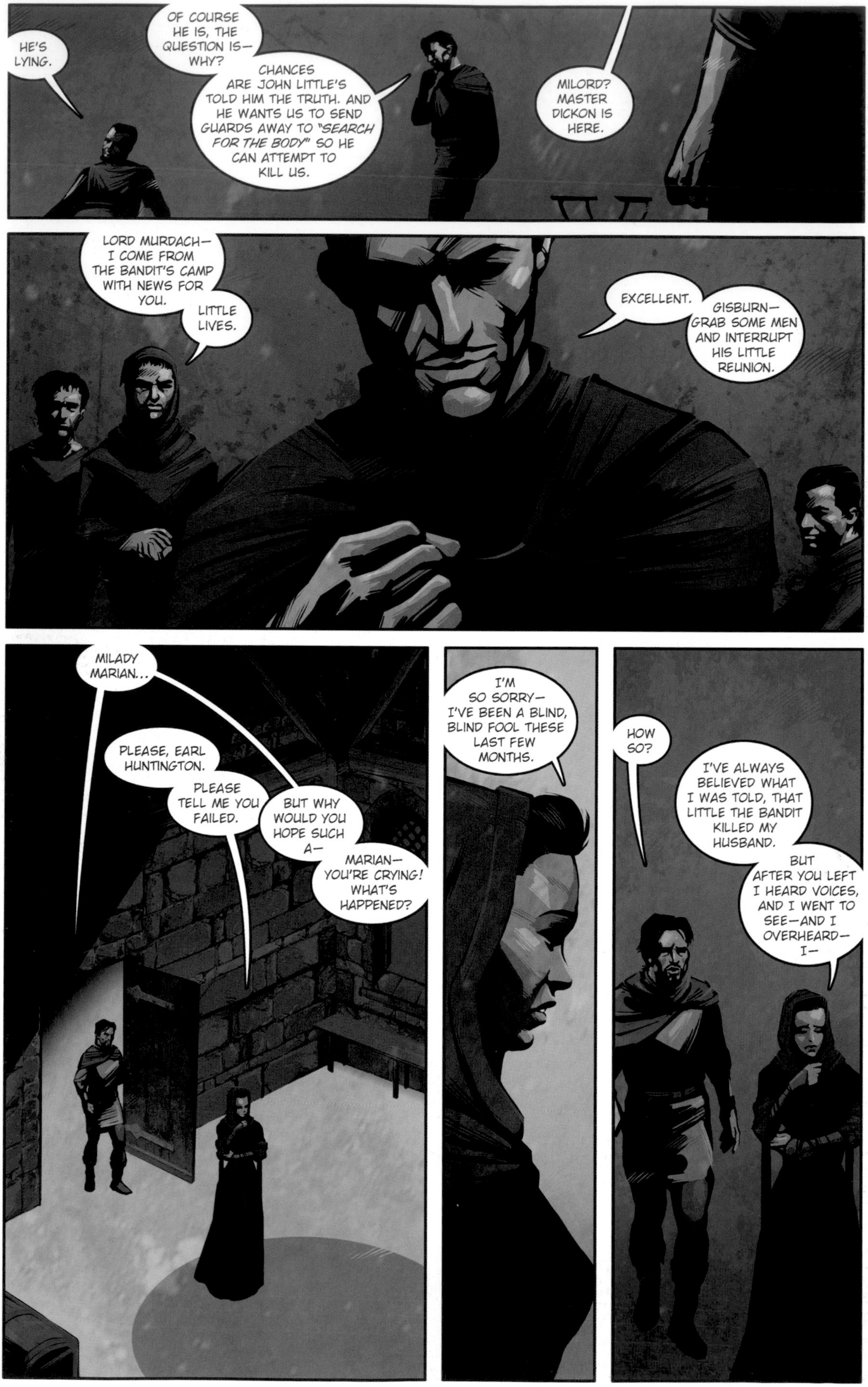
HE'S LYING.
OF COURSE HE IS, THE QUESTION IS— WHY?
CHANCES ARE JOHN LITTLE'S TOLD HIM THE TRUTH. AND HE WANTS US TO SEND GUARDS AWAY TO "SEARCH FOR THE BODY" SO HE CAN ATTEMPT TO KILL US.
MILORD? MASTER DICKON IS HERE.
LORD MURDACH— I COME FROM THE BANDIT'S CAMP WITH NEWS FOR YOU.
LITTLE LIVES.
EXCELLENT.
GISBURN— GRAB SOME MEN AND INTERRUPT HIS LITTLE REUNION.
MILADY MARIAN...
PLEASE, EARL HUNTINGTON.
PLEASE TELL ME YOU FAILED.
BUT WHY WOULD YOU HOPE SUCH A—
MARIAN— YOU'RE CRYING! WHAT'S HAPPENED?
I'M SO SORRY— I'VE BEEN A BLIND, BLIND FOOL THESE LAST FEW MONTHS.
HOW SO?
I'VE ALWAYS BELIEVED WHAT I WAS TOLD, THAT LITTLE THE BANDIT KILLED MY HUSBAND.
BUT AFTER YOU LEFT I HEARD VOICES, AND I WENT TO SEE—AND I OVERHEARD— I—

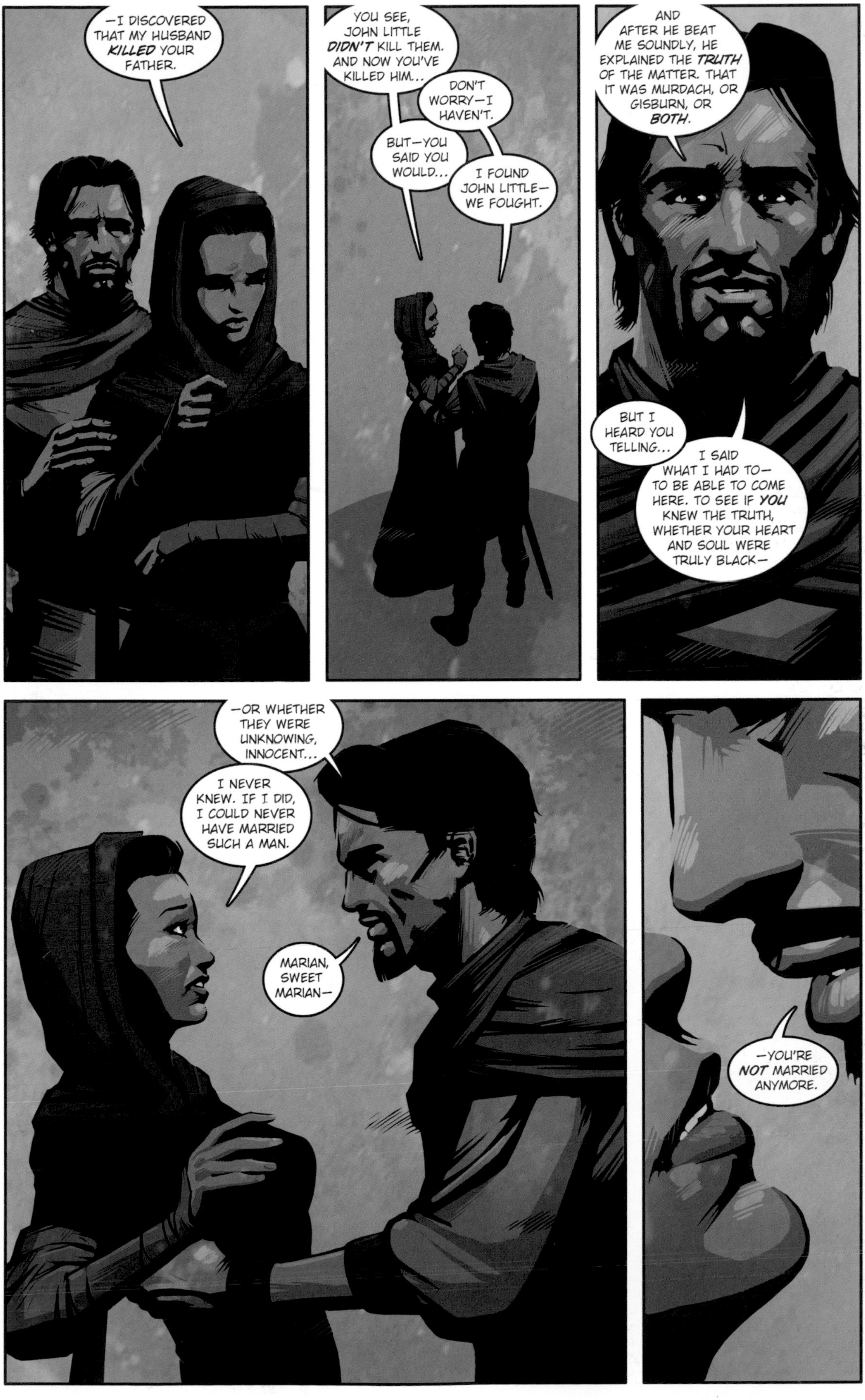
—I DISCOVERED THAT MY HUSBAND KILLED YOUR FATHER.
YOU SEE, JOHN LITTLE DIDN'T KILL THEM. AND NOW YOU'VE KILLED HIM...
DON'T WORRY—I HAVEN'T.
BUT—YOU SAID YOU WOULD...
I FOUND JOHN LITTLE—WE FOUGHT.
AND AFTER HE BEAT ME SOUNDLY, HE EXPLAINED THE TRUTH OF THE MATTER. THAT IT WAS MURDACH, OR GISBURN, OR BOTH.
BUT I HEARD YOU TELLING...
I SAID WHAT I HAD TO—TO BE ABLE TO COME HERE. TO SEE IF YOU KNEW THE TRUTH, WHETHER YOUR HEART AND SOUL WERE TRULY BLACK—
—OR WHETHER THEY WERE UNKNOWING, INNOCENT...
I NEVER KNEW. IF I DID, I COULD NEVER HAVE MARRIED SUCH A MAN.
MARIAN, SWEET MARIAN—
—YOU'RE NOT MARRIED ANYMORE.

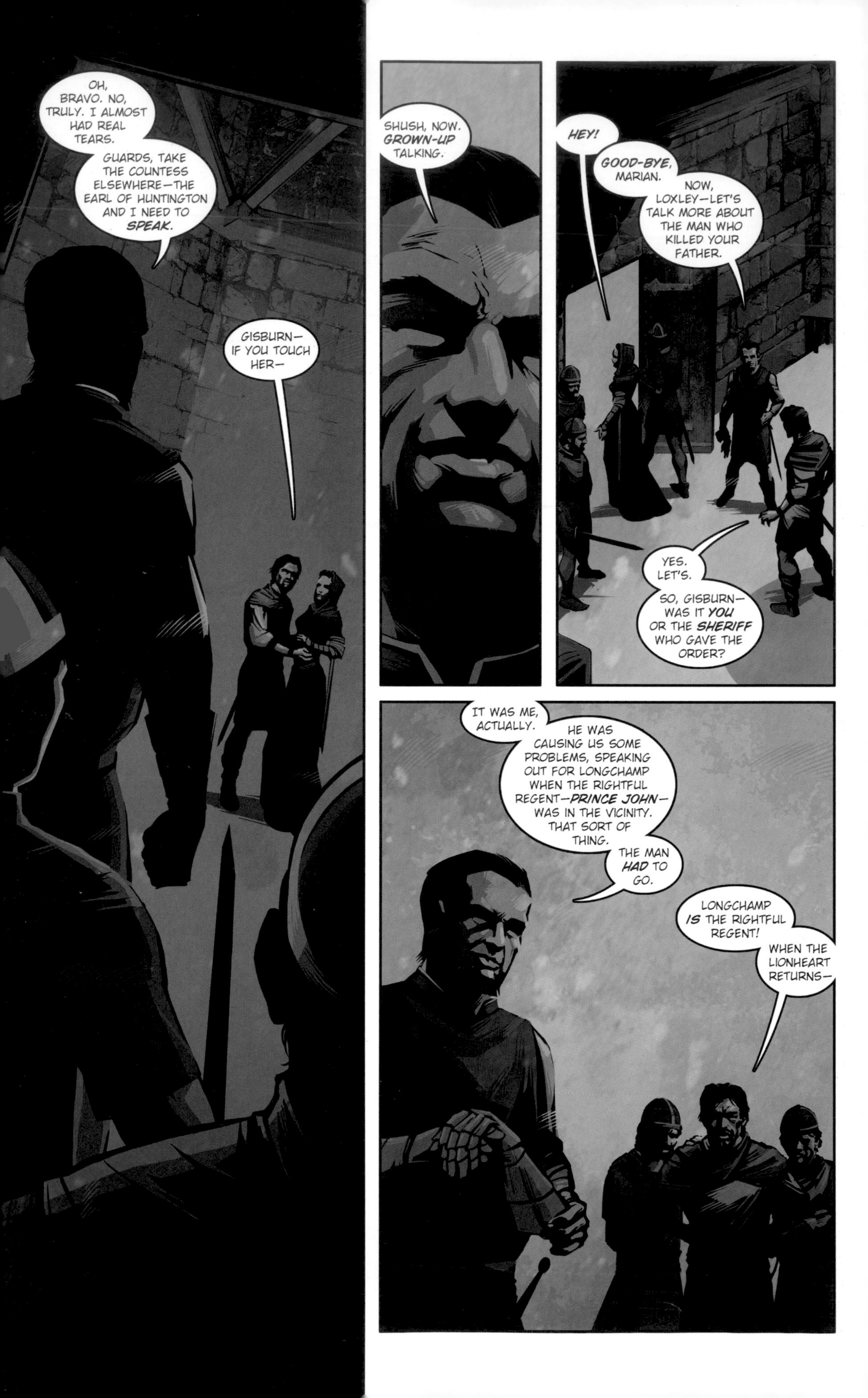
OH, BRAVO. NO, TRULY. I ALMOST HAD REAL TEARS.
GUARDS, TAKE THE COUNTESS ELSEWHERE—THE EARL OF HUNTINGTON AND I NEED TO SPEAK.
GISBURN—IF YOU TOUCH HER—
SHUSH, NOW. GROWN-UP TALKING.
HEY!
GOOD-BYE, MARIAN.
NOW, LOXLEY—LET'S TALK MORE ABOUT THE MAN WHO KILLED YOUR FATHER.
YES. LET'S.
SO, GISBURN—WAS IT YOU OR THE SHERIFF WHO GAVE THE ORDER?
IT WAS ME, ACTUALLY.
HE WAS CAUSING US SOME PROBLEMS, SPEAKING OUT FOR LONGCHAMP WHEN THE RIGHTFUL REGENT—PRINCE JOHN—WAS IN THE VICINITY. THAT SORT OF THING.
THE MAN HAD TO GO.
LONGCHAMP IS THE RIGHTFUL REGENT!
WHEN THE LIONHEART RETURNS—

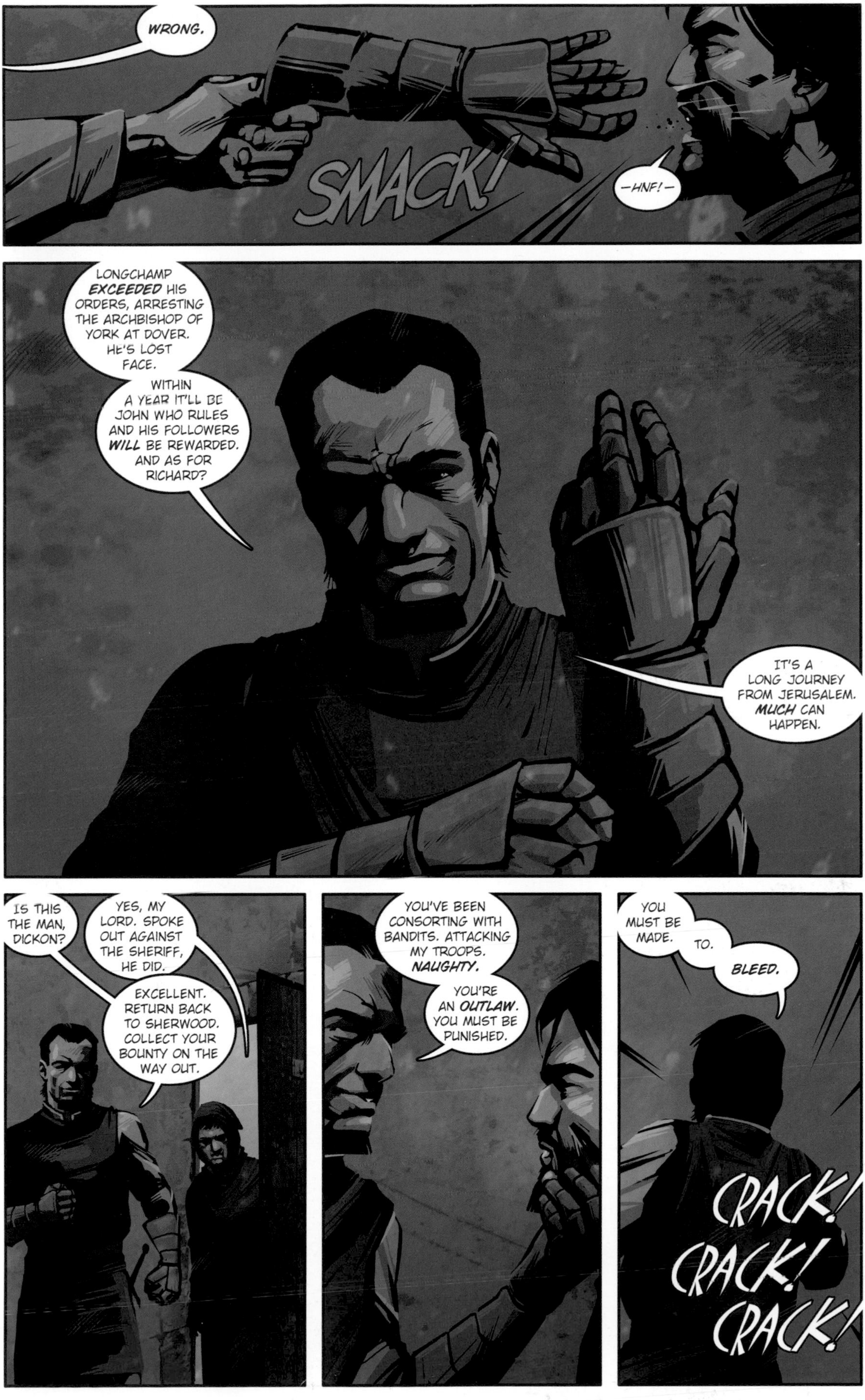
WRONG.
SMACK!
—HNF!—
LONGCHAMP EXCEEDED HIS ORDERS, ARRESTING THE ARCHBISHOP OF YORK AT DOVER. HE'S LOST FACE.
WITHIN A YEAR IT'LL BE JOHN WHO RULES AND HIS FOLLOWERS WILL BE REWARDED. AND AS FOR RICHARD?
IT'S A LONG JOURNEY FROM JERUSALEM. MUCH CAN HAPPEN.
IS THIS THE MAN, DICKON?
YES, MY LORD. SPOKE OUT AGAINST THE SHERIFF, HE DID.
EXCELLENT. RETURN BACK TO SHERWOOD. COLLECT YOUR BOUNTY ON THE WAY OUT.
YOU'VE BEEN CONSORTING WITH BANDITS. ATTACKING MY TROOPS. NAUGHTY.
YOU'RE AN OUTLAW. YOU MUST BE PUNISHED.
YOU MUST BE MADE.
TO.
BLEED.
CRACK! CRACK! CRACK!

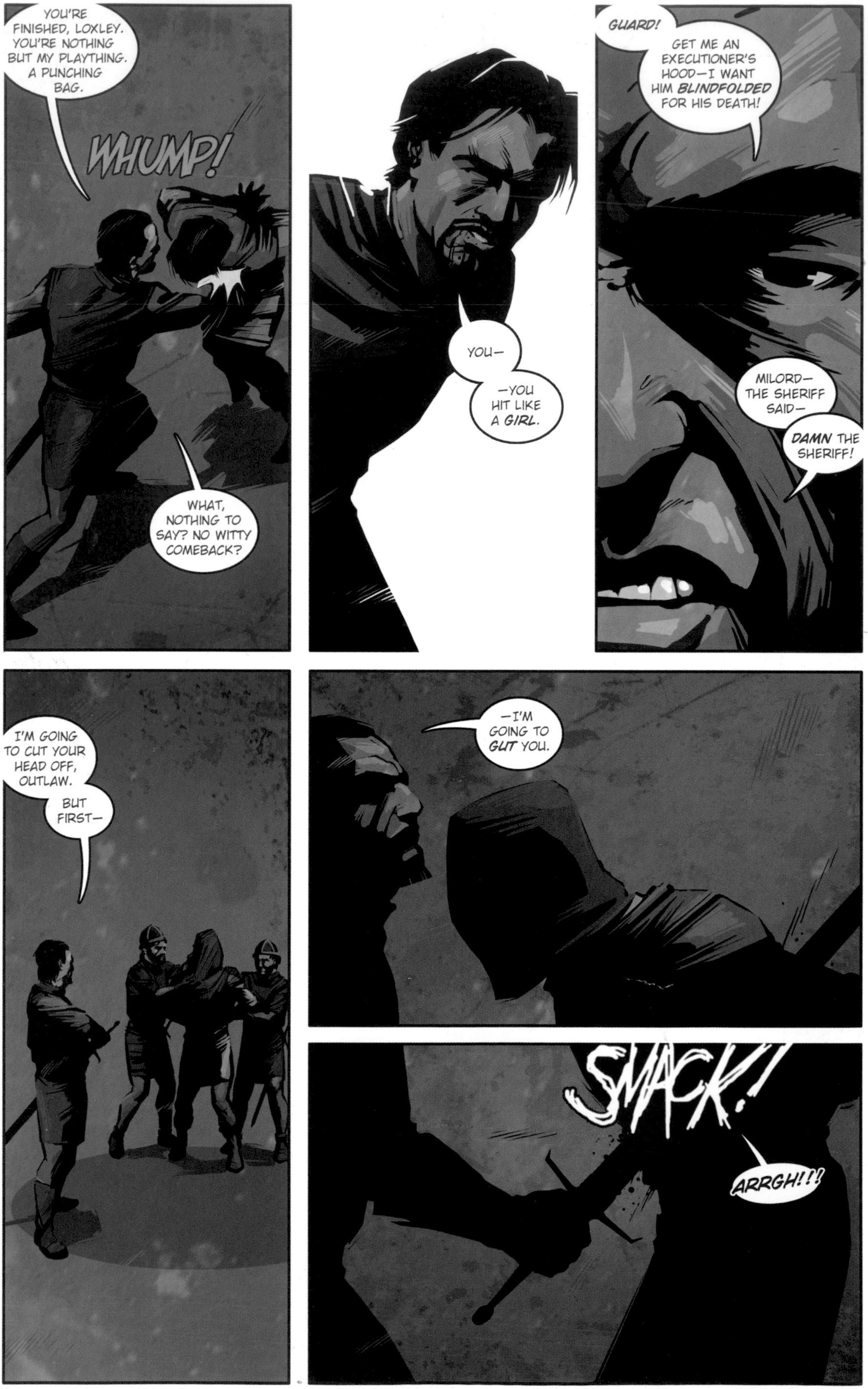
YOU'RE FINISHED, LOXLEY. YOU'RE NOTHING BUT MY PLAYTHING. A PUNCHING BAG.
WHUMP!
WHAT, NOTHING TO SAY? NO WITTY COMEBACK?
YOU—
—YOU HIT LIKE A GIRL.
GUARD!
GET ME AN EXECUTIONER'S HOOD—I WANT HIM BLINDFOLDED FOR HIS DEATH!
MILORD— THE SHERIFF SAID—
DAMN THE SHERIFF!
I'M GOING TO CUT YOUR HEAD OFF, OUTLAW.
BUT FIRST—
—I'M GOING TO GUT YOU.
SMACK!
ARRGH!!!

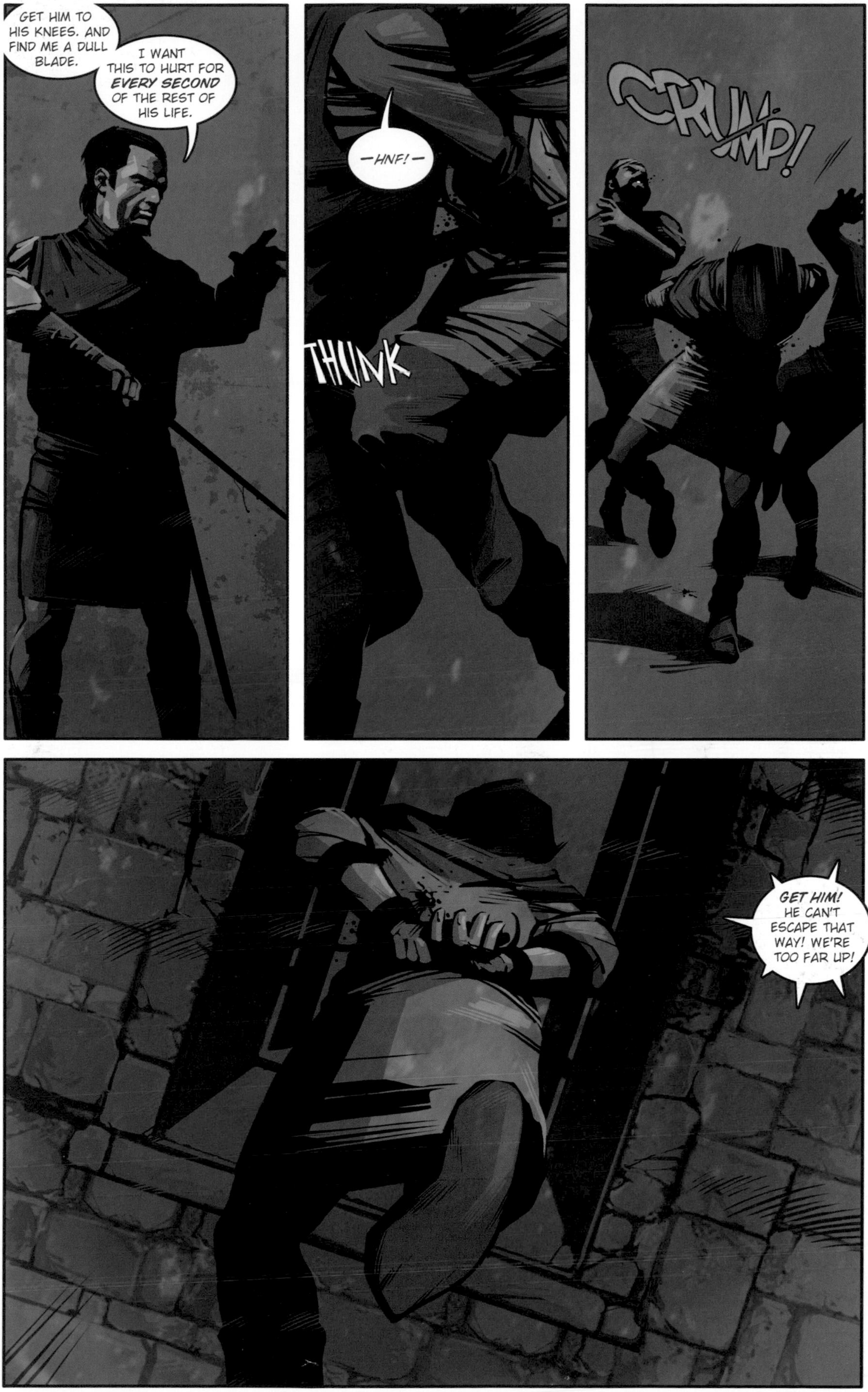
GET HIM TO HIS KNEES. AND FIND ME A DULL BLADE.
I WANT THIS TO HURT FOR **EVERY SECOND** OF THE REST OF HIS LIFE.
—HNF!—
THUNK
CRUMP!
GET HIM! HE CAN'T ESCAPE THAT WAY! WE'RE TOO FAR UP!

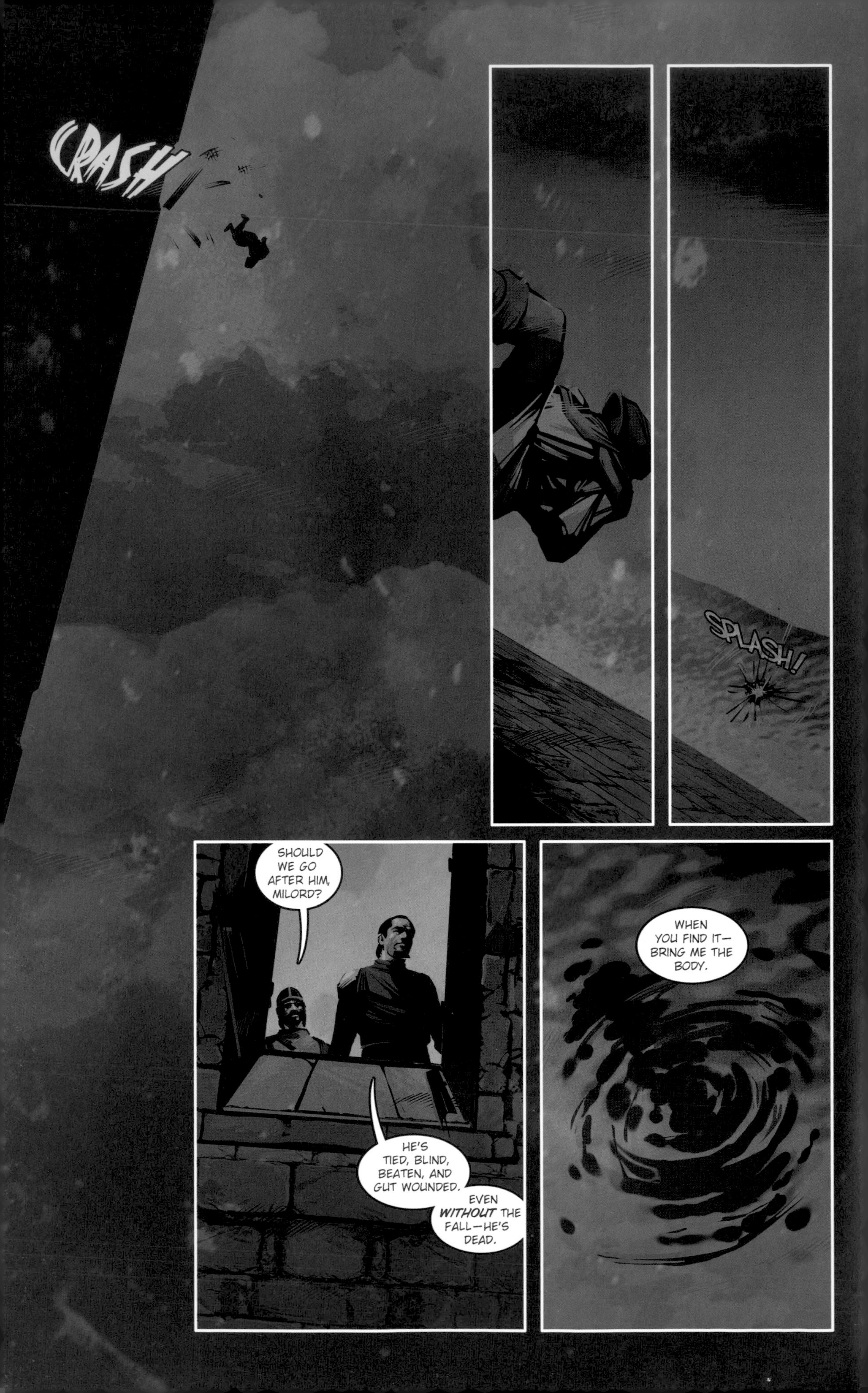
CRASH
SPLASH!
SHOULD WE GO AFTER HIM, MILORD?
HE'S TIED, BLIND, BEATEN, AND GUT WOUNDED.
EVEN *WITHOUT* THE FALL—HE'S DEAD.
WHEN YOU FIND IT—BRING ME THE BODY.

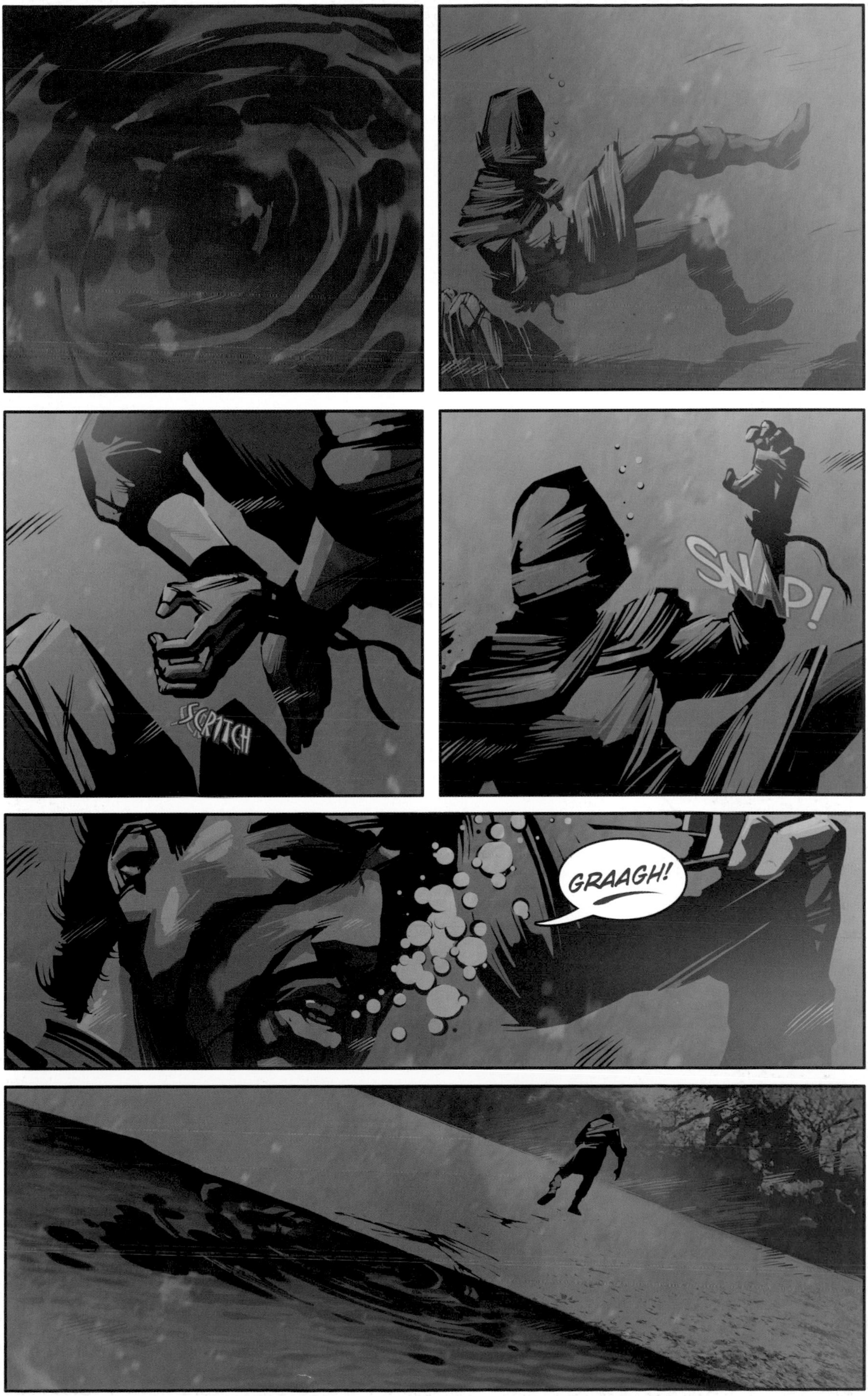
SCRITCH
SNAP!
GRAAGH!

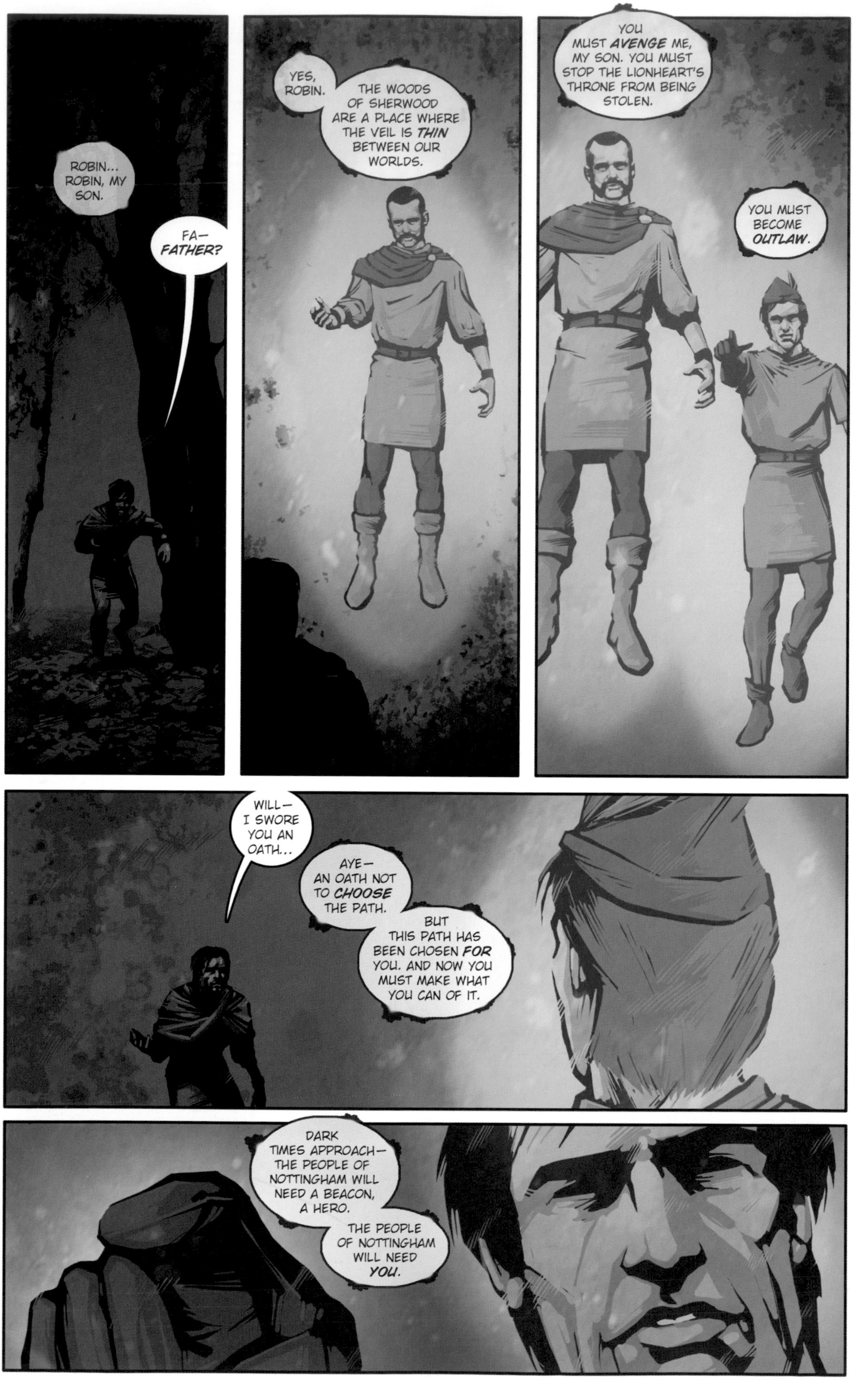
ROBIN... ROBIN, MY SON.
FA— FATHER?
YES, ROBIN.
THE WOODS OF SHERWOOD ARE A PLACE WHERE THE VEIL IS THIN BETWEEN OUR WORLDS.
YOU MUST AVENGE ME, MY SON. YOU MUST STOP THE LIONHEART'S THRONE FROM BEING STOLEN.
YOU MUST BECOME OUTLAW.
WILL— I SWORE YOU AN OATH...
AYE— AN OATH NOT TO CHOOSE THE PATH.
BUT THIS PATH HAS BEEN CHOSEN FOR YOU. AND NOW YOU MUST MAKE WHAT YOU CAN OF IT.
DARK TIMES APPROACH— THE PEOPLE OF NOTTINGHAM WILL NEED A BEACON, A HERO.
THE PEOPLE OF NOTTINGHAM WILL NEED YOU.

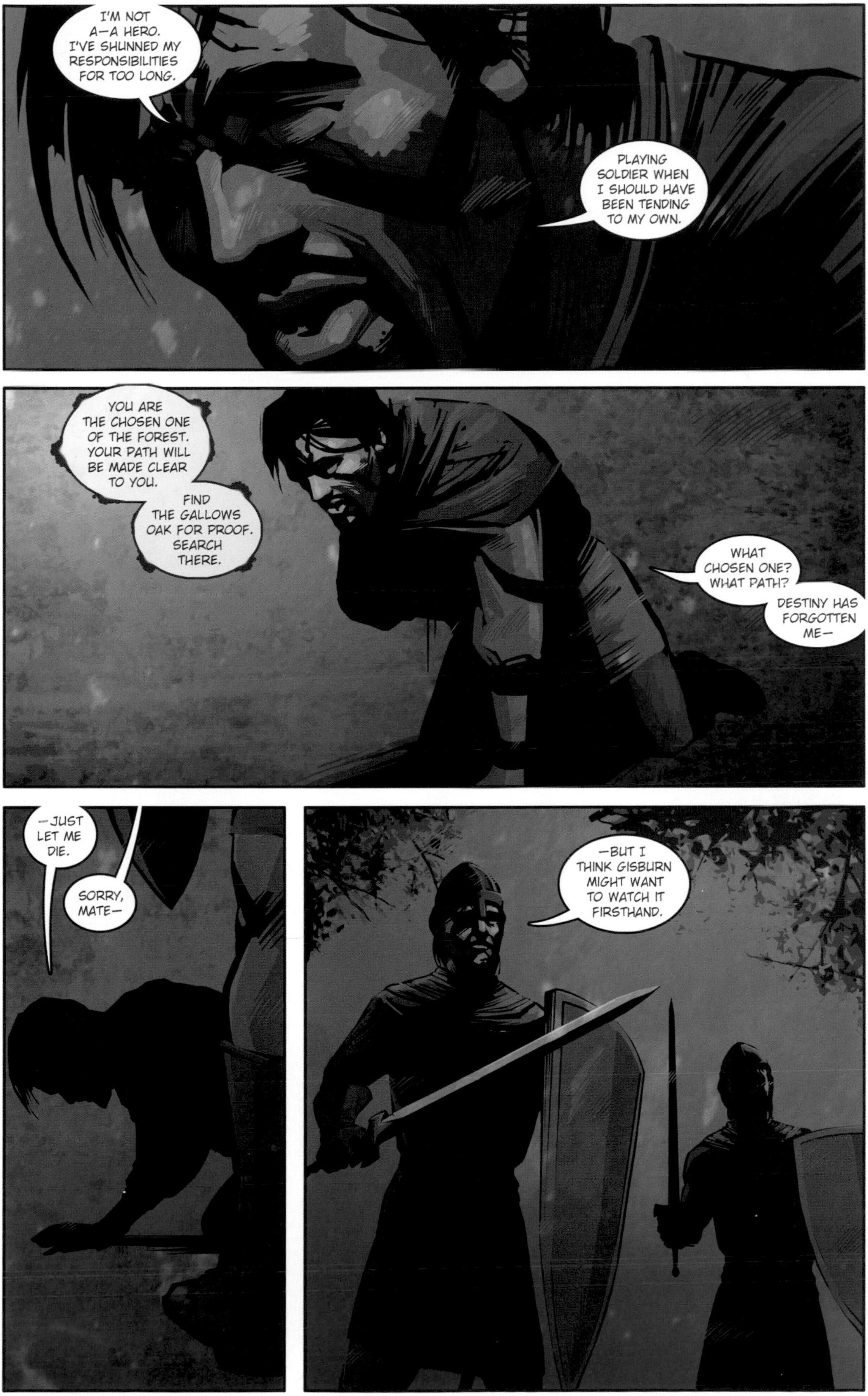
I'M NOT A—A HERO. I'VE SHUNNED MY RESPONSIBILITIES FOR TOO LONG.
PLAYING SOLDIER WHEN I SHOULD HAVE BEEN TENDING TO MY OWN.
YOU ARE THE CHOSEN ONE OF THE FOREST. YOUR PATH WILL BE MADE CLEAR TO YOU.
FIND THE GALLOWS OAK FOR PROOF. SEARCH THERE.
WHAT CHOSEN ONE? WHAT PATH?
DESTINY HAS FORGOTTEN ME—
—JUST LET ME DIE.
SORRY, MATE—
—BUT I THINK GISBURN MIGHT WANT TO WATCH IT FIRSTHAND.

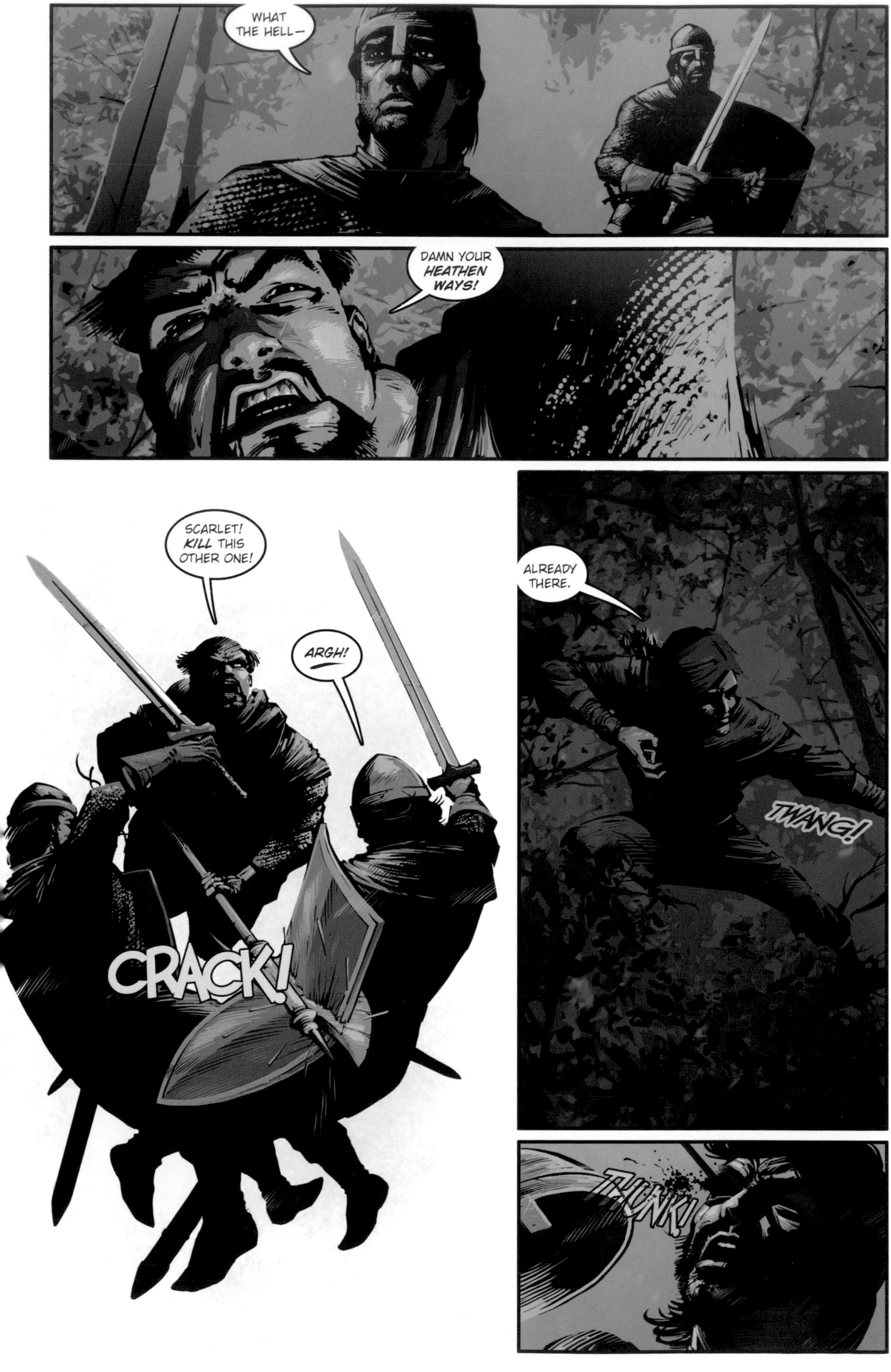
WHAT THE HELL—
DAMN YOUR HEATHEN WAYS!
SCARLET! KILL THIS OTHER ONE!
ARGH!
CRACK!
ALREADY THERE.
TWANG!
THUNK!

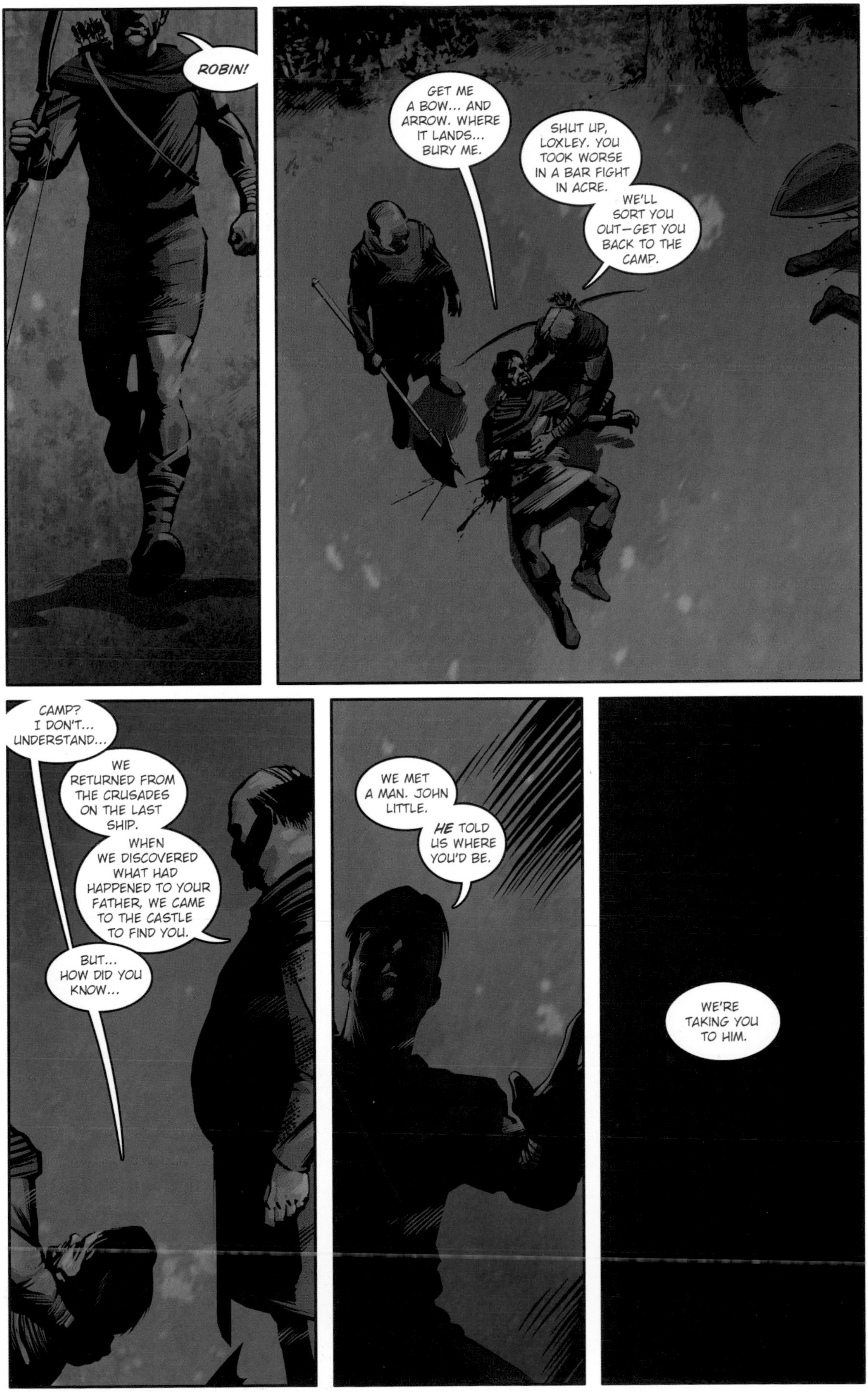
ROBIN!
GET ME A BOW... AND ARROW. WHERE IT LANDS... BURY ME.
SHUT UP, LOXLEY. YOU TOOK WORSE IN A BAR FIGHT IN ACRE.
WE'LL SORT YOU OUT—GET YOU BACK TO THE CAMP.
CAMP? I DON'T... UNDERSTAND...
WE RETURNED FROM THE CRUSADES ON THE LAST SHIP.
WHEN WE DISCOVERED WHAT HAD HAPPENED TO YOUR FATHER, WE CAME TO THE CASTLE TO FIND YOU.
BUT... HOW DID YOU KNOW...
WE MET A MAN. JOHN LITTLE.
HE TOLD US WHERE YOU'D BE.
WE'RE TAKING YOU TO HIM.

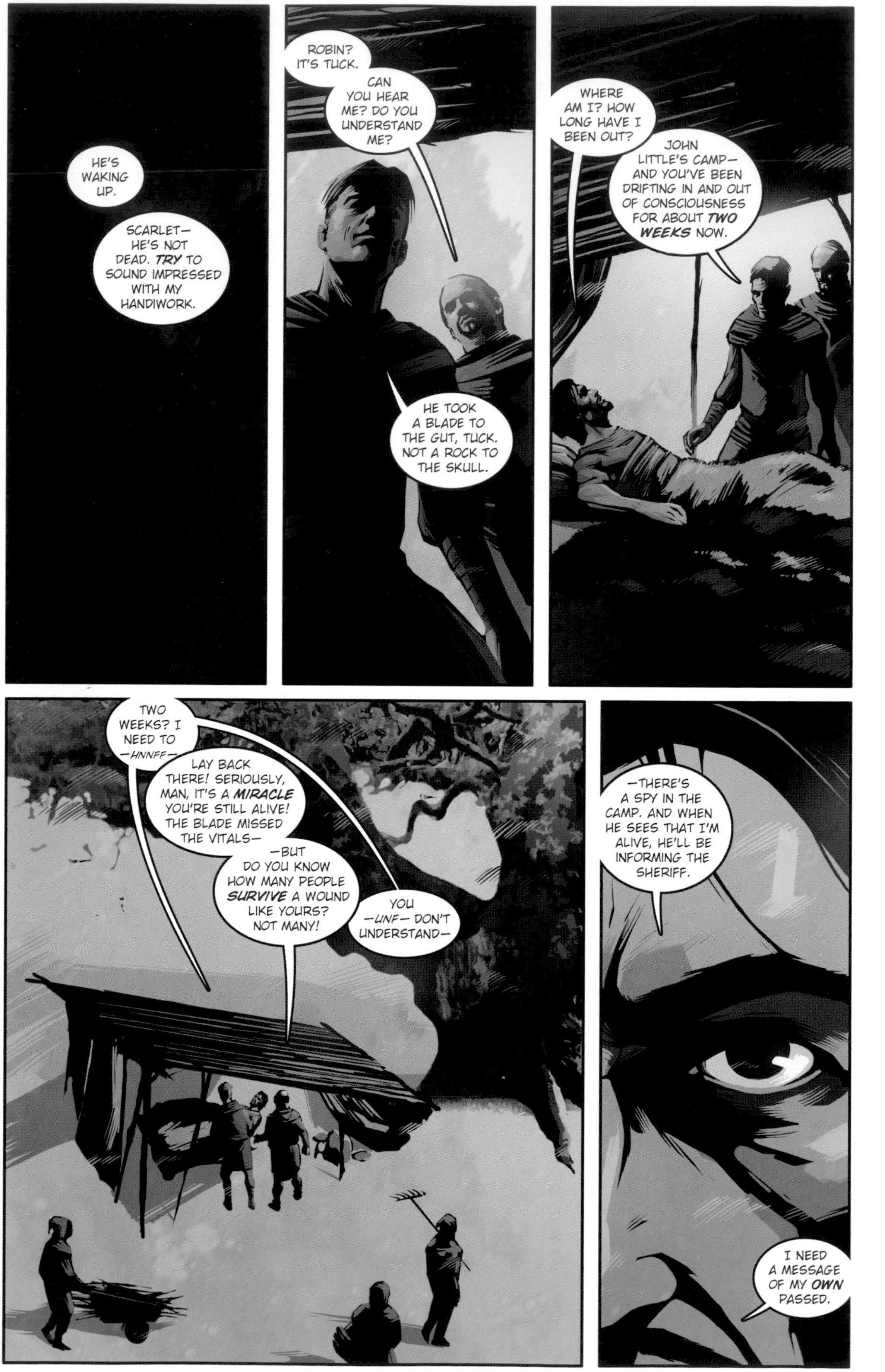
HE'S WAKING UP.
SCARLET— HE'S NOT DEAD. TRY TO SOUND IMPRESSED WITH MY HANDIWORK.
ROBIN? IT'S TUCK.
CAN YOU HEAR ME? DO YOU UNDERSTAND ME?
HE TOOK A BLADE TO THE GUT, TUCK. NOT A ROCK TO THE SKULL.
WHERE AM I? HOW LONG HAVE I BEEN OUT?
JOHN LITTLE'S CAMP— AND YOU'VE BEEN DRIFTING IN AND OUT OF CONSCIOUSNESS FOR ABOUT TWO WEEKS NOW.
TWO WEEKS? I NEED TO —HNNFF—
LAY BACK THERE! SERIOUSLY, MAN, IT'S A MIRACLE YOU'RE STILL ALIVE! THE BLADE MISSED THE VITALS—
—BUT DO YOU KNOW HOW MANY PEOPLE SURVIVE A WOUND LIKE YOURS? NOT MANY!
YOU —UNF— DON'T UNDERSTAND—
—THERE'S A SPY IN THE CAMP. AND WHEN HE SEES THAT I'M ALIVE, HE'LL BE INFORMING THE SHERIFF.
I NEED A MESSAGE OF MY OWN PASSED.

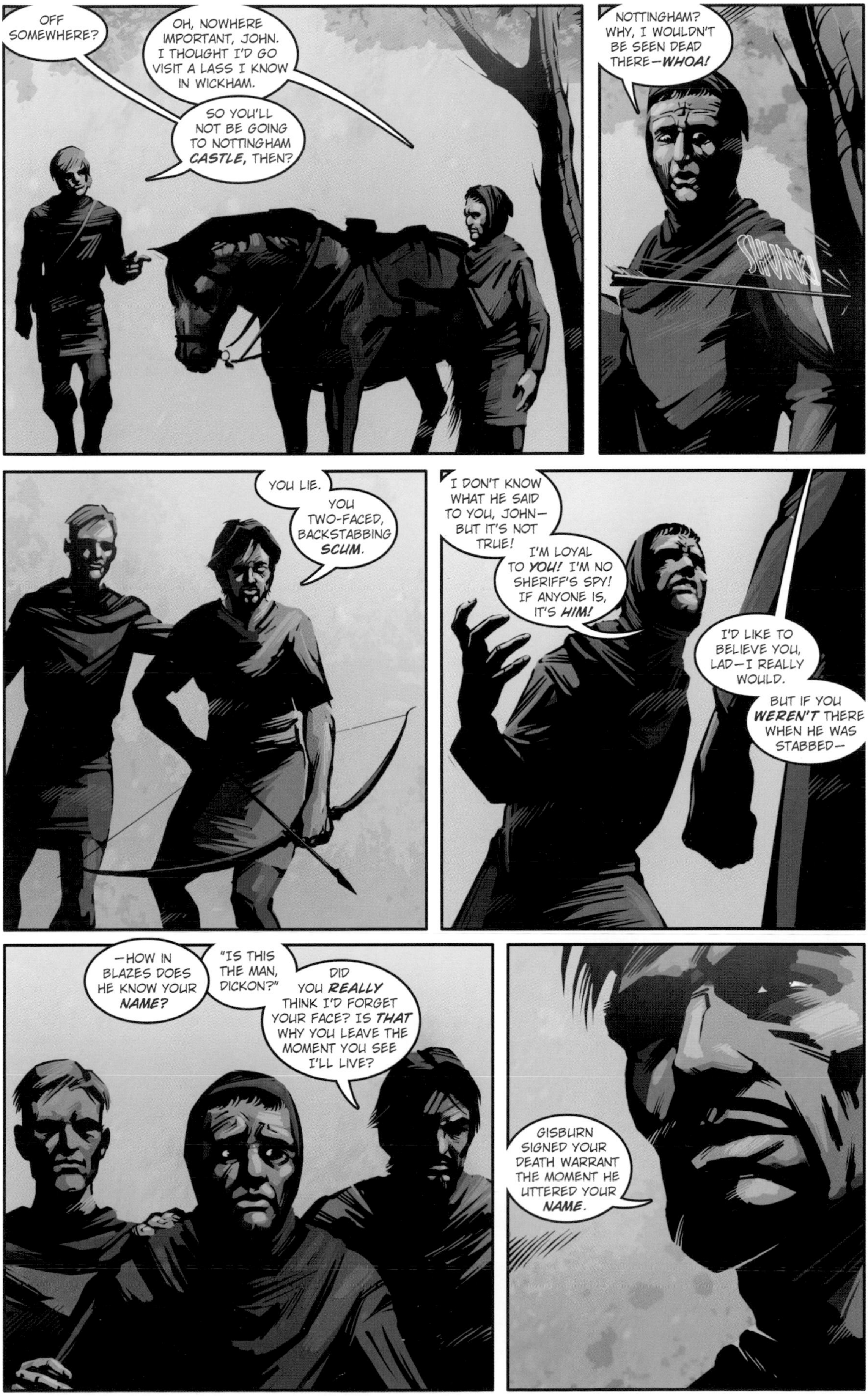
OFF SOMEWHERE?
OH, NOWHERE IMPORTANT, JOHN. I THOUGHT I'D GO VISIT A LASS I KNOW IN WICKHAM.
SO YOU'LL NOT BE GOING TO NOTTINGHAM CASTLE, THEN?
NOTTINGHAM? WHY, I WOULDN'T BE SEEN DEAD THERE—WHOA!
SHUNK!
YOU LIE.
YOU TWO-FACED, BACKSTABBING SCUM.
I DON'T KNOW WHAT HE SAID TO YOU, JOHN—BUT IT'S NOT TRUE!
I'M LOYAL TO YOU! I'M NO SHERIFF'S SPY! IF ANYONE IS, IT'S HIM!
I'D LIKE TO BELIEVE YOU, LAD—I REALLY WOULD.
BUT IF YOU WEREN'T THERE WHEN HE WAS STABBED—
—HOW IN BLAZES DOES HE KNOW YOUR NAME?
"IS THIS THE MAN, DICKON?"
DID YOU REALLY THINK I'D FORGET YOUR FACE? IS THAT WHY YOU LEAVE THE MOMENT YOU SEE I'LL LIVE?
GISBURN SIGNED YOUR DEATH WARRANT THE MOMENT HE UTTERED YOUR NAME.

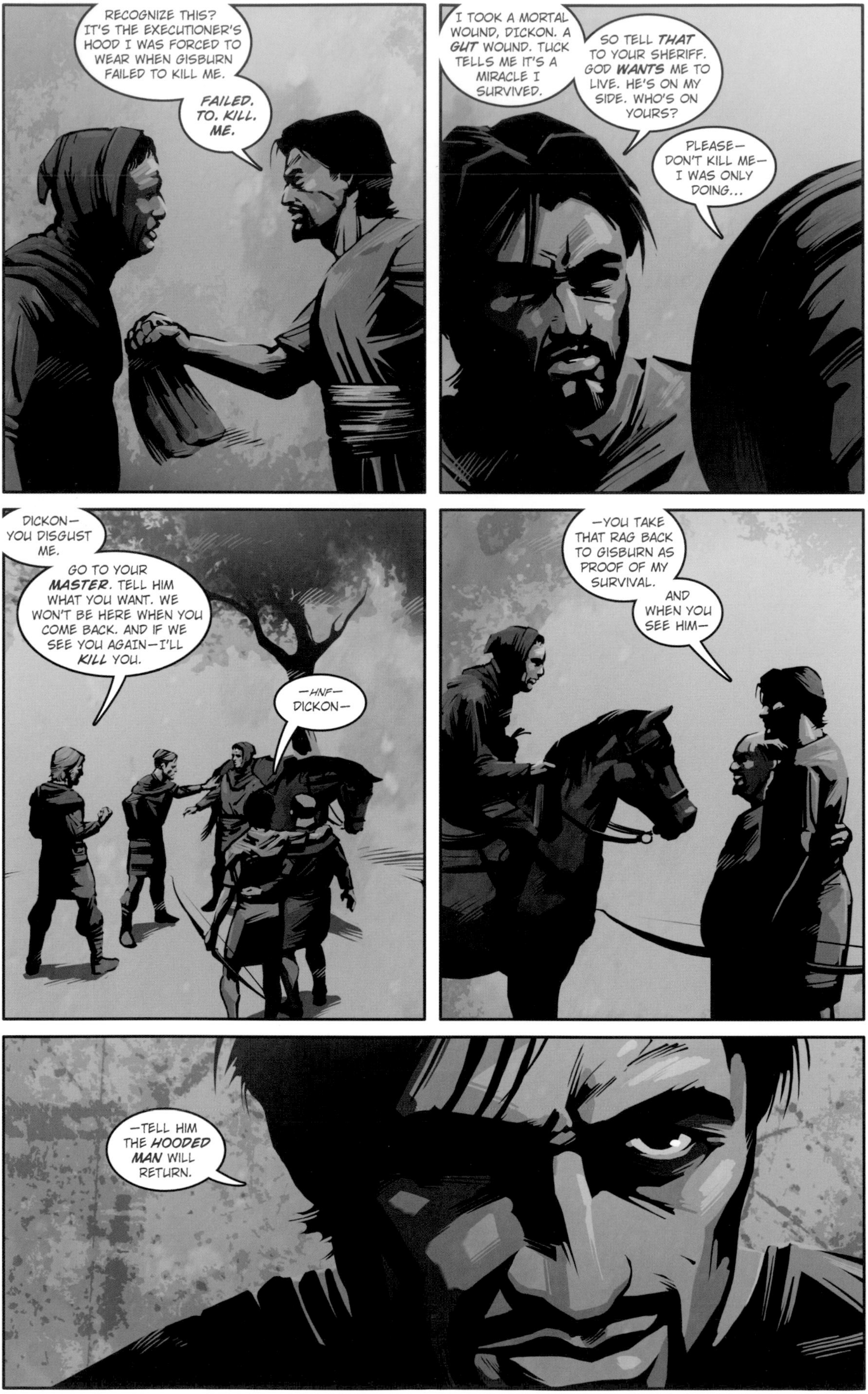

RECOGNIZE THIS? IT'S THE EXECUTIONER'S HOOD I WAS FORCED TO WEAR WHEN GISBURN FAILED TO KILL ME.
FAILED. TO. KILL. ME.
I TOOK A MORTAL WOUND, DICKON. A GUT WOUND. TUCK TELLS ME IT'S A MIRACLE I SURVIVED.
SO TELL THAT TO YOUR SHERIFF. GOD WANTS ME TO LIVE. HE'S ON MY SIDE. WHO'S ON YOURS?
PLEASE— DON'T KILL ME— I WAS ONLY DOING...
DICKON— YOU DISGUST ME.
GO TO YOUR MASTER. TELL HIM WHAT YOU WANT. WE WON'T BE HERE WHEN YOU COME BACK. AND IF WE SEE YOU AGAIN—I'LL KILL YOU.
—HNF— DICKON—
—YOU TAKE THAT RAG BACK TO GISBURN AS PROOF OF MY SURVIVAL.
AND WHEN YOU SEE HIM—
—TELL HIM THE HOODED MAN WILL RETURN.

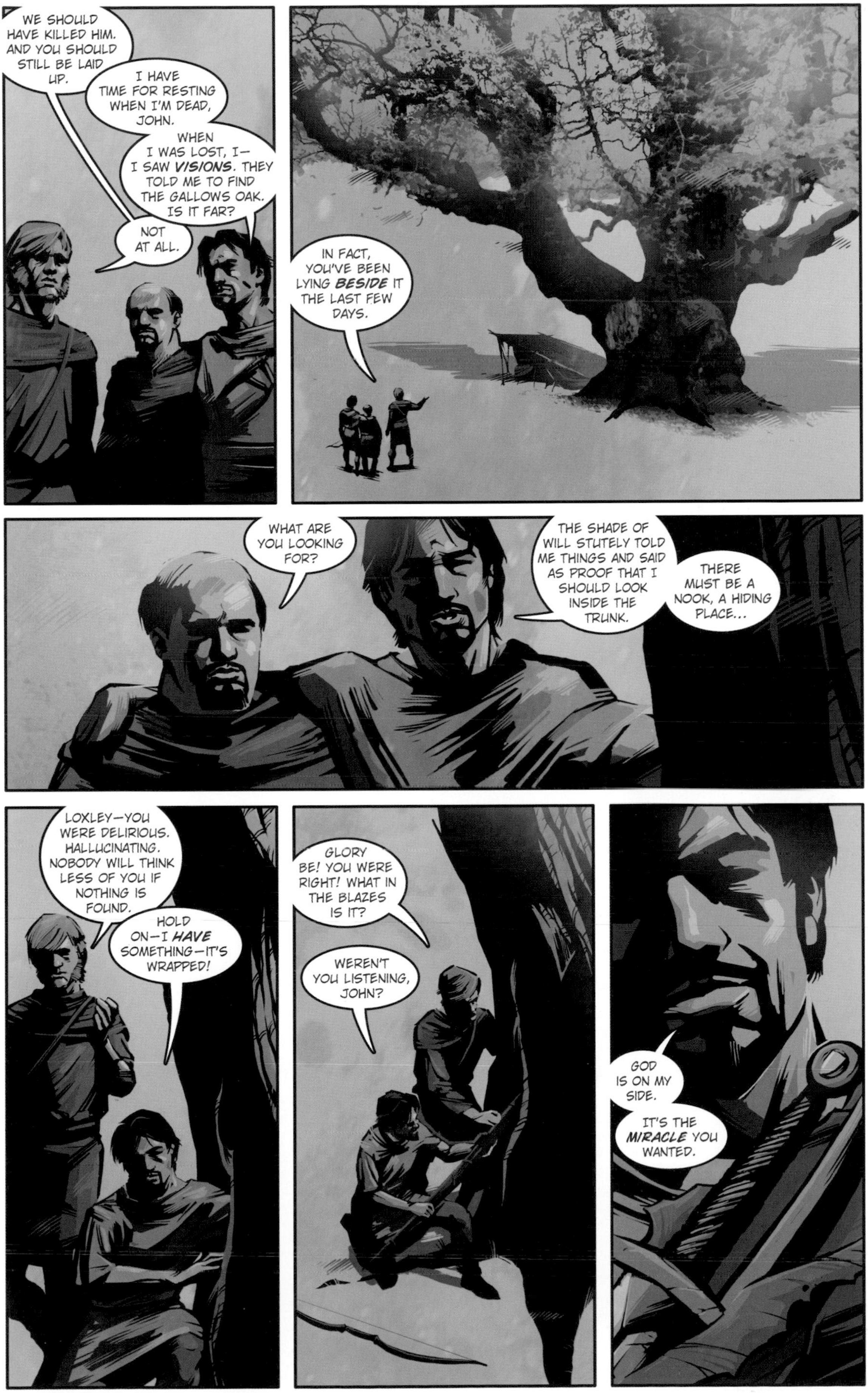
WE SHOULD HAVE KILLED HIM. AND YOU SHOULD STILL BE LAID UP.
I HAVE TIME FOR RESTING WHEN I'M DEAD, JOHN.
WHEN I WAS LOST, I— I SAW ***VISIONS***. THEY TOLD ME TO FIND THE GALLOWS OAK. IS IT FAR?
NOT AT ALL.
IN FACT, YOU'VE BEEN LYING ***BESIDE*** IT THE LAST FEW DAYS.
WHAT ARE YOU LOOKING FOR?
THE SHADE OF WILL STUTELY TOLD ME THINGS AND SAID AS PROOF THAT I SHOULD LOOK INSIDE THE TRUNK.
THERE MUST BE A NOOK, A HIDING PLACE...
LOXLEY—YOU WERE DELIRIOUS. HALLUCINATING. NOBODY WILL THINK LESS OF YOU IF NOTHING IS FOUND.
HOLD ON—I ***HAVE*** SOMETHING—IT'S WRAPPED!
GLORY BE! YOU WERE RIGHT! WHAT IN THE BLAZES IS IT?
WEREN'T YOU LISTENING, JOHN?
GOD IS ON MY SIDE.
IT'S THE ***MIRACLE*** YOU WANTED.

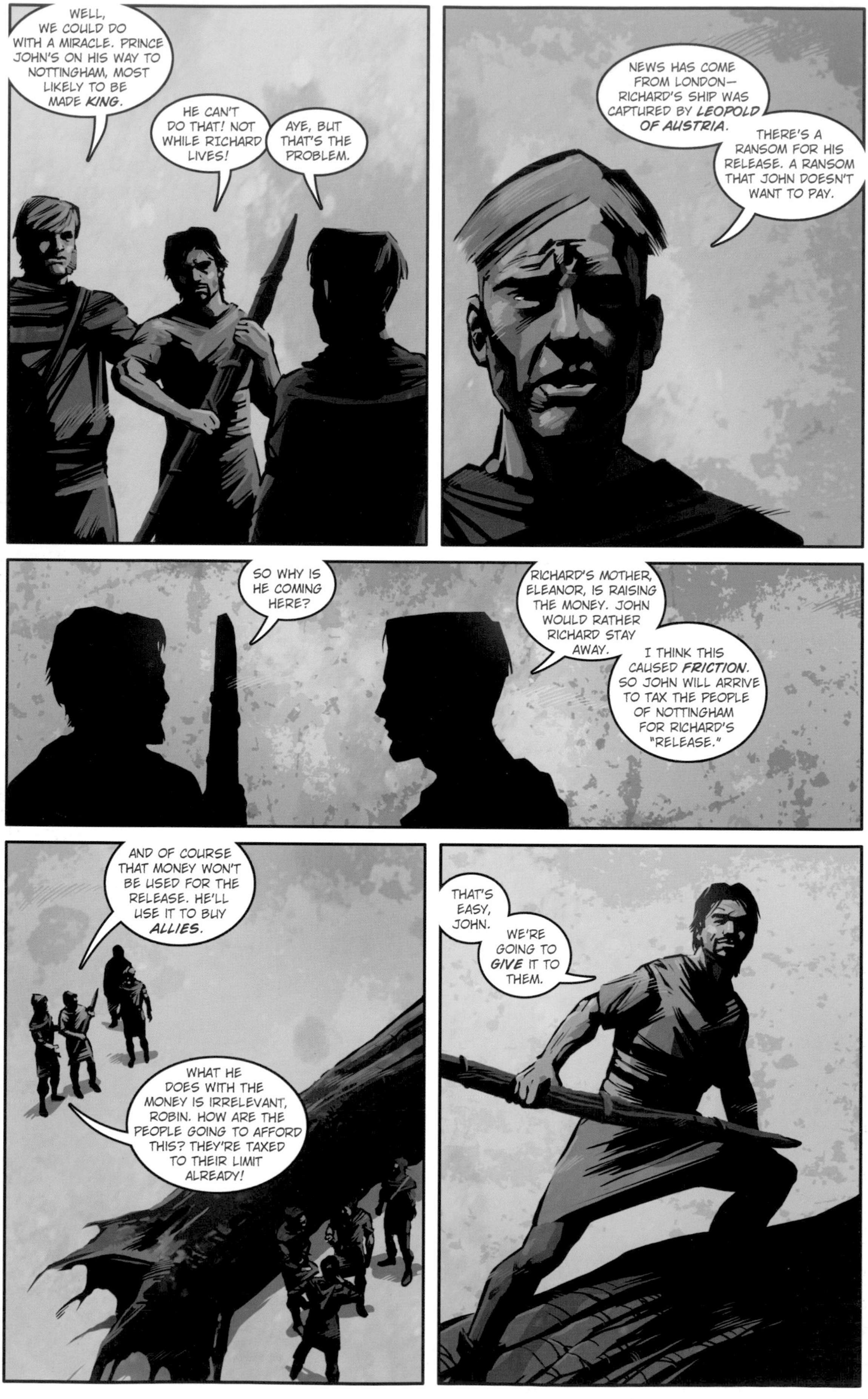
WELL, WE COULD DO WITH A MIRACLE. PRINCE JOHN'S ON HIS WAY TO NOTTINGHAM, MOST LIKELY TO BE MADE KING.
HE CAN'T DO THAT! NOT WHILE RICHARD LIVES!
AYE, BUT THAT'S THE PROBLEM.
NEWS HAS COME FROM LONDON— RICHARD'S SHIP WAS CAPTURED BY LEOPOLD OF AUSTRIA.
THERE'S A RANSOM FOR HIS RELEASE. A RANSOM THAT JOHN DOESN'T WANT TO PAY.
SO WHY IS HE COMING HERE?
RICHARD'S MOTHER, ELEANOR, IS RAISING THE MONEY. JOHN WOULD RATHER RICHARD STAY AWAY.
I THINK THIS CAUSED FRICTION. SO JOHN WILL ARRIVE TO TAX THE PEOPLE OF NOTTINGHAM FOR RICHARD'S "RELEASE."
AND OF COURSE THAT MONEY WON'T BE USED FOR THE RELEASE. HE'LL USE IT TO BUY ALLIES.
WHAT HE DOES WITH THE MONEY IS IRRELEVANT, ROBIN. HOW ARE THE PEOPLE GOING TO AFFORD THIS? THEY'RE TAXED TO THEIR LIMIT ALREADY!
THAT'S EASY, JOHN.
WE'RE GOING TO GIVE IT TO THEM.

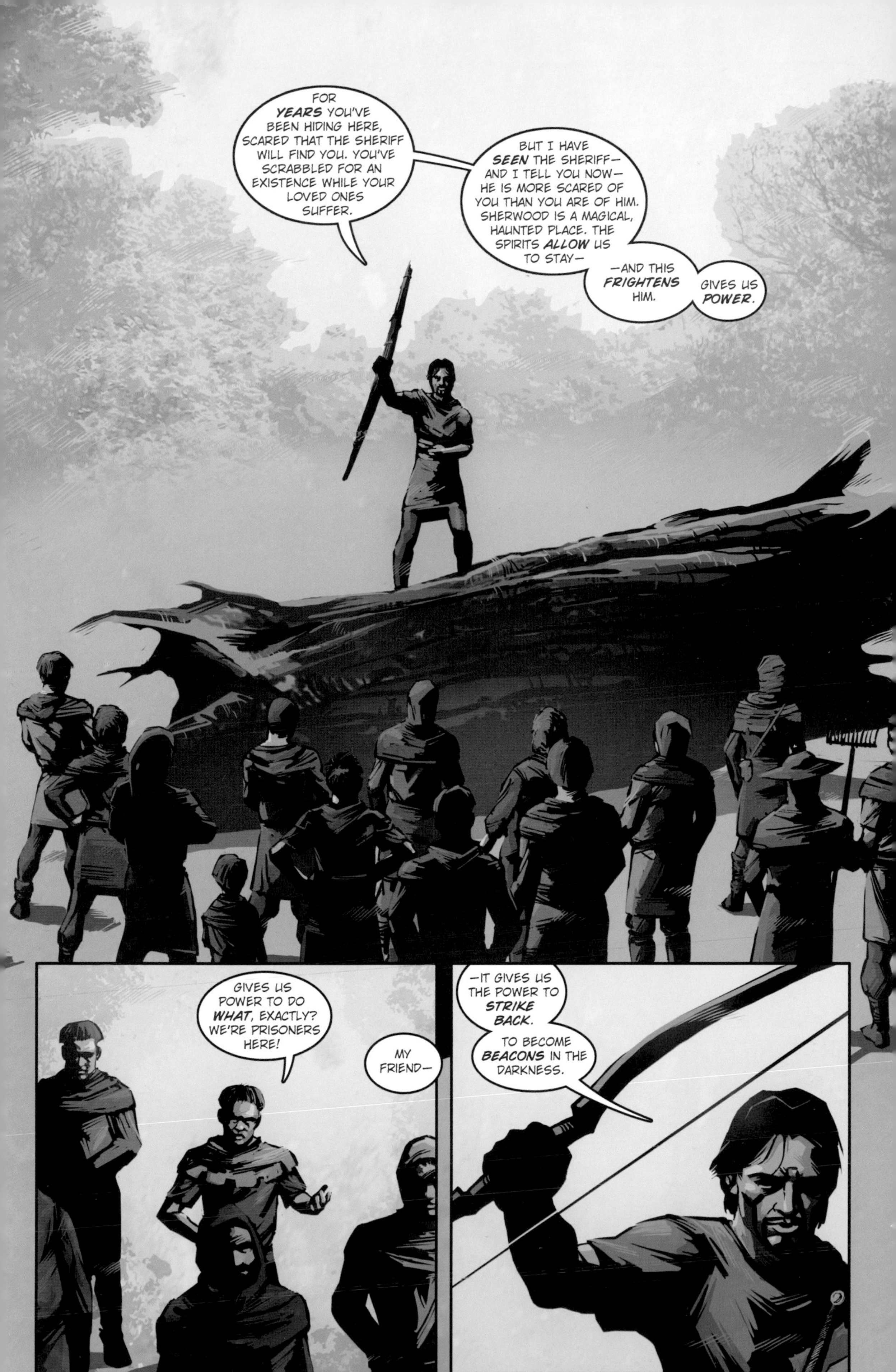
FOR YEARS YOU'VE BEEN HIDING HERE, SCARED THAT THE SHERIFF WILL FIND YOU. YOU'VE SCRABBLED FOR AN EXISTENCE WHILE YOUR LOVED ONES SUFFER.
BUT I HAVE SEEN THE SHERIFF— AND I TELL YOU NOW— HE IS MORE SCARED OF YOU THAN YOU ARE OF HIM. SHERWOOD IS A MAGICAL, HAUNTED PLACE. THE SPIRITS ALLOW US TO STAY—
—AND THIS FRIGHTENS HIM.
GIVES US POWER.
GIVES US POWER TO DO WHAT, EXACTLY? WE'RE PRISONERS HERE!
MY FRIEND—
—IT GIVES US THE POWER TO STRIKE BACK.
TO BECOME BEACONS IN THE DARKNESS.

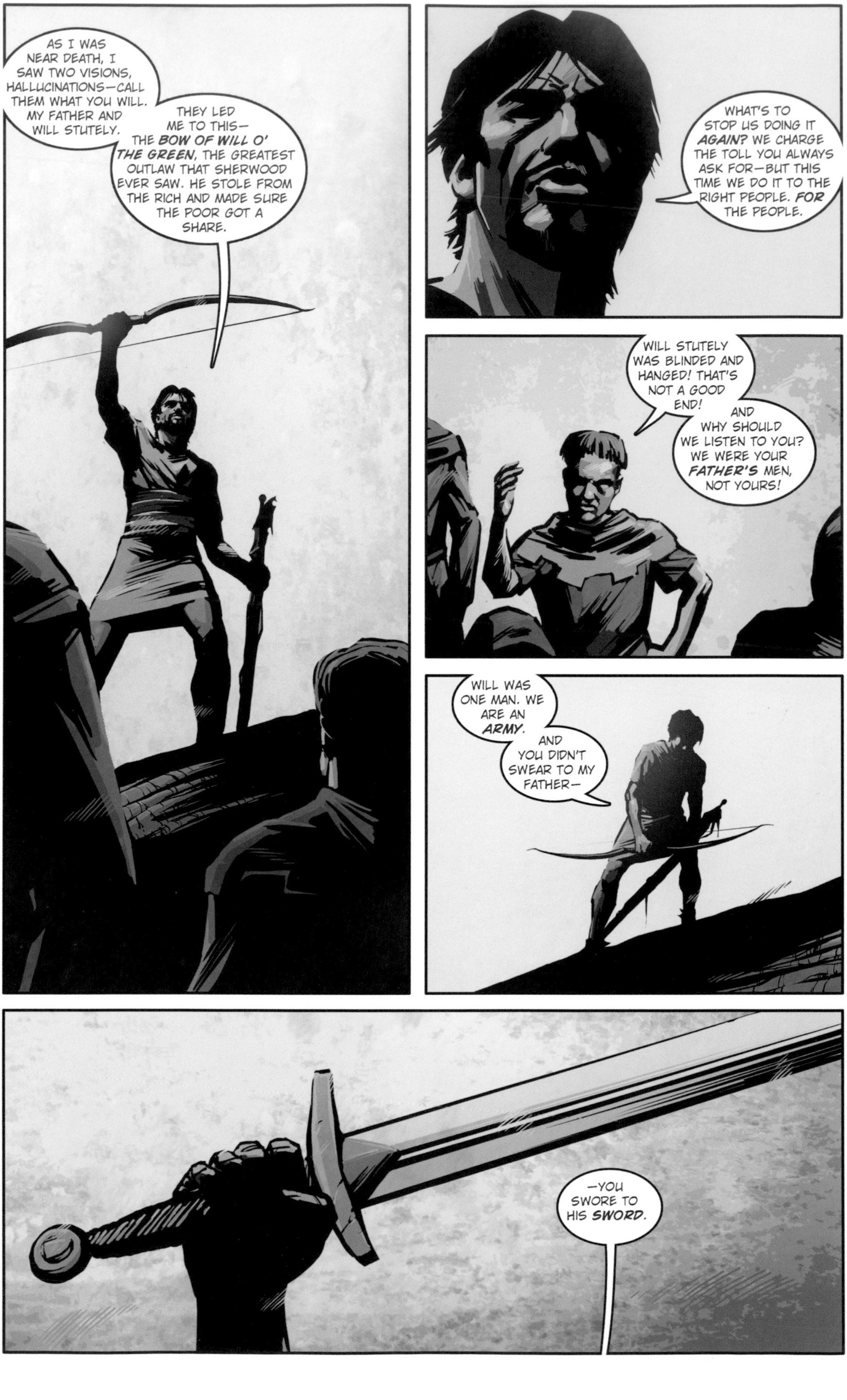
AS I WAS NEAR DEATH, I SAW TWO VISIONS, HALLUCINATIONS—CALL THEM WHAT YOU WILL. MY FATHER AND WILL STUTELY.
THEY LED ME TO THIS— THE ***BOW OF WILL O' THE GREEN***, THE GREATEST OUTLAW THAT SHERWOOD EVER SAW. HE STOLE FROM THE RICH AND MADE SURE THE POOR GOT A SHARE.
WHAT'S TO STOP US DOING IT ***AGAIN?*** WE CHARGE THE TOLL YOU ALWAYS ASK FOR—BUT THIS TIME WE DO IT TO THE RIGHT PEOPLE. ***FOR*** THE PEOPLE.
WILL STUTELY WAS BLINDED AND HANGED! THAT'S NOT A GOOD END!
AND WHY SHOULD WE LISTEN TO YOU? WE WERE YOUR ***FATHER'S*** MEN, NOT YOURS!
WILL WAS ONE MAN. WE ARE AN ***ARMY***.
AND YOU DIDN'T SWEAR TO MY FATHER—
—YOU SWORE TO HIS ***SWORD***.

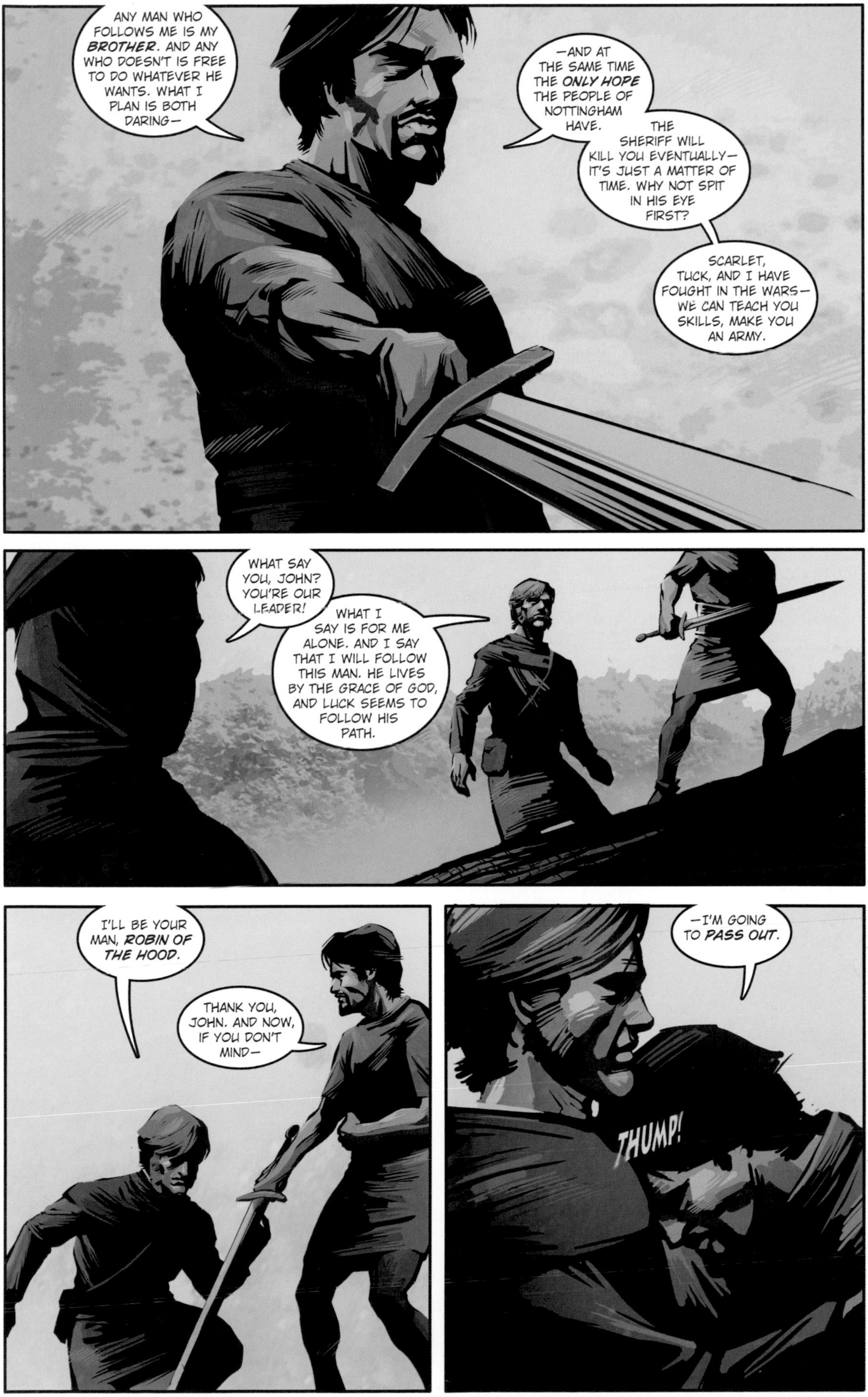
ANY MAN WHO FOLLOWS ME IS MY BROTHER. AND ANY WHO DOESN'T IS FREE TO DO WHATEVER HE WANTS. WHAT I PLAN IS BOTH DARING—
—AND AT THE SAME TIME THE ONLY HOPE THE PEOPLE OF NOTTINGHAM HAVE.
THE SHERIFF WILL KILL YOU EVENTUALLY—IT'S JUST A MATTER OF TIME. WHY NOT SPIT IN HIS EYE FIRST?
SCARLET, TUCK, AND I HAVE FOUGHT IN THE WARS—WE CAN TEACH YOU SKILLS, MAKE YOU AN ARMY.
WHAT SAY YOU, JOHN? YOU'RE OUR LEADER!
WHAT I SAY IS FOR ME ALONE. AND I SAY THAT I WILL FOLLOW THIS MAN. HE LIVES BY THE GRACE OF GOD, AND LUCK SEEMS TO FOLLOW HIS PATH.
I'LL BE YOUR MAN, ROBIN OF THE HOOD.
THANK YOU, JOHN. AND NOW, IF YOU DON'T MIND—
—I'M GOING TO PASS OUT.
THUMP!

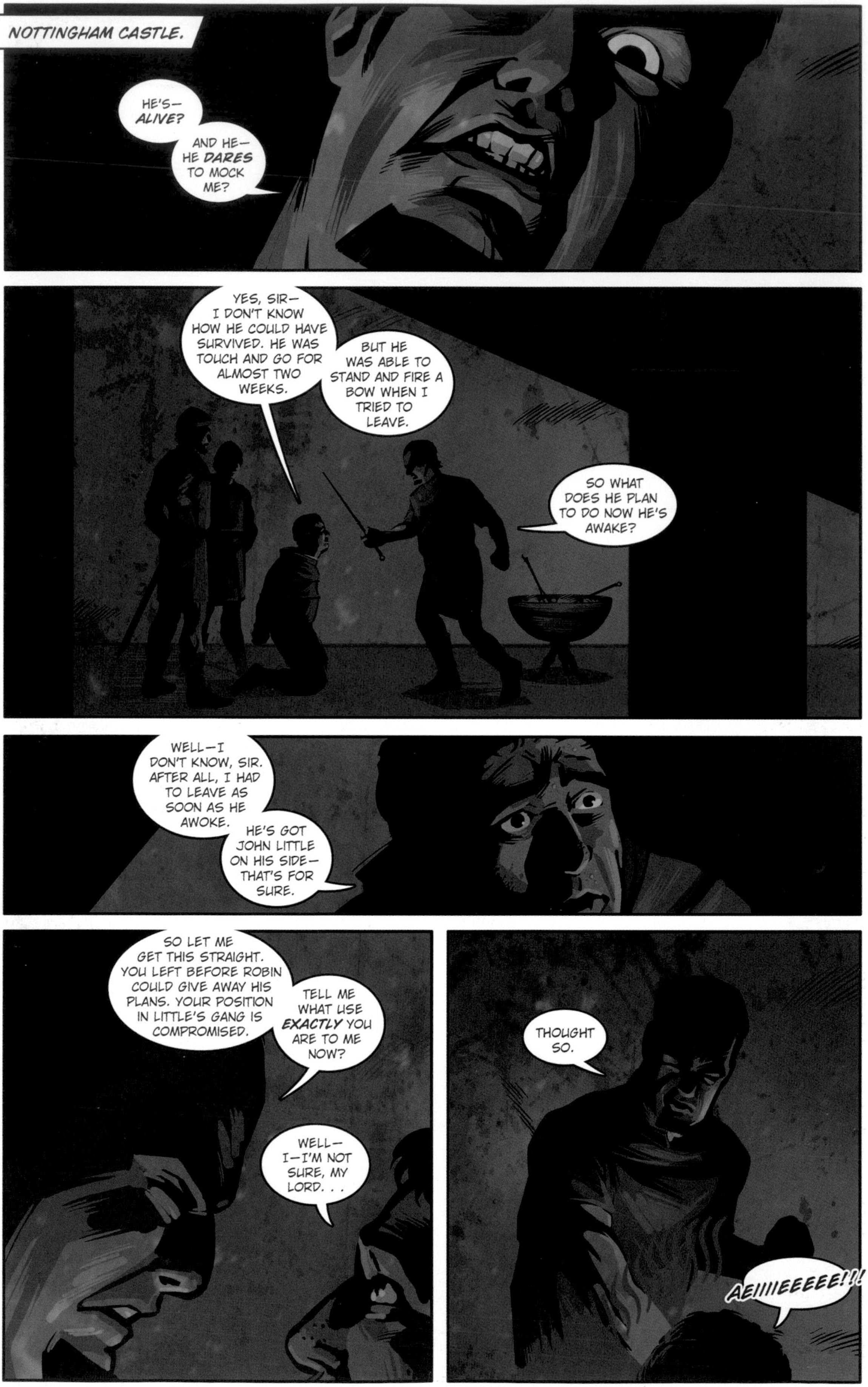
NOTTINGHAM CASTLE.
HE'S— *ALIVE?*
AND HE— HE **DARES** TO MOCK ME?
YES, SIR— I DON'T KNOW HOW HE COULD HAVE SURVIVED. HE WAS TOUCH AND GO FOR ALMOST TWO WEEKS.
BUT HE WAS ABLE TO STAND AND FIRE A BOW WHEN I TRIED TO LEAVE.
SO WHAT DOES HE PLAN TO DO NOW HE'S AWAKE?
WELL—I DON'T KNOW, SIR. AFTER ALL, I HAD TO LEAVE AS SOON AS HE AWOKE.
HE'S GOT JOHN LITTLE ON HIS SIDE— THAT'S FOR SURE.
SO LET ME GET THIS STRAIGHT. YOU LEFT BEFORE ROBIN COULD GIVE AWAY HIS PLANS. YOUR POSITION IN LITTLE'S GANG IS COMPROMISED.
TELL ME WHAT USE ***EXACTLY*** YOU ARE TO ME NOW?
WELL— I—I'M NOT SURE, MY LORD. . .
THOUGHT SO.
AEIIIIEEEEE!!!

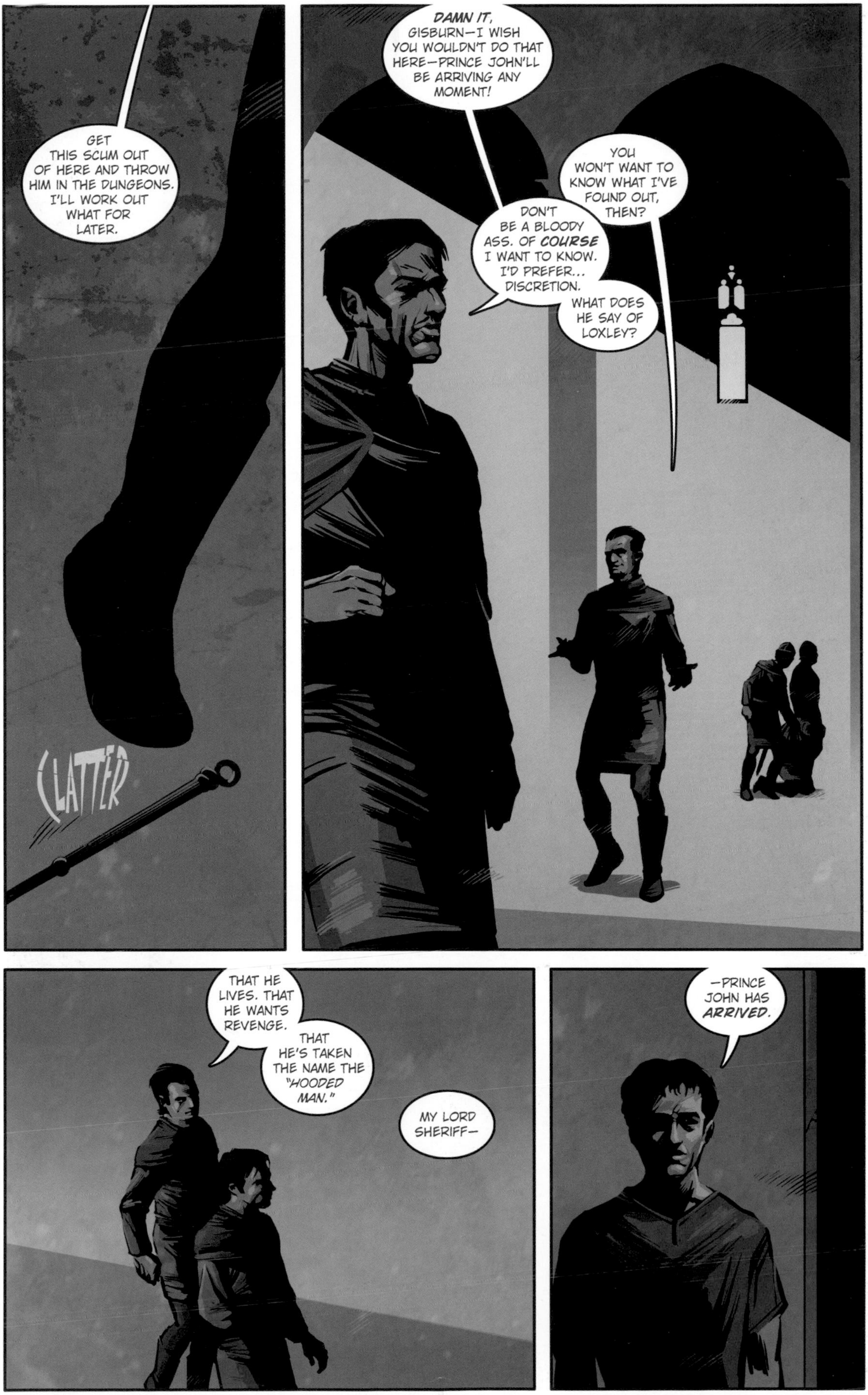
GET THIS SCUM OUT OF HERE AND THROW HIM IN THE DUNGEONS. I'LL WORK OUT WHAT FOR LATER.
CLATTER
DAMN IT, GISBURN—I WISH YOU WOULDN'T DO THAT HERE—PRINCE JOHN'LL BE ARRIVING ANY MOMENT!
YOU WON'T WANT TO KNOW WHAT I'VE FOUND OUT, THEN?
DON'T BE A BLOODY ASS. OF COURSE I WANT TO KNOW. I'D PREFER... DISCRETION.
WHAT DOES HE SAY OF LOXLEY?
THAT HE LIVES. THAT HE WANTS REVENGE.
THAT HE'S TAKEN THE NAME THE "HOODED MAN."
MY LORD SHERIFF—
—PRINCE JOHN HAS ARRIVED.

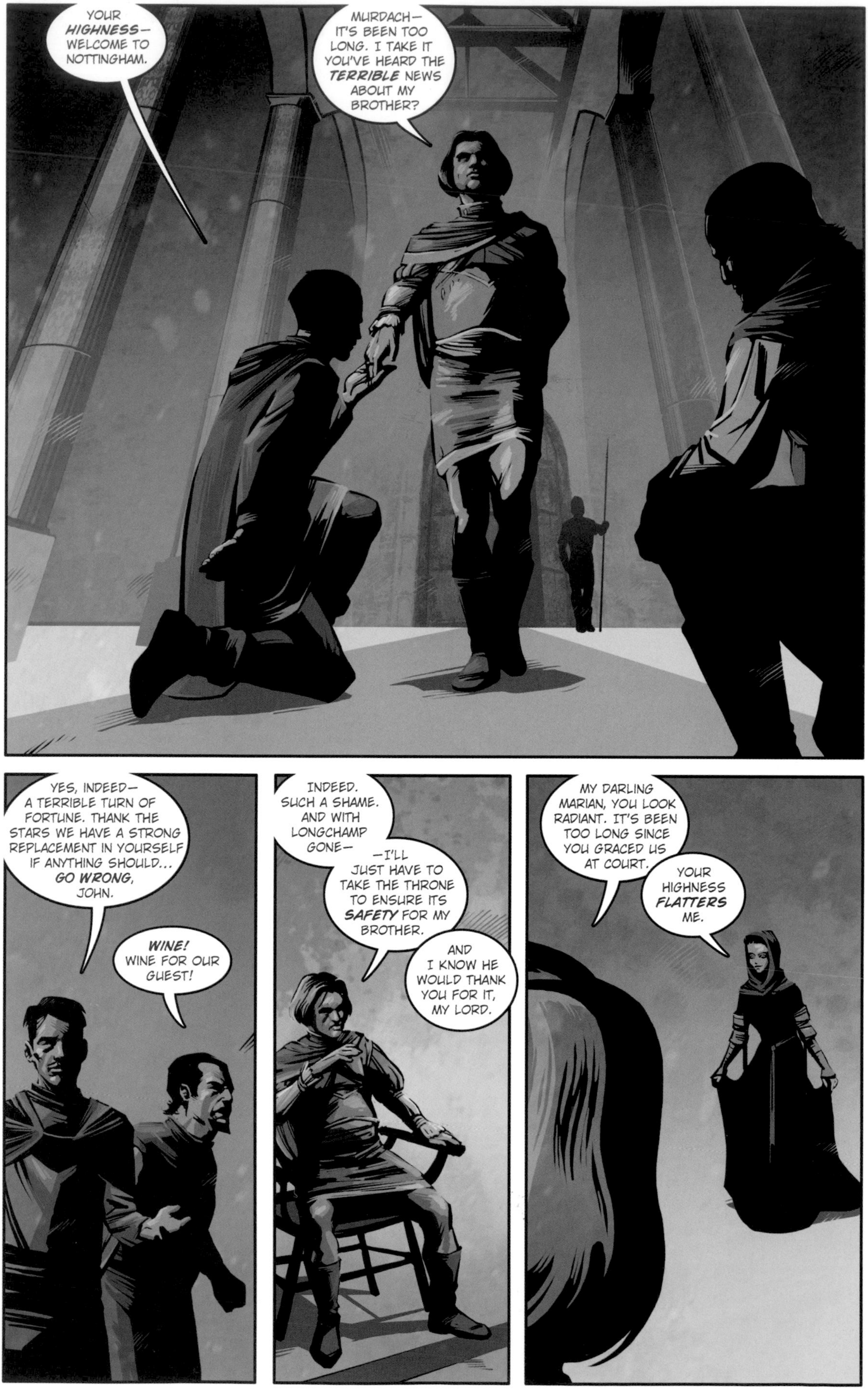
YOUR HIGHNESS— WELCOME TO NOTTINGHAM.
MURDACH— IT'S BEEN TOO LONG. I TAKE IT YOU'VE HEARD THE TERRIBLE NEWS ABOUT MY BROTHER?
YES, INDEED— A TERRIBLE TURN OF FORTUNE. THANK THE STARS WE HAVE A STRONG REPLACEMENT IN YOURSELF IF ANYTHING SHOULD... GO WRONG, JOHN.
WINE! WINE FOR OUR GUEST!
INDEED. SUCH A SHAME. AND WITH LONGCHAMP GONE—
—I'LL JUST HAVE TO TAKE THE THRONE TO ENSURE ITS SAFETY FOR MY BROTHER.
AND I KNOW HE WOULD THANK YOU FOR IT, MY LORD.
MY DARLING MARIAN, YOU LOOK RADIANT. IT'S BEEN TOO LONG SINCE YOU GRACED US AT COURT.
YOUR HIGHNESS FLATTERS ME.

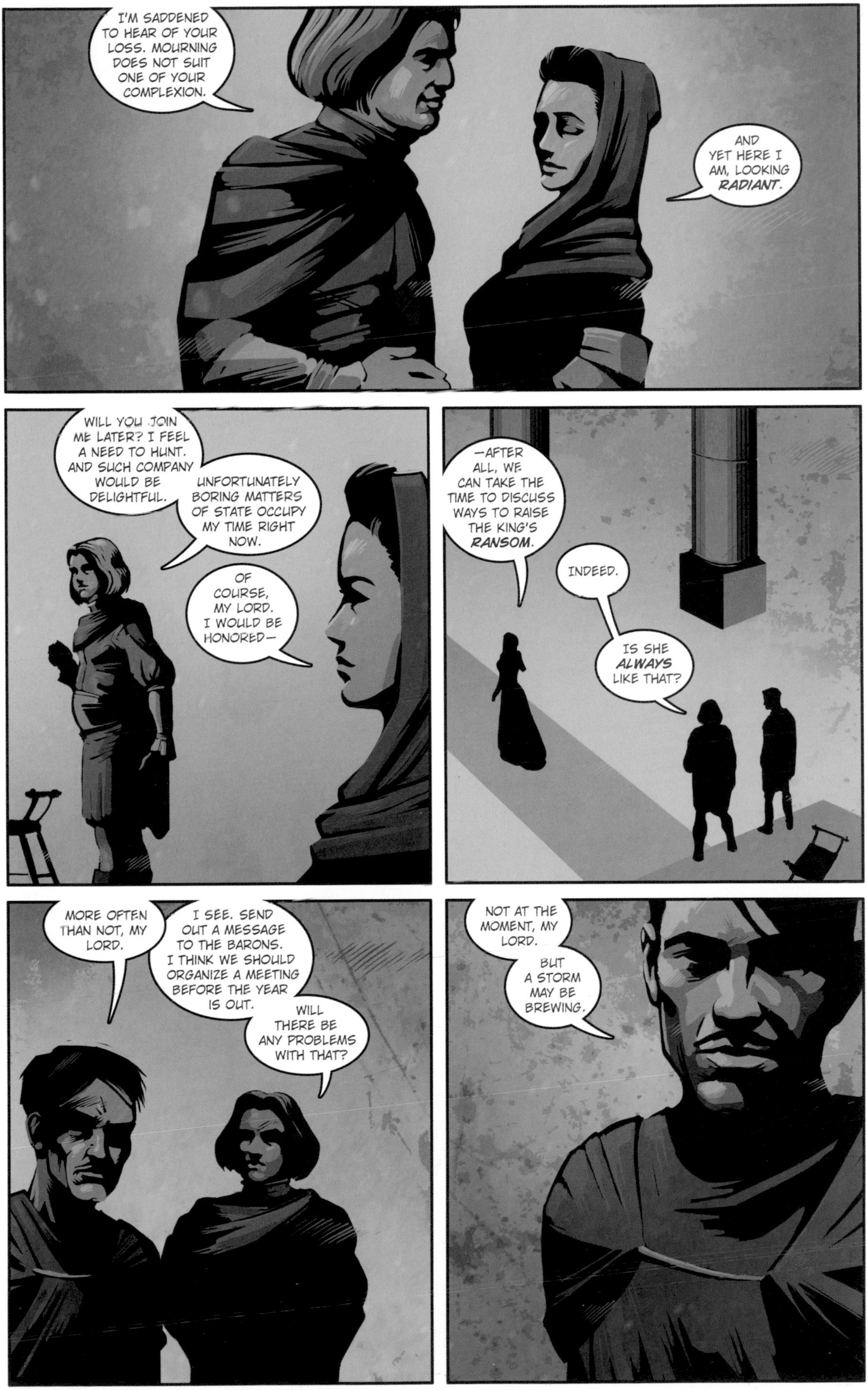
I'M SADDENED TO HEAR OF YOUR LOSS. MOURNING DOES NOT SUIT ONE OF YOUR COMPLEXION.
AND YET HERE I AM, LOOKING *RADIANT*.
WILL YOU JOIN ME LATER? I FEEL A NEED TO HUNT. AND SUCH COMPANY WOULD BE DELIGHTFUL.
UNFORTUNATELY BORING MATTERS OF STATE OCCUPY MY TIME RIGHT NOW.
OF COURSE, MY LORD. I WOULD BE HONORED—
—AFTER ALL, WE CAN TAKE THE TIME TO DISCUSS WAYS TO RAISE THE KING'S *RANSOM*.
INDEED.
IS SHE *ALWAYS* LIKE THAT?
MORE OFTEN THAN NOT, MY LORD.
I SEE. SEND OUT A MESSAGE TO THE BARONS. I THINK WE SHOULD ORGANIZE A MEETING BEFORE THE YEAR IS OUT.
WILL THERE BE ANY PROBLEMS WITH THAT?
NOT AT THE MOMENT, MY LORD.
BUT A STORM MAY BE BREWING.

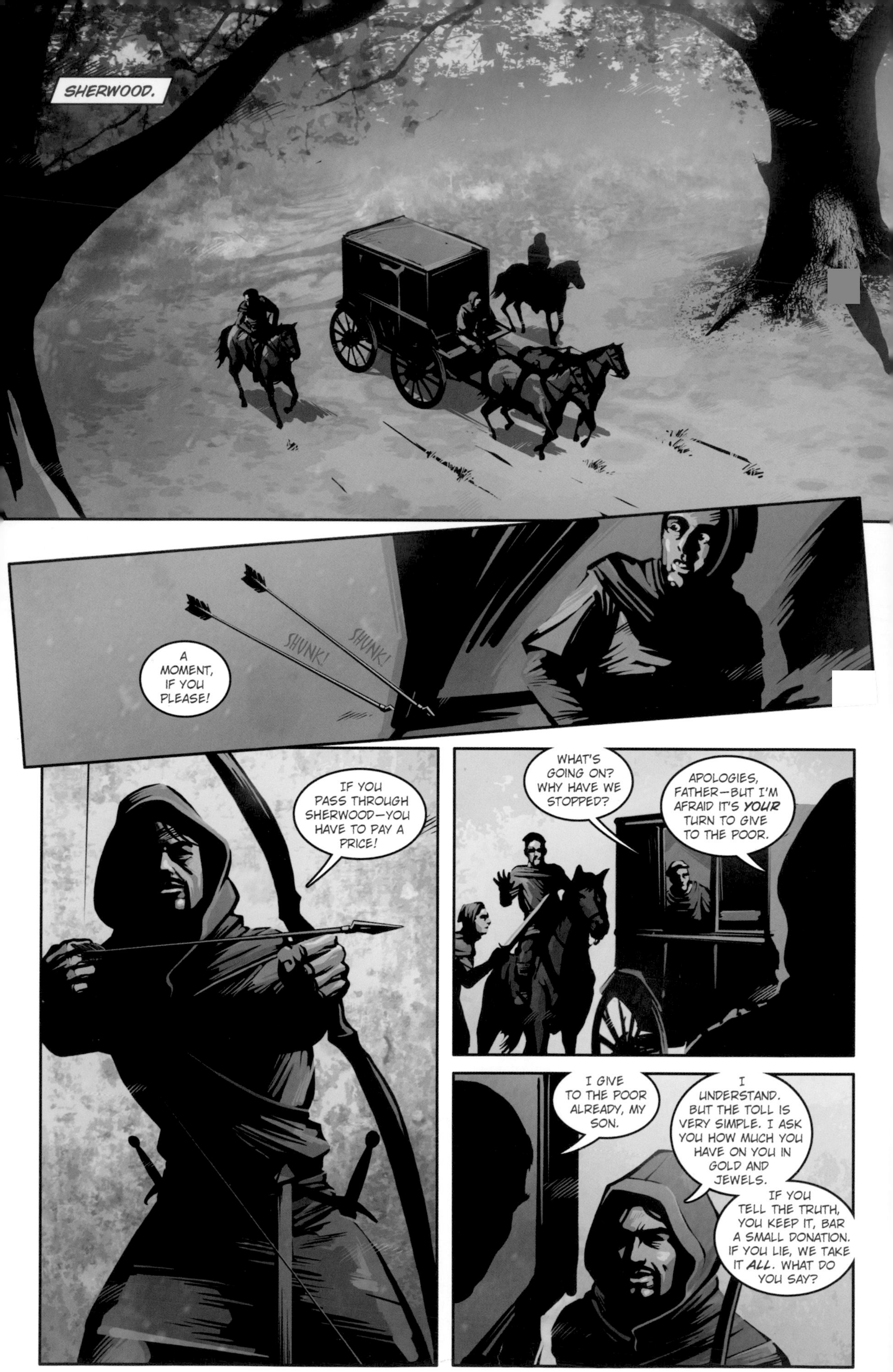
SHERWOOD.
SHUNK!
SHUNK!
A MOMENT, IF YOU PLEASE!
IF YOU PASS THROUGH SHERWOOD—YOU HAVE TO PAY A PRICE!
WHAT'S GOING ON? WHY HAVE WE STOPPED?
APOLOGIES, FATHER—BUT I'M AFRAID IT'S *YOUR* TURN TO GIVE TO THE POOR.
I GIVE TO THE POOR ALREADY, MY SON.
I UNDERSTAND. BUT THE TOLL IS VERY SIMPLE. I ASK YOU HOW MUCH YOU HAVE ON YOU IN GOLD AND JEWELS.
IF YOU TELL THE TRUTH, YOU KEEP IT, BAR A SMALL DONATION. IF YOU LIE, WE TAKE IT *ALL*. WHAT DO YOU SAY?

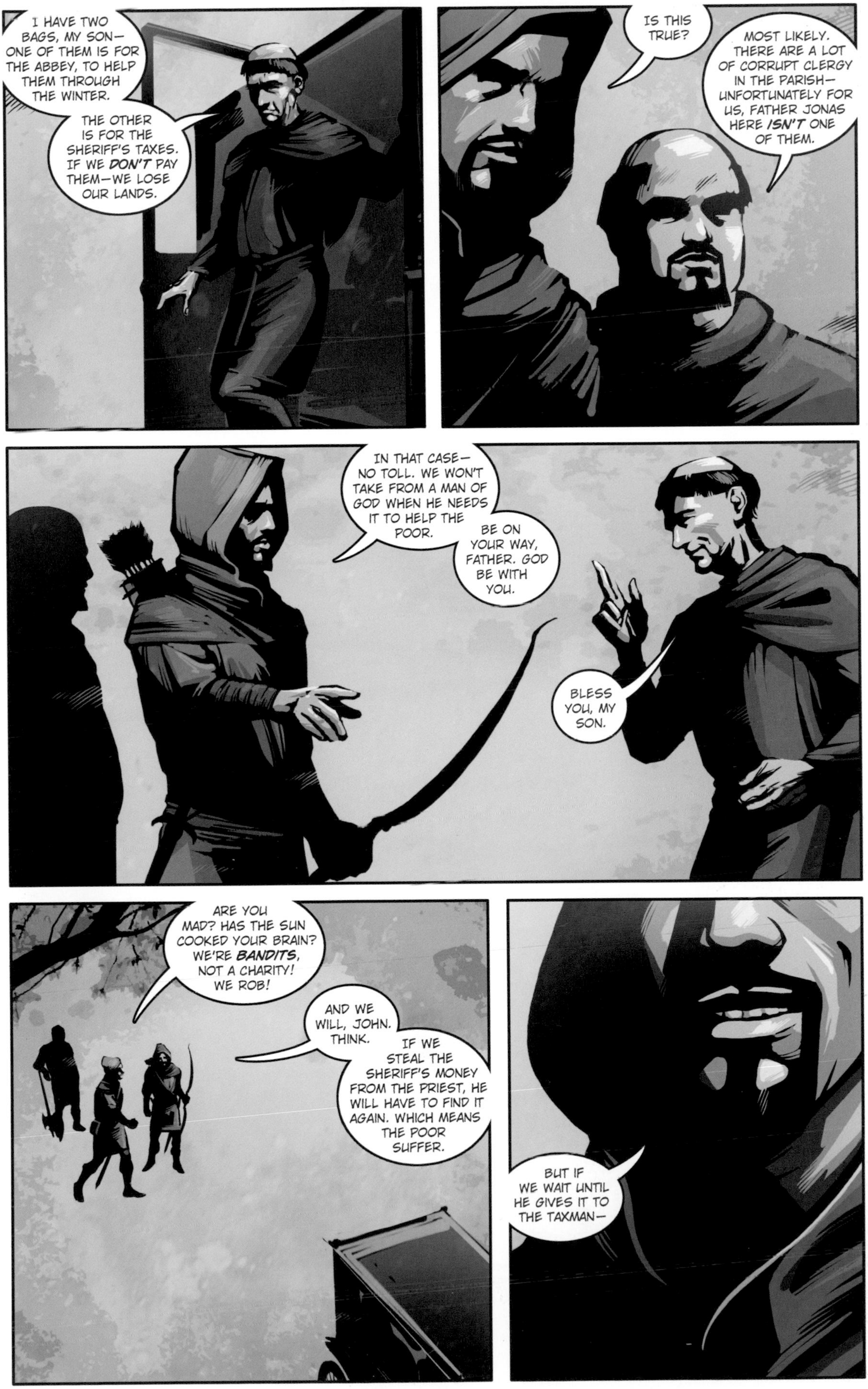
I HAVE TWO BAGS, MY SON—ONE OF THEM IS FOR THE ABBEY, TO HELP THEM THROUGH THE WINTER.
THE OTHER IS FOR THE SHERIFF'S TAXES. IF WE *DON'T* PAY THEM—WE LOSE OUR LANDS.
IS THIS TRUE?
MOST LIKELY. THERE ARE A LOT OF CORRUPT CLERGY IN THE PARISH—UNFORTUNATELY FOR US, FATHER JONAS HERE *ISN'T* ONE OF THEM.
IN THAT CASE—NO TOLL. WE WON'T TAKE FROM A MAN OF GOD WHEN HE NEEDS IT TO HELP THE POOR.
BE ON YOUR WAY, FATHER. GOD BE WITH YOU.
BLESS YOU, MY SON.
ARE YOU MAD? HAS THE SUN COOKED YOUR BRAIN? WE'RE *BANDITS*, NOT A CHARITY! WE ROB!
AND WE WILL, JOHN. THINK.
IF WE STEAL THE SHERIFF'S MONEY FROM THE PRIEST, HE WILL HAVE TO FIND IT AGAIN. WHICH MEANS THE POOR SUFFER.
BUT IF WE WAIT UNTIL HE GIVES IT TO THE TAXMAN—

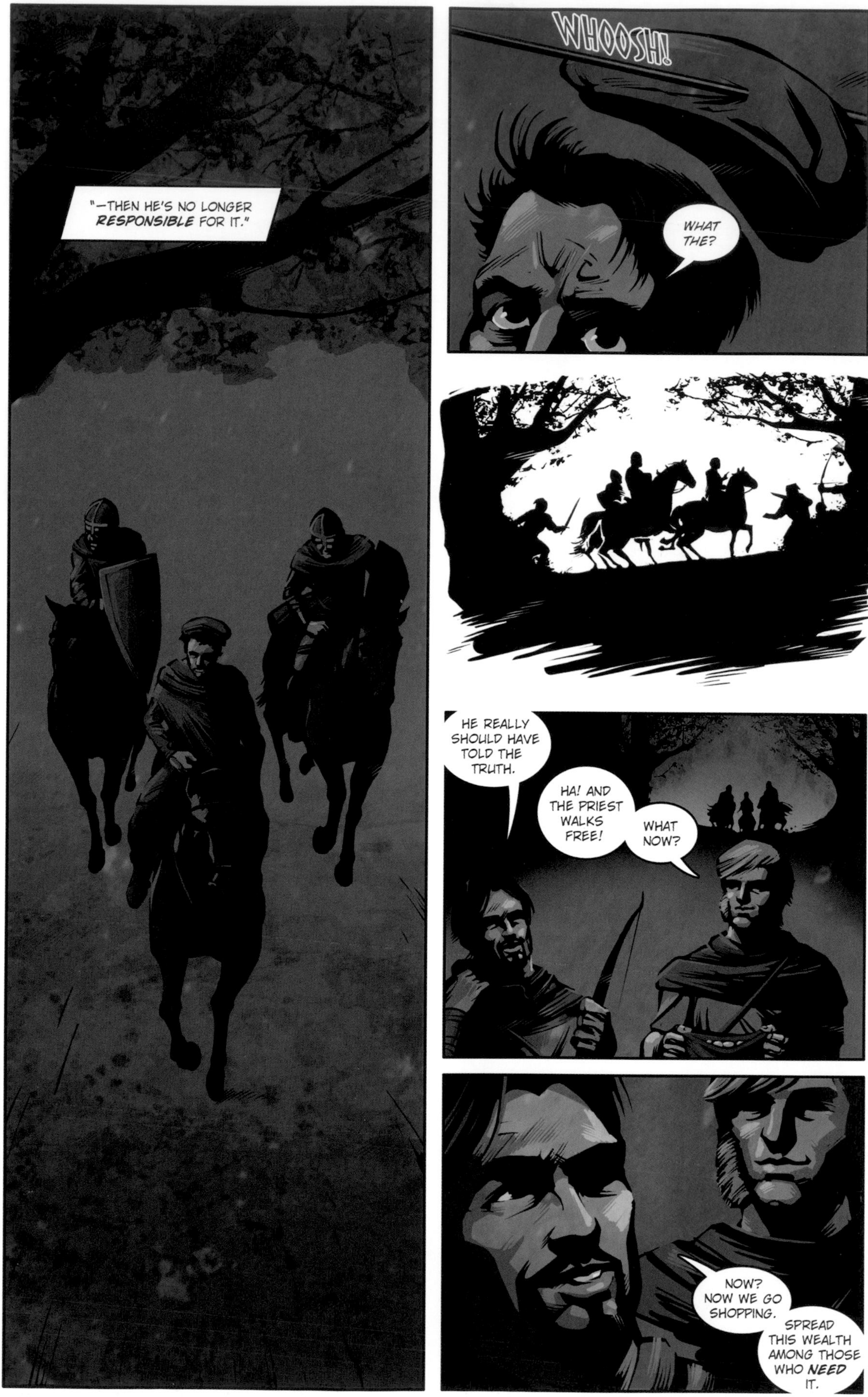
"—THEN HE'S NO LONGER *RESPONSIBLE* FOR IT."
WHOOSH!
WHAT THE?
HE REALLY SHOULD HAVE TOLD THE TRUTH.
HA! AND THE PRIEST WALKS FREE!
WHAT NOW?
NOW? NOW WE GO SHOPPING.
SPREAD THIS WEALTH AMONG THOSE WHO *NEED* IT.

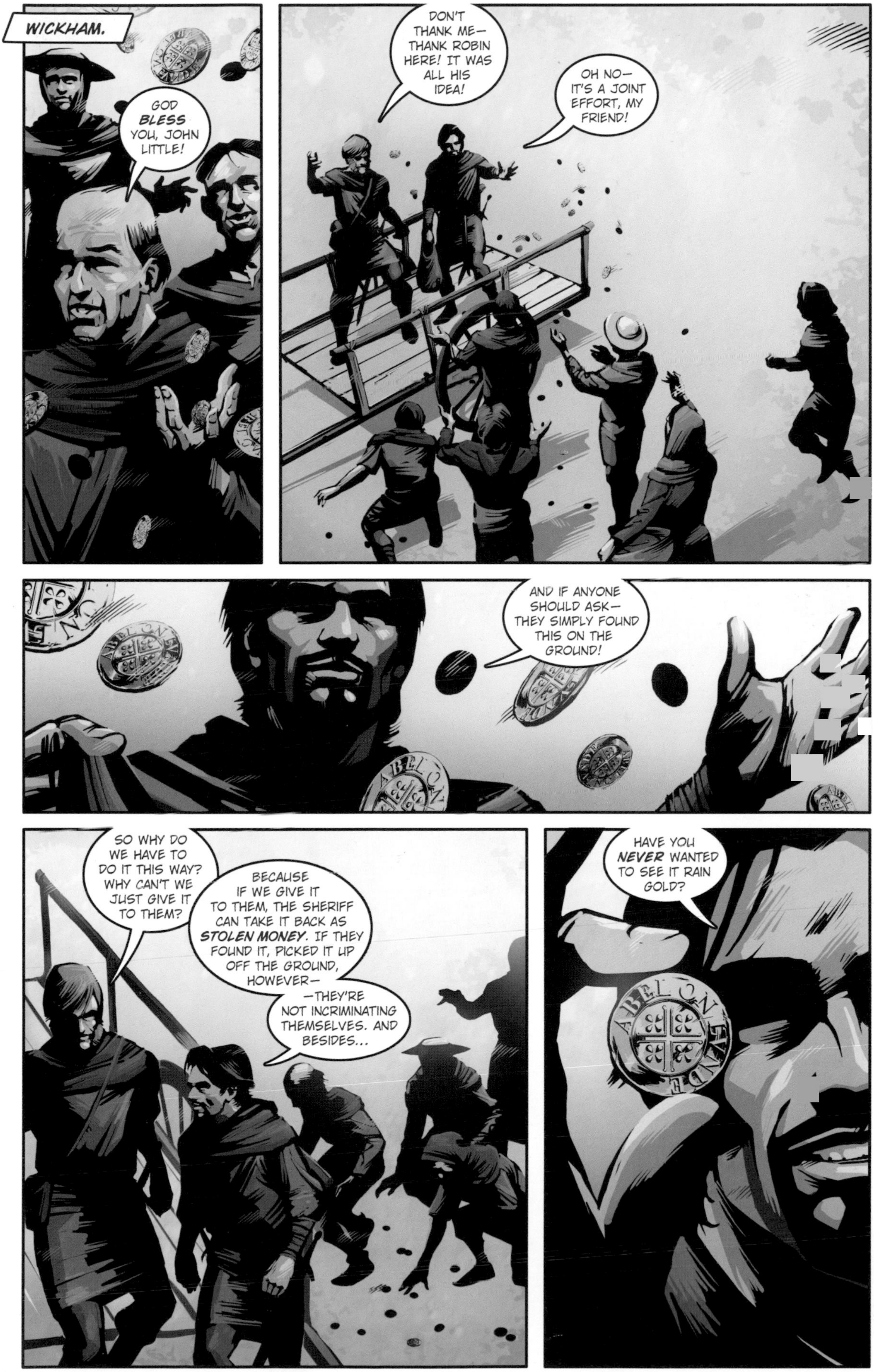
WICKHAM.
GOD BLESS YOU, JOHN LITTLE!
DON'T THANK ME— THANK ROBIN HERE! IT WAS ALL HIS IDEA!
OH NO— IT'S A JOINT EFFORT, MY FRIEND!
AND IF ANYONE SHOULD ASK— THEY SIMPLY FOUND THIS ON THE GROUND!
SO WHY DO WE HAVE TO DO IT THIS WAY? WHY CAN'T WE JUST GIVE IT TO THEM?
BECAUSE IF WE GIVE IT TO THEM, THE SHERIFF CAN TAKE IT BACK AS STOLEN MONEY. IF THEY FOUND IT, PICKED IT UP OFF THE GROUND, HOWEVER—
—THEY'RE NOT INCRIMINATING THEMSELVES. AND BESIDES...
HAVE YOU NEVER WANTED TO SEE IT RAIN GOLD?

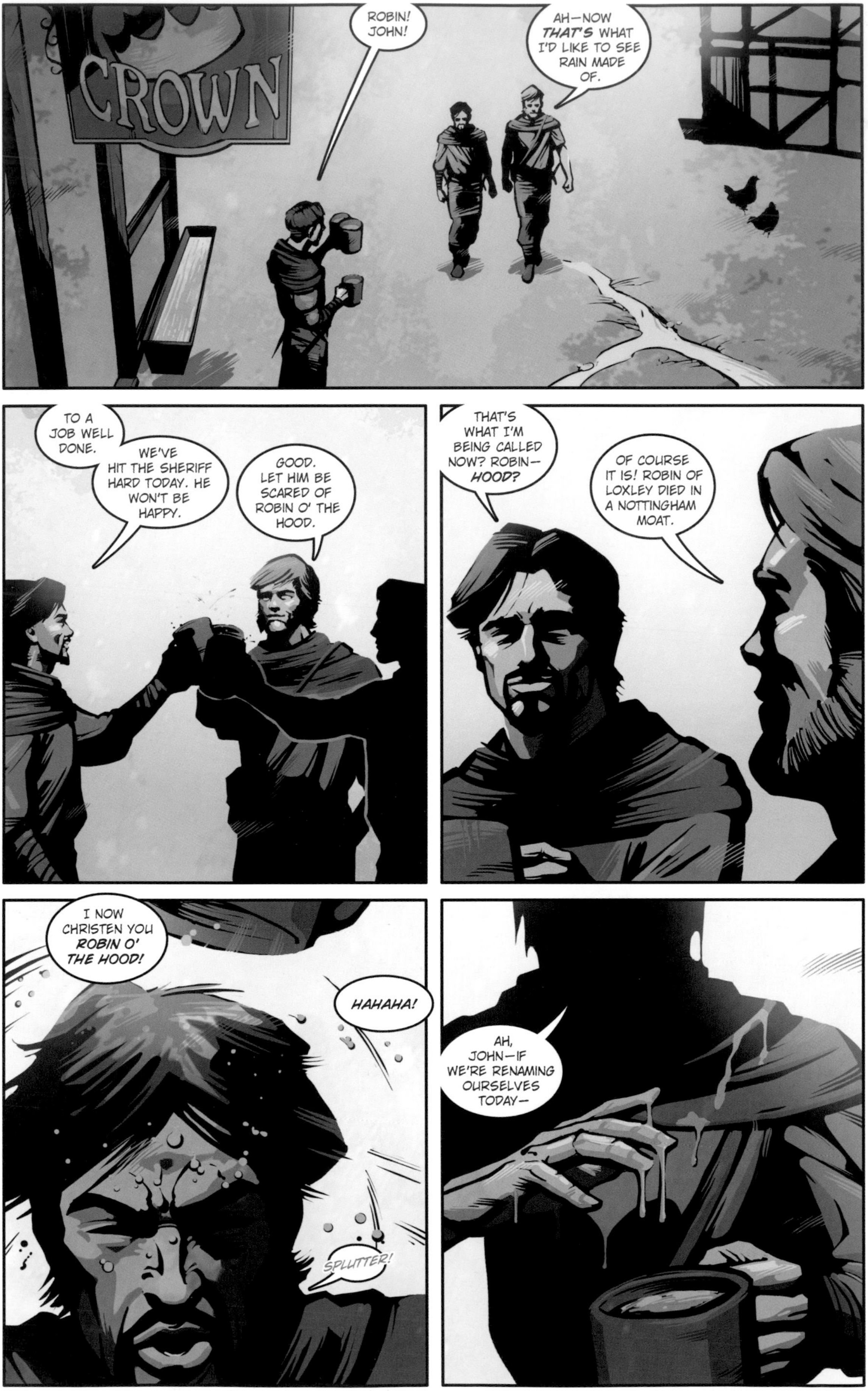
CROWN
ROBIN! JOHN!
AH—NOW ***THAT'S*** WHAT I'D LIKE TO SEE RAIN MADE OF.
TO A JOB WELL DONE.
WE'VE HIT THE SHERIFF HARD TODAY. HE WON'T BE HAPPY.
GOOD. LET HIM BE SCARED OF ROBIN O' THE HOOD.
THAT'S WHAT I'M BEING CALLED NOW? ROBIN—***HOOD?***
OF COURSE IT IS! ROBIN OF LOXLEY DIED IN A NOTTINGHAM MOAT.
I NOW CHRISTEN YOU ***ROBIN O' THE HOOD!***
HAHAHA!
SPLUTTER!
AH, JOHN—IF WE'RE RENAMING OURSELVES TODAY—

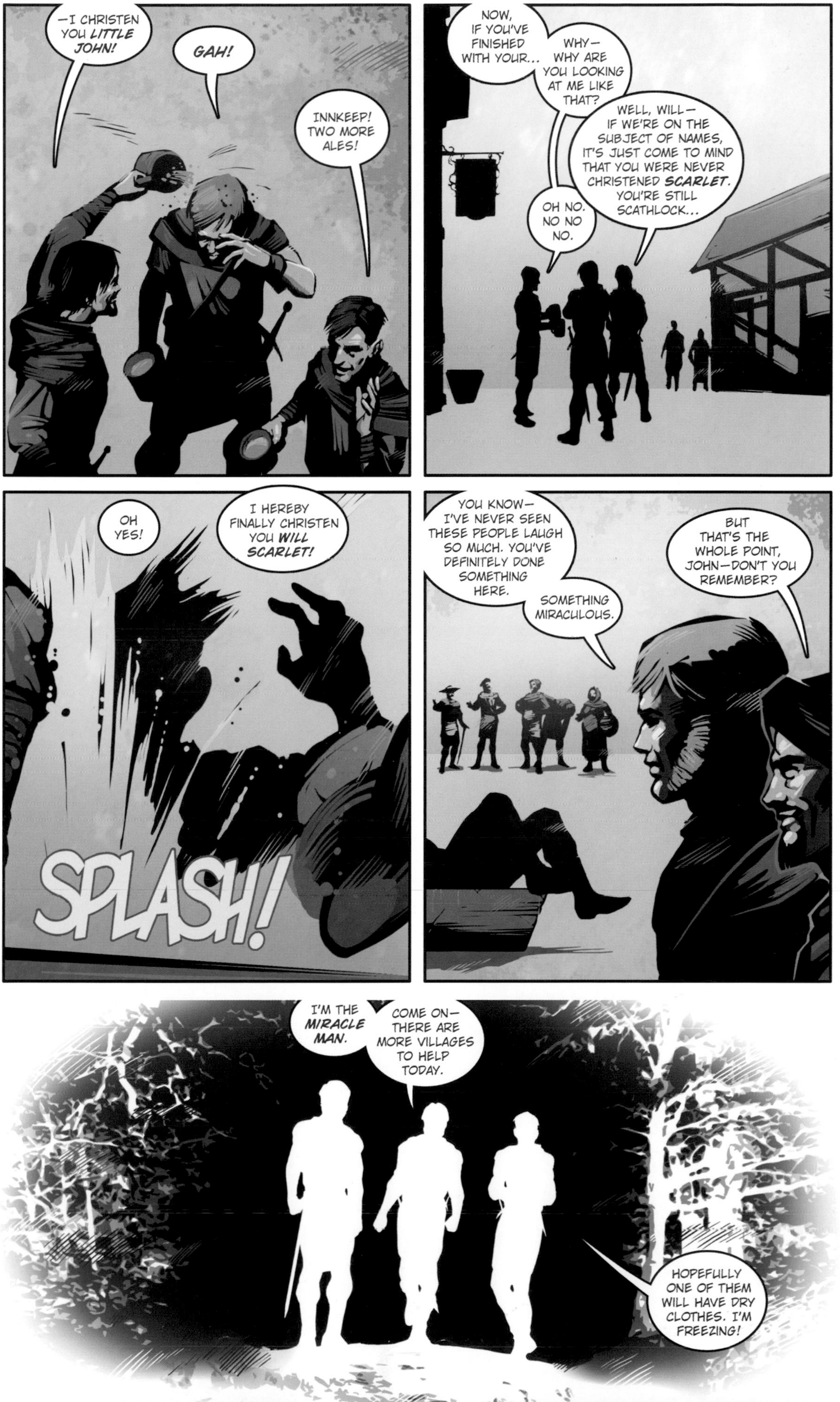
—I CHRISTEN YOU LITTLE JOHN!
GAH!
INNKEEP! TWO MORE ALES!
NOW, IF YOU'VE FINISHED WITH YOUR...
WHY— WHY ARE YOU LOOKING AT ME LIKE THAT?
WELL, WILL— IF WE'RE ON THE SUBJECT OF NAMES, IT'S JUST COME TO MIND THAT YOU WERE NEVER CHRISTENED SCARLET. YOU'RE STILL SCATHLOCK...
OH NO. NO NO NO.
OH YES!
I HEREBY FINALLY CHRISTEN YOU WILL SCARLET!
SPLASH!
YOU KNOW— I'VE NEVER SEEN THESE PEOPLE LAUGH SO MUCH. YOU'VE DEFINITELY DONE SOMETHING HERE.
SOMETHING MIRACULOUS.
BUT THAT'S THE WHOLE POINT, JOHN—DON'T YOU REMEMBER?
I'M THE MIRACLE MAN.
COME ON— THERE ARE MORE VILLAGES TO HELP TODAY.
HOPEFULLY ONE OF THEM WILL HAVE DRY CLOTHES. I'M FREEZING!

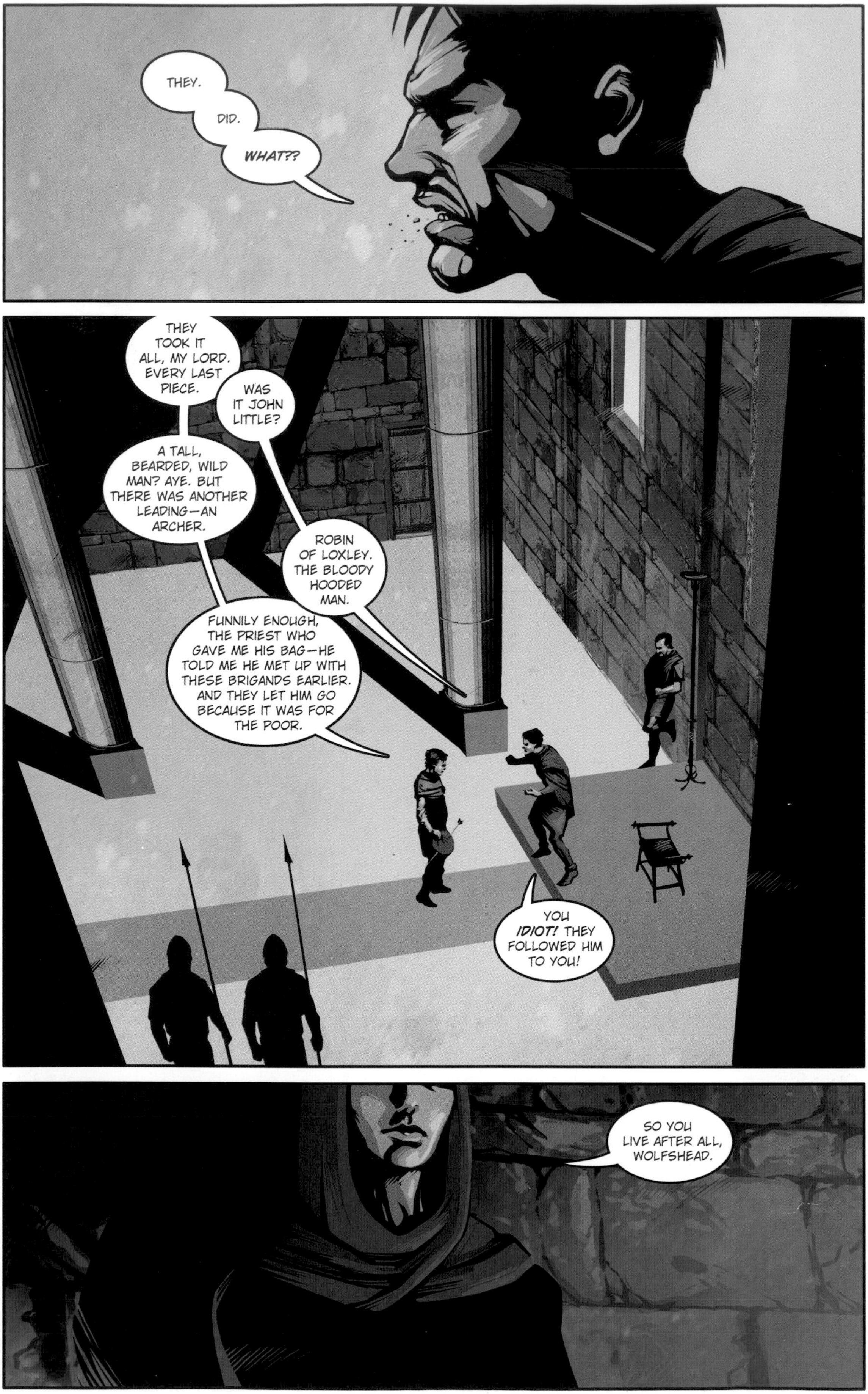
THEY.
DID.
WHAT??
THEY TOOK IT ALL, MY LORD. EVERY LAST PIECE.
WAS IT JOHN LITTLE?
A TALL, BEARDED, WILD MAN? AYE. BUT THERE WAS ANOTHER LEADING—AN ARCHER.
ROBIN OF LOXLEY. THE BLOODY HOODED MAN.
FUNNILY ENOUGH, THE PRIEST WHO GAVE ME HIS BAG—HE TOLD ME HE MET UP WITH THESE BRIGANDS EARLIER. AND THEY LET HIM GO BECAUSE IT WAS FOR THE POOR.
YOU IDIOT! THEY FOLLOWED HIM TO YOU!
SO YOU LIVE AFTER ALL, WOLFSHEAD.

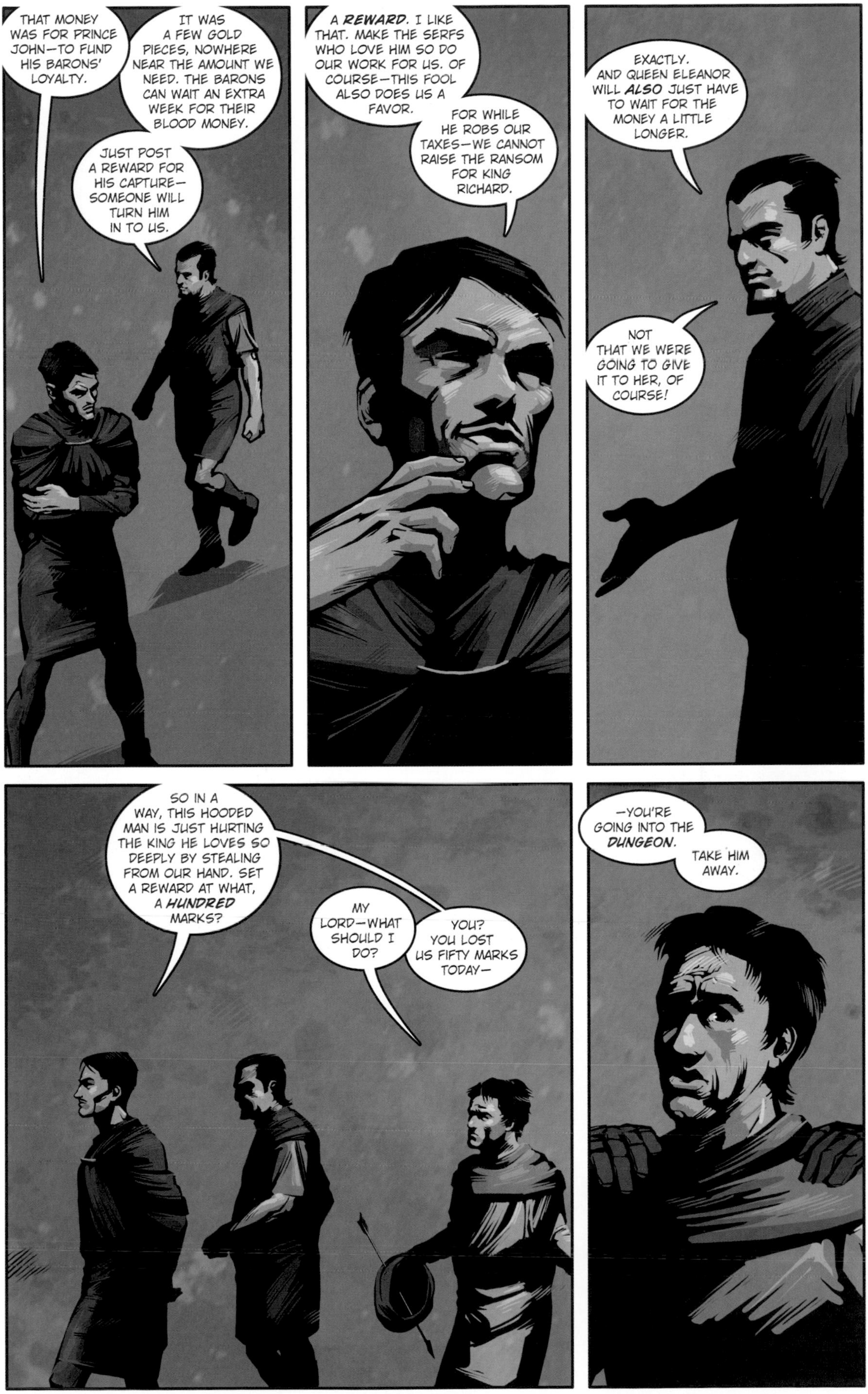
THAT MONEY WAS FOR PRINCE JOHN—TO FUND HIS BARONS' LOYALTY.
IT WAS A FEW GOLD PIECES, NOWHERE NEAR THE AMOUNT WE NEED. THE BARONS CAN WAIT AN EXTRA WEEK FOR THEIR BLOOD MONEY.
JUST POST A REWARD FOR HIS CAPTURE—SOMEONE WILL TURN HIM IN TO US.
A REWARD. I LIKE THAT. MAKE THE SERFS WHO LOVE HIM SO DO OUR WORK FOR US. OF COURSE—THIS FOOL ALSO DOES US A FAVOR.
FOR WHILE HE ROBS OUR TAXES—WE CANNOT RAISE THE RANSOM FOR KING RICHARD.
EXACTLY. AND QUEEN ELEANOR WILL ALSO JUST HAVE TO WAIT FOR THE MONEY A LITTLE LONGER.
NOT THAT WE WERE GOING TO GIVE IT TO HER, OF COURSE!
SO IN A WAY, THIS HOODED MAN IS JUST HURTING THE KING HE LOVES SO DEEPLY BY STEALING FROM OUR HAND. SET A REWARD AT WHAT, A HUNDRED MARKS?
MY LORD—WHAT SHOULD I DO?
YOU? YOU LOST US FIFTY MARKS TODAY—
—YOU'RE GOING INTO THE DUNGEON.
TAKE HIM AWAY.

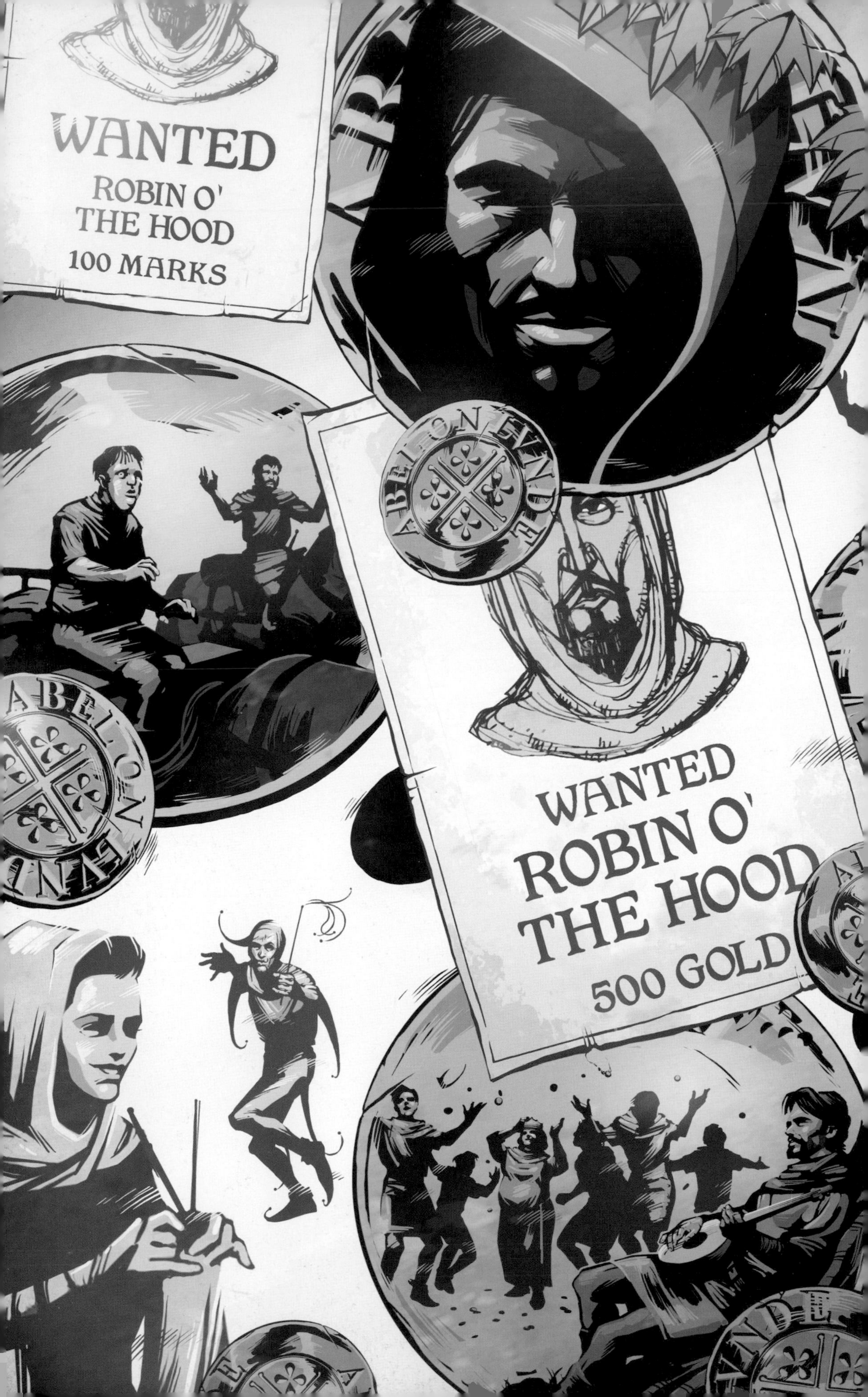
WANTED
ROBIN O'
THE HOOD
100 MARKS
WANTED
ROBIN O'
THE HOOD
500 GOLD

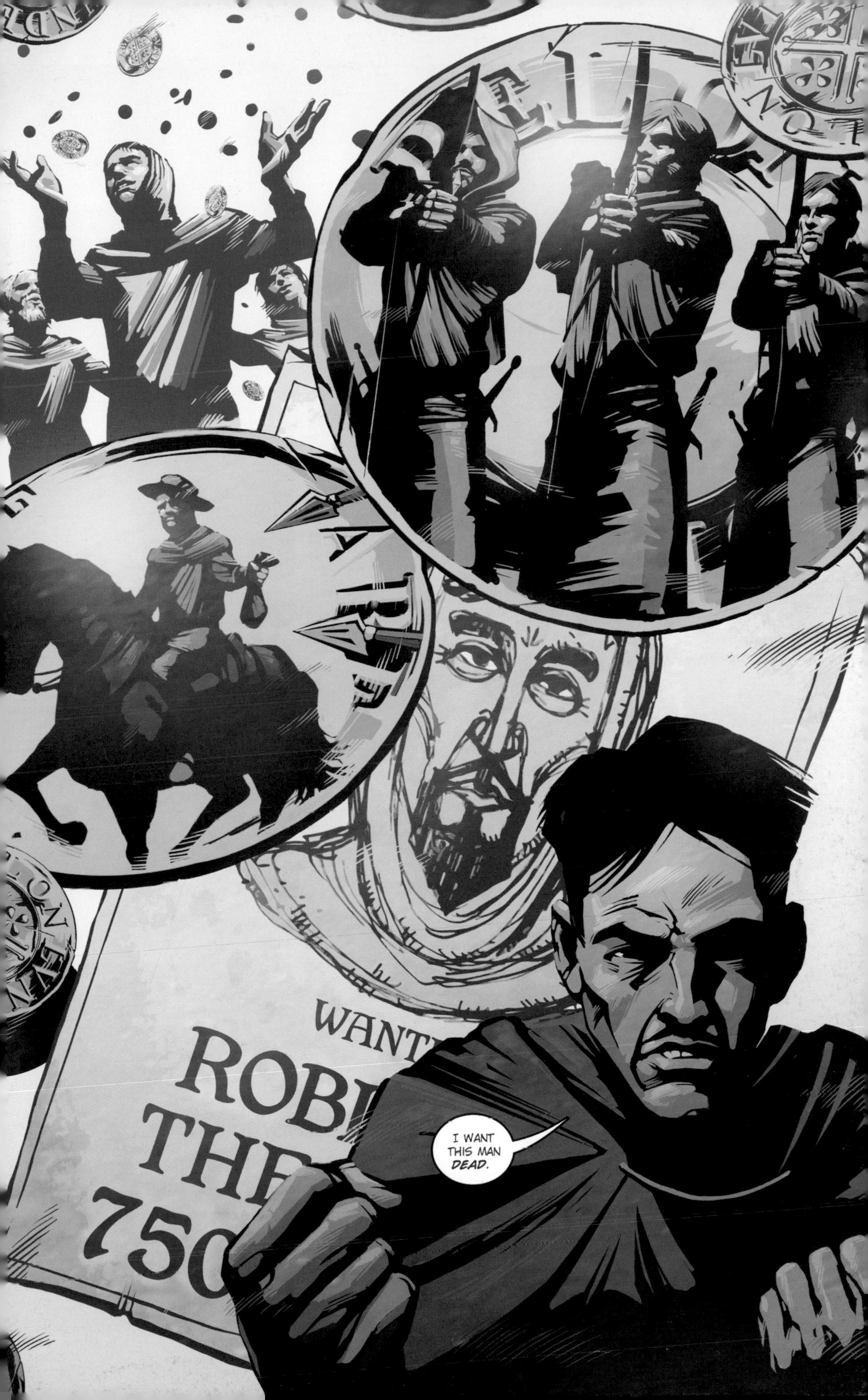
I WANT THIS MAN DEAD.

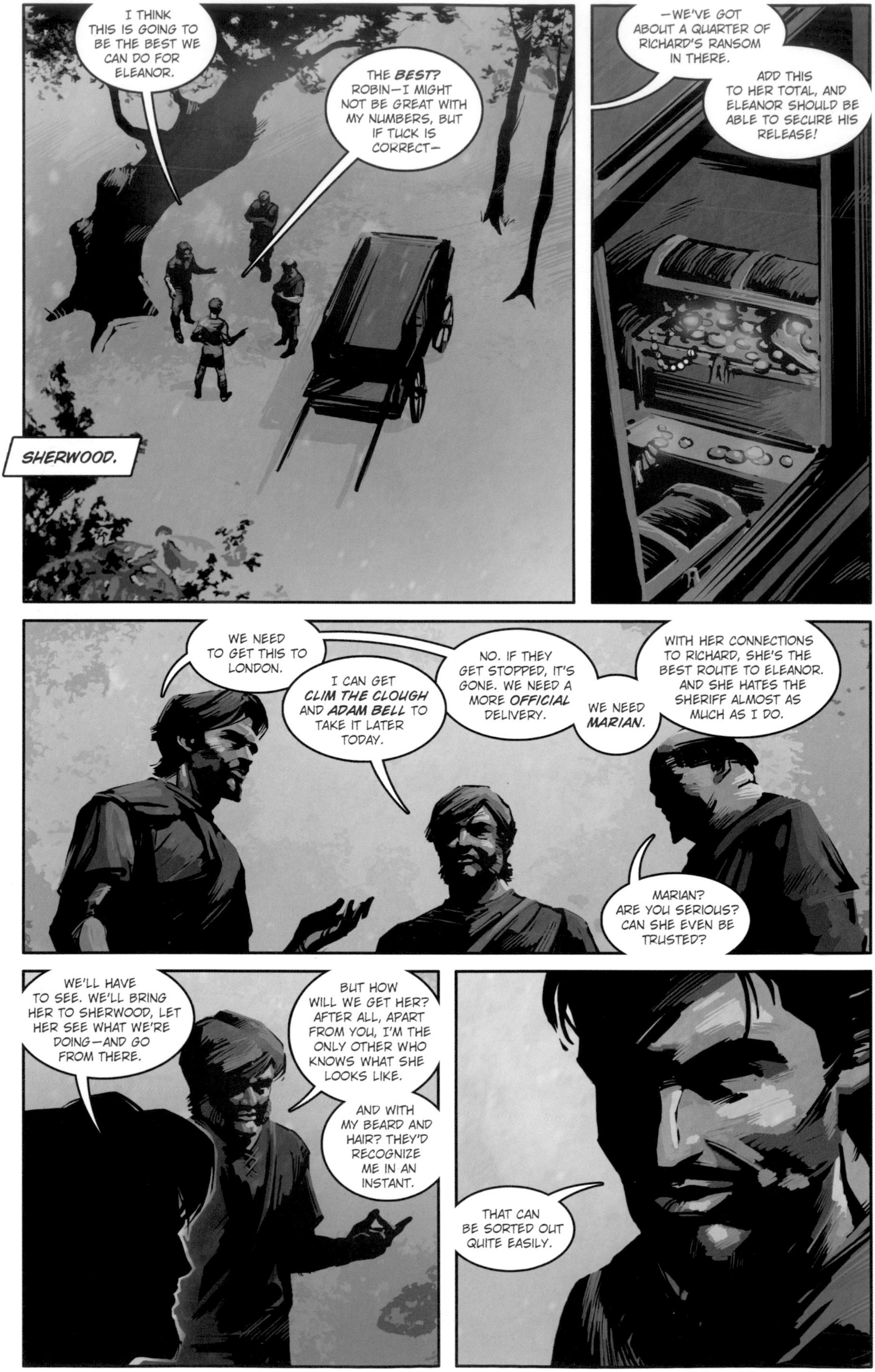
I THINK THIS IS GOING TO BE THE BEST WE CAN DO FOR ELEANOR.
THE BEST? ROBIN—I MIGHT NOT BE GREAT WITH MY NUMBERS, BUT IF TUCK IS CORRECT—
SHERWOOD.
—WE'VE GOT ABOUT A QUARTER OF RICHARD'S RANSOM IN THERE.
ADD THIS TO HER TOTAL, AND ELEANOR SHOULD BE ABLE TO SECURE HIS RELEASE!
WE NEED TO GET THIS TO LONDON.
I CAN GET CLIM THE CLOUGH AND ADAM BELL TO TAKE IT LATER TODAY.
NO. IF THEY GET STOPPED, IT'S GONE. WE NEED A MORE OFFICIAL DELIVERY.
WE NEED MARIAN.
WITH HER CONNECTIONS TO RICHARD, SHE'S THE BEST ROUTE TO ELEANOR. AND SHE HATES THE SHERIFF ALMOST AS MUCH AS I DO.
MARIAN? ARE YOU SERIOUS? CAN SHE EVEN BE TRUSTED?
WE'LL HAVE TO SEE. WE'LL BRING HER TO SHERWOOD, LET HER SEE WHAT WE'RE DOING—AND GO FROM THERE.
BUT HOW WILL WE GET HER? AFTER ALL, APART FROM YOU, I'M THE ONLY OTHER WHO KNOWS WHAT SHE LOOKS LIKE.
AND WITH MY BEARD AND HAIR? THEY'D RECOGNIZE ME IN AN INSTANT.
THAT CAN BE SORTED OUT QUITE EASILY.

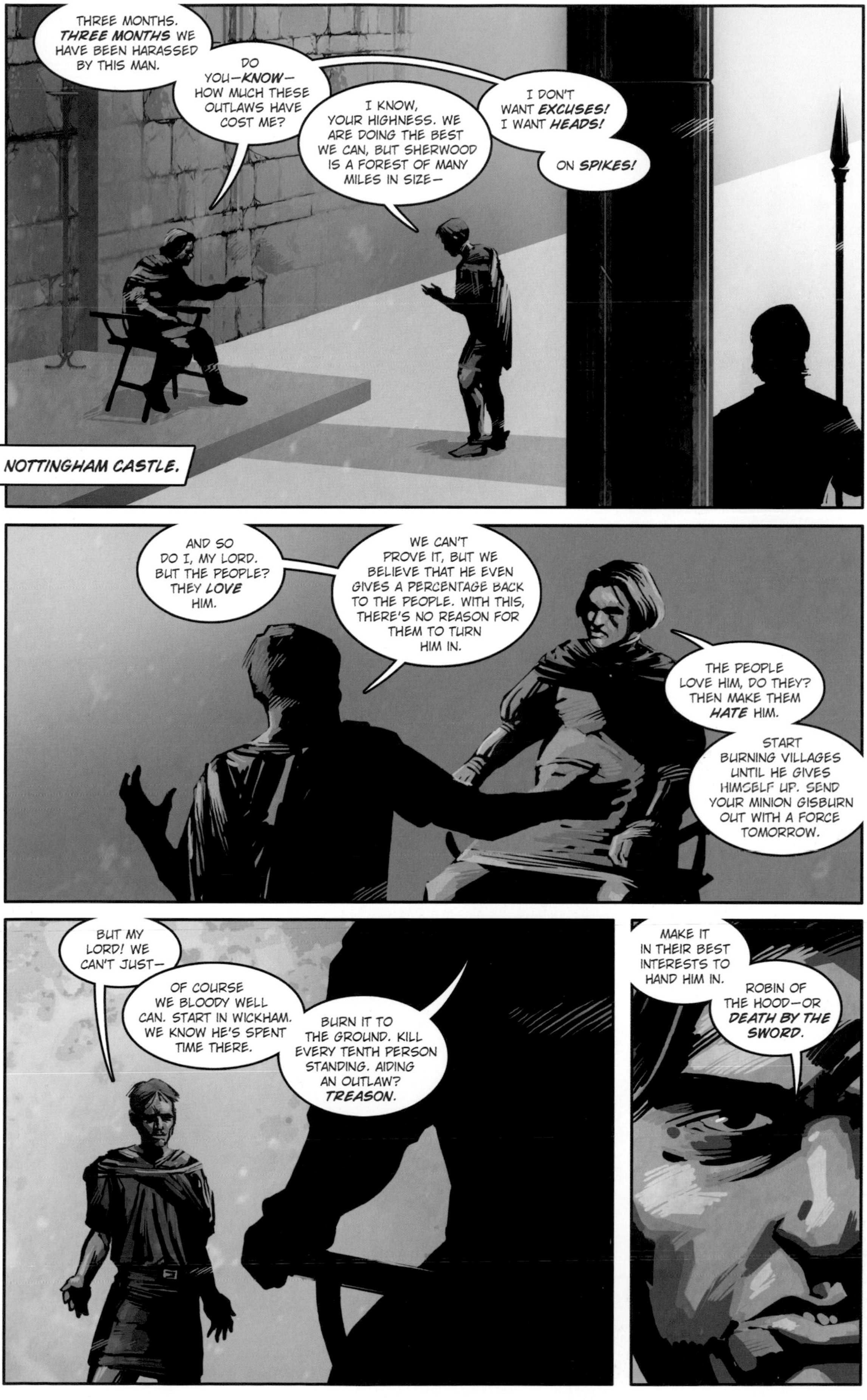
THREE MONTHS. THREE MONTHS WE HAVE BEEN HARASSED BY THIS MAN.
DO YOU—KNOW—HOW MUCH THESE OUTLAWS HAVE COST ME?
I KNOW, YOUR HIGHNESS. WE ARE DOING THE BEST WE CAN, BUT SHERWOOD IS A FOREST OF MANY MILES IN SIZE—
I DON'T WANT EXCUSES! I WANT HEADS!
ON SPIKES!
NOTTINGHAM CASTLE.
AND SO DO I, MY LORD. BUT THE PEOPLE? THEY LOVE HIM.
WE CAN'T PROVE IT, BUT WE BELIEVE THAT HE EVEN GIVES A PERCENTAGE BACK TO THE PEOPLE. WITH THIS, THERE'S NO REASON FOR THEM TO TURN HIM IN.
THE PEOPLE LOVE HIM, DO THEY? THEN MAKE THEM HATE HIM.
START BURNING VILLAGES UNTIL HE GIVES HIMSELF UP. SEND YOUR MINION GISBURN OUT WITH A FORCE TOMORROW.
BUT MY LORD! WE CAN'T JUST—
OF COURSE WE BLOODY WELL CAN. START IN WICKHAM. WE KNOW HE'S SPENT TIME THERE.
BURN IT TO THE GROUND. KILL EVERY TENTH PERSON STANDING. AIDING AN OUTLAW? TREASON.
MAKE IT IN THEIR BEST INTERESTS TO HAND HIM IN.
ROBIN OF THE HOOD—OR DEATH BY THE SWORD.

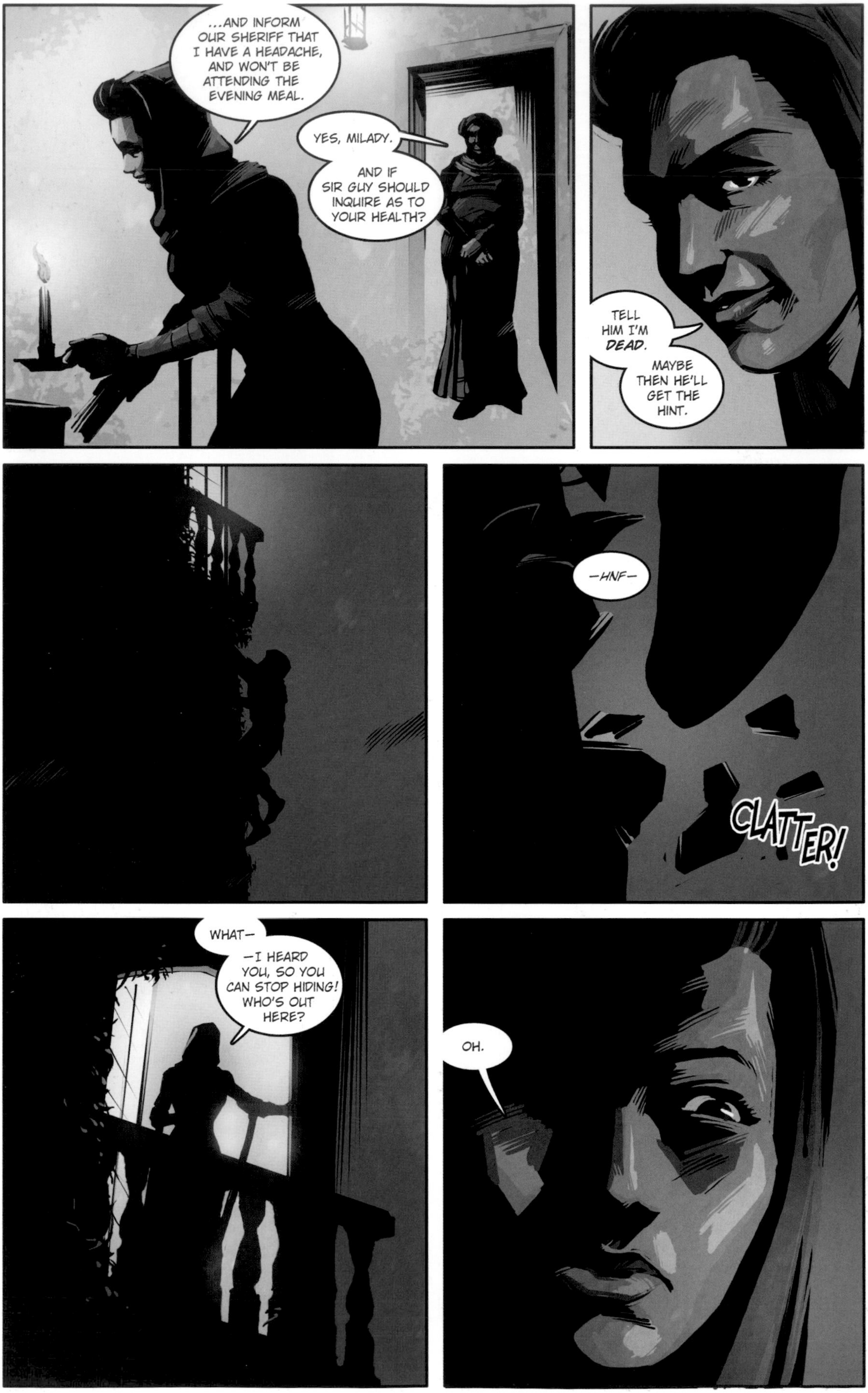
...AND INFORM OUR SHERIFF THAT I HAVE A HEADACHE, AND WON'T BE ATTENDING THE EVENING MEAL.
YES, MILADY.
AND IF SIR GUY SHOULD INQUIRE AS TO YOUR HEALTH?
TELL HIM I'M *DEAD*.
MAYBE THEN HE'LL GET THE HINT.
—HNF—
CLATTER!
WHAT—
—I HEARD YOU, SO YOU CAN STOP HIDING! WHO'S OUT HERE?
OH.

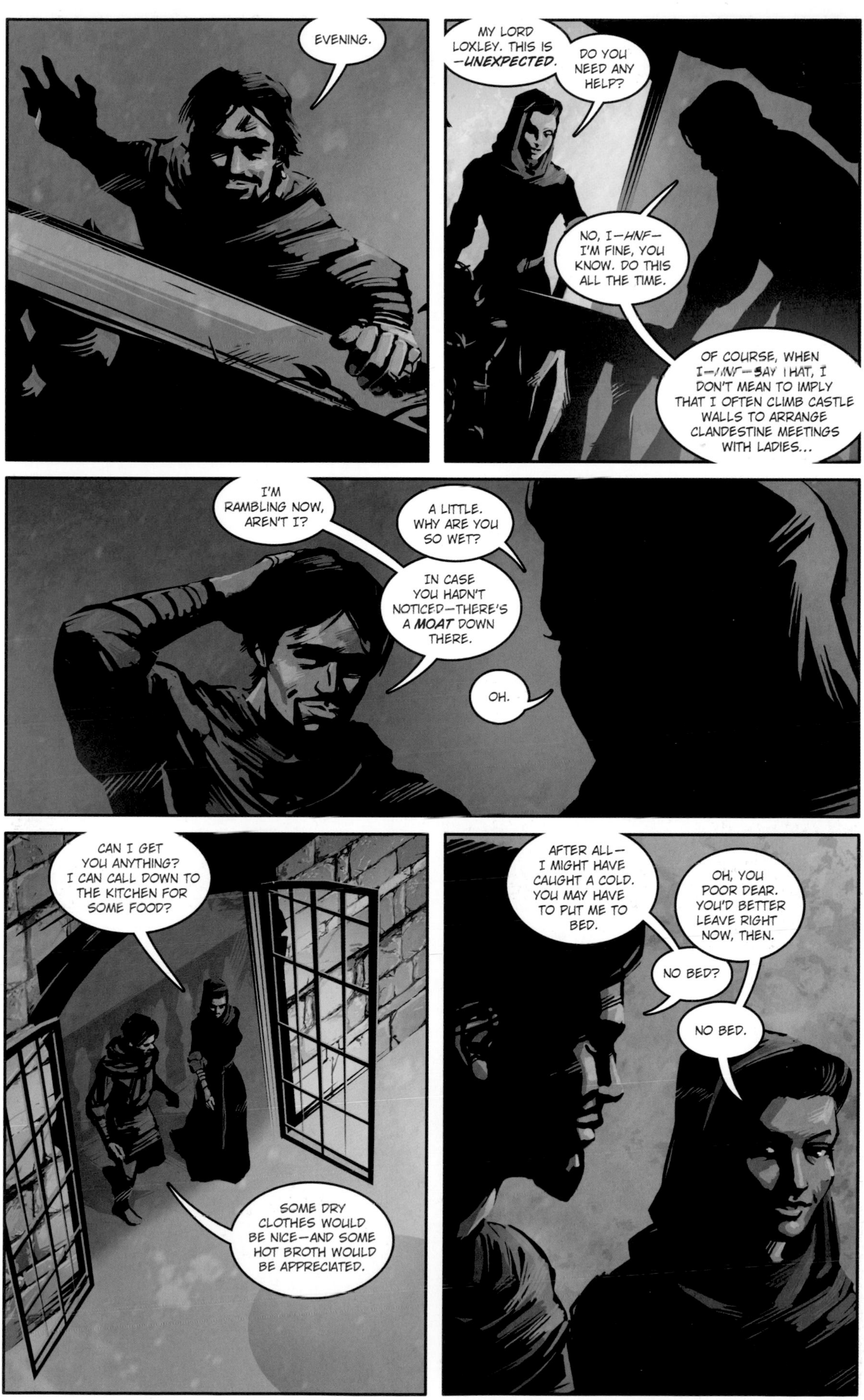
EVENING.
MY LORD LOXLEY. THIS IS —*UNEXPECTED*.
DO YOU NEED ANY HELP?
NO, I—*HNF*— I'M FINE, YOU KNOW. DO THIS ALL THE TIME.
OF COURSE, WHEN I—*HNF*—SAY THAT, I DON'T MEAN TO IMPLY THAT I OFTEN CLIMB CASTLE WALLS TO ARRANGE CLANDESTINE MEETINGS WITH LADIES...
I'M RAMBLING NOW, AREN'T I?
A LITTLE. WHY ARE YOU SO WET?
IN CASE YOU HADN'T NOTICED—THERE'S A *MOAT* DOWN THERE.
OH.
CAN I GET YOU ANYTHING? I CAN CALL DOWN TO THE KITCHEN FOR SOME FOOD?
SOME DRY CLOTHES WOULD BE NICE—AND SOME HOT BROTH WOULD BE APPRECIATED.
AFTER ALL— I MIGHT HAVE CAUGHT A COLD. YOU MAY HAVE TO PUT ME TO BED.
OH, YOU POOR DEAR. YOU'D BETTER LEAVE RIGHT NOW, THEN.
NO BED?
NO BED.

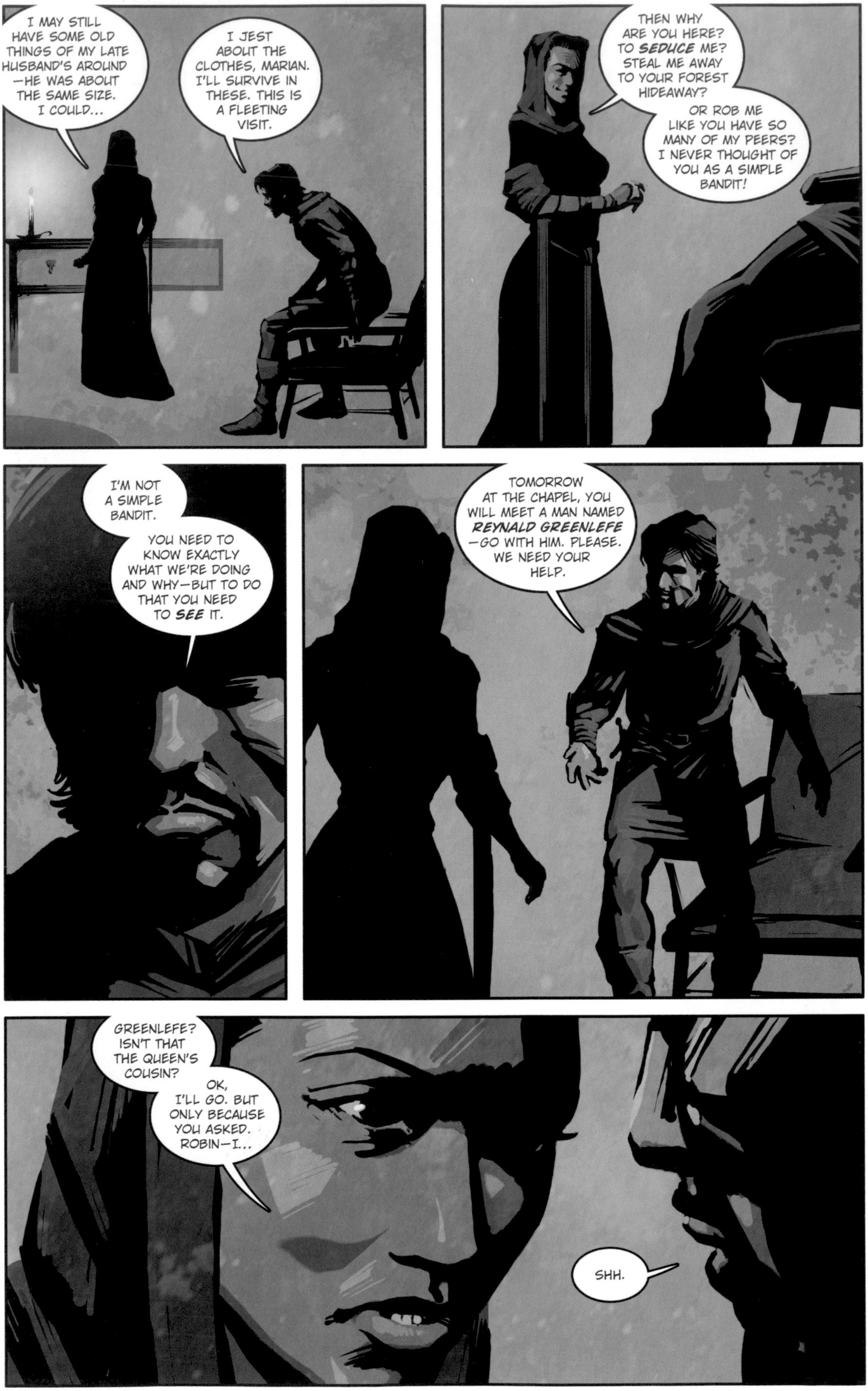
I MAY STILL HAVE SOME OLD THINGS OF MY LATE HUSBAND'S AROUND —HE WAS ABOUT THE SAME SIZE. I COULD...
I JEST ABOUT THE CLOTHES, MARIAN. I'LL SURVIVE IN THESE. THIS IS A FLEETING VISIT.
THEN WHY ARE YOU HERE? TO SEDUCE ME? STEAL ME AWAY TO YOUR FOREST HIDEAWAY?
OR ROB ME LIKE YOU HAVE SO MANY OF MY PEERS? I NEVER THOUGHT OF YOU AS A SIMPLE BANDIT!
I'M NOT A SIMPLE BANDIT.
YOU NEED TO KNOW EXACTLY WHAT WE'RE DOING AND WHY—BUT TO DO THAT YOU NEED TO SEE IT.
TOMORROW AT THE CHAPEL, YOU WILL MEET A MAN NAMED REYNALD GREENLEFE —GO WITH HIM. PLEASE. WE NEED YOUR HELP.
GREENLEFE? ISN'T THAT THE QUEEN'S COUSIN?
OK, I'LL GO. BUT ONLY BECAUSE YOU ASKED. ROBIN—I...
SHH.

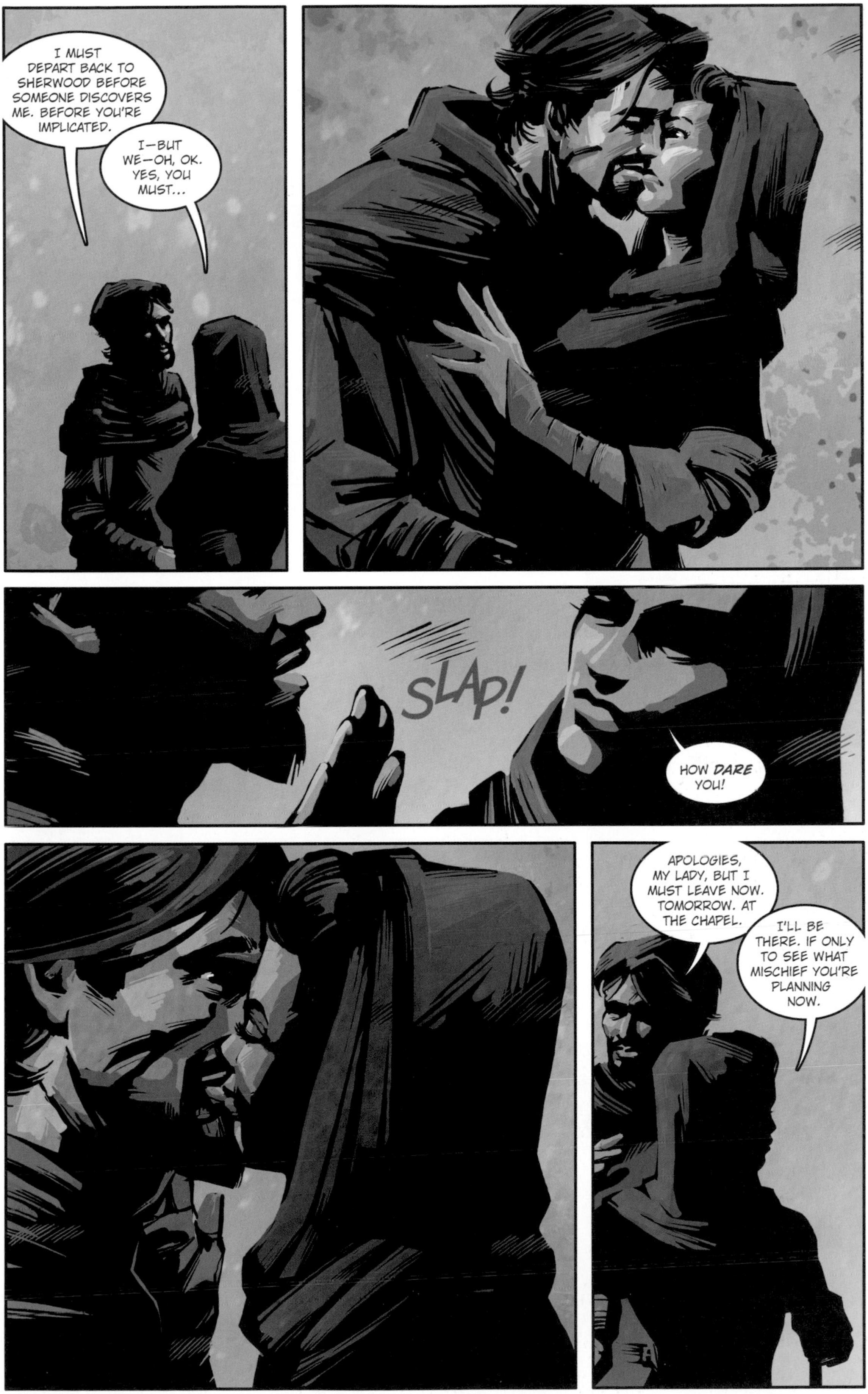
I MUST DEPART BACK TO SHERWOOD BEFORE SOMEONE DISCOVERS ME. BEFORE YOU'RE IMPLICATED.
I—BUT WE—OH, OK. YES, YOU MUST...
SLAP!
HOW DARE YOU!
APOLOGIES, MY LADY, BUT I MUST LEAVE NOW. TOMORROW. AT THE CHAPEL.
I'LL BE THERE. IF ONLY TO SEE WHAT MISCHIEF YOU'RE PLANNING NOW.

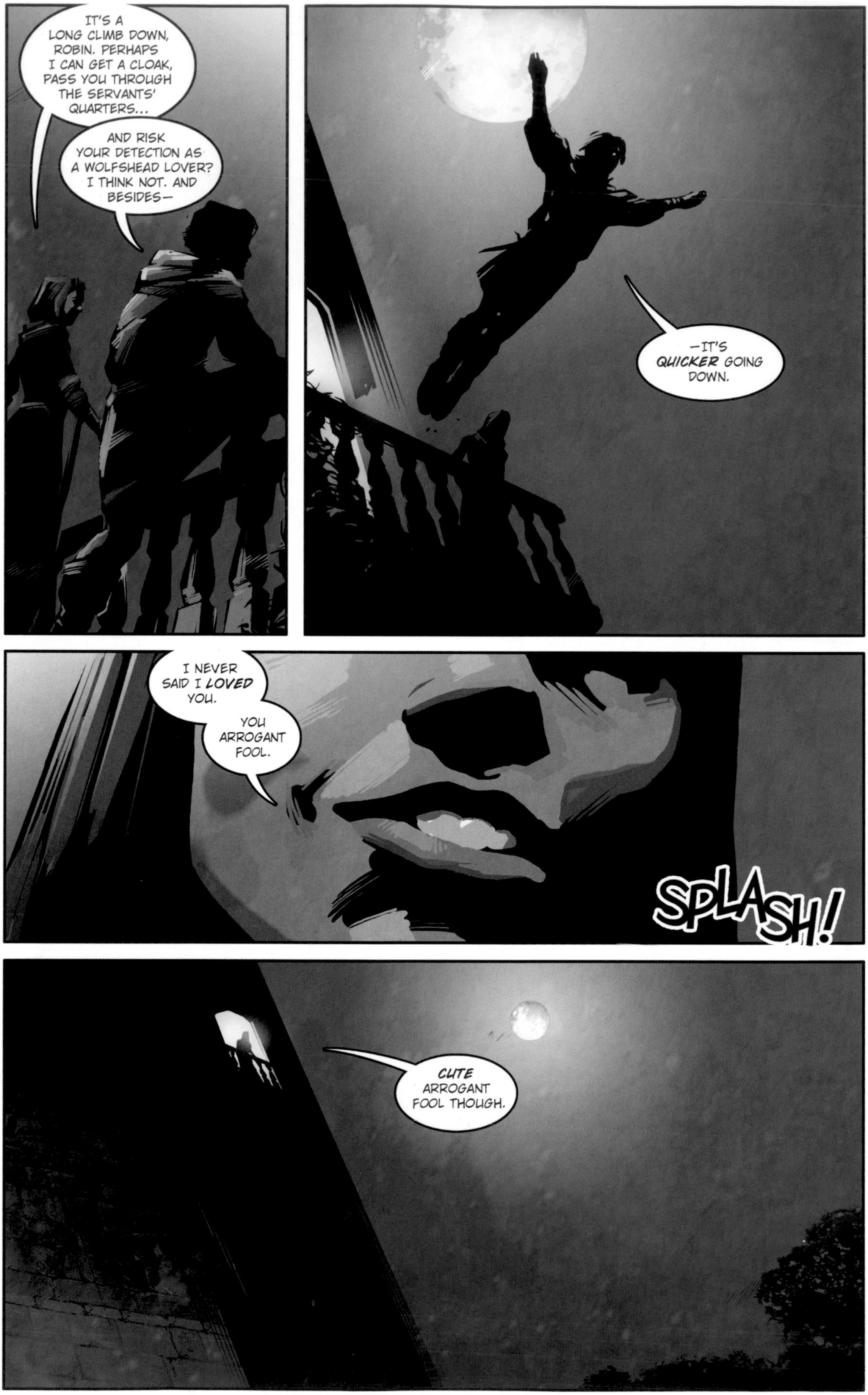
IT'S A LONG CLIMB DOWN, ROBIN. PERHAPS I CAN GET A CLOAK, PASS YOU THROUGH THE SERVANTS' QUARTERS...
AND RISK YOUR DETECTION AS A WOLFSHEAD LOVER? I THINK NOT. AND BESIDES—
—IT'S QUICKER GOING DOWN.
I NEVER SAID I LOVED YOU.
YOU ARROGANT FOOL.
SPLASH!
CUTE ARROGANT FOOL THOUGH.

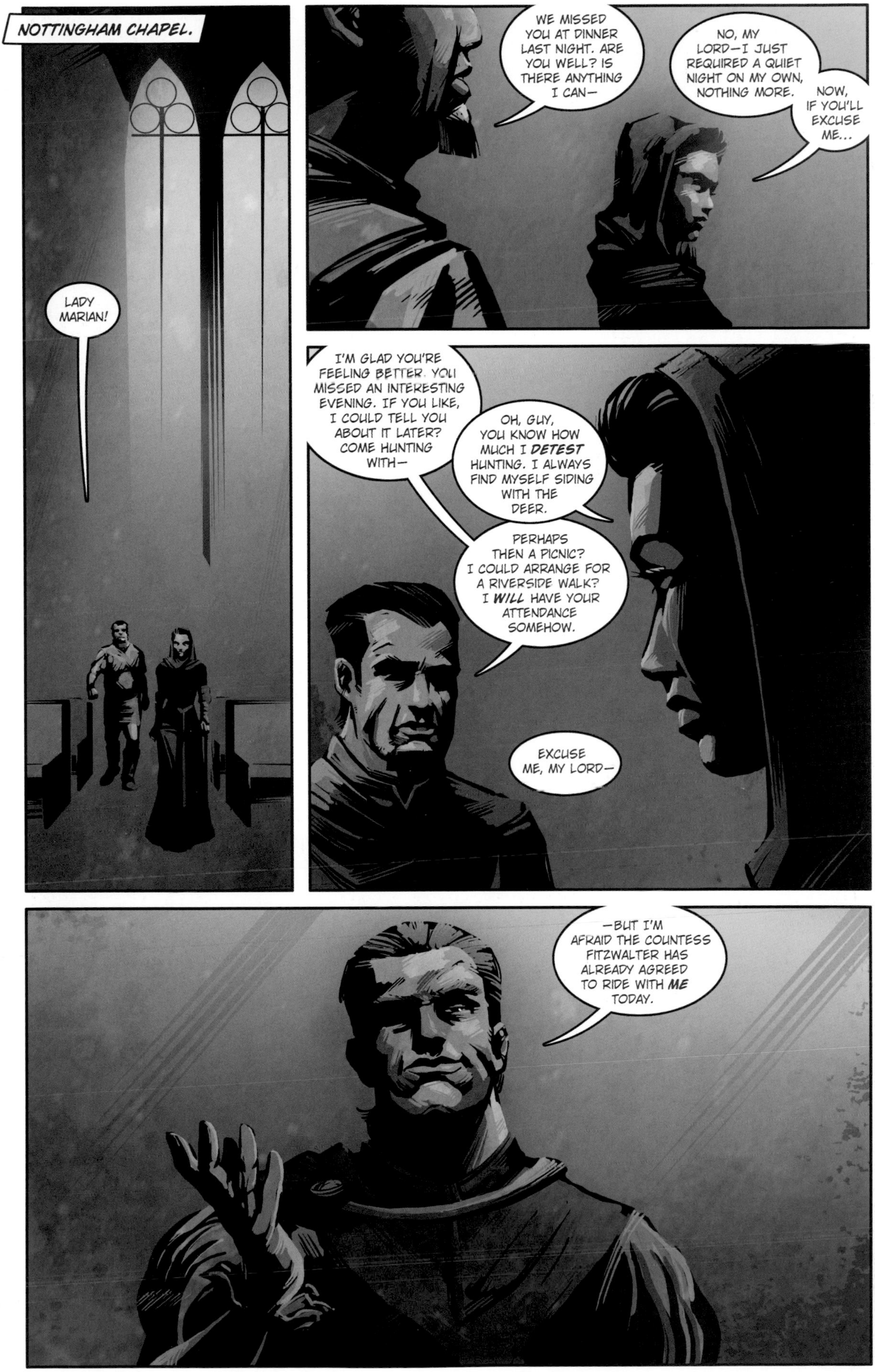
NOTTINGHAM CHAPEL.
LADY MARIAN!
WE MISSED YOU AT DINNER LAST NIGHT. ARE YOU WELL? IS THERE ANYTHING I CAN—
NO, MY LORD—I JUST REQUIRED A QUIET NIGHT ON MY OWN, NOTHING MORE.
NOW, IF YOU'LL EXCUSE ME...
I'M GLAD YOU'RE FEELING BETTER. YOU MISSED AN INTERESTING EVENING. IF YOU LIKE, I COULD TELL YOU ABOUT IT LATER? COME HUNTING WITH—
OH, GUY, YOU KNOW HOW MUCH I DETEST HUNTING. I ALWAYS FIND MYSELF SIDING WITH THE DEER.
PERHAPS THEN A PICNIC? I COULD ARRANGE FOR A RIVERSIDE WALK? I WILL HAVE YOUR ATTENDANCE SOMEHOW.
EXCUSE ME, MY LORD—
—BUT I'M AFRAID THE COUNTESS FITZWALTER HAS ALREADY AGREED TO RIDE WITH ME TODAY.

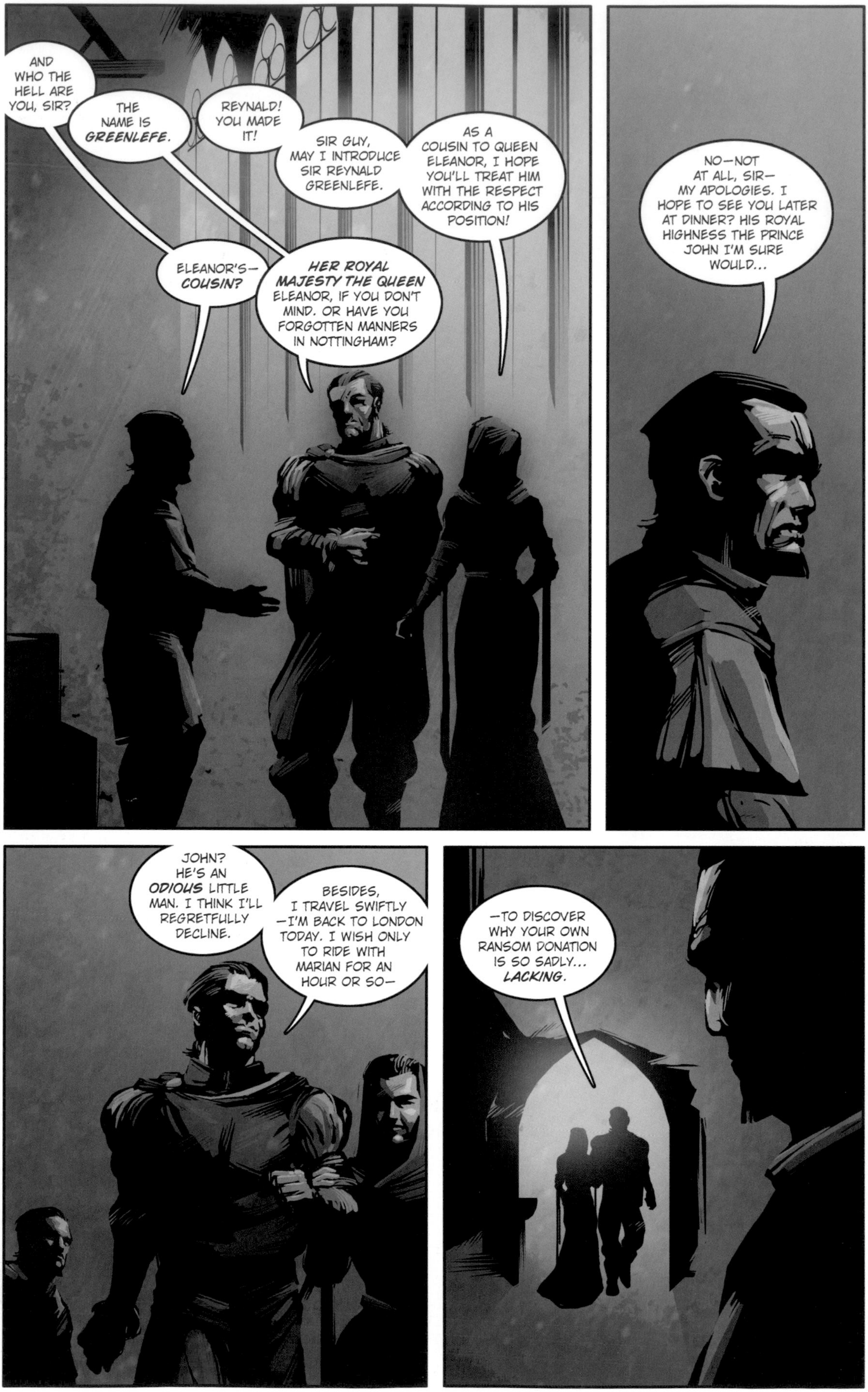
AND WHO THE HELL ARE YOU, SIR?
THE NAME IS GREENLEFE.
REYNALD! YOU MADE IT!
SIR GUY, MAY I INTRODUCE SIR REYNALD GREENLEFE.
AS A COUSIN TO QUEEN ELEANOR, I HOPE YOU'LL TREAT HIM WITH THE RESPECT ACCORDING TO HIS POSITION!
ELEANOR'S—COUSIN?
HER ROYAL MAJESTY THE QUEEN ELEANOR, IF YOU DON'T MIND. OR HAVE YOU FORGOTTEN MANNERS IN NOTTINGHAM?
NO—NOT AT ALL, SIR—MY APOLOGIES. I HOPE TO SEE YOU LATER AT DINNER? HIS ROYAL HIGHNESS THE PRINCE JOHN I'M SURE WOULD...
JOHN? HE'S AN ODIOUS LITTLE MAN. I THINK I'LL REGRETFULLY DECLINE.
BESIDES, I TRAVEL SWIFTLY—I'M BACK TO LONDON TODAY. I WISH ONLY TO RIDE WITH MARIAN FOR AN HOUR OR SO—
—TO DISCOVER WHY YOUR OWN RANSOM DONATION IS SO SADLY... LACKING.

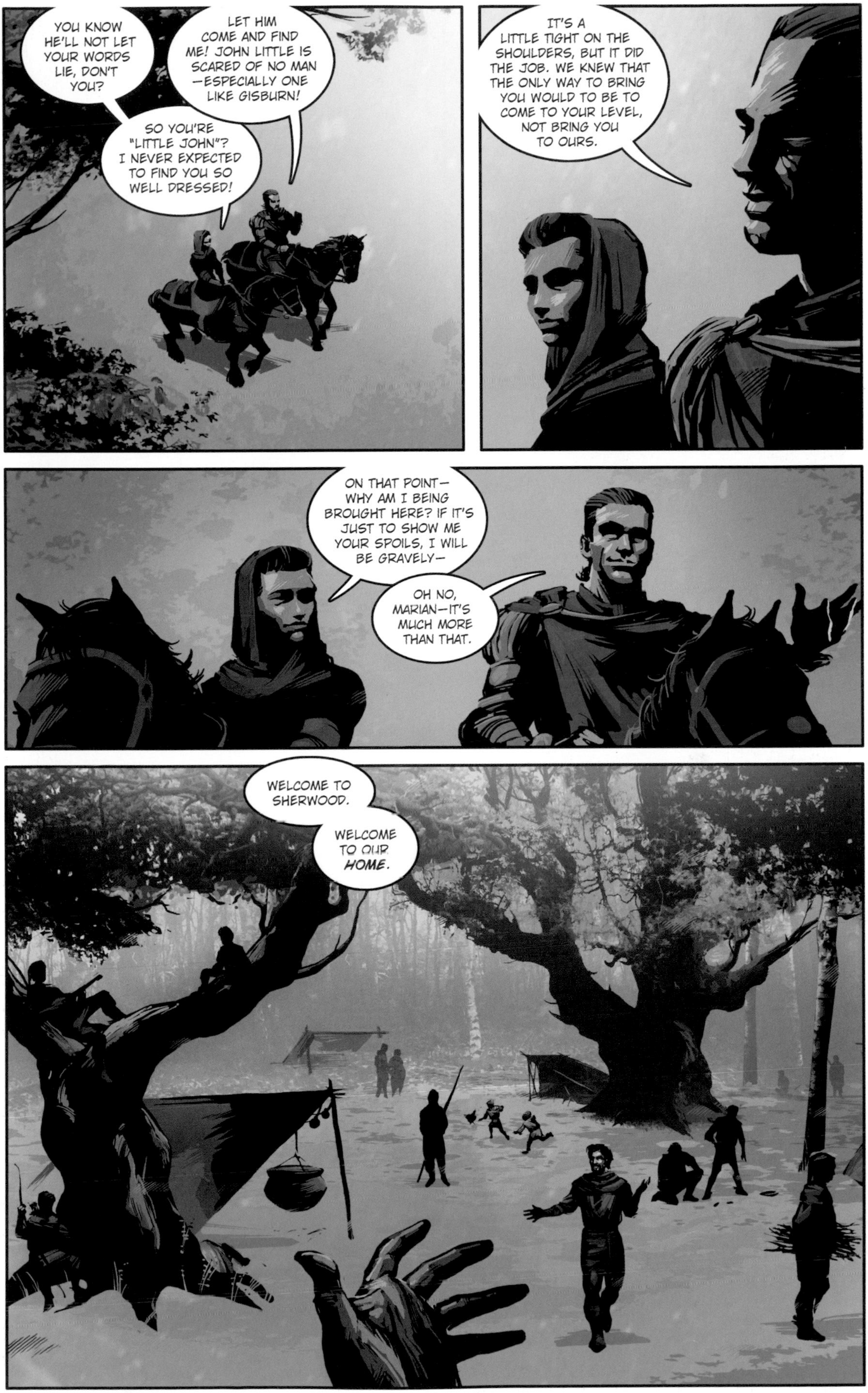
YOU KNOW HE'LL NOT LET YOUR WORDS LIE, DON'T YOU?
LET HIM COME AND FIND ME! JOHN LITTLE IS SCARED OF NO MAN —ESPECIALLY ONE LIKE GISBURN!
SO YOU'RE "LITTLE JOHN"? I NEVER EXPECTED TO FIND YOU SO WELL DRESSED!
IT'S A LITTLE TIGHT ON THE SHOULDERS, BUT IT DID THE JOB. WE KNEW THAT THE ONLY WAY TO BRING YOU WOULD TO BE TO COME TO YOUR LEVEL, NOT BRING YOU TO OURS.
ON THAT POINT— WHY AM I BEING BROUGHT HERE? IF IT'S JUST TO SHOW ME YOUR SPOILS, I WILL BE GRAVELY—
OH NO, MARIAN—IT'S MUCH MORE THAN THAT.
WELCOME TO SHERWOOD.
WELCOME TO OUR *HOME*.

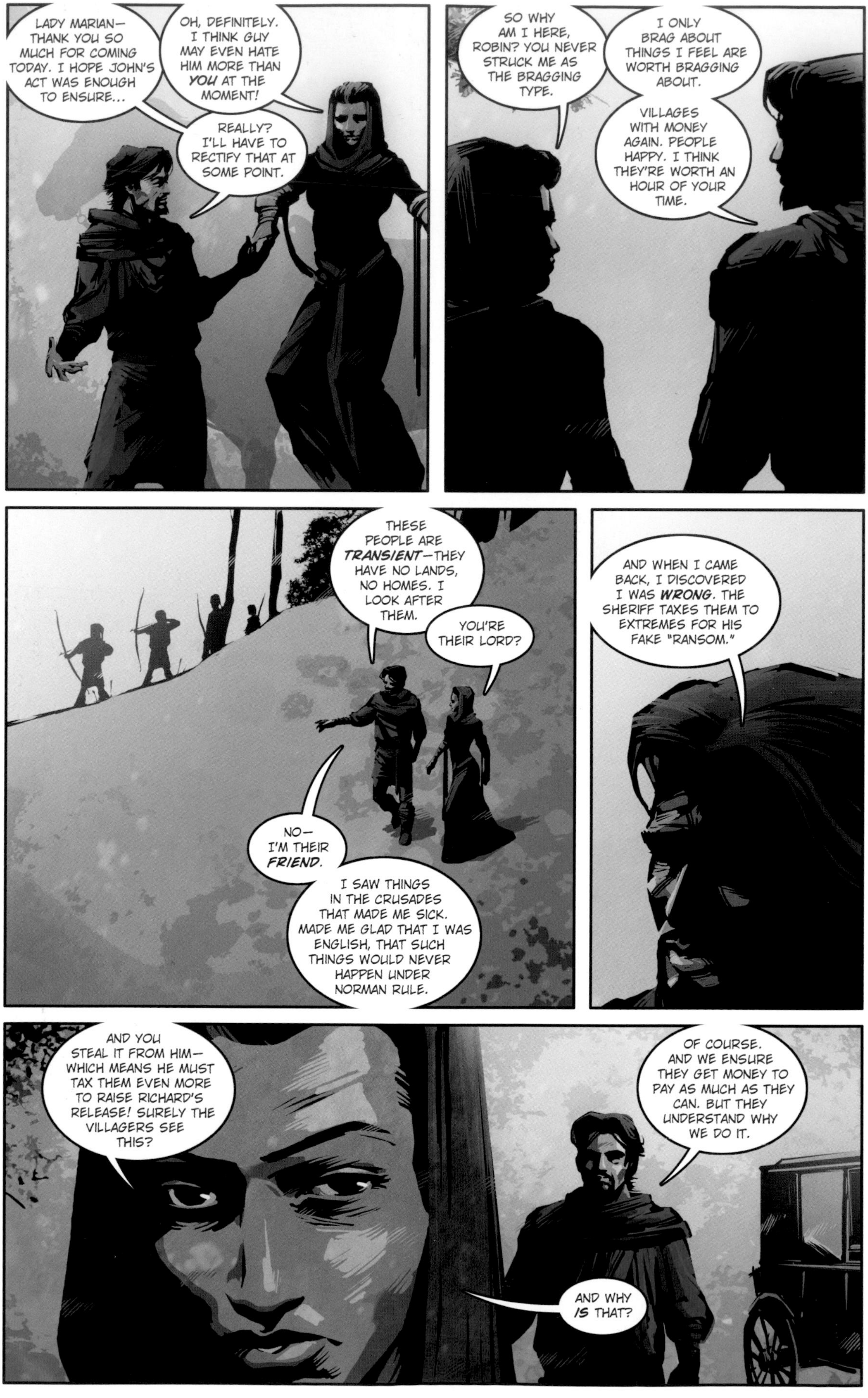
LADY MARIAN— THANK YOU SO MUCH FOR COMING TODAY. I HOPE JOHN'S ACT WAS ENOUGH TO ENSURE...
OH, DEFINITELY. I THINK GUY MAY EVEN HATE HIM MORE THAN *YOU* AT THE MOMENT!
REALLY? I'LL HAVE TO RECTIFY THAT AT SOME POINT.
SO WHY AM I HERE, ROBIN? YOU NEVER STRUCK ME AS THE BRAGGING TYPE.
I ONLY BRAG ABOUT THINGS I FEEL ARE WORTH BRAGGING ABOUT.
VILLAGES WITH MONEY AGAIN. PEOPLE HAPPY. I THINK THEY'RE WORTH AN HOUR OF YOUR TIME.
THESE PEOPLE ARE *TRANSIENT*—THEY HAVE NO LANDS, NO HOMES. I LOOK AFTER THEM.
YOU'RE THEIR LORD?
NO— I'M THEIR *FRIEND*.
I SAW THINGS IN THE CRUSADES THAT MADE ME SICK. MADE ME GLAD THAT I WAS ENGLISH, THAT SUCH THINGS WOULD NEVER HAPPEN UNDER NORMAN RULE.
AND WHEN I CAME BACK, I DISCOVERED I WAS *WRONG*. THE SHERIFF TAXES THEM TO EXTREMES FOR HIS FAKE "RANSOM."
AND YOU STEAL IT FROM HIM— WHICH MEANS HE MUST TAX THEM EVEN MORE TO RAISE RICHARD'S RELEASE! SURELY THE VILLAGERS SEE THIS?
OF COURSE. AND WE ENSURE THEY GET MONEY TO PAY AS MUCH AS THEY CAN. BUT THEY UNDERSTAND WHY WE DO IT.
AND WHY *IS* THAT?

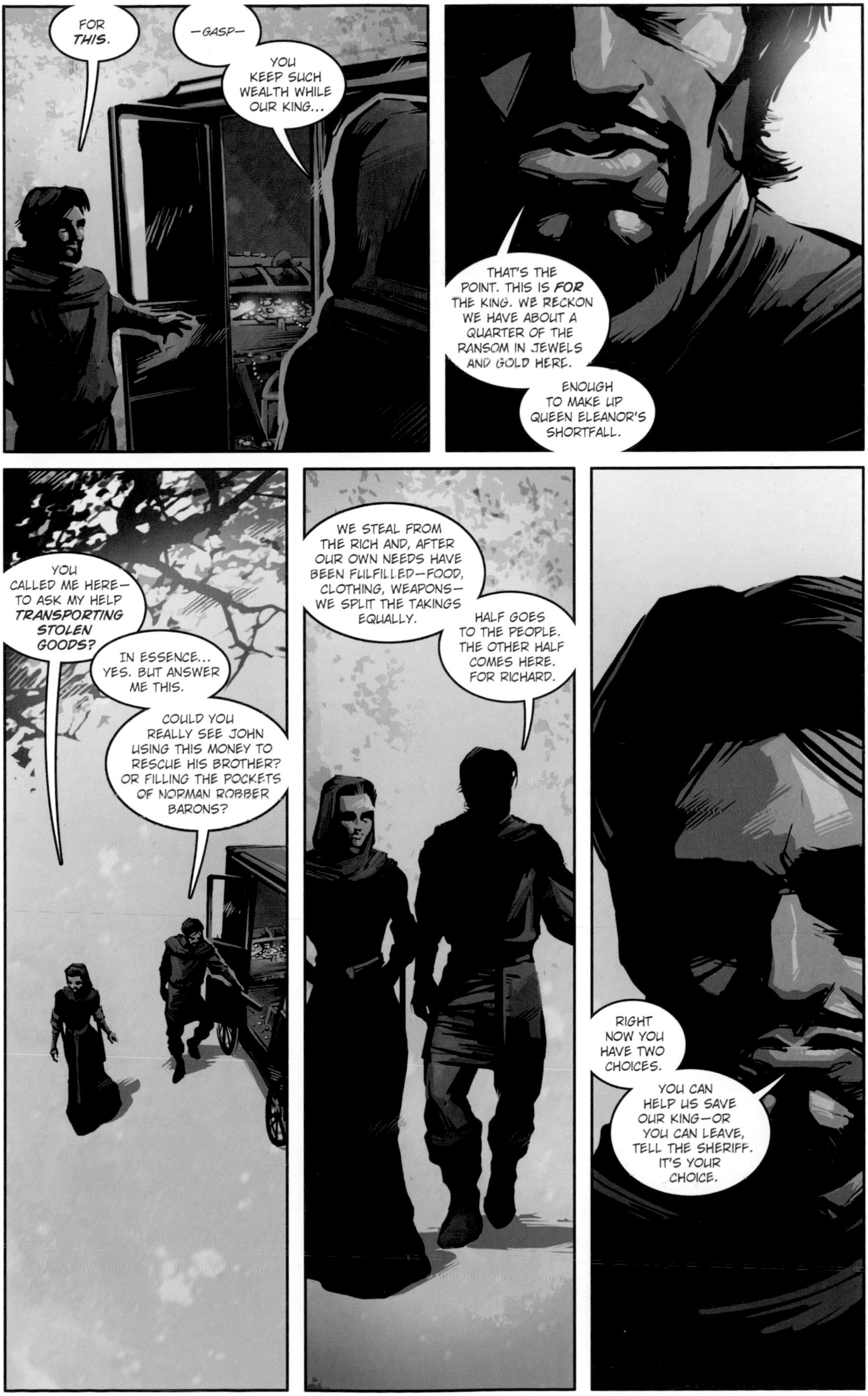
FOR THIS.
—GASP—
YOU KEEP SUCH WEALTH WHILE OUR KING...
THAT'S THE POINT. THIS IS FOR THE KING. WE RECKON WE HAVE ABOUT A QUARTER OF THE RANSOM IN JEWELS AND GOLD HERE.
ENOUGH TO MAKE UP QUEEN ELEANOR'S SHORTFALL.
YOU CALLED ME HERE—TO ASK MY HELP TRANSPORTING STOLEN GOODS?
IN ESSENCE... YES. BUT ANSWER ME THIS.
COULD YOU REALLY SEE JOHN USING THIS MONEY TO RESCUE HIS BROTHER? OR FILLING THE POCKETS OF NORMAN ROBBER BARONS?
WE STEAL FROM THE RICH AND, AFTER OUR OWN NEEDS HAVE BEEN FULFILLED—FOOD, CLOTHING, WEAPONS—WE SPLIT THE TAKINGS EQUALLY.
HALF GOES TO THE PEOPLE. THE OTHER HALF COMES HERE. FOR RICHARD.
RIGHT NOW YOU HAVE TWO CHOICES.
YOU CAN HELP US SAVE OUR KING—OR YOU CAN LEAVE, TELL THE SHERIFF. IT'S YOUR CHOICE.

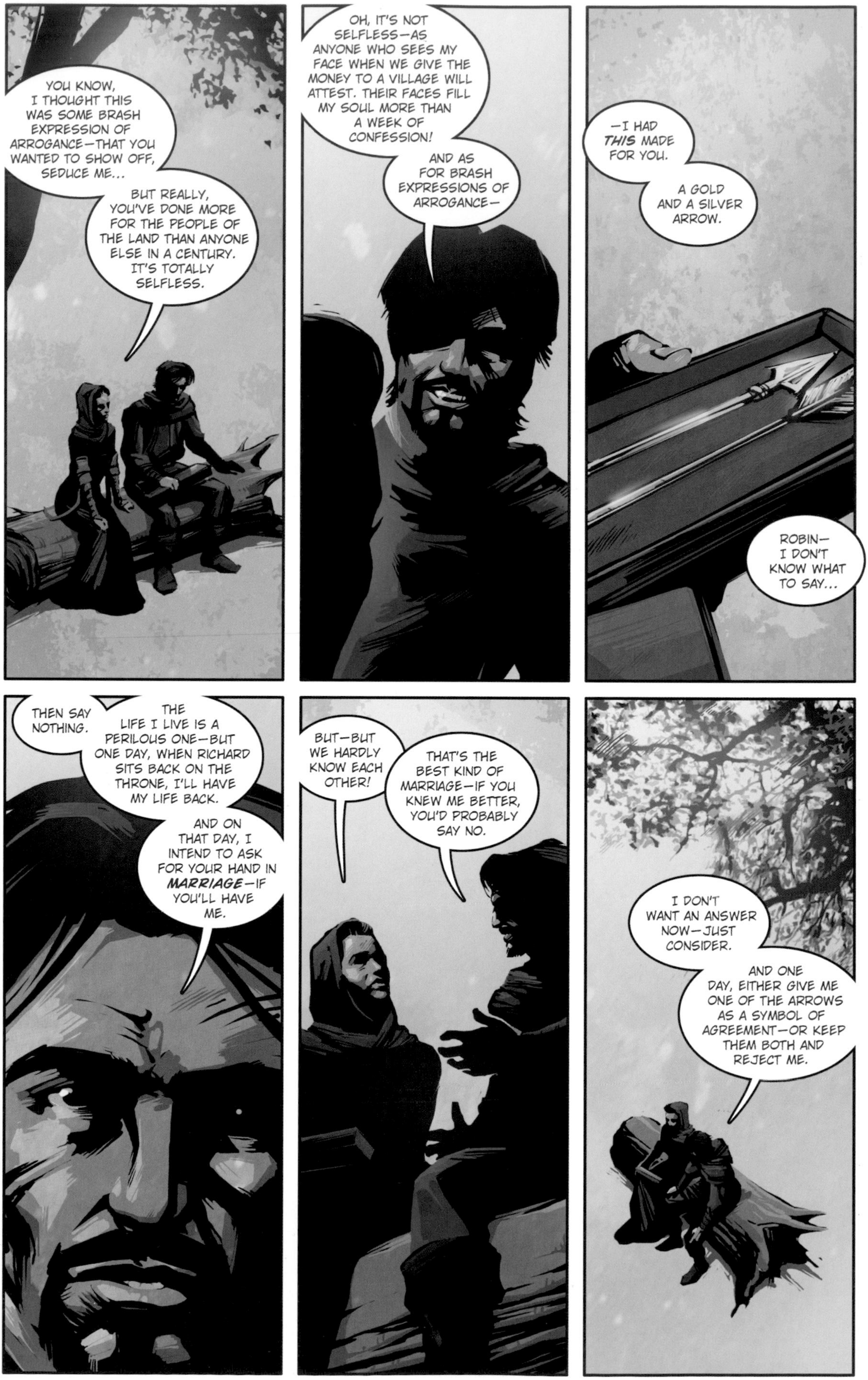
YOU KNOW, I THOUGHT THIS WAS SOME BRASH EXPRESSION OF ARROGANCE—THAT YOU WANTED TO SHOW OFF, SEDUCE ME...
BUT REALLY, YOU'VE DONE MORE FOR THE PEOPLE OF THE LAND THAN ANYONE ELSE IN A CENTURY. IT'S TOTALLY SELFLESS.
OH, IT'S NOT SELFLESS—AS ANYONE WHO SEES MY FACE WHEN WE GIVE THE MONEY TO A VILLAGE WILL ATTEST. THEIR FACES FILL MY SOUL MORE THAN A WEEK OF CONFESSION!
AND AS FOR BRASH EXPRESSIONS OF ARROGANCE—
—I HAD *THIS* MADE FOR YOU.
A GOLD AND A SILVER ARROW.
ROBIN—I DON'T KNOW WHAT TO SAY...
THEN SAY NOTHING.
THE LIFE I LIVE IS A PERILOUS ONE—BUT ONE DAY, WHEN RICHARD SITS BACK ON THE THRONE, I'LL HAVE MY LIFE BACK.
AND ON THAT DAY, I INTEND TO ASK FOR YOUR HAND IN ***MARRIAGE***—IF YOU'LL HAVE ME.
BUT—BUT WE HARDLY KNOW EACH OTHER!
THAT'S THE BEST KIND OF MARRIAGE—IF YOU KNEW ME BETTER, YOU'D PROBABLY SAY NO.
I DON'T WANT AN ANSWER NOW—JUST CONSIDER.
AND ONE DAY, EITHER GIVE ME ONE OF THE ARROWS AS A SYMBOL OF AGREEMENT—OR KEEP THEM BOTH AND REJECT ME.

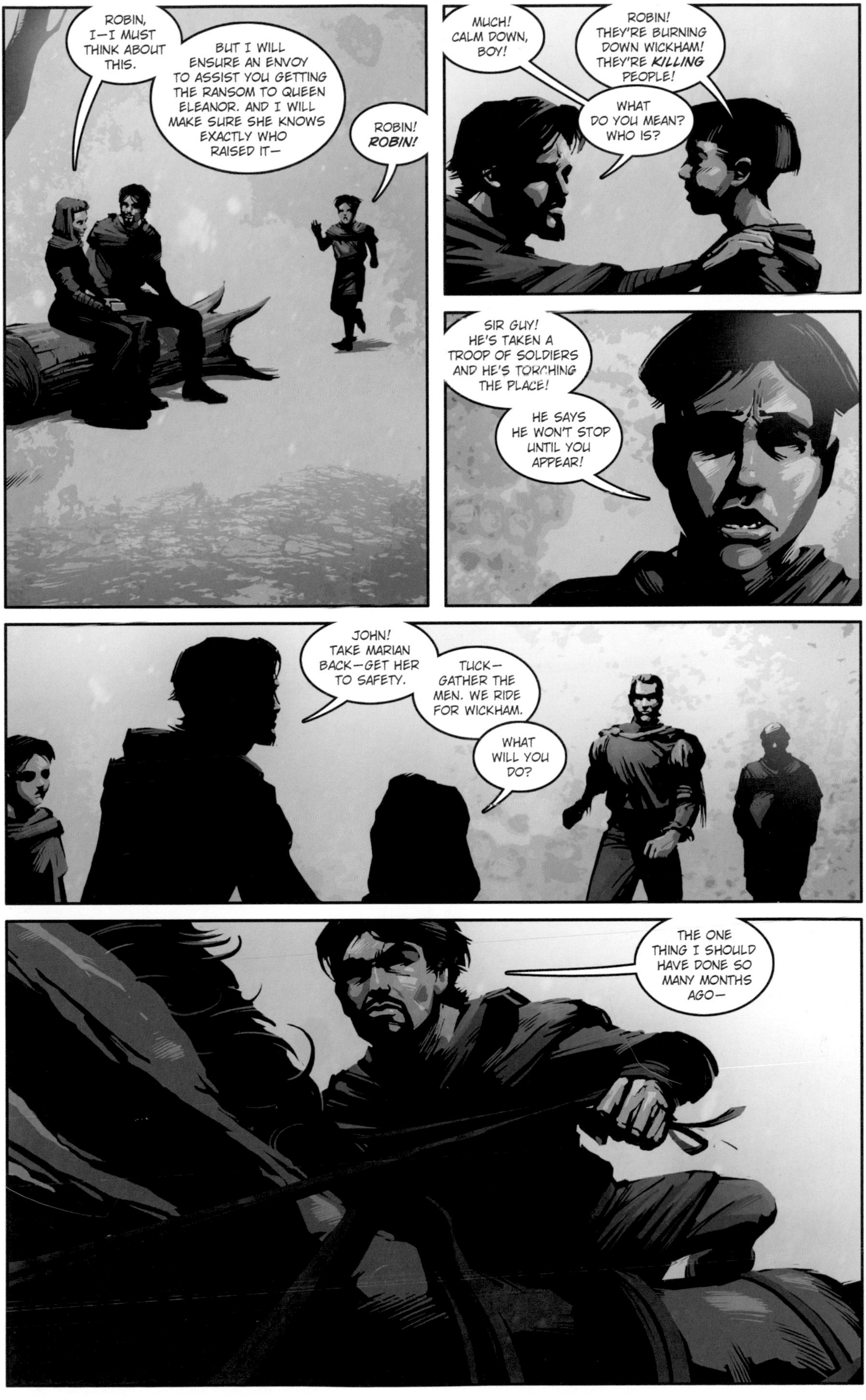
ROBIN, I—I MUST THINK ABOUT THIS.
BUT I WILL ENSURE AN ENVOY TO ASSIST YOU GETTING THE RANSOM TO QUEEN ELEANOR. AND I WILL MAKE SURE SHE KNOWS EXACTLY WHO RAISED IT—
ROBIN! ROBIN!
MUCH! CALM DOWN, BOY!
ROBIN! THEY'RE BURNING DOWN WICKHAM! THEY'RE KILLING PEOPLE!
WHAT DO YOU MEAN? WHO IS?
SIR GUY! HE'S TAKEN A TROOP OF SOLDIERS AND HE'S TORCHING THE PLACE!
HE SAYS HE WON'T STOP UNTIL YOU APPEAR!
JOHN! TAKE MARIAN BACK—GET HER TO SAFETY.
TUCK—GATHER THE MEN. WE RIDE FOR WICKHAM.
WHAT WILL YOU DO?
THE ONE THING I SHOULD HAVE DONE SO MANY MONTHS AGO—

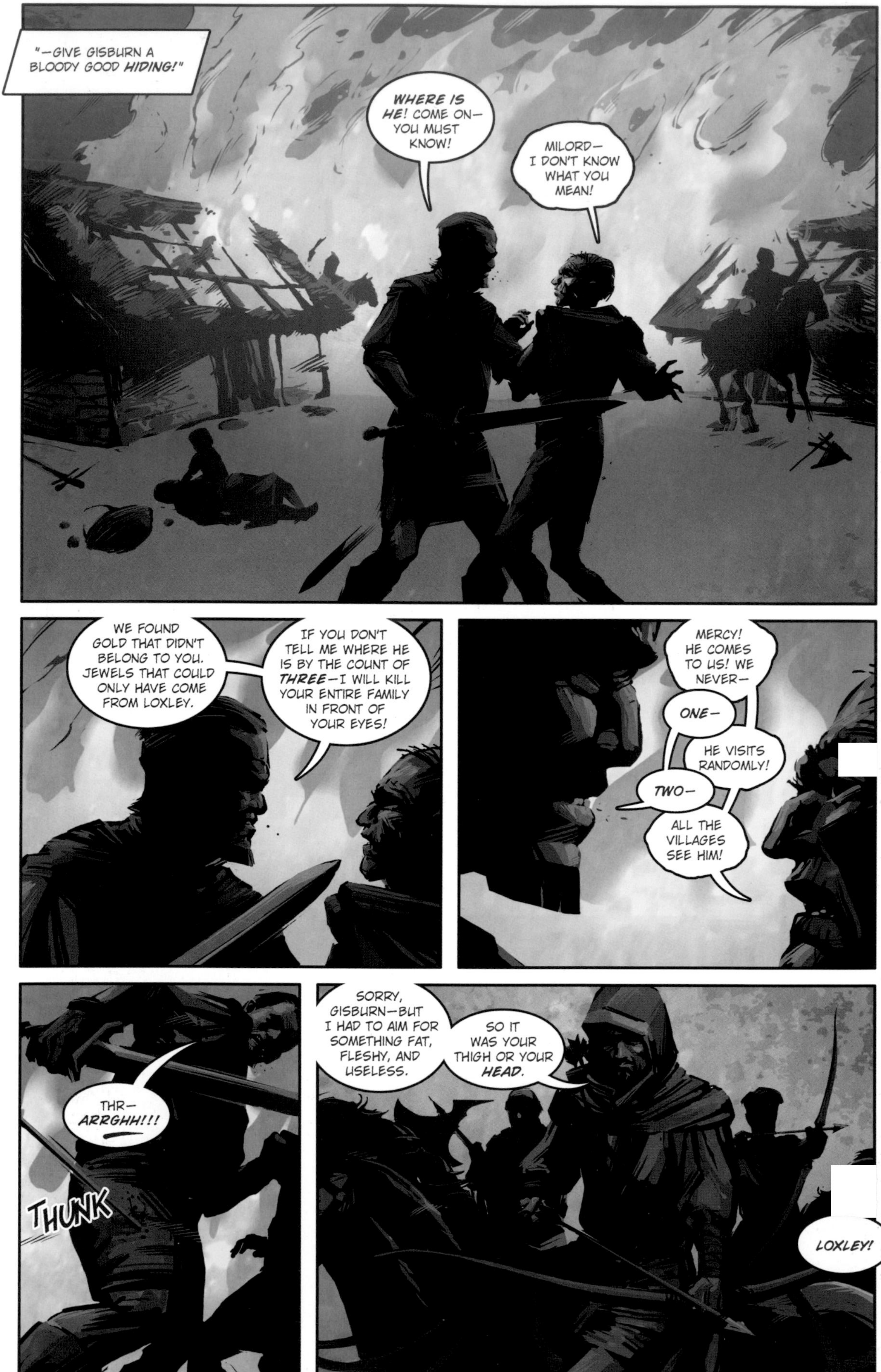
"—GIVE GISBURN A BLOODY GOOD HIDING!"
WHERE IS HE! COME ON— YOU MUST KNOW!
MILORD— I DON'T KNOW WHAT YOU MEAN!
WE FOUND GOLD THAT DIDN'T BELONG TO YOU. JEWELS THAT COULD ONLY HAVE COME FROM LOXLEY.
IF YOU DON'T TELL ME WHERE HE IS BY THE COUNT OF THREE—I WILL KILL YOUR ENTIRE FAMILY IN FRONT OF YOUR EYES!
MERCY! HE COMES TO US! WE NEVER—
ONE—
HE VISITS RANDOMLY!
TWO—
ALL THE VILLAGES SEE HIM!
THR—ARRGHH!!!
THUNK
SORRY, GISBURN—BUT I HAD TO AIM FOR SOMETHING FAT, FLESHY, AND USELESS.
SO IT WAS YOUR THIGH OR YOUR HEAD.
LOXLEY!

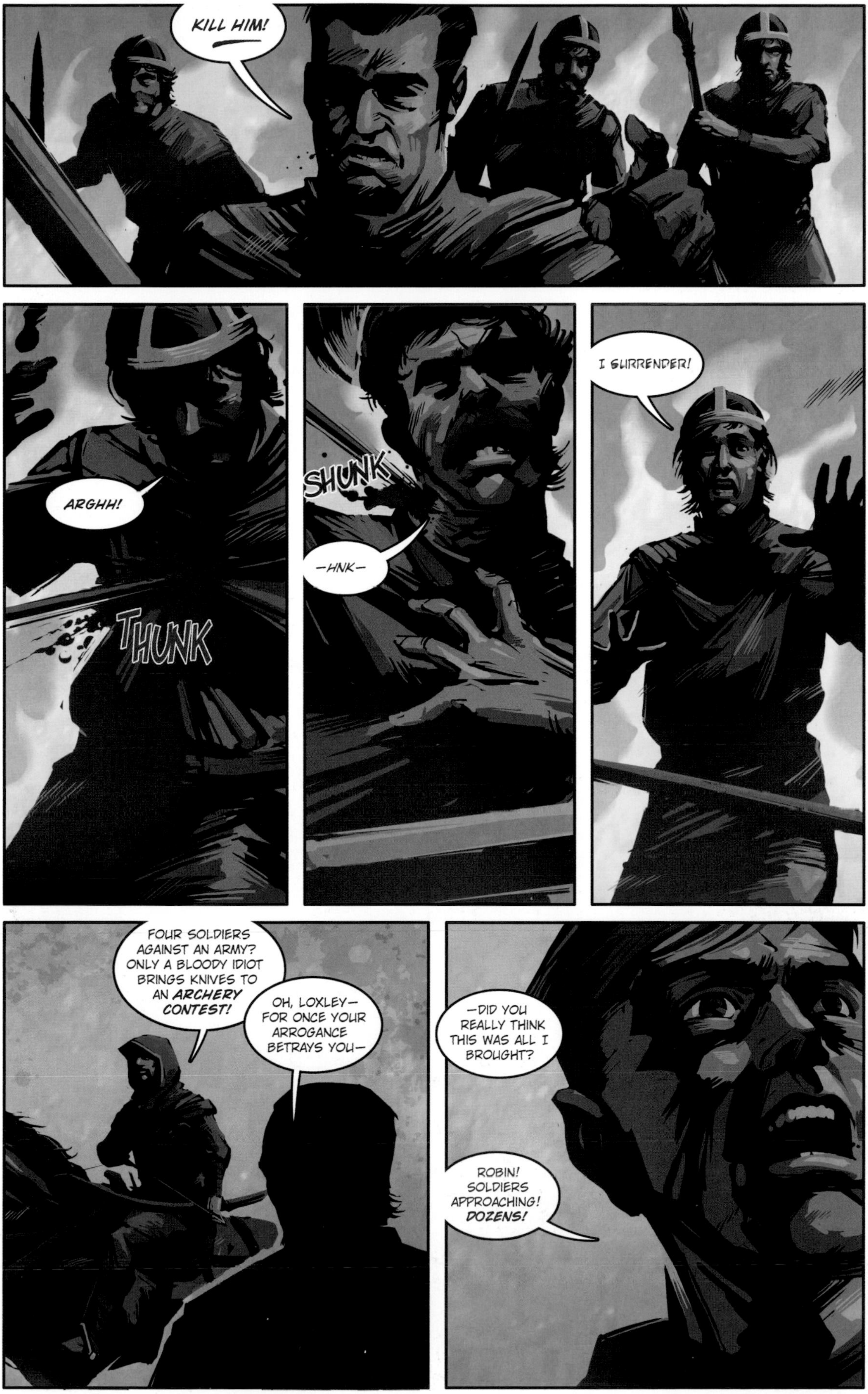
KILL HIM!
ARGHH!
THUNK
SHUNK
—HNK—
I SURRENDER!
FOUR SOLDIERS AGAINST AN ARMY? ONLY A BLOODY IDIOT BRINGS KNIVES TO AN ARCHERY CONTEST!
OH, LOXLEY— FOR ONCE YOUR ARROGANCE BETRAYS YOU—
—DID YOU REALLY THINK THIS WAS ALL I BROUGHT?
ROBIN! SOLDIERS APPROACHING! DOZENS!

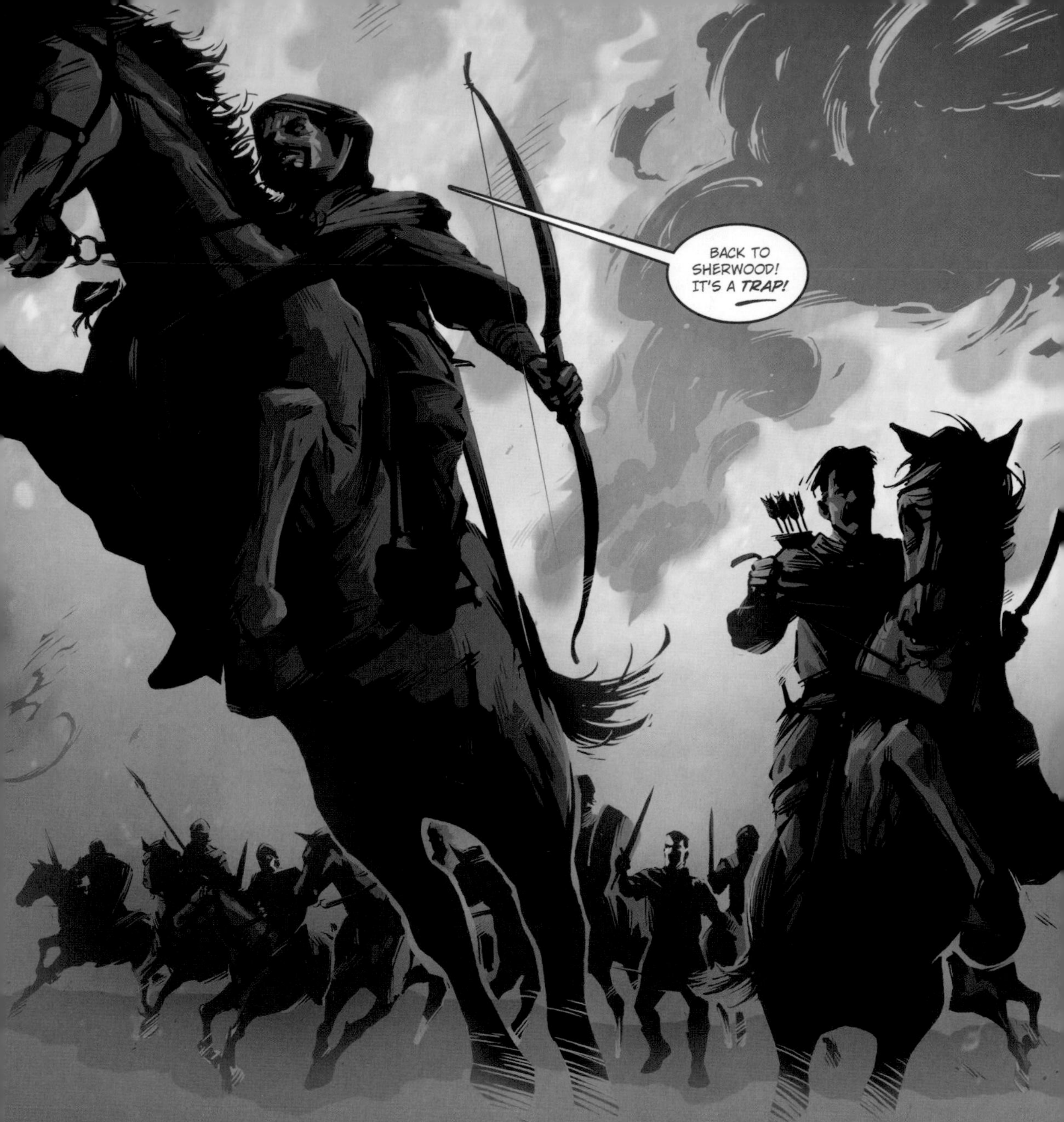
BACK TO SHERWOOD! IT'S A *TRAP!*

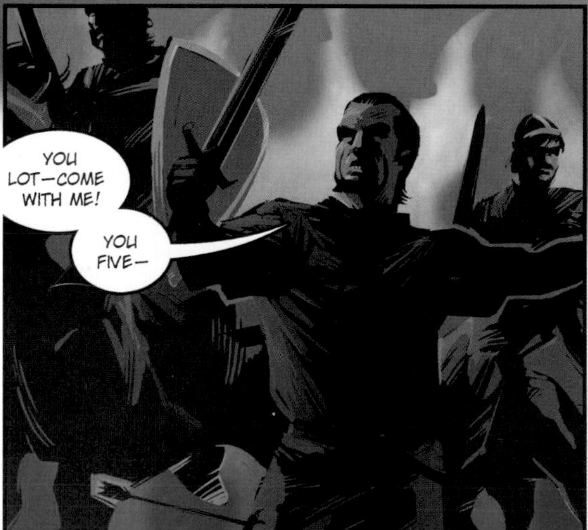
YOU LOT—COME WITH ME!
YOU FIVE—

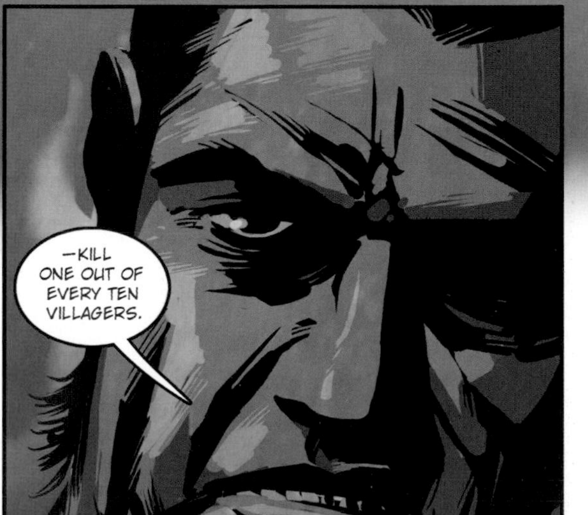
—KILL ONE OUT OF EVERY TEN VILLAGERS.

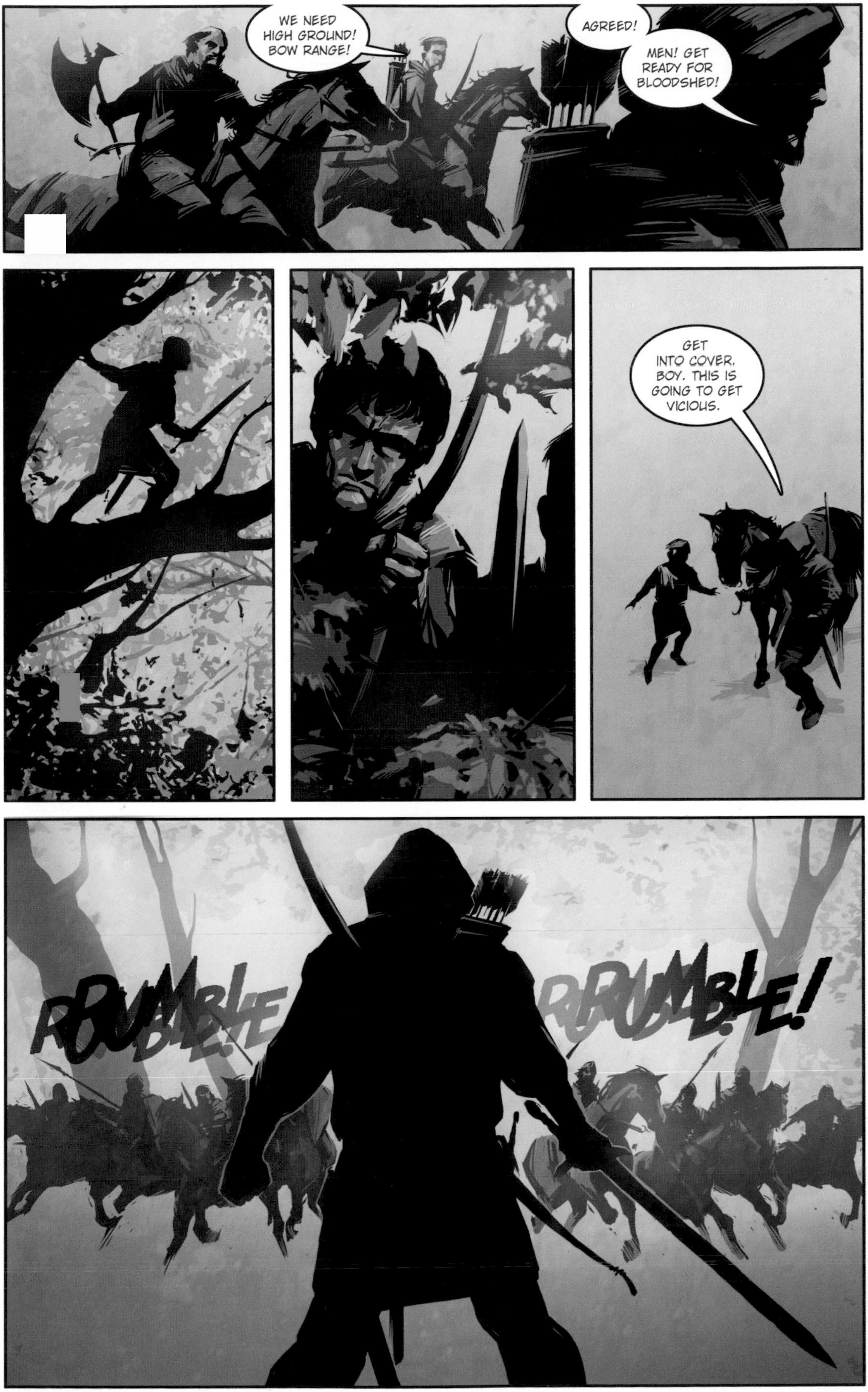
WE NEED HIGH GROUND! BOW RANGE!
AGREED!
MEN! GET READY FOR BLOODSHED!
GET INTO COVER, BOY. THIS IS GOING TO GET VICIOUS.

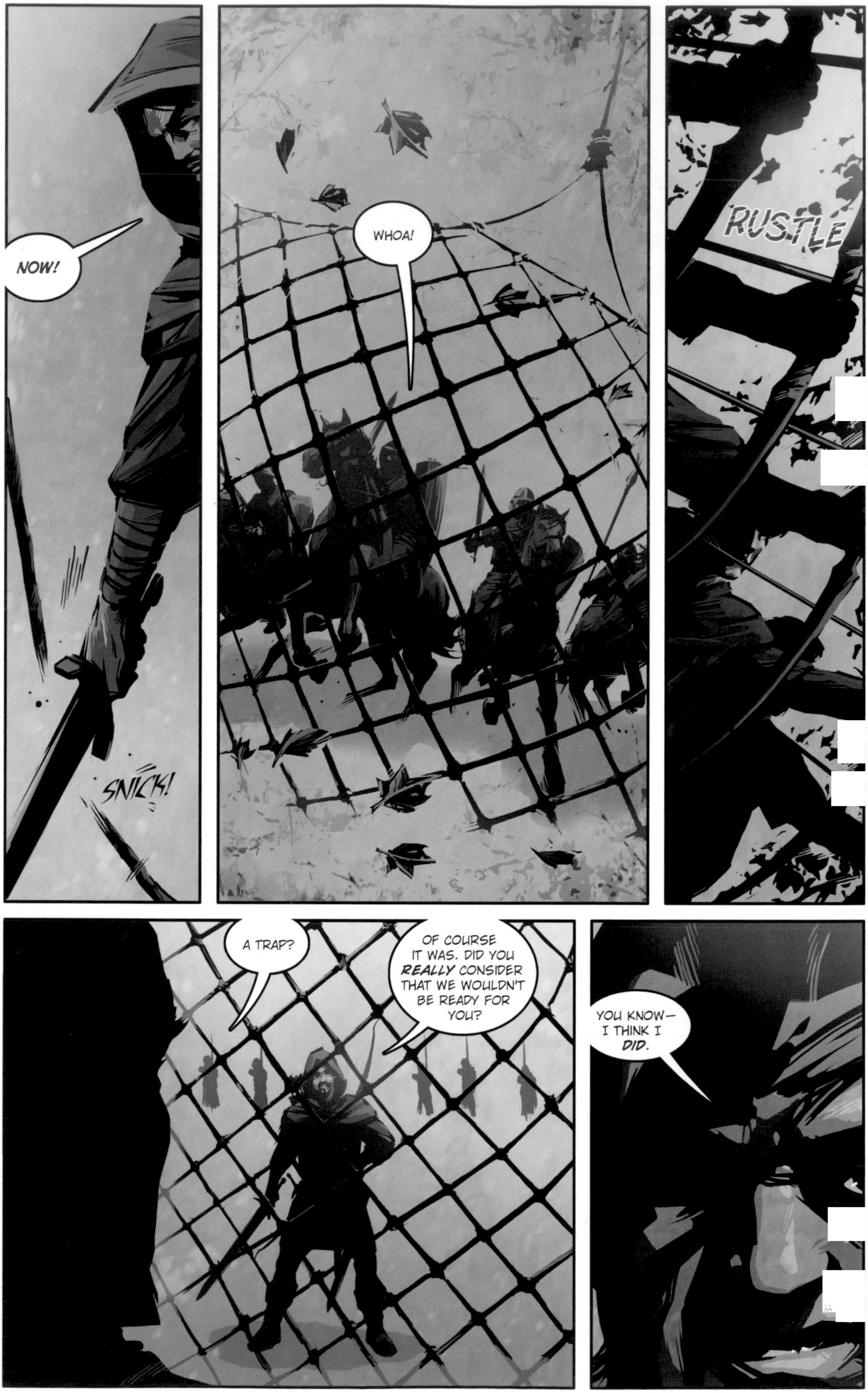
NOW!
SNICK!
WHOA!
RUSTLE
A TRAP?
OF COURSE IT WAS. DID YOU *REALLY* CONSIDER THAT WE WOULDN'T BE READY FOR YOU?
YOU KNOW— I THINK I *DID*.

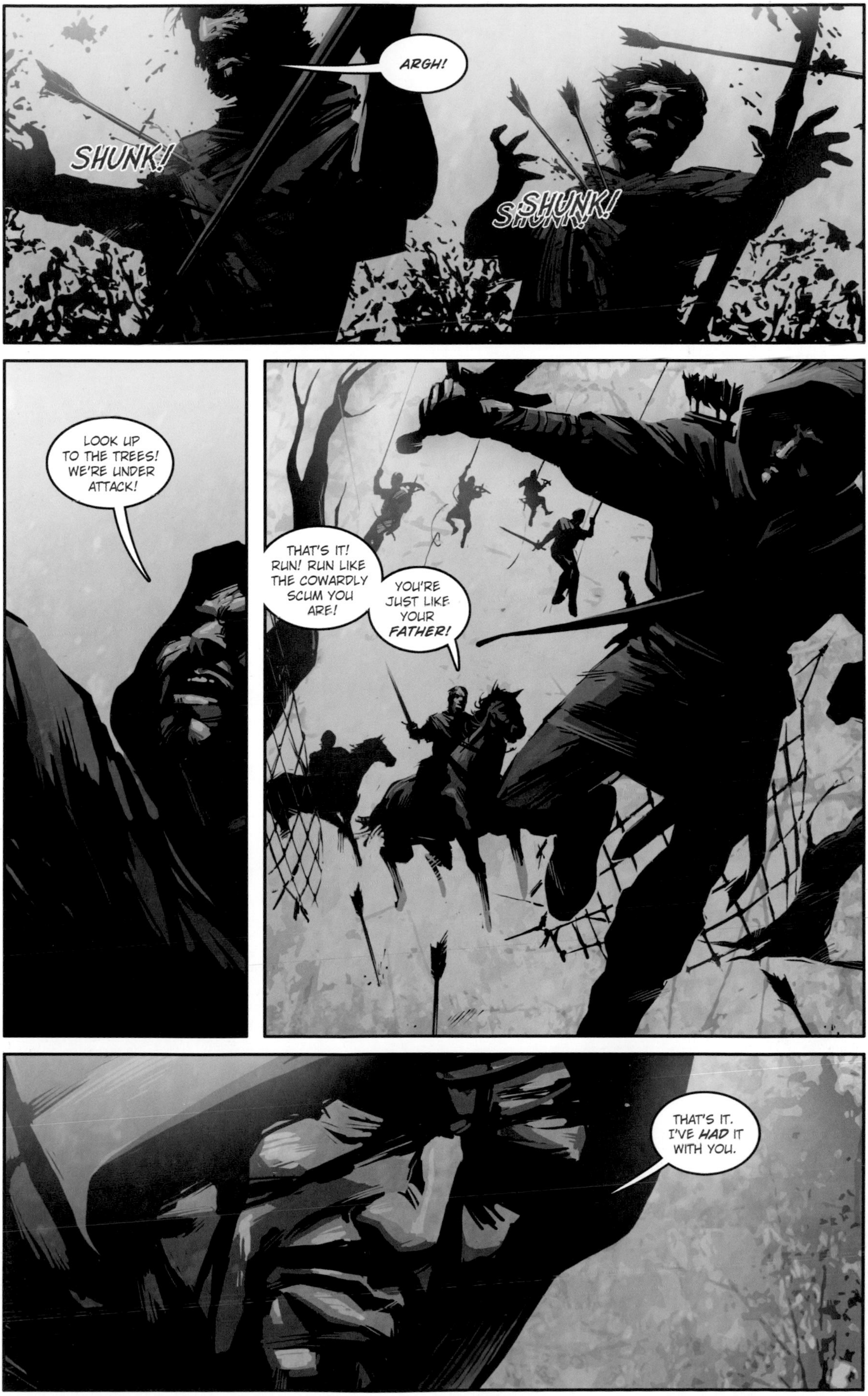
ARGH!
SHUNK!
SHUNK!
LOOK UP TO THE TREES! WE'RE UNDER ATTACK!
THAT'S IT! RUN! RUN LIKE THE COWARDLY SCUM YOU ARE!
YOU'RE JUST LIKE YOUR FATHER!
THAT'S IT. I'VE HAD IT WITH YOU.

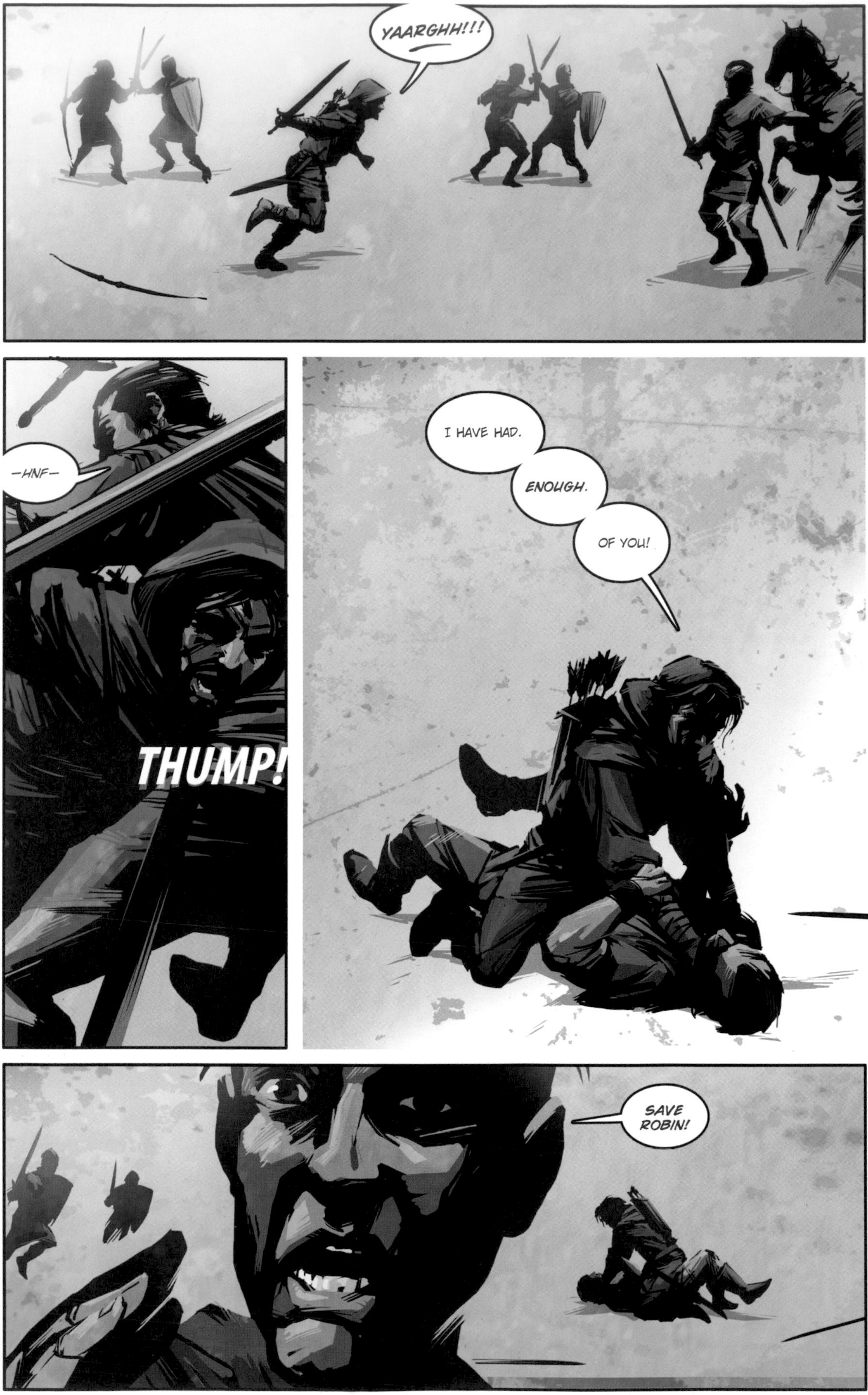
YAARGHH!!!
-HNF-
THUMP!
I HAVE HAD.
ENOUGH.
OF YOU!
SAVE ROBIN!

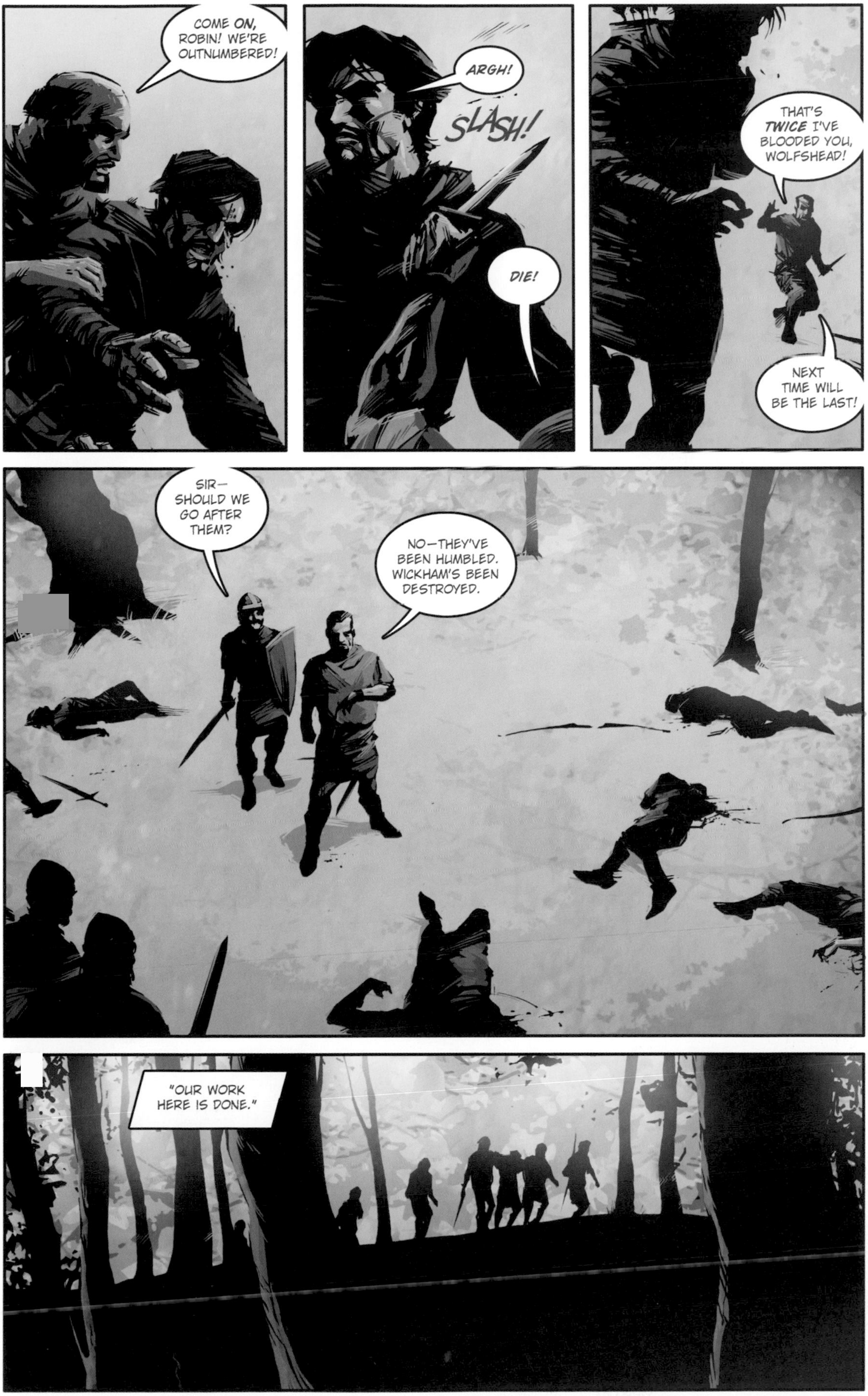
COME ON, ROBIN! WE'RE OUTNUMBERED!
ARGH!
SLASH!
DIE!
THAT'S TWICE I'VE BLOODED YOU, WOLFSHEAD!
NEXT TIME WILL BE THE LAST!
SIR— SHOULD WE GO AFTER THEM?
NO—THEY'VE BEEN HUMBLED. WICKHAM'S BEEN DESTROYED.
"OUR WORK HERE IS DONE."

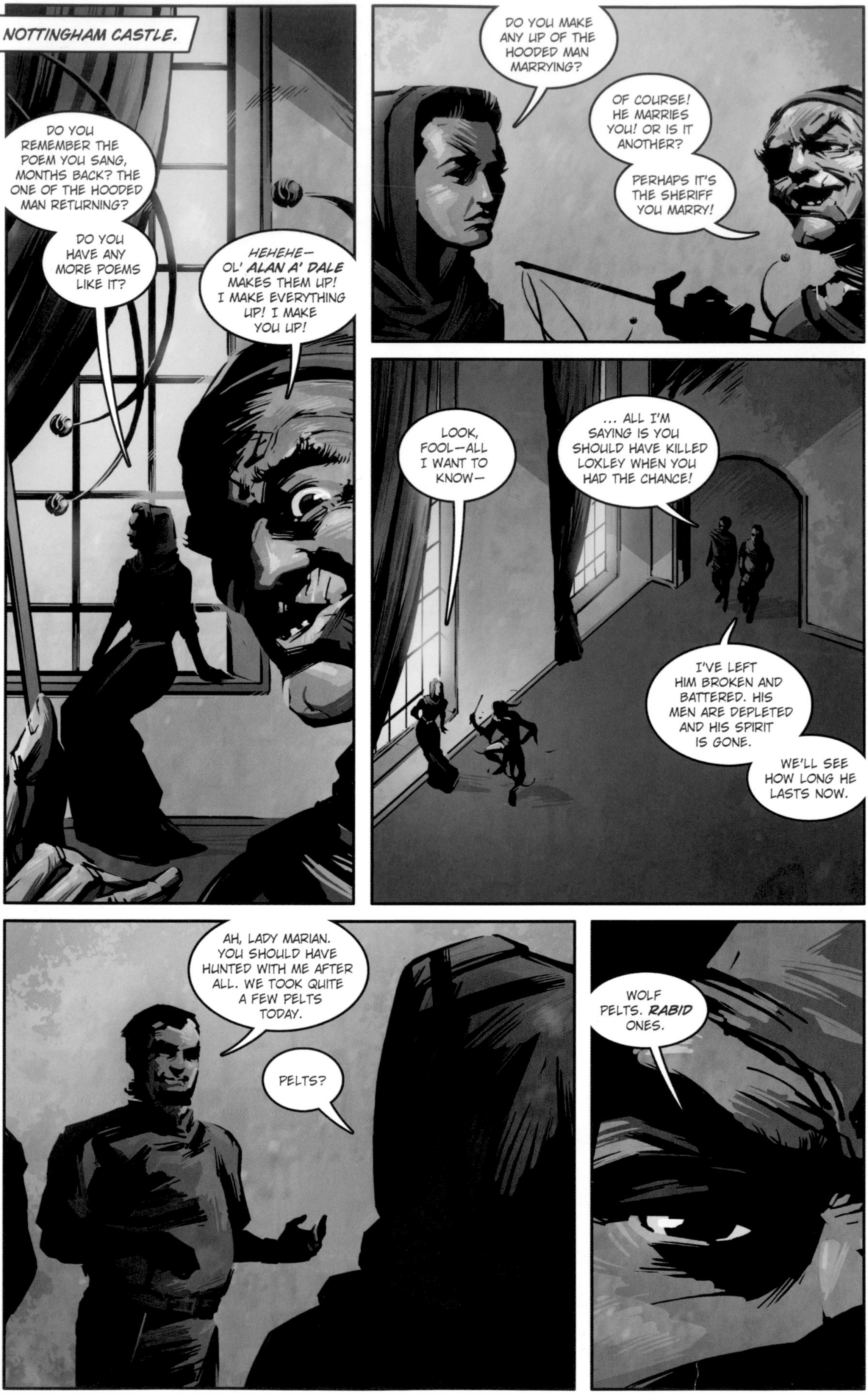
NOTTINGHAM CASTLE.
DO YOU REMEMBER THE POEM YOU SANG, MONTHS BACK? THE ONE OF THE HOODED MAN RETURNING?
DO YOU HAVE ANY MORE POEMS LIKE IT?
HEHEHE— OL' ALAN A' DALE MAKES THEM UP! I MAKE EVERYTHING UP! I MAKE YOU UP!
DO YOU MAKE ANY UP OF THE HOODED MAN MARRYING?
OF COURSE! HE MARRIES YOU! OR IS IT ANOTHER?
PERHAPS IT'S THE SHERIFF YOU MARRY!
LOOK, FOOL—ALL I WANT TO KNOW—
... ALL I'M SAYING IS YOU SHOULD HAVE KILLED LOXLEY WHEN YOU HAD THE CHANCE!
I'VE LEFT HIM BROKEN AND BATTERED. HIS MEN ARE DEPLETED AND HIS SPIRIT IS GONE.
WE'LL SEE HOW LONG HE LASTS NOW.
AH, LADY MARIAN. YOU SHOULD HAVE HUNTED WITH ME AFTER ALL. WE TOOK QUITE A FEW PELTS TODAY.
PELTS?
WOLF PELTS. RABID ONES.

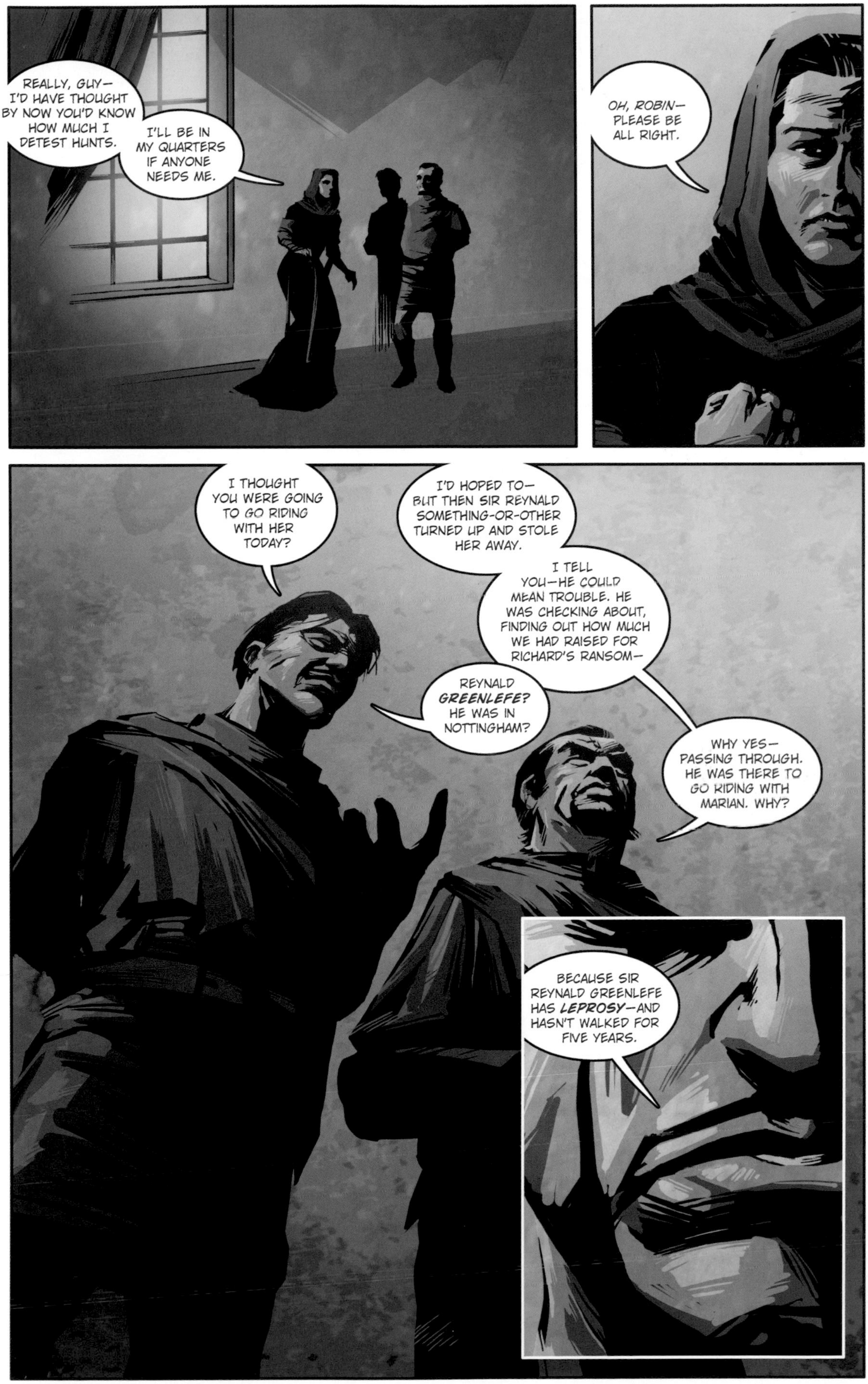
REALLY, GUY—I'D HAVE THOUGHT BY NOW YOU'D KNOW HOW MUCH I DETEST HUNTS.
I'LL BE IN MY QUARTERS IF ANYONE NEEDS ME.
OH, ROBIN—PLEASE BE ALL RIGHT.
I THOUGHT YOU WERE GOING TO GO RIDING WITH HER TODAY?
I'D HOPED TO—BUT THEN SIR REYNALD SOMETHING-OR-OTHER TURNED UP AND STOLE HER AWAY.
I TELL YOU—HE COULD MEAN TROUBLE. HE WAS CHECKING ABOUT, FINDING OUT HOW MUCH WE HAD RAISED FOR RICHARD'S RANSOM—
REYNALD GREENLEFE? HE WAS IN NOTTINGHAM?
WHY YES—PASSING THROUGH. HE WAS THERE TO GO RIDING WITH MARIAN. WHY?
BECAUSE SIR REYNALD GREENLEFE HAS LEPROSY—AND HASN'T WALKED FOR FIVE YEARS.

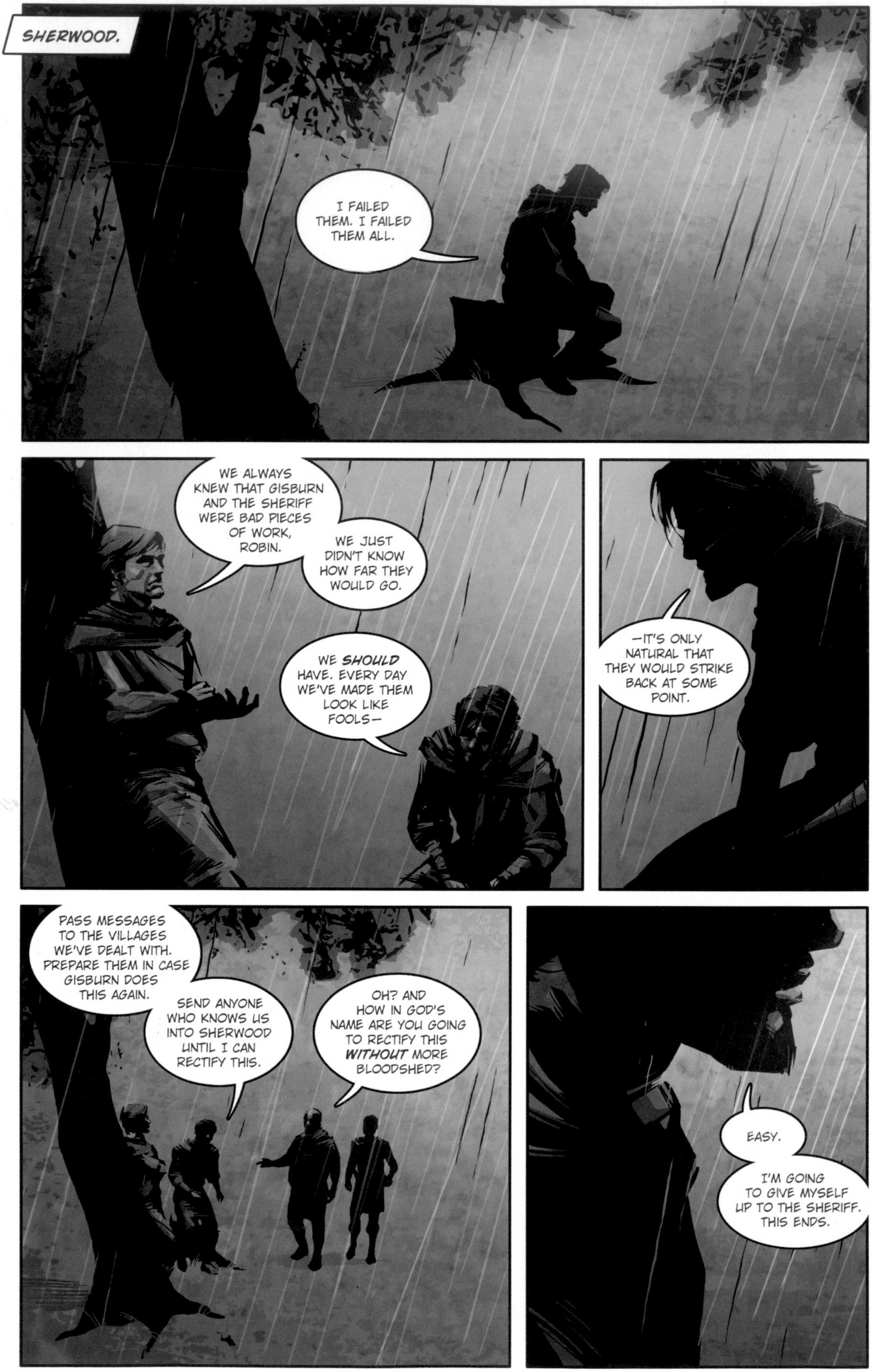
SHERWOOD.
I FAILED THEM. I FAILED THEM ALL.
WE ALWAYS KNEW THAT GISBURN AND THE SHERIFF WERE BAD PIECES OF WORK, ROBIN.
WE JUST DIDN'T KNOW HOW FAR THEY WOULD GO.
WE SHOULD HAVE. EVERY DAY WE'VE MADE THEM LOOK LIKE FOOLS—
—IT'S ONLY NATURAL THAT THEY WOULD STRIKE BACK AT SOME POINT.
PASS MESSAGES TO THE VILLAGES WE'VE DEALT WITH. PREPARE THEM IN CASE GISBURN DOES THIS AGAIN.
SEND ANYONE WHO KNOWS US INTO SHERWOOD UNTIL I CAN RECTIFY THIS.
OH? AND HOW IN GOD'S NAME ARE YOU GOING TO RECTIFY THIS WITHOUT MORE BLOODSHED?
EASY.
I'M GOING TO GIVE MYSELF UP TO THE SHERIFF. THIS ENDS.

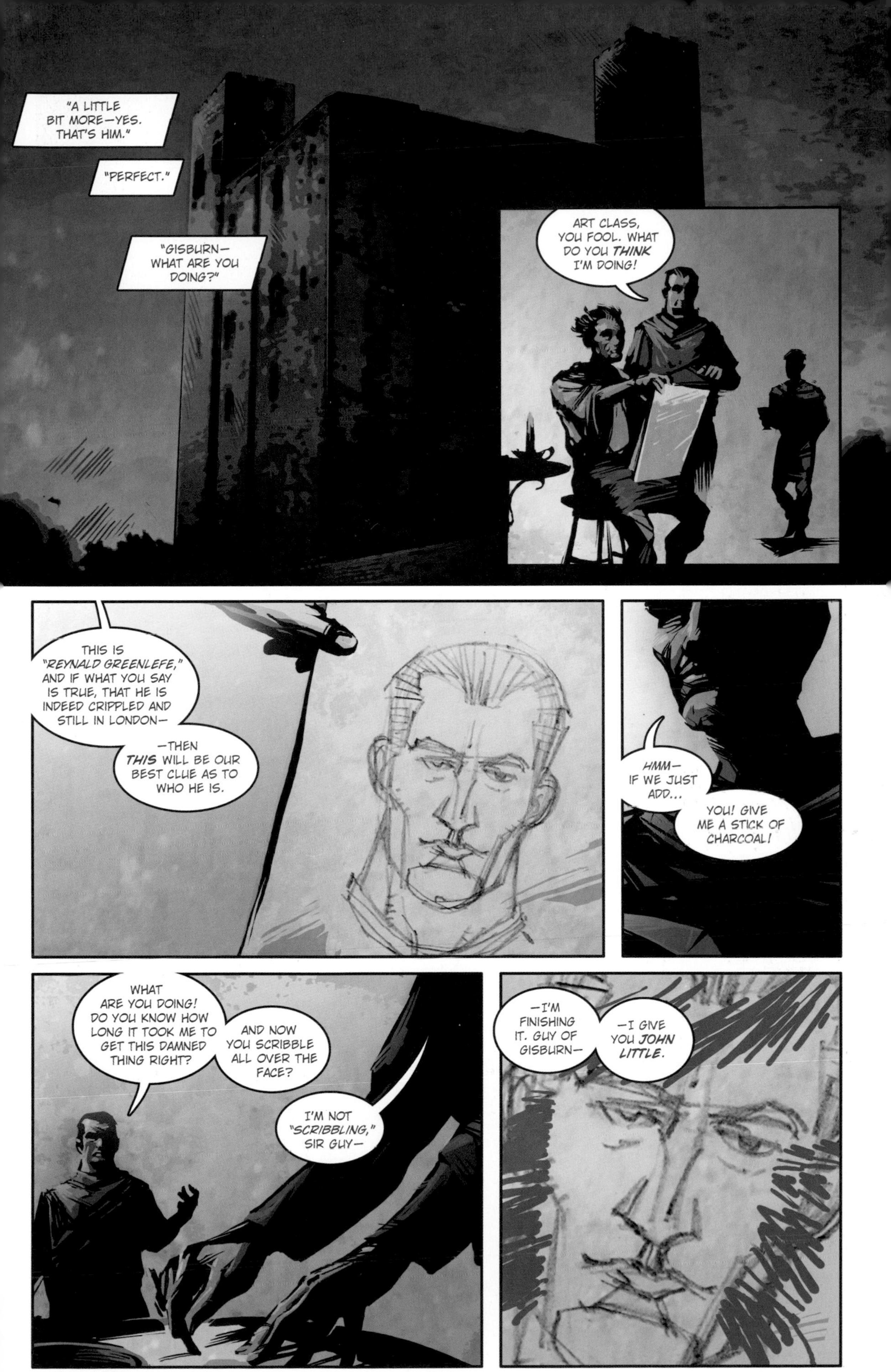
"A LITTLE BIT MORE—YES. THAT'S HIM."
"PERFECT."
"GISBURN—WHAT ARE YOU DOING?"
ART CLASS, YOU FOOL. WHAT DO YOU *THINK* I'M DOING!
THIS IS "*REYNALD GREENLEFE,*" AND IF WHAT YOU SAY IS TRUE, THAT HE IS INDEED CRIPPLED AND STILL IN LONDON—
—THEN *THIS* WILL BE OUR BEST CLUE AS TO WHO HE IS.
HMM—IF WE JUST ADD...
YOU! GIVE ME A STICK OF CHARCOAL!
WHAT ARE YOU DOING! DO YOU KNOW HOW LONG IT TOOK ME TO GET THIS DAMNED THING RIGHT?
AND NOW YOU SCRIBBLE ALL OVER THE FACE?
I'M NOT "*SCRIBBLING,*" SIR GUY—
—I'M FINISHING IT. GUY OF GISBURN—
—I GIVE YOU *JOHN LITTLE*.

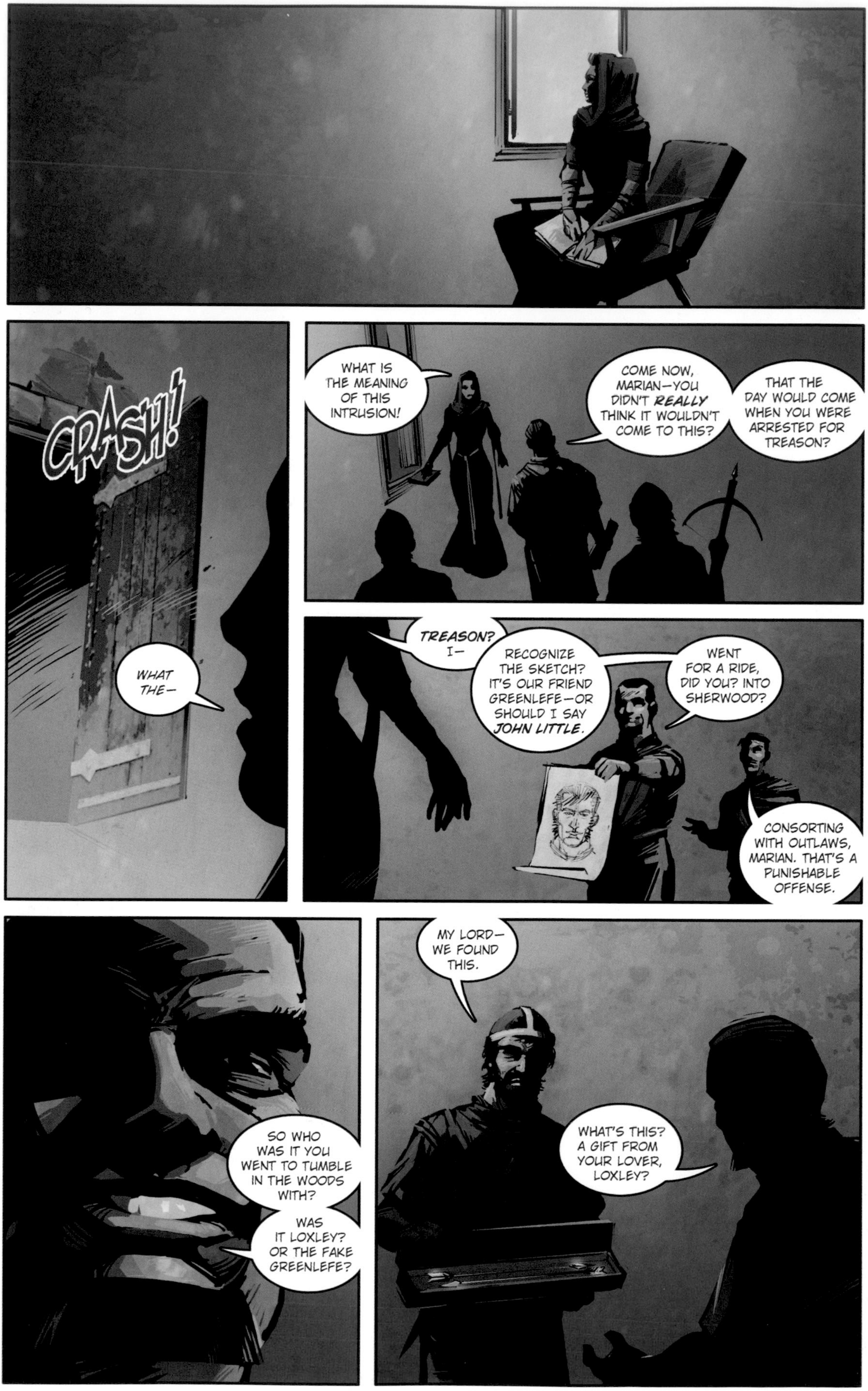
CRASH!
WHAT THE—
WHAT IS THE MEANING OF THIS INTRUSION!
COME NOW, MARIAN—YOU DIDN'T *REALLY* THINK IT WOULDN'T COME TO THIS?
THAT THE DAY WOULD COME WHEN YOU WERE ARRESTED FOR TREASON?
TREASON? I—
RECOGNIZE THE SKETCH? IT'S OUR FRIEND GREENLEFE—OR SHOULD I SAY ***JOHN LITTLE***.
WENT FOR A RIDE, DID YOU? INTO SHERWOOD?
CONSORTING WITH OUTLAWS, MARIAN. THAT'S A PUNISHABLE OFFENSE.
SO WHO WAS IT YOU WENT TO TUMBLE IN THE WOODS WITH?
WAS IT LOXLEY? OR THE FAKE GREENLEFE?
MY LORD— WE FOUND THIS.
WHAT'S THIS? A GIFT FROM YOUR LOVER, LOXLEY?

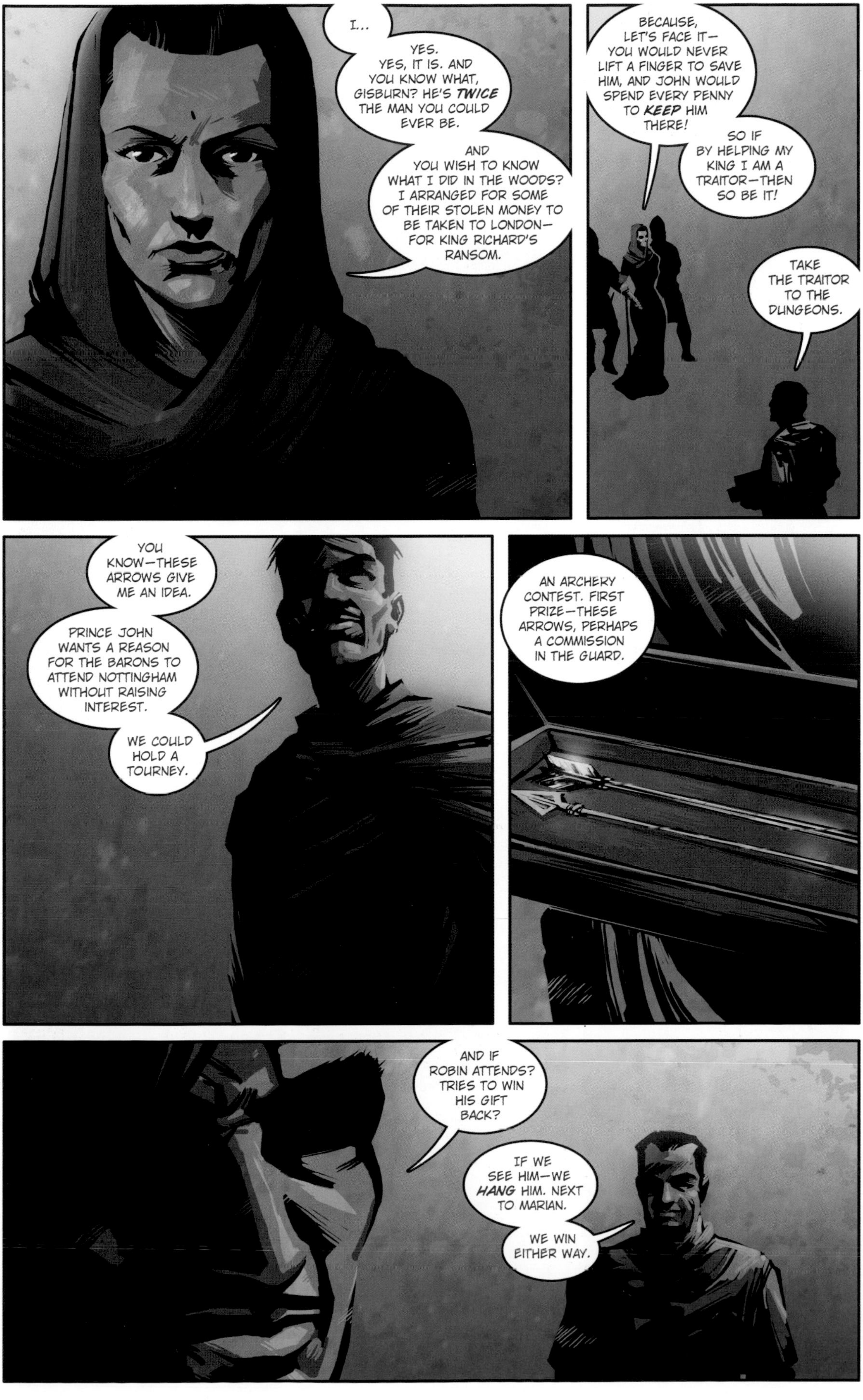
I...
YES. YES, IT IS. AND YOU KNOW WHAT, GISBURN? HE'S TWICE THE MAN YOU COULD EVER BE.
AND YOU WISH TO KNOW WHAT I DID IN THE WOODS? I ARRANGED FOR SOME OF THEIR STOLEN MONEY TO BE TAKEN TO LONDON—FOR KING RICHARD'S RANSOM.
BECAUSE, LET'S FACE IT—YOU WOULD NEVER LIFT A FINGER TO SAVE HIM, AND JOHN WOULD SPEND EVERY PENNY TO KEEP HIM THERE!
SO IF BY HELPING MY KING I AM A TRAITOR—THEN SO BE IT!
TAKE THE TRAITOR TO THE DUNGEONS.
YOU KNOW—THESE ARROWS GIVE ME AN IDEA.
PRINCE JOHN WANTS A REASON FOR THE BARONS TO ATTEND NOTTINGHAM WITHOUT RAISING INTEREST.
WE COULD HOLD A TOURNEY.
AN ARCHERY CONTEST. FIRST PRIZE—THESE ARROWS, PERHAPS A COMMISSION IN THE GUARD.
AND IF ROBIN ATTENDS? TRIES TO WIN HIS GIFT BACK?
IF WE SEE HIM—WE HANG HIM. NEXT TO MARIAN.
WE WIN EITHER WAY.

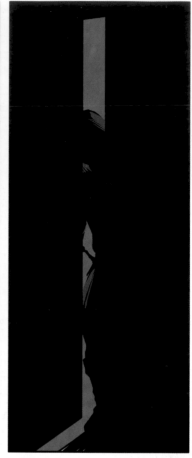

—HMMMF!—

GOOD EVENING, SHERIFF.

I THINK WE NEED TO TALK.

HOW DARE YOU—I COULD CALL THE GUARDS—

AND BY THE TIME THEY GOT HERE, YOUR THROAT WOULD BE CUT AND YOU WOULD BE DEAD.

SO SHUT UP AND LISTEN.

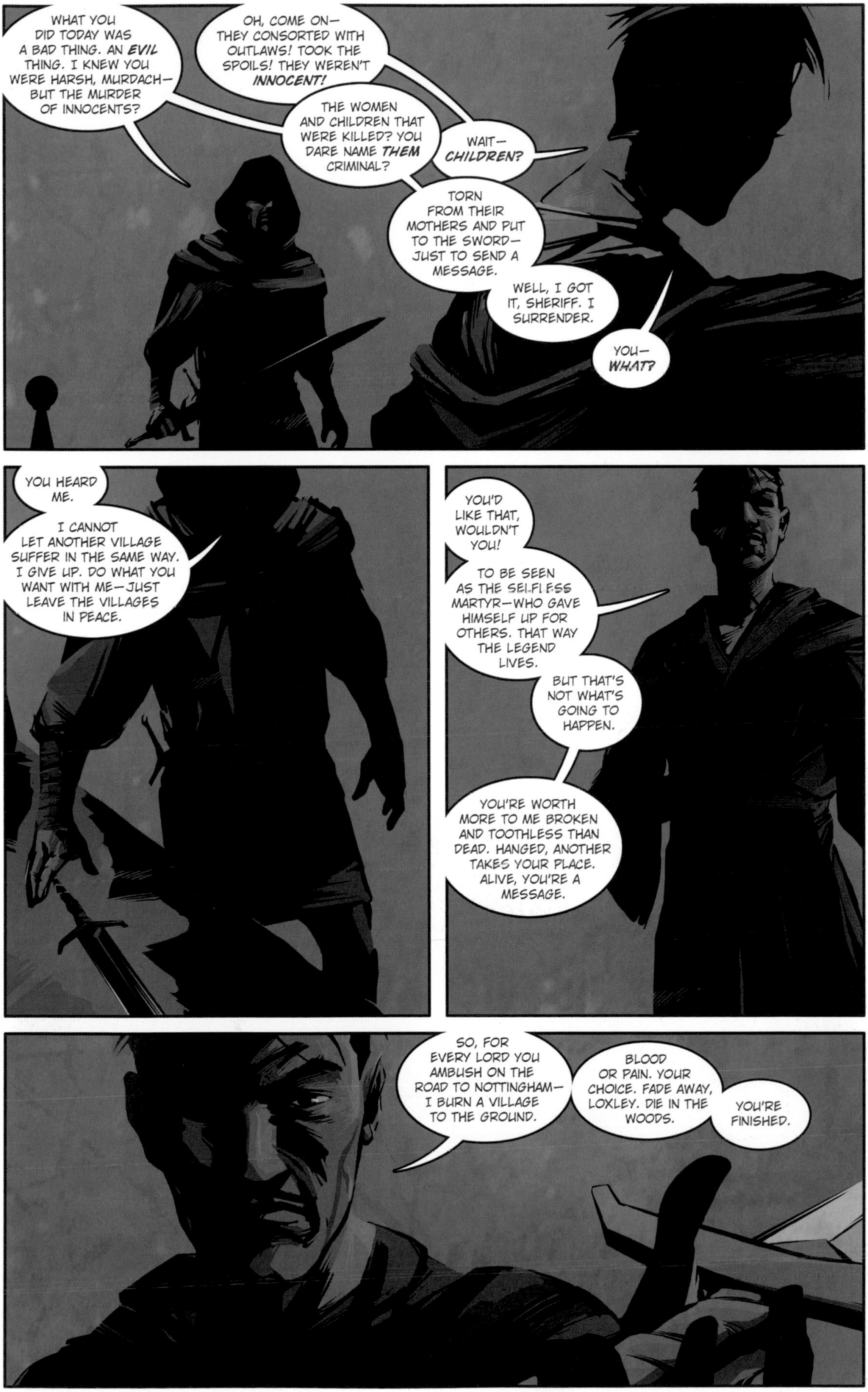
WHAT YOU DID TODAY WAS A BAD THING. AN EVIL THING. I KNEW YOU WERE HARSH, MURDACH— BUT THE MURDER OF INNOCENTS?
OH, COME ON— THEY CONSORTED WITH OUTLAWS! TOOK THE SPOILS! THEY WEREN'T INNOCENT!
THE WOMEN AND CHILDREN THAT WERE KILLED? YOU DARE NAME THEM CRIMINAL?
WAIT— CHILDREN?
TORN FROM THEIR MOTHERS AND PUT TO THE SWORD— JUST TO SEND A MESSAGE.
WELL, I GOT IT, SHERIFF. I SURRENDER.
YOU— WHAT?
YOU HEARD ME.
I CANNOT LET ANOTHER VILLAGE SUFFER IN THE SAME WAY. I GIVE UP. DO WHAT YOU WANT WITH ME—JUST LEAVE THE VILLAGES IN PEACE.
YOU'D LIKE THAT, WOULDN'T YOU!
TO BE SEEN AS THE SELFLESS MARTYR—WHO GAVE HIMSELF UP FOR OTHERS. THAT WAY THE LEGEND LIVES.
BUT THAT'S NOT WHAT'S GOING TO HAPPEN.
YOU'RE WORTH MORE TO ME BROKEN AND TOOTHLESS THAN DEAD. HANGED, ANOTHER TAKES YOUR PLACE. ALIVE, YOU'RE A MESSAGE.
SO, FOR EVERY LORD YOU AMBUSH ON THE ROAD TO NOTTINGHAM— I BURN A VILLAGE TO THE GROUND.
BLOOD OR PAIN. YOUR CHOICE. FADE AWAY, LOXLEY. DIE IN THE WOODS.
YOU'RE FINISHED.

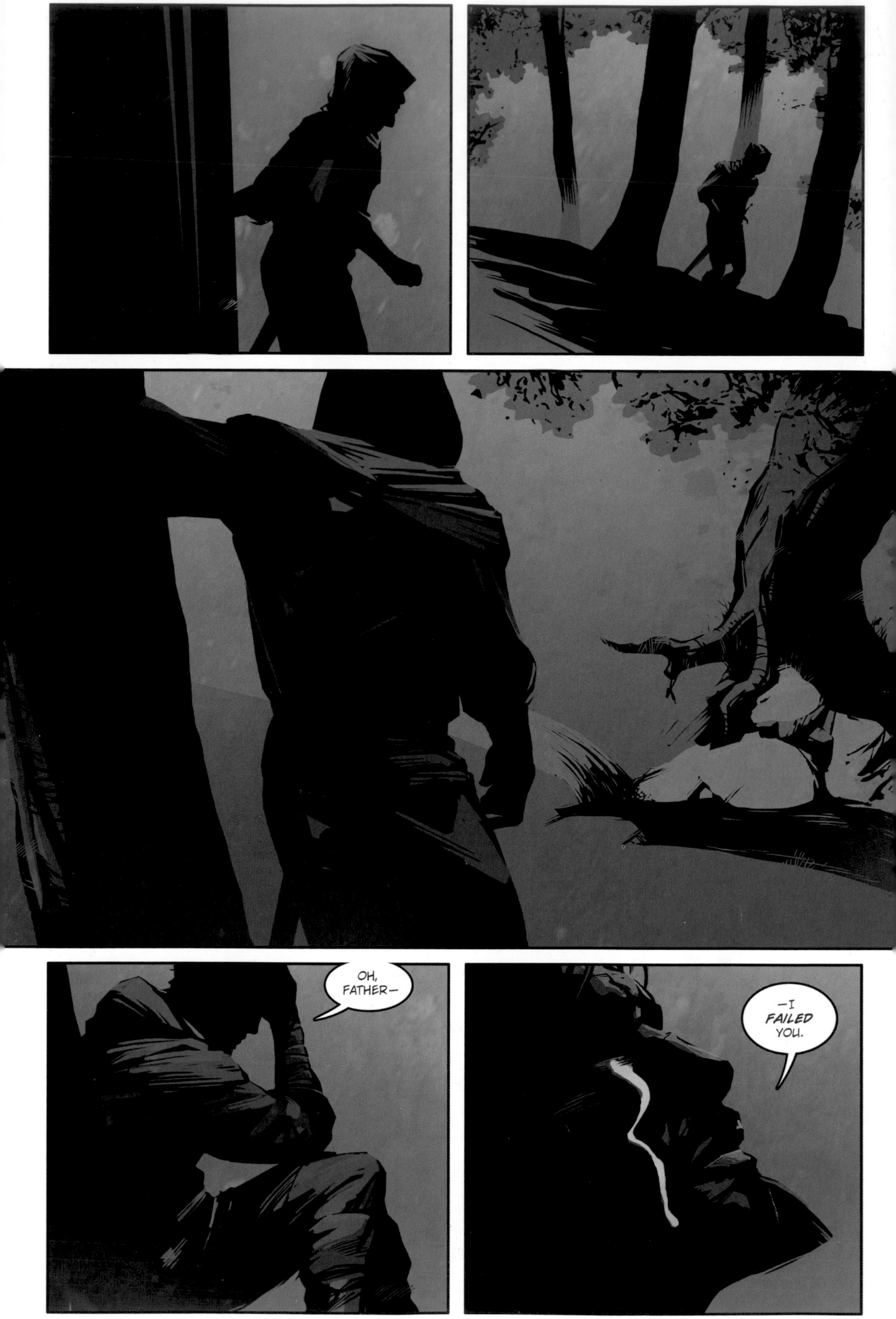
OH, FATHER—
—I *FAILED* YOU.

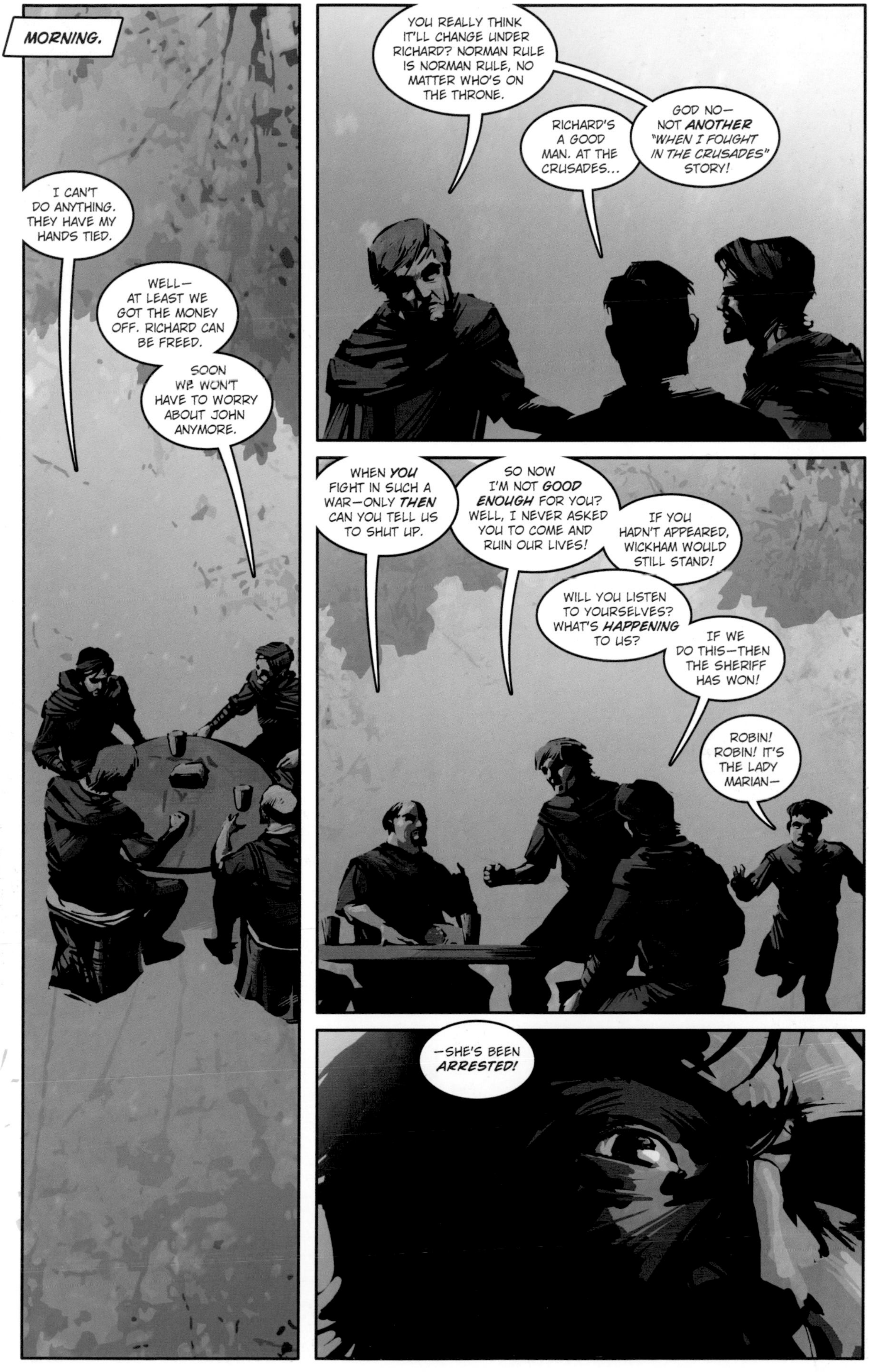
MORNING.
I CAN'T DO ANYTHING. THEY HAVE MY HANDS TIED.
WELL— AT LEAST WE GOT THE MONEY OFF. RICHARD CAN BE FREED.
SOON WE WON'T HAVE TO WORRY ABOUT JOHN ANYMORE.
YOU REALLY THINK IT'LL CHANGE UNDER RICHARD? NORMAN RULE IS NORMAN RULE, NO MATTER WHO'S ON THE THRONE.
RICHARD'S A GOOD MAN. AT THE CRUSADES...
GOD NO— NOT ANOTHER "WHEN I FOUGHT IN THE CRUSADES" STORY!
WHEN YOU FIGHT IN SUCH A WAR—ONLY THEN CAN YOU TELL US TO SHUT UP.
SO NOW I'M NOT GOOD ENOUGH FOR YOU? WELL, I NEVER ASKED YOU TO COME AND RUIN OUR LIVES!
IF YOU HADN'T APPEARED, WICKHAM WOULD STILL STAND!
WILL YOU LISTEN TO YOURSELVES? WHAT'S HAPPENING TO US?
IF WE DO THIS—THEN THE SHERIFF HAS WON!
ROBIN! ROBIN! IT'S THE LADY MARIAN—
—SHE'S BEEN ARRESTED!

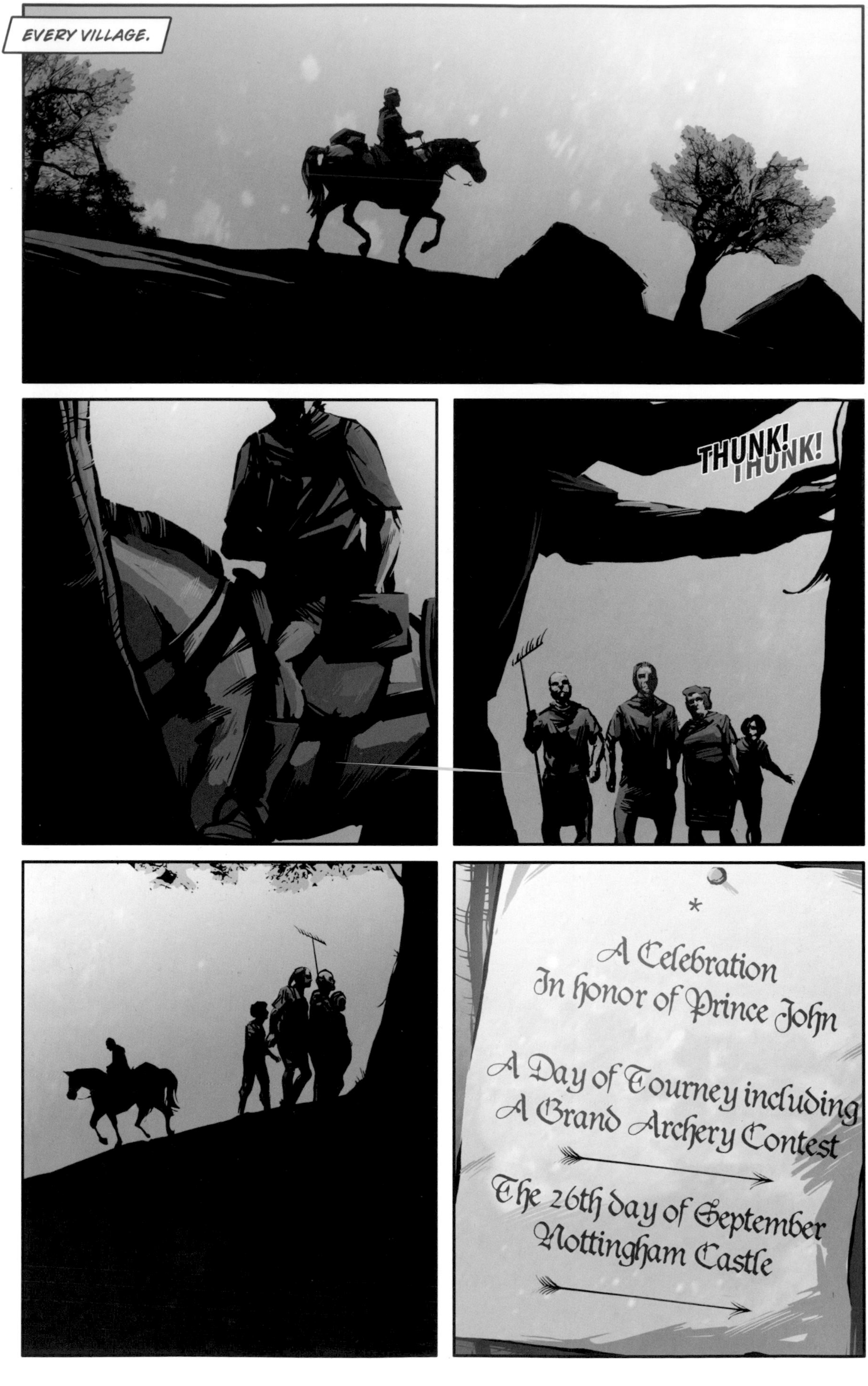
EVERY VILLAGE.
THUNK! THUNK!
A Celebration
In honor of Prince John
A Day of Tourney including
A Grand Archery Contest
The 26th day of September
Nottingham Castle

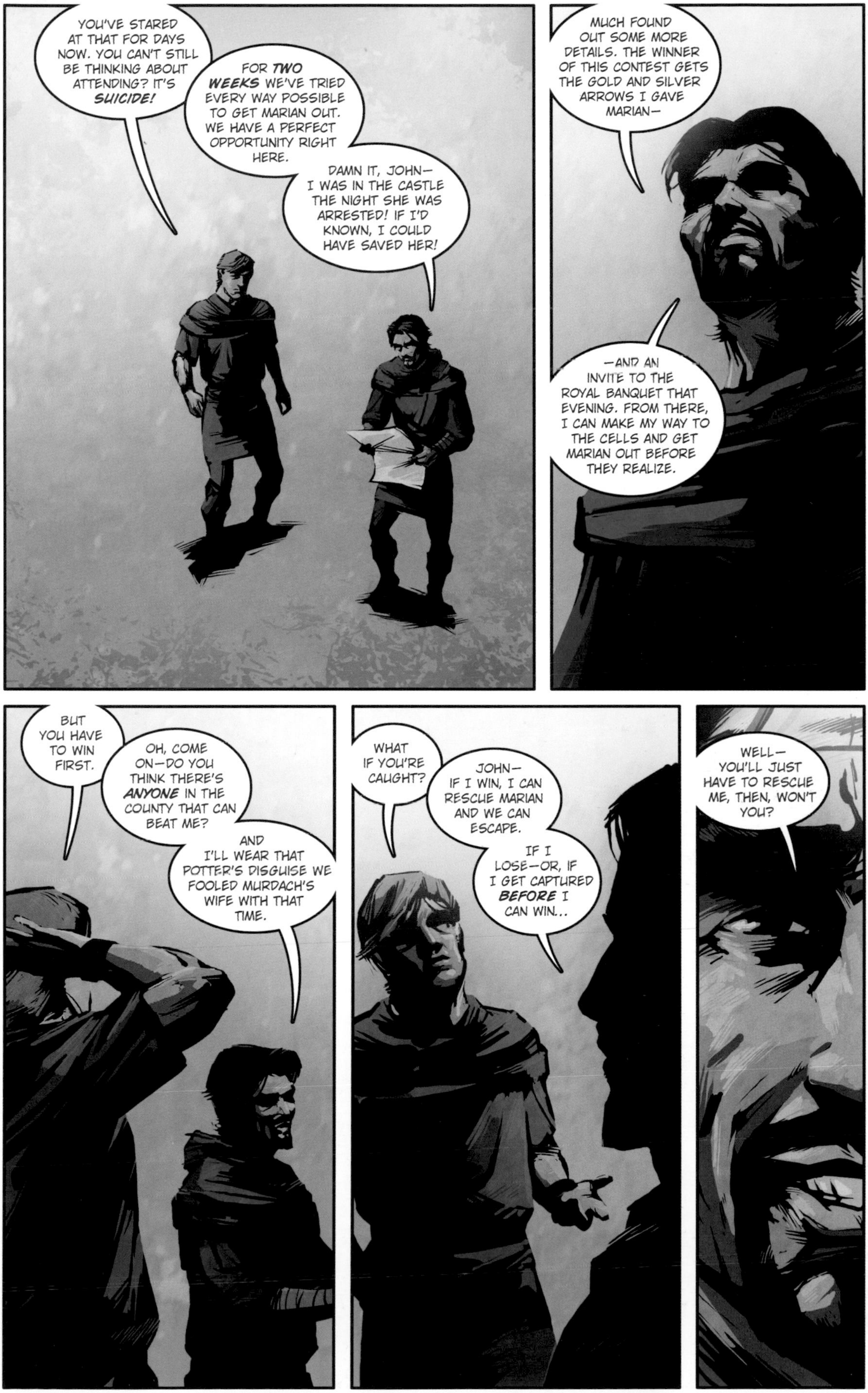
YOU'VE STARED AT THAT FOR DAYS NOW. YOU CAN'T STILL BE THINKING ABOUT ATTENDING? IT'S SUICIDE!
FOR TWO WEEKS WE'VE TRIED EVERY WAY POSSIBLE TO GET MARIAN OUT. WE HAVE A PERFECT OPPORTUNITY RIGHT HERE.
DAMN IT, JOHN— I WAS IN THE CASTLE THE NIGHT SHE WAS ARRESTED! IF I'D KNOWN, I COULD HAVE SAVED HER!
MUCH FOUND OUT SOME MORE DETAILS. THE WINNER OF THIS CONTEST GETS THE GOLD AND SILVER ARROWS I GAVE MARIAN—
—AND AN INVITE TO THE ROYAL BANQUET THAT EVENING. FROM THERE, I CAN MAKE MY WAY TO THE CELLS AND GET MARIAN OUT BEFORE THEY REALIZE.
BUT YOU HAVE TO WIN FIRST.
OH, COME ON—DO YOU THINK THERE'S ANYONE IN THE COUNTY THAT CAN BEAT ME?
AND I'LL WEAR THAT POTTER'S DISGUISE WE FOOLED MURDACH'S WIFE WITH THAT TIME.
WHAT IF YOU'RE CAUGHT?
JOHN— IF I WIN, I CAN RESCUE MARIAN AND WE CAN ESCAPE.
IF I LOSE—OR, IF I GET CAPTURED BEFORE I CAN WIN...
WELL— YOU'LL JUST HAVE TO RESCUE ME, THEN, WON'T YOU?

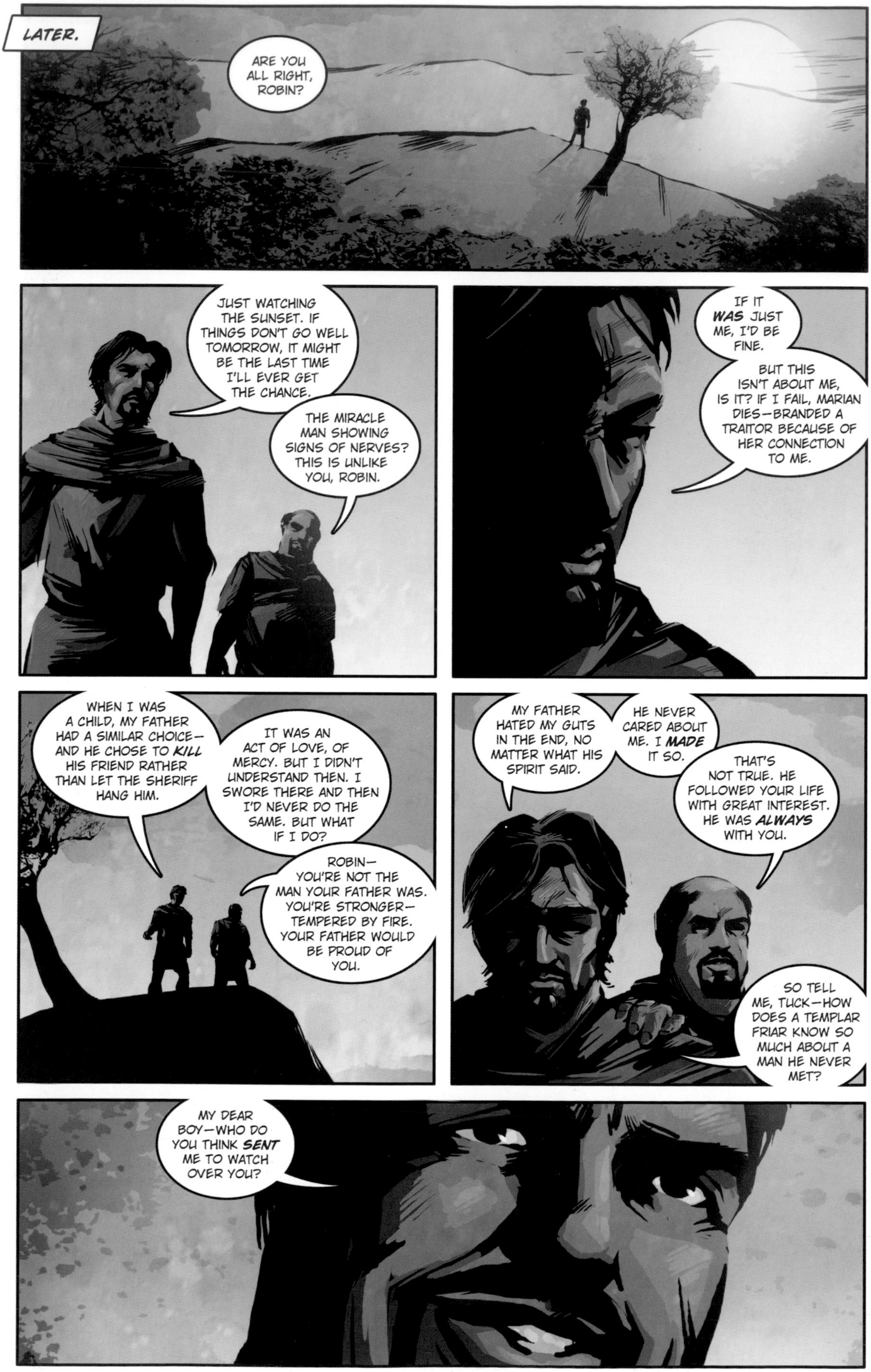
LATER.
ARE YOU ALL RIGHT, ROBIN?
JUST WATCHING THE SUNSET. IF THINGS DON'T GO WELL TOMORROW, IT MIGHT BE THE LAST TIME I'LL EVER GET THE CHANCE.
THE MIRACLE MAN SHOWING SIGNS OF NERVES? THIS IS UNLIKE YOU, ROBIN.
IF IT *WAS* JUST ME, I'D BE FINE.
BUT THIS ISN'T ABOUT ME, IS IT? IF I FAIL, MARIAN DIES—BRANDED A TRAITOR BECAUSE OF HER CONNECTION TO ME.
WHEN I WAS A CHILD, MY FATHER HAD A SIMILAR CHOICE—AND HE CHOSE TO *KILL* HIS FRIEND RATHER THAN LET THE SHERIFF HANG HIM.
IT WAS AN ACT OF LOVE, OF MERCY. BUT I DIDN'T UNDERSTAND THEN. I SWORE THERE AND THEN I'D NEVER DO THE SAME. BUT WHAT IF I DO?
ROBIN—YOU'RE NOT THE MAN YOUR FATHER WAS. YOU'RE STRONGER—TEMPERED BY FIRE. YOUR FATHER WOULD BE PROUD OF YOU.
MY FATHER HATED MY GUTS IN THE END, NO MATTER WHAT HIS SPIRIT SAID.
HE NEVER CARED ABOUT ME. I *MADE* IT SO.
THAT'S NOT TRUE. HE FOLLOWED YOUR LIFE WITH GREAT INTEREST. HE WAS *ALWAYS* WITH YOU.
SO TELL ME, TUCK—HOW DOES A TEMPLAR FRIAR KNOW SO MUCH ABOUT A MAN HE NEVER MET?
MY DEAR BOY—WHO DO YOU THINK *SENT* ME TO WATCH OVER YOU?

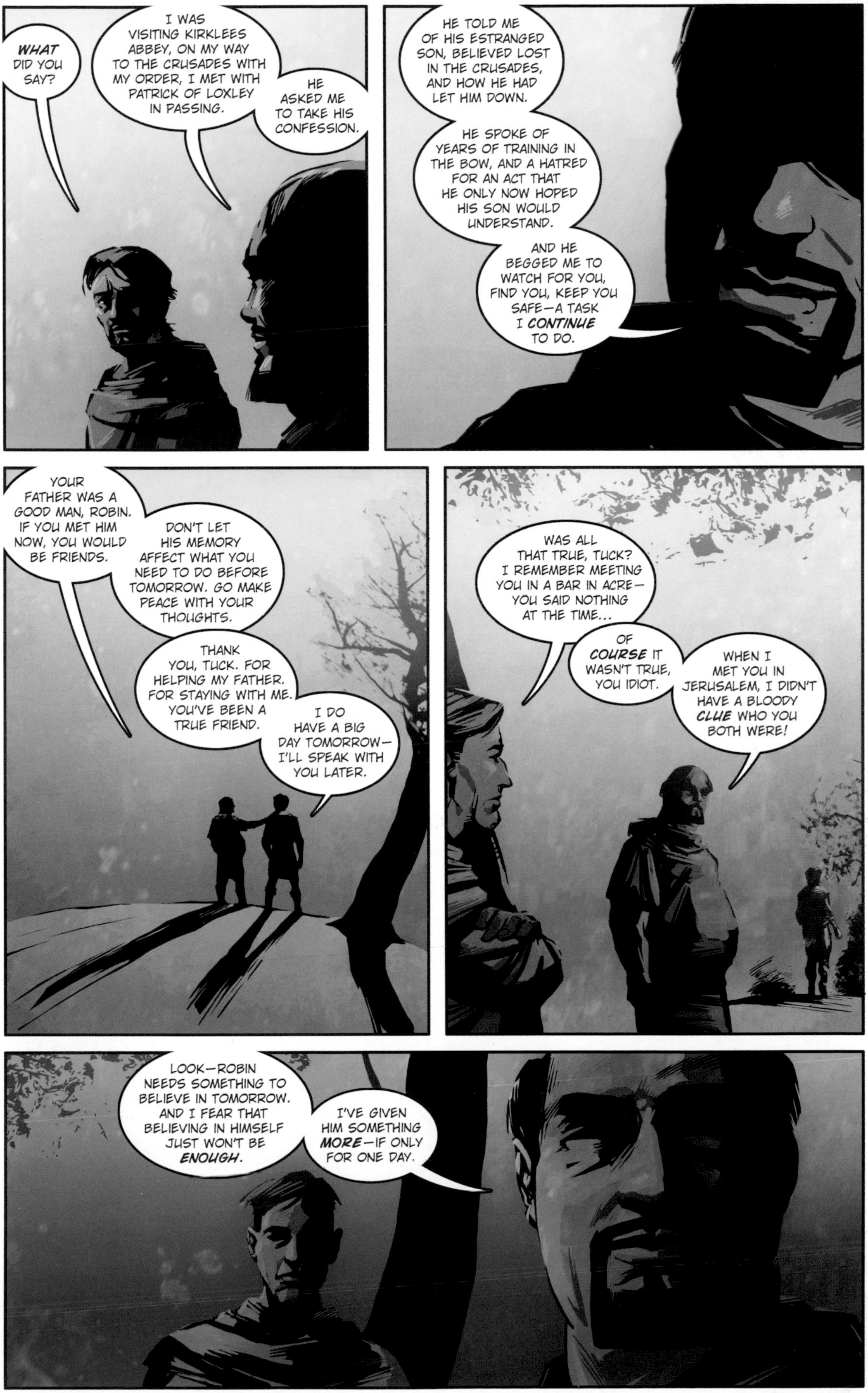
WHAT DID YOU SAY?
I WAS VISITING KIRKLEES ABBEY, ON MY WAY TO THE CRUSADES WITH MY ORDER, I MET WITH PATRICK OF LOXLEY IN PASSING.
HE ASKED ME TO TAKE HIS CONFESSION.
HE TOLD ME OF HIS ESTRANGED SON, BELIEVED LOST IN THE CRUSADES, AND HOW HE HAD LET HIM DOWN.
HE SPOKE OF YEARS OF TRAINING IN THE BOW, AND A HATRED FOR AN ACT THAT HE ONLY NOW HOPED HIS SON WOULD UNDERSTAND.
AND HE BEGGED ME TO WATCH FOR YOU, FIND YOU, KEEP YOU SAFE—A TASK I CONTINUE TO DO.
YOUR FATHER WAS A GOOD MAN, ROBIN. IF YOU MET HIM NOW, YOU WOULD BE FRIENDS.
DON'T LET HIS MEMORY AFFECT WHAT YOU NEED TO DO BEFORE TOMORROW. GO MAKE PEACE WITH YOUR THOUGHTS.
THANK YOU, TUCK. FOR HELPING MY FATHER. FOR STAYING WITH ME. YOU'VE BEEN A TRUE FRIEND.
I DO HAVE A BIG DAY TOMORROW—I'LL SPEAK WITH YOU LATER.
WAS ALL THAT TRUE, TUCK? I REMEMBER MEETING YOU IN A BAR IN ACRE—YOU SAID NOTHING AT THE TIME...
OF COURSE IT WASN'T TRUE, YOU IDIOT.
WHEN I MET YOU IN JERUSALEM, I DIDN'T HAVE A BLOODY CLUE WHO YOU BOTH WERE!
LOOK—ROBIN NEEDS SOMETHING TO BELIEVE IN TOMORROW. AND I FEAR THAT BELIEVING IN HIMSELF JUST WON'T BE ENOUGH.
I'VE GIVEN HIM SOMETHING MORE—IF ONLY FOR ONE DAY.

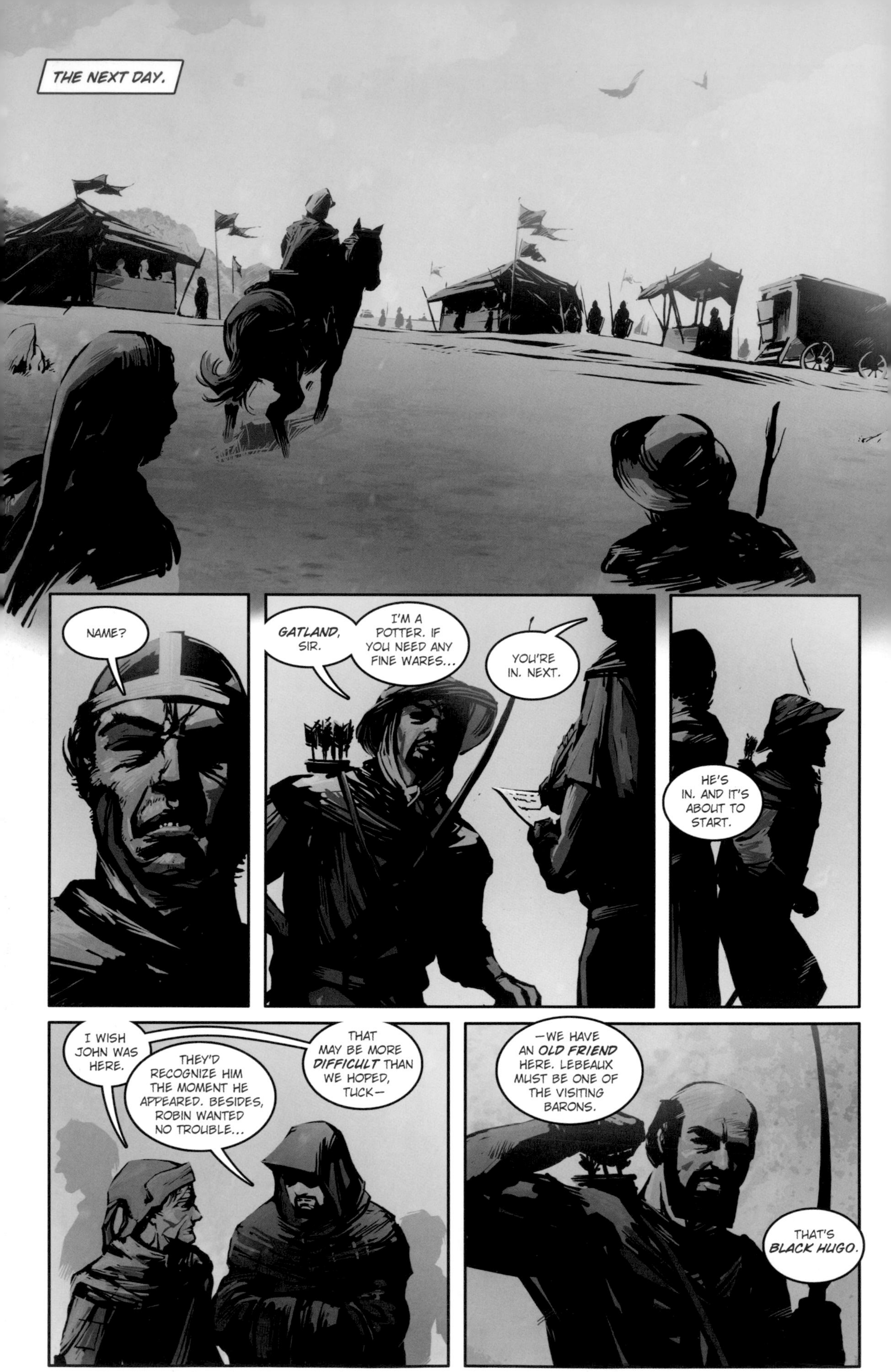
THE NEXT DAY.
NAME?
GATLAND, SIR.
I'M A POTTER. IF YOU NEED ANY FINE WARES...
YOU'RE IN. NEXT.
HE'S IN. AND IT'S ABOUT TO START.
I WISH JOHN WAS HERE.
THEY'D RECOGNIZE HIM THE MOMENT HE APPEARED. BESIDES, ROBIN WANTED NO TROUBLE...
THAT MAY BE MORE DIFFICULT THAN WE HOPED, TUCK—
—WE HAVE AN OLD FRIEND HERE. LEBEAUX MUST BE ONE OF THE VISITING BARONS.
THAT'S BLACK HUGO.

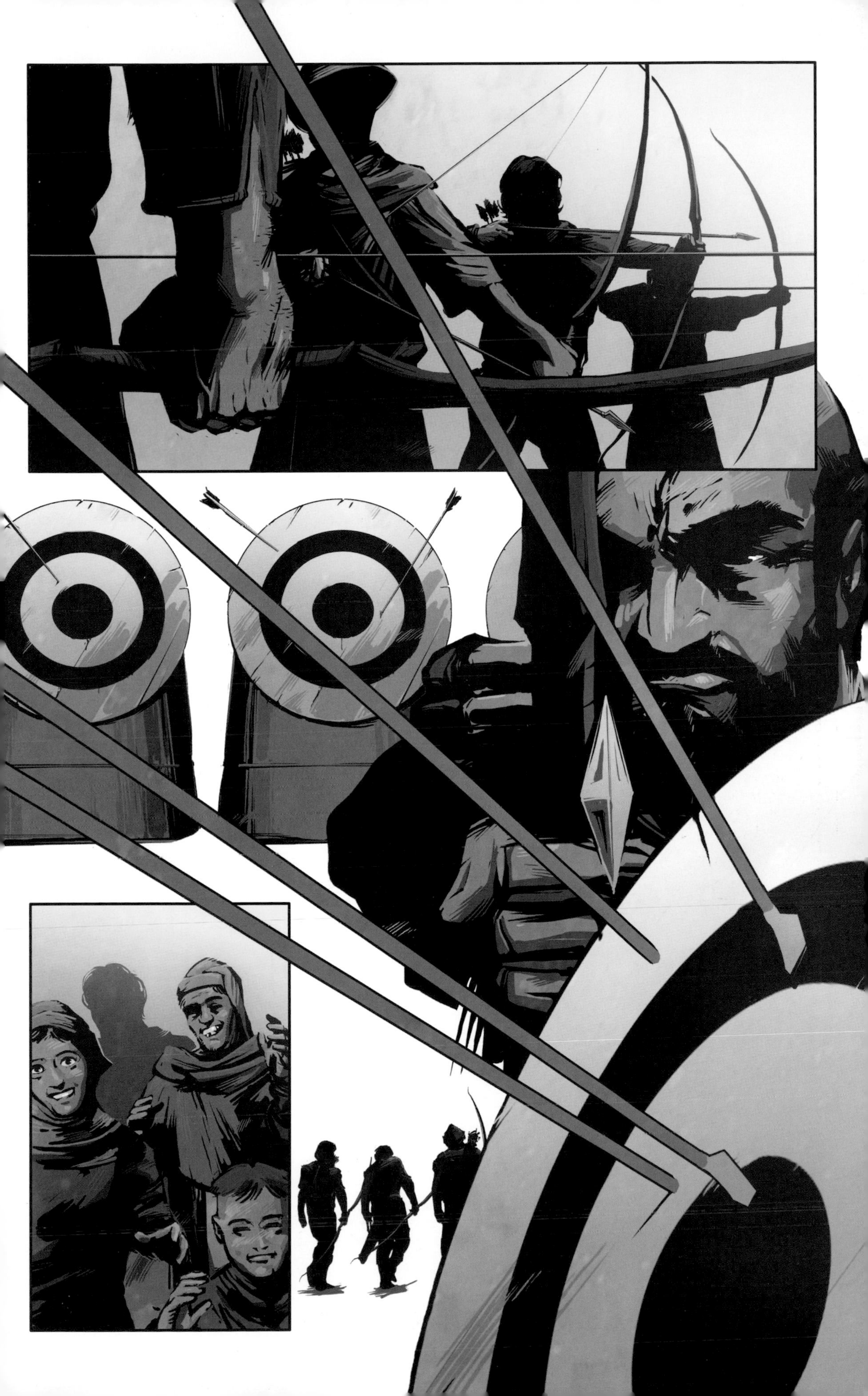

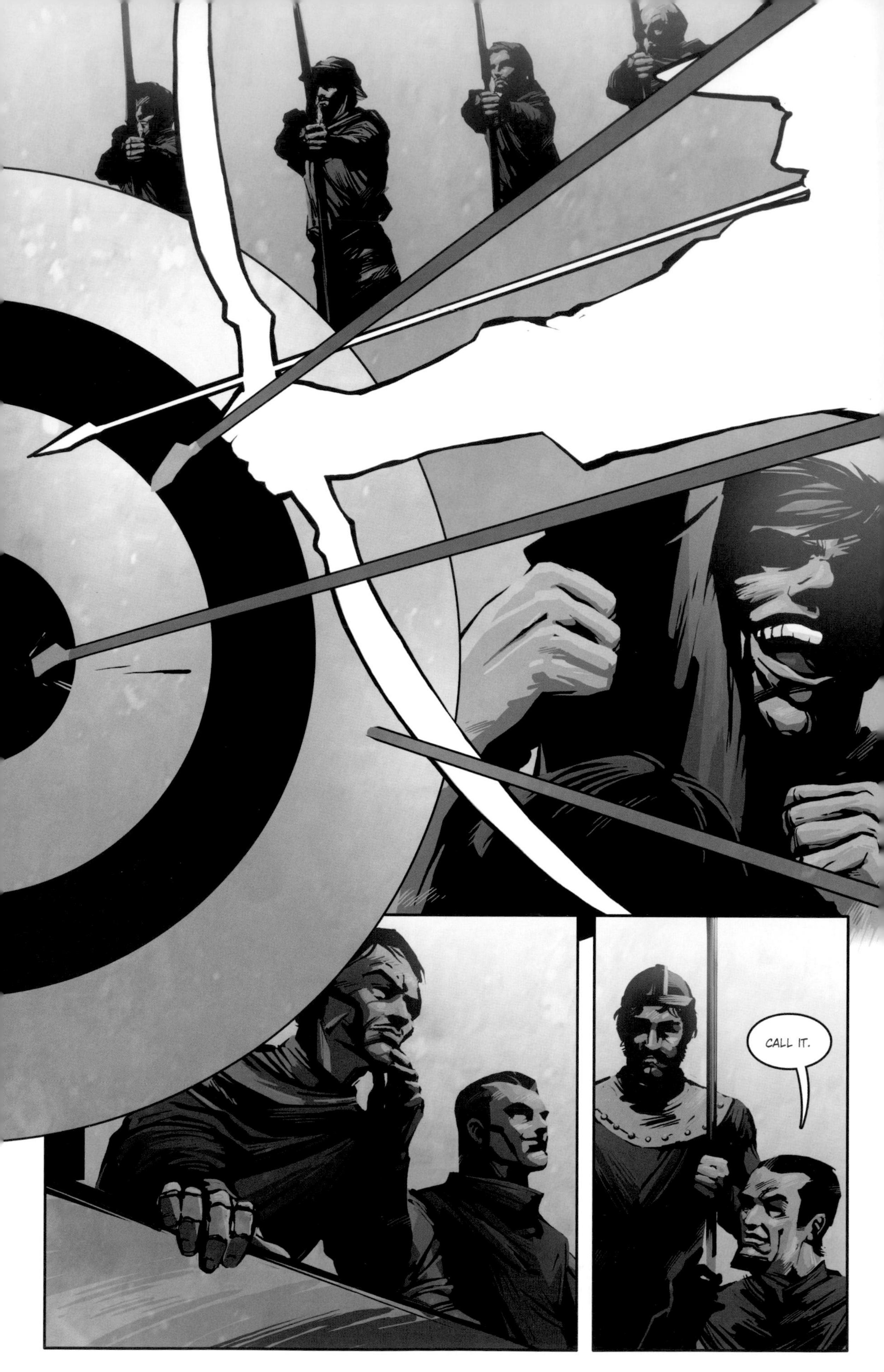
CALL IT.

CONGRATULATIONS, HUGO AND THE OLD POTTER—

—OR SHOULD I SAY *LOXLEY!*

WELL DEDUCED, GISBURN. TELL ME—

—DID YOU WORK IT OUT *ALONE?* OR DID YOU HAVE HELP?

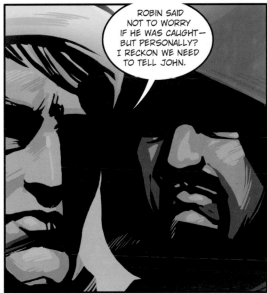

ROBIN SAID NOT TO WORRY IF HE WAS CAUGHT— BUT PERSONALLY? I RECKON WE NEED TO TELL JOHN.

MY LORD GISBURN—I UNDERSTAND THAT YOU WISH THIS MAN DEAD.

BUT CAN WE AT LEAST *FINISH* THIS? I NEED TO PROVE ONCE AND FOR ALL I AM THE BETTER ARCHER.

THE LAST TIME THEY MET—LOXLEY *CHEATED* HUGO, AND HIS FRIEND SPEARED MY SHOULDER.

LET US SEE THE MAN DEFEATED BEFORE CAPTURED.

OF COURSE— WE CAN WAIT. *FINISH THE CONTEST.*

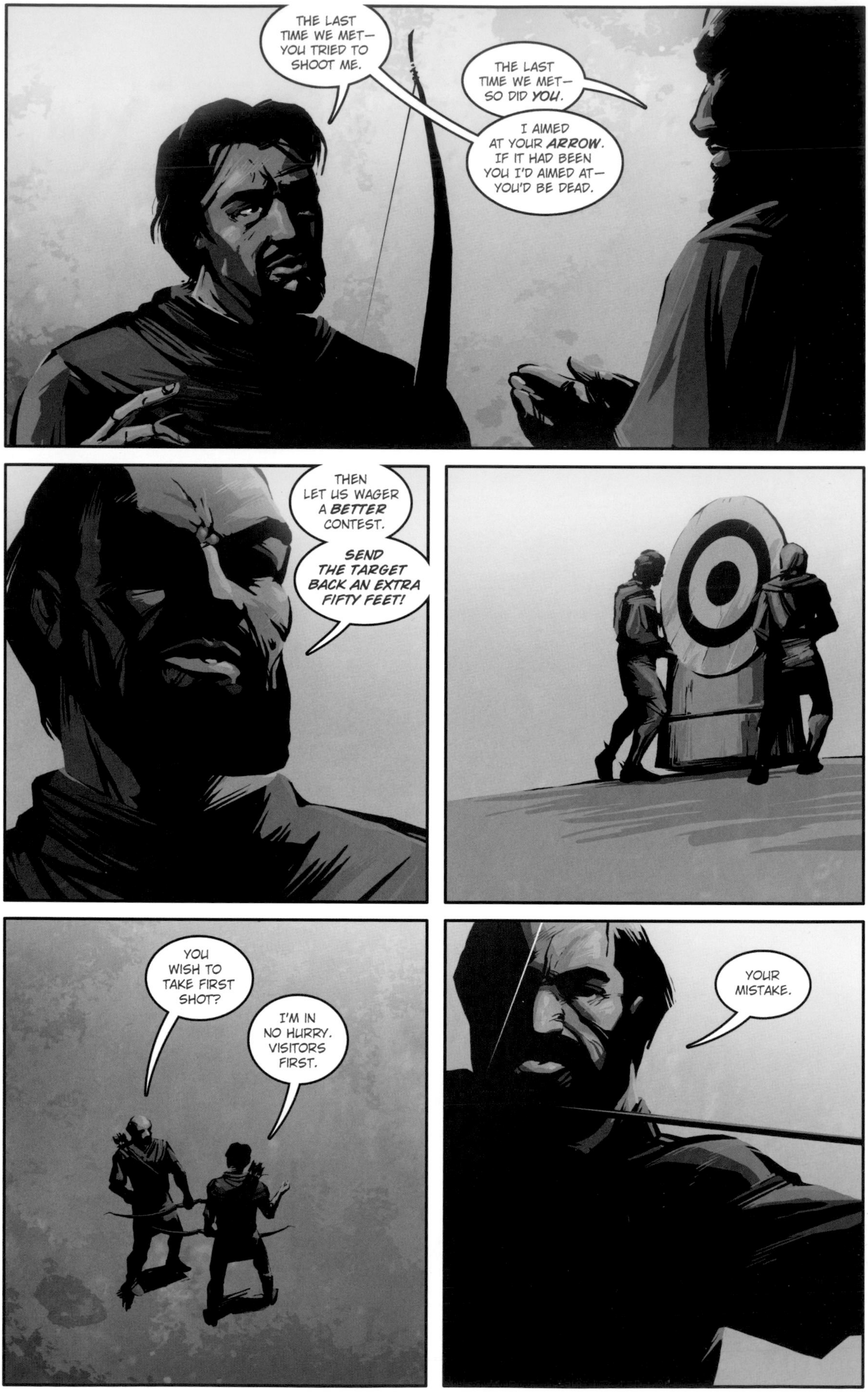
THE LAST TIME WE MET— YOU TRIED TO SHOOT ME.
THE LAST TIME WE MET— SO DID *YOU*.
I AIMED AT YOUR ***ARROW***. IF IT HAD BEEN YOU I'D AIMED AT— YOU'D BE DEAD.
THEN LET US WAGER A ***BETTER*** CONTEST.
SEND THE TARGET BACK AN EXTRA FIFTY FEET!
YOU WISH TO TAKE FIRST SHOT?
I'M IN NO HURRY. VISITORS FIRST.
YOUR MISTAKE.

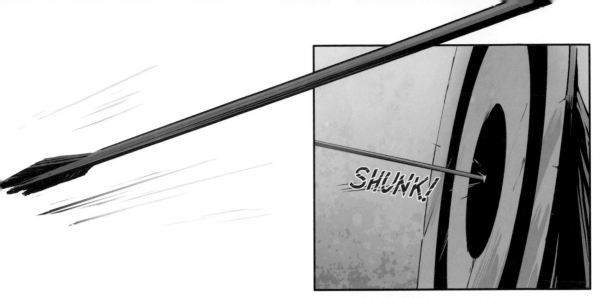

SHUNK!

YESSS!

DEAD CENTER, ENGLISHMAN.

NOBODY IS GOOD ENOUGH TO BETTER A SHOT LIKE THAT.

YOU'RE WRONG, HUGO—

—AS YOU WERE WRONG IN JERUSALEM.

WHEN I BEAT YOU.

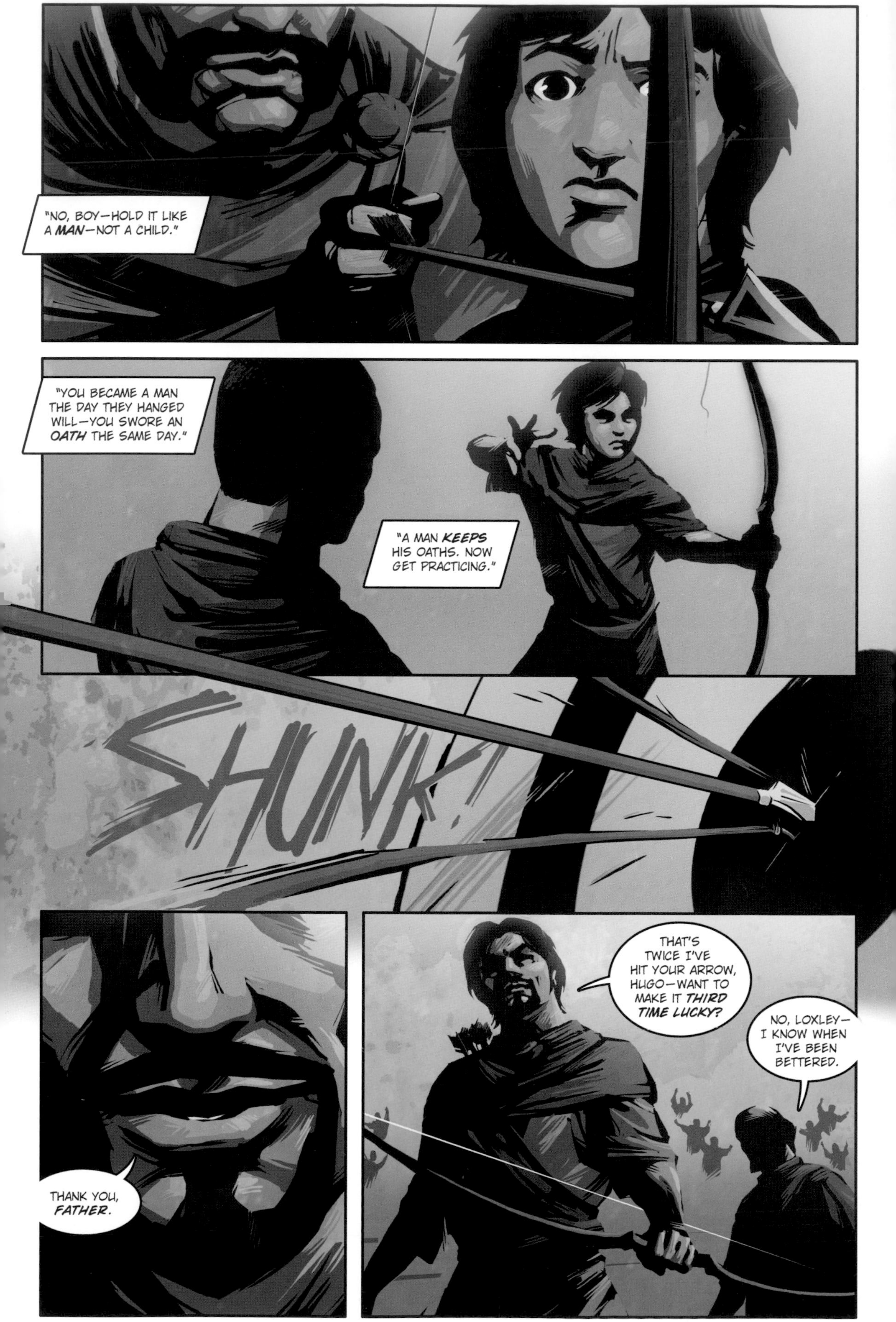
"NO, BOY—HOLD IT LIKE A MAN—NOT A CHILD."
"YOU BECAME A MAN THE DAY THEY HANGED WILL—YOU SWORE AN OATH THE SAME DAY."
"A MAN KEEPS HIS OATHS. NOW GET PRACTICING."
SHUNK!
THANK YOU, FATHER.
THAT'S TWICE I'VE HIT YOUR ARROW, HUGO—WANT TO MAKE IT THIRD TIME LUCKY?
NO, LOXLEY—I KNOW WHEN I'VE BEEN BETTERED.

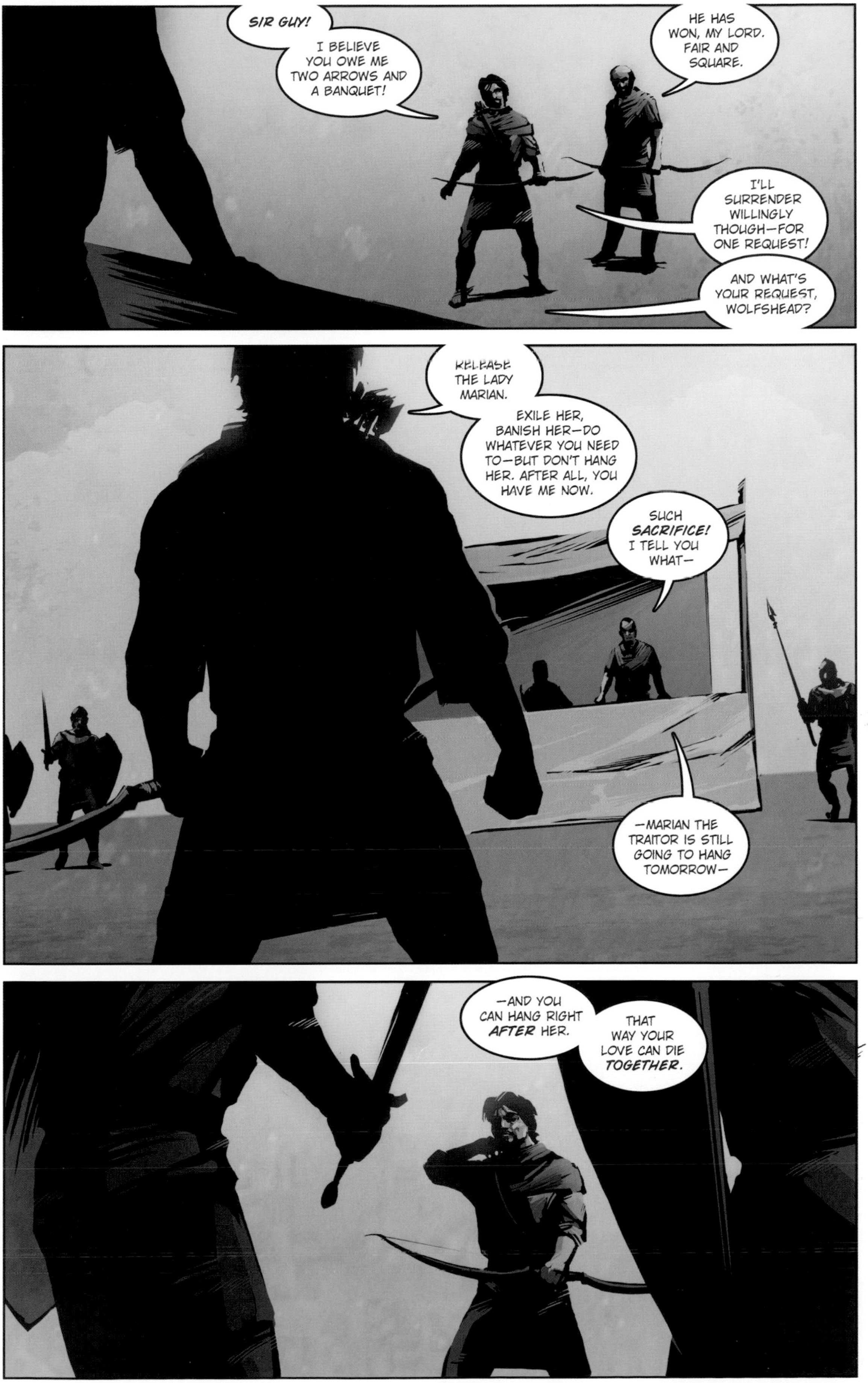
SIR GUY!
I BELIEVE YOU OWE ME TWO ARROWS AND A BANQUET!
HE HAS WON, MY LORD. FAIR AND SQUARE.
I'LL SURRENDER WILLINGLY THOUGH—FOR ONE REQUEST!
AND WHAT'S YOUR REQUEST, WOLFSHEAD?
RELEASE THE LADY MARIAN.
EXILE HER, BANISH HER—DO WHATEVER YOU NEED TO—BUT DON'T HANG HER. AFTER ALL, YOU HAVE ME NOW.
SUCH SACRIFICE! I TELL YOU WHAT—
—MARIAN THE TRAITOR IS STILL GOING TO HANG TOMORROW—
—AND YOU CAN HANG RIGHT AFTER HER.
THAT WAY YOUR LOVE CAN DIE TOGETHER.

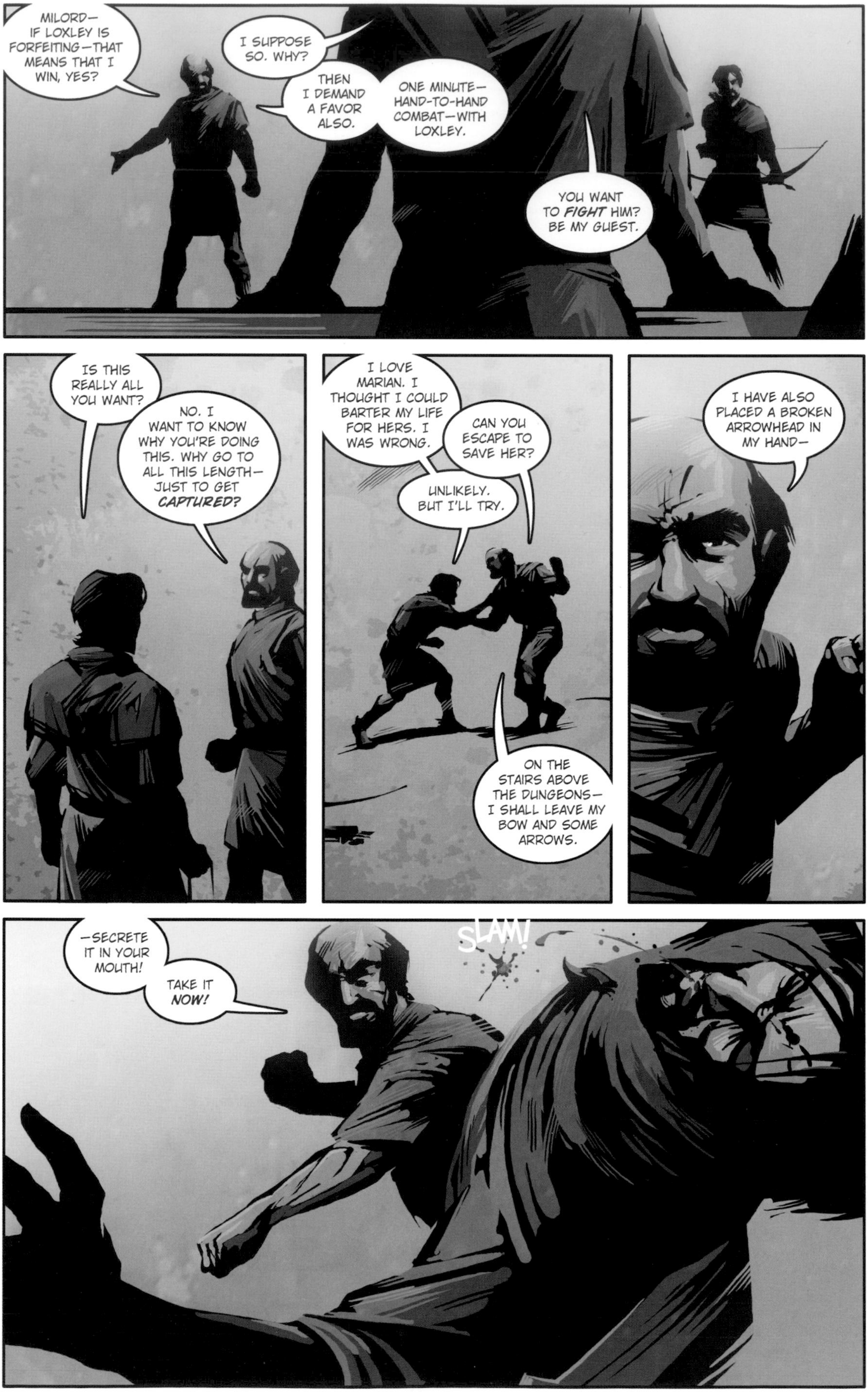
MILORD— IF LOXLEY IS FORFEITING—THAT MEANS THAT I WIN, YES?
I SUPPOSE SO. WHY?
THEN I DEMAND A FAVOR ALSO.
ONE MINUTE— HAND-TO-HAND COMBAT—WITH LOXLEY.
YOU WANT TO FIGHT HIM? BE MY GUEST.
IS THIS REALLY ALL YOU WANT?
NO. I WANT TO KNOW WHY YOU'RE DOING THIS. WHY GO TO ALL THIS LENGTH— JUST TO GET CAPTURED?
I LOVE MARIAN. I THOUGHT I COULD BARTER MY LIFE FOR HERS. I WAS WRONG.
CAN YOU ESCAPE TO SAVE HER?
UNLIKELY. BUT I'LL TRY.
ON THE STAIRS ABOVE THE DUNGEONS— I SHALL LEAVE MY BOW AND SOME ARROWS.
I HAVE ALSO PLACED A BROKEN ARROWHEAD IN MY HAND—
—SECRETE IT IN YOUR MOUTH!
TAKE IT NOW!
SLAM!

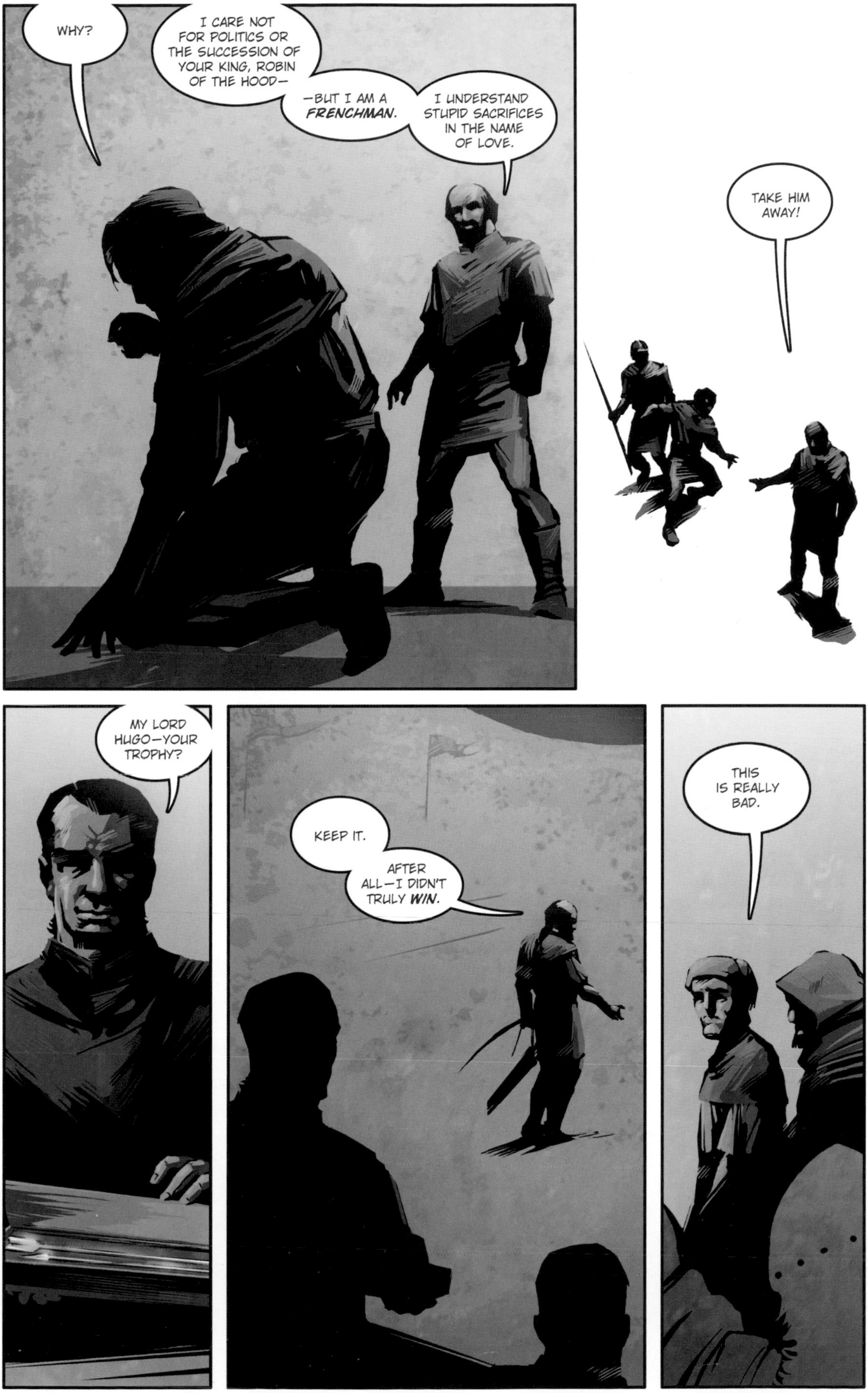
WHY?
I CARE NOT FOR POLITICS OR THE SUCCESSION OF YOUR KING, ROBIN OF THE HOOD—
—BUT I AM A FRENCHMAN.
I UNDERSTAND STUPID SACRIFICES IN THE NAME OF LOVE.
TAKE HIM AWAY!
MY LORD HUGO—YOUR TROPHY?
KEEP IT.
AFTER ALL—I DIDN'T TRULY WIN.
THIS IS REALLY BAD.

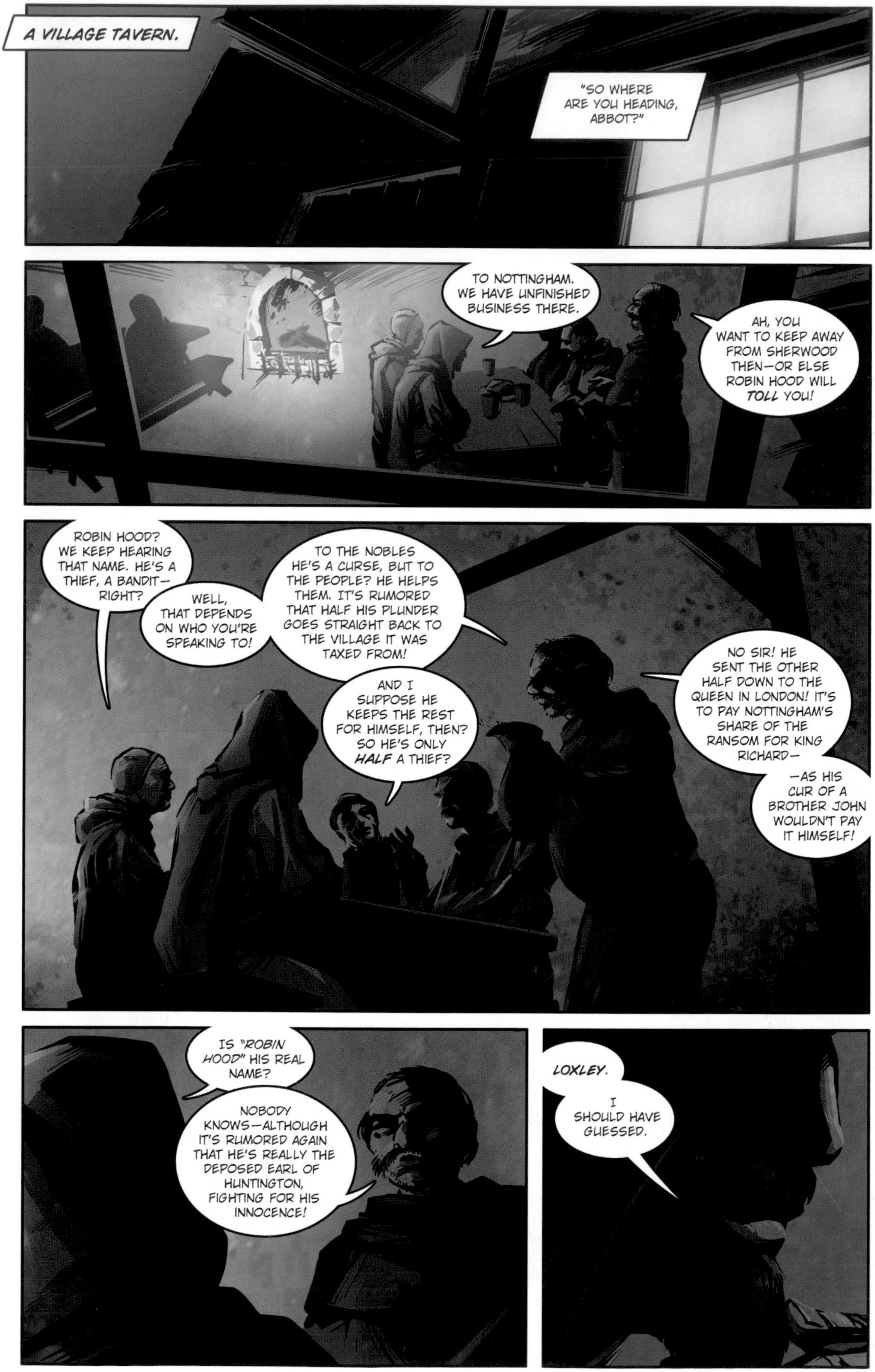
A VILLAGE TAVERN.
"SO WHERE ARE YOU HEADING, ABBOT?"
TO NOTTINGHAM. WE HAVE UNFINISHED BUSINESS THERE.
AH, YOU WANT TO KEEP AWAY FROM SHERWOOD THEN—OR ELSE ROBIN HOOD WILL *TOLL* YOU!
ROBIN HOOD? WE KEEP HEARING THAT NAME. HE'S A THIEF, A BANDIT—RIGHT?
WELL, THAT DEPENDS ON WHO YOU'RE SPEAKING TO!
TO THE NOBLES HE'S A CURSE, BUT TO THE PEOPLE? HE HELPS THEM. IT'S RUMORED THAT HALF HIS PLUNDER GOES STRAIGHT BACK TO THE VILLAGE IT WAS TAXED FROM!
AND I SUPPOSE HE KEEPS THE REST FOR HIMSELF, THEN? SO HE'S ONLY *HALF* A THIEF?
NO SIR! HE SENT THE OTHER HALF DOWN TO THE QUEEN IN LONDON! IT'S TO PAY NOTTINGHAM'S SHARE OF THE RANSOM FOR KING RICHARD—
—AS HIS CUR OF A BROTHER JOHN WOULDN'T PAY IT HIMSELF!
IS *"ROBIN HOOD"* HIS REAL NAME?
NOBODY KNOWS—ALTHOUGH IT'S RUMORED AGAIN THAT HE'S REALLY THE DEPOSED EARL OF HUNTINGTON, FIGHTING FOR HIS INNOCENCE!
LOXLEY.
I SHOULD HAVE GUESSED.

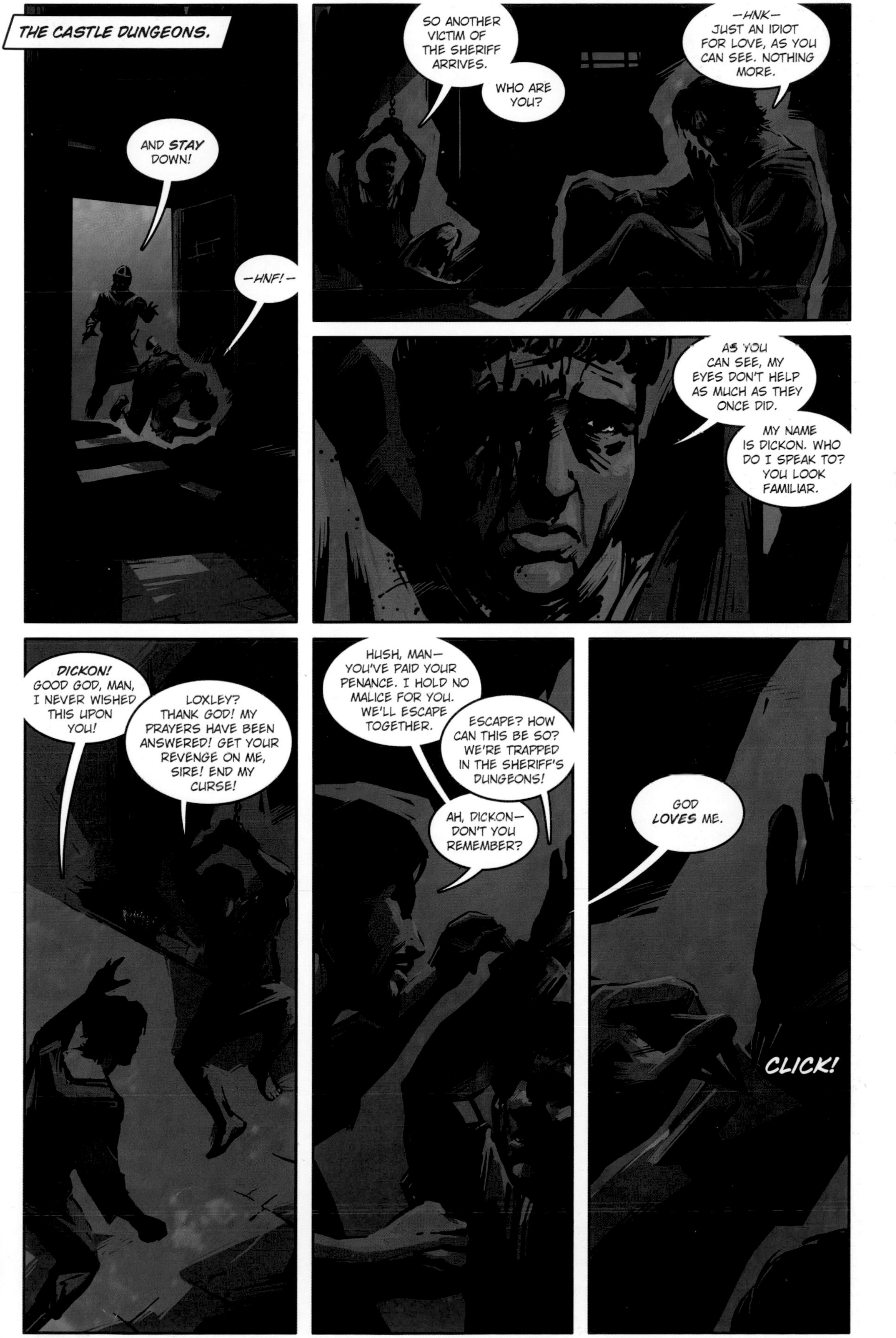
THE CASTLE DUNGEONS.
AND STAY DOWN!
—HNF!—
SO ANOTHER VICTIM OF THE SHERIFF ARRIVES.
WHO ARE YOU?
—HNK— JUST AN IDIOT FOR LOVE, AS YOU CAN SEE. NOTHING MORE.
AS YOU CAN SEE, MY EYES DON'T HELP AS MUCH AS THEY ONCE DID.
MY NAME IS DICKON. WHO DO I SPEAK TO? YOU LOOK FAMILIAR.
DICKON! GOOD GOD, MAN, I NEVER WISHED THIS UPON YOU!
LOXLEY? THANK GOD! MY PRAYERS HAVE BEEN ANSWERED! GET YOUR REVENGE ON ME, SIRE! END MY CURSE!
HUSH, MAN— YOU'VE PAID YOUR PENANCE. I HOLD NO MALICE FOR YOU. WE'LL ESCAPE TOGETHER.
ESCAPE? HOW CAN THIS BE SO? WE'RE TRAPPED IN THE SHERIFF'S DUNGEONS!
AH, DICKON— DON'T YOU REMEMBER?
GOD LOVES ME.
CLICK!

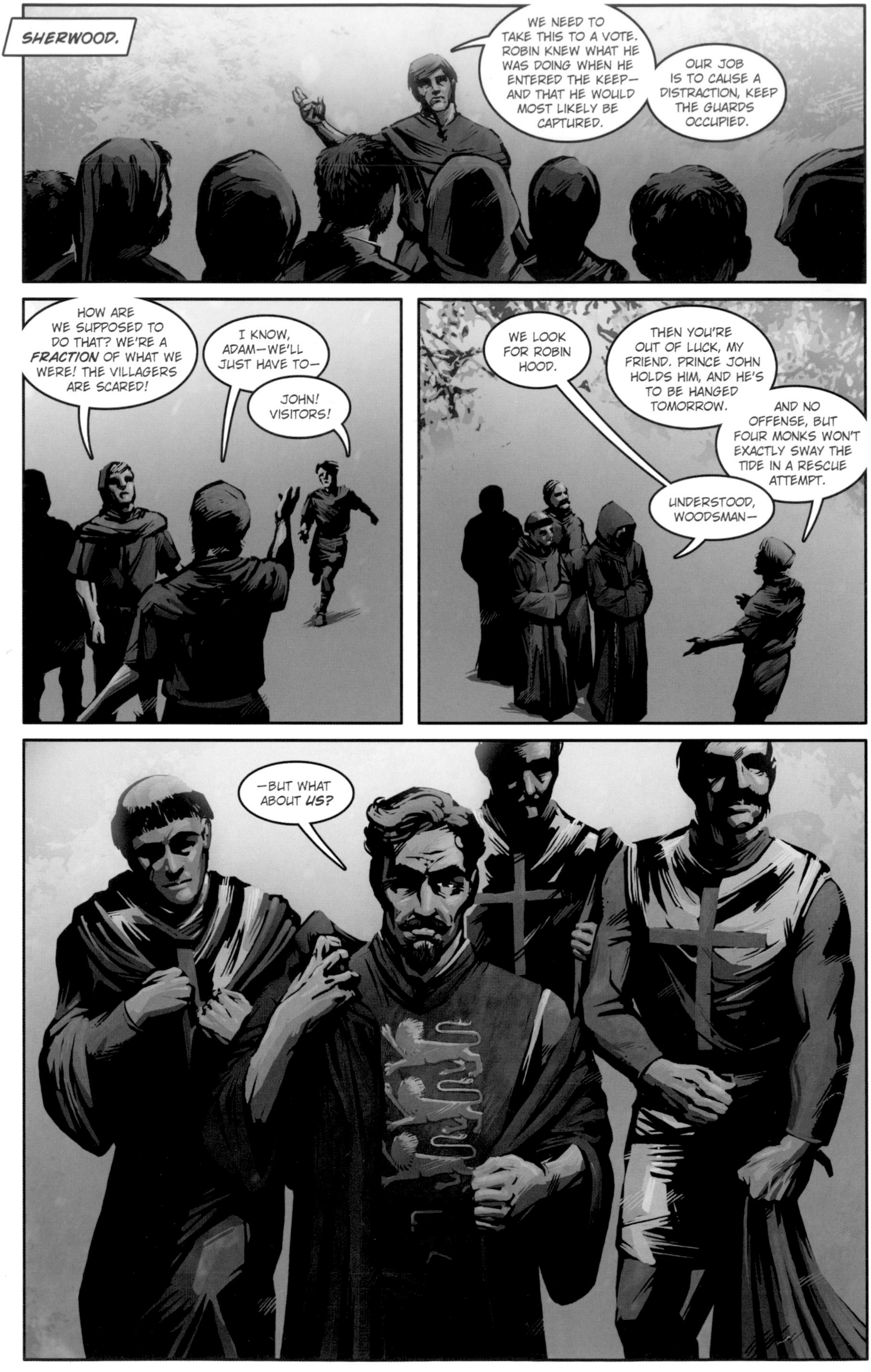
SHERWOOD.
WE NEED TO TAKE THIS TO A VOTE. ROBIN KNEW WHAT HE WAS DOING WHEN HE ENTERED THE KEEP— AND THAT HE WOULD MOST LIKELY BE CAPTURED.
OUR JOB IS TO CAUSE A DISTRACTION, KEEP THE GUARDS OCCUPIED.
HOW ARE WE SUPPOSED TO DO THAT? WE'RE A *FRACTION* OF WHAT WE WERE! THE VILLAGERS ARE SCARED!
I KNOW, ADAM—WE'LL JUST HAVE TO—
JOHN! VISITORS!
WE LOOK FOR ROBIN HOOD.
THEN YOU'RE OUT OF LUCK, MY FRIEND. PRINCE JOHN HOLDS HIM, AND HE'S TO BE HANGED TOMORROW.
AND NO OFFENSE, BUT FOUR MONKS WON'T EXACTLY SWAY THE TIDE IN A RESCUE ATTEMPT.
UNDERSTOOD, WOODSMAN—
—BUT WHAT ABOUT *US?*

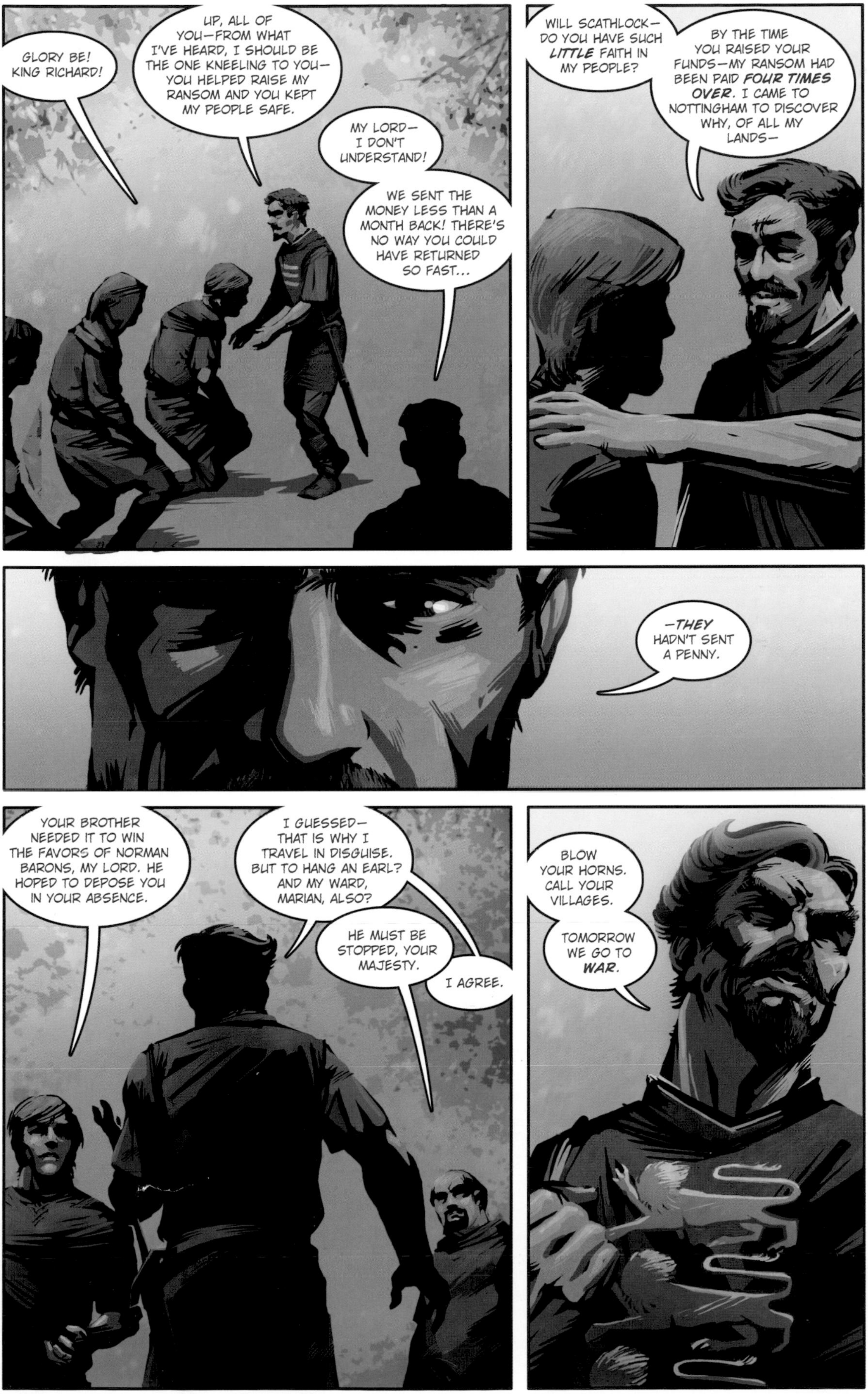
GLORY BE! KING RICHARD!
UP, ALL OF YOU—FROM WHAT I'VE HEARD, I SHOULD BE THE ONE KNEELING TO YOU—YOU HELPED RAISE MY RANSOM AND YOU KEPT MY PEOPLE SAFE.
MY LORD—I DON'T UNDERSTAND!
WE SENT THE MONEY LESS THAN A MONTH BACK! THERE'S NO WAY YOU COULD HAVE RETURNED SO FAST...
WILL SCATHLOCK—DO YOU HAVE SUCH LITTLE FAITH IN MY PEOPLE?
BY THE TIME YOU RAISED YOUR FUNDS—MY RANSOM HAD BEEN PAID FOUR TIMES OVER. I CAME TO NOTTINGHAM TO DISCOVER WHY, OF ALL MY LANDS—
—THEY HADN'T SENT A PENNY.
YOUR BROTHER NEEDED IT TO WIN THE FAVORS OF NORMAN BARONS, MY LORD. HE HOPED TO DEPOSE YOU IN YOUR ABSENCE.
I GUESSED—THAT IS WHY I TRAVEL IN DISGUISE. BUT TO HANG AN EARL? AND MY WARD, MARIAN, ALSO?
HE MUST BE STOPPED, YOUR MAJESTY.
I AGREE.
BLOW YOUR HORNS. CALL YOUR VILLAGES.
TOMORROW WE GO TO WAR.

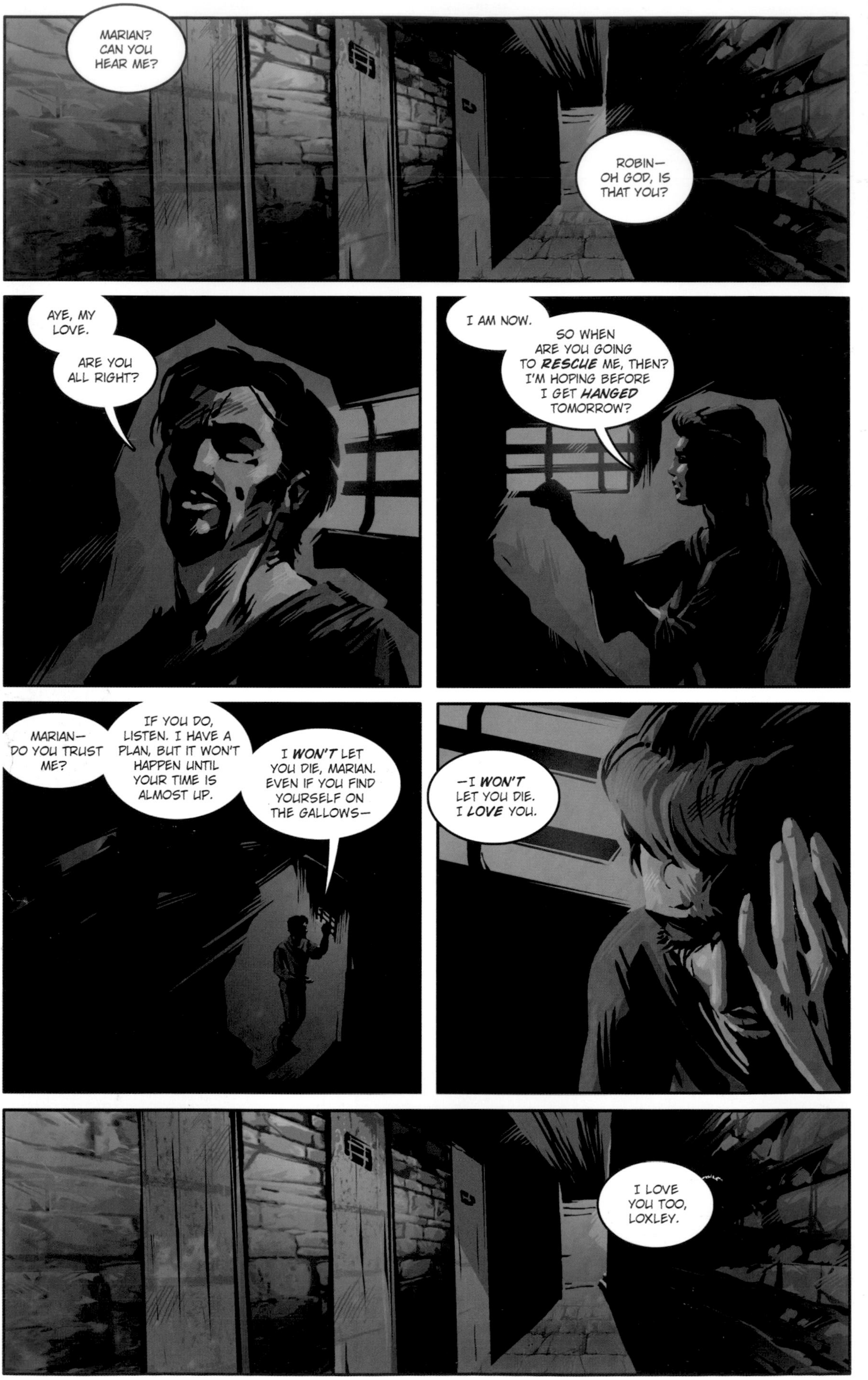
MARIAN?
CAN YOU
HEAR ME?
ROBIN—
OH GOD, IS
THAT YOU?
AYE, MY
LOVE.
ARE YOU
ALL RIGHT?
I AM NOW.
SO WHEN
ARE YOU GOING
TO **RESCUE** ME, THEN?
I'M HOPING BEFORE
I GET **HANGED**
TOMORROW?
MARIAN—
DO YOU TRUST
ME?
IF YOU DO,
LISTEN. I HAVE A
PLAN, BUT IT WON'T
HAPPEN UNTIL
YOUR TIME IS
ALMOST UP.
I **WON'T** LET
YOU DIE, MARIAN.
EVEN IF YOU FIND
YOURSELF ON
THE GALLOWS—
—I **WON'T**
LET YOU DIE.
I **LOVE** YOU.
I LOVE
YOU TOO,
LOXLEY.

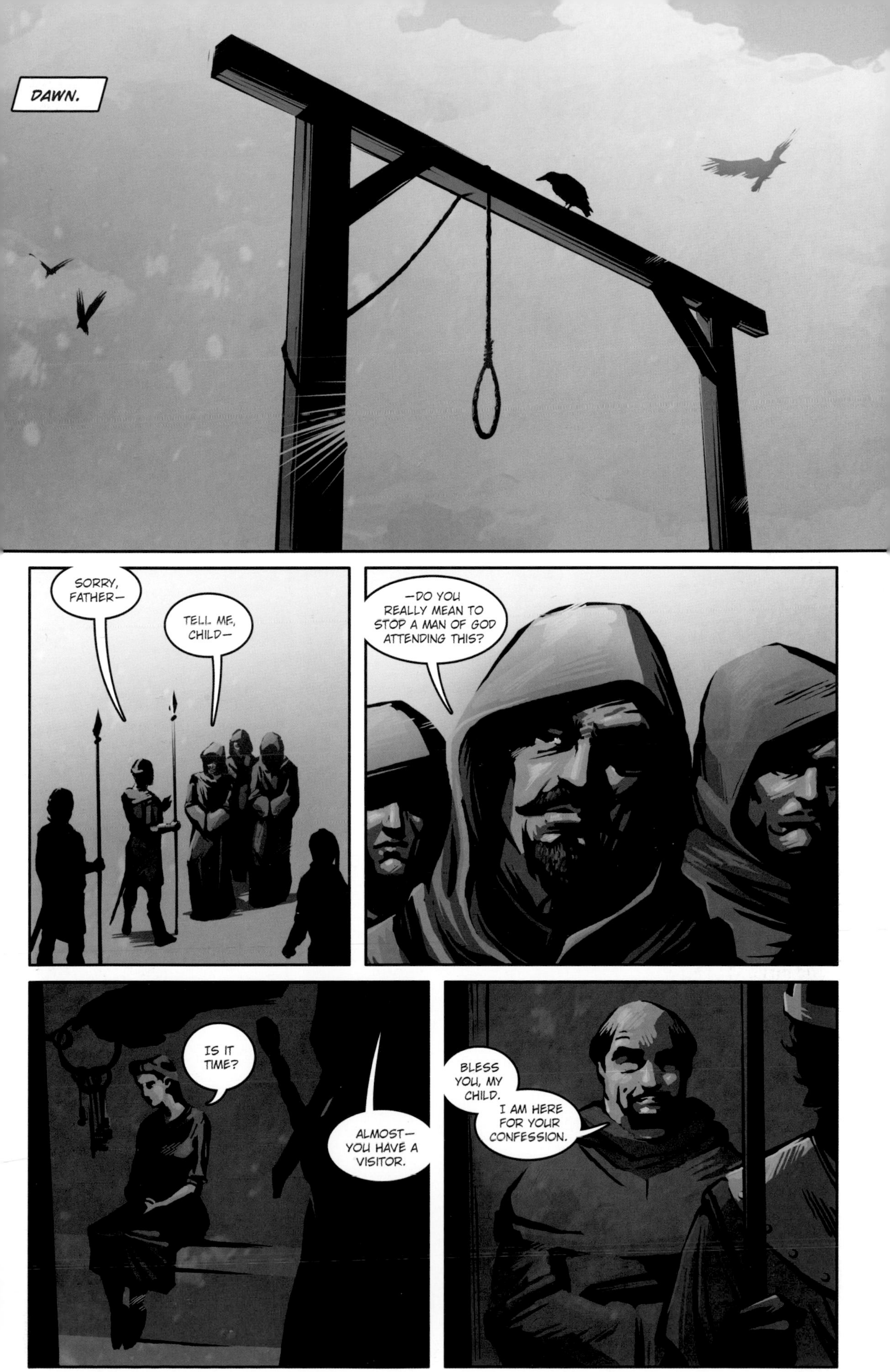
DAWN.
SORRY, FATHER—
TELL ME, CHILD—
—DO YOU REALLY MEAN TO STOP A MAN OF GOD ATTENDING THIS?
IS IT TIME?
ALMOST— YOU HAVE A VISITOR.
BLESS YOU, MY CHILD.
I AM HERE FOR YOUR CONFESSION.

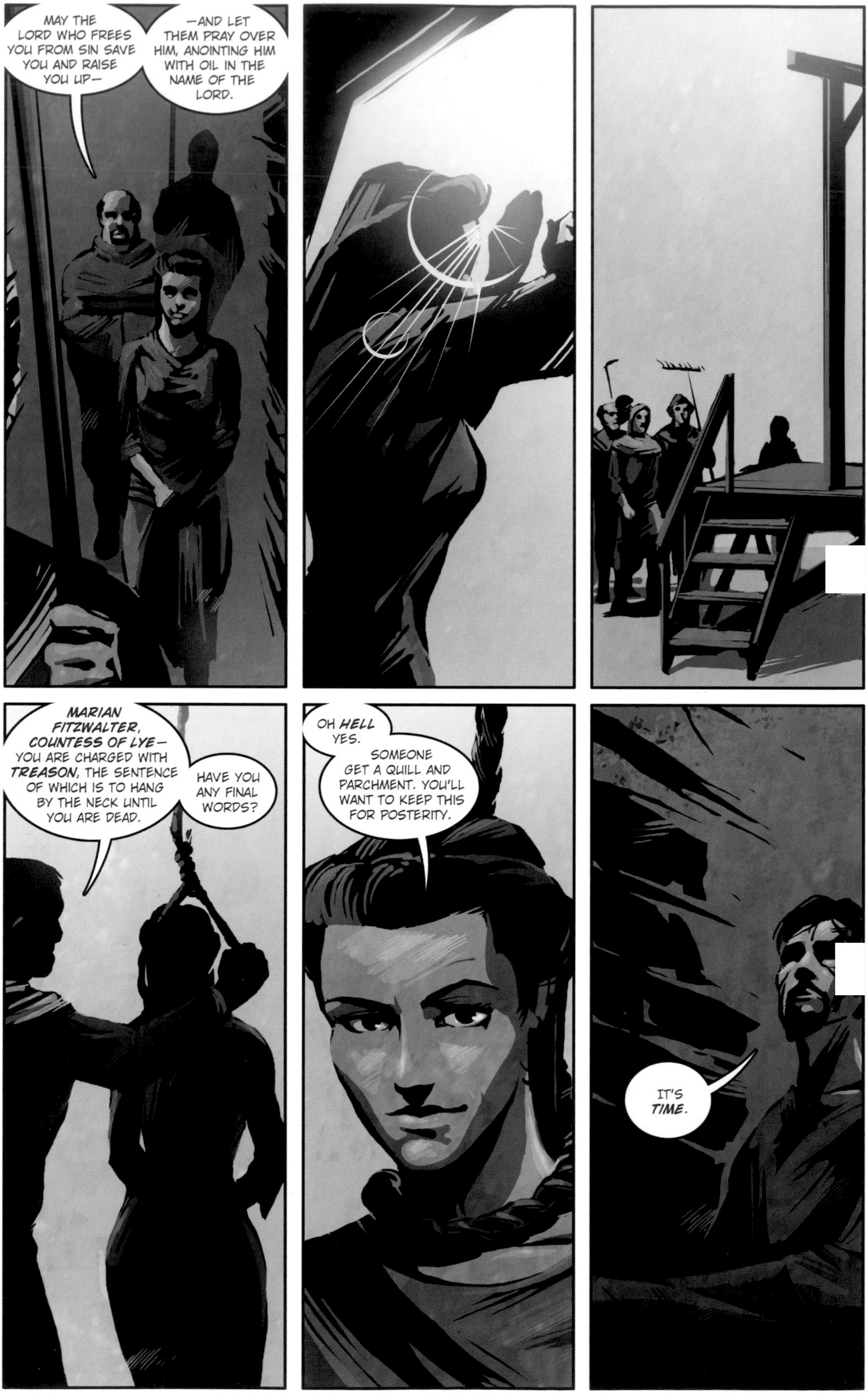
MAY THE LORD WHO FREES YOU FROM SIN SAVE YOU AND RAISE YOU UP—
—AND LET THEM PRAY OVER HIM, ANOINTING HIM WITH OIL IN THE NAME OF THE LORD.
MARIAN FITZWALTER, COUNTESS OF LYE—YOU ARE CHARGED WITH TREASON, THE SENTENCE OF WHICH IS TO HANG BY THE NECK UNTIL YOU ARE DEAD.
HAVE YOU ANY FINAL WORDS?
OH HELL YES.
SOMEONE GET A QUILL AND PARCHMENT. YOU'LL WANT TO KEEP THIS FOR POSTERITY.
IT'S TIME.

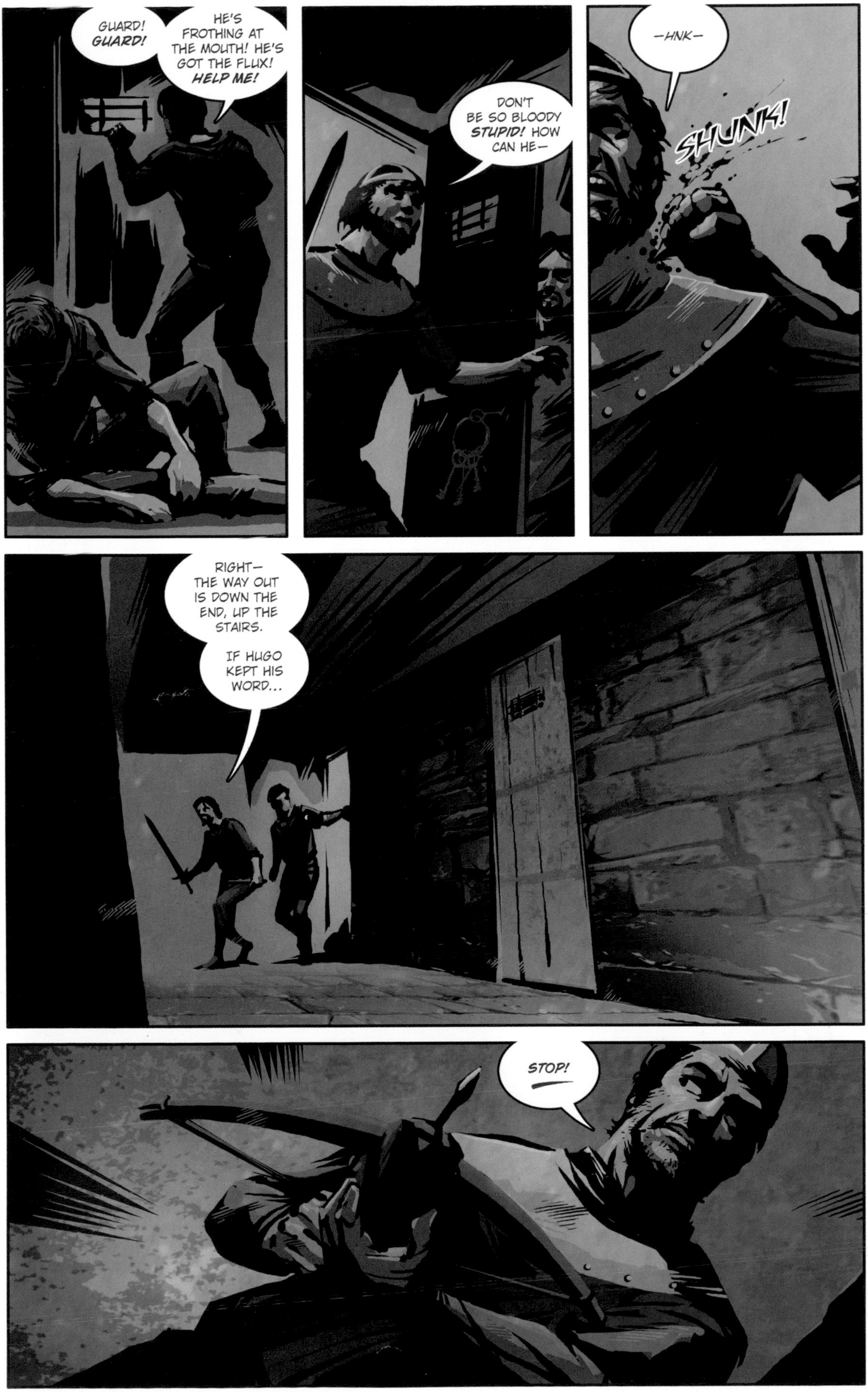
GUARD! **GUARD!**
HE'S FROTHING AT THE MOUTH! HE'S GOT THE FLUX! **HELP ME!**
DON'T BE SO BLOODY **STUPID!** HOW CAN HE—
—HNK—
SHUNK!
RIGHT— THE WAY OUT IS DOWN THE END, UP THE STAIRS.
IF HUGO KEPT HIS WORD...
STOP!

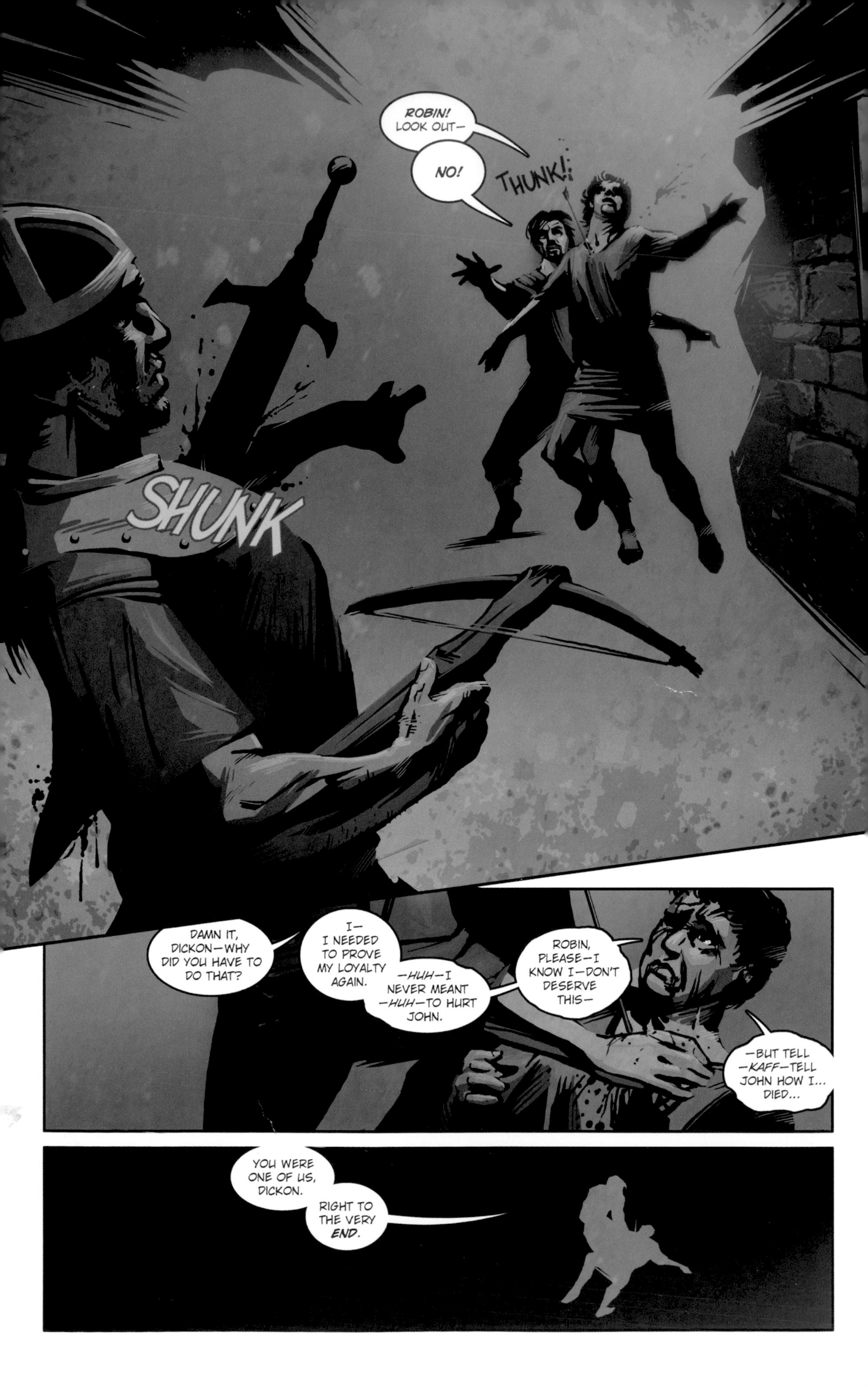
ROBIN! LOOK OUT—
NO!
THUNK!
SHUNK
DAMN IT, DICKON—WHY DID YOU HAVE TO DO THAT?
I— I NEEDED TO PROVE MY LOYALTY AGAIN.
—HUH—I NEVER MEANT —HUH—TO HURT JOHN.
ROBIN, PLEASE—I KNOW I—DON'T DESERVE THIS—
—BUT TELL —KAFF—TELL JOHN HOW I... DIED...
YOU WERE ONE OF US, DICKON.
RIGHT TO THE VERY END.

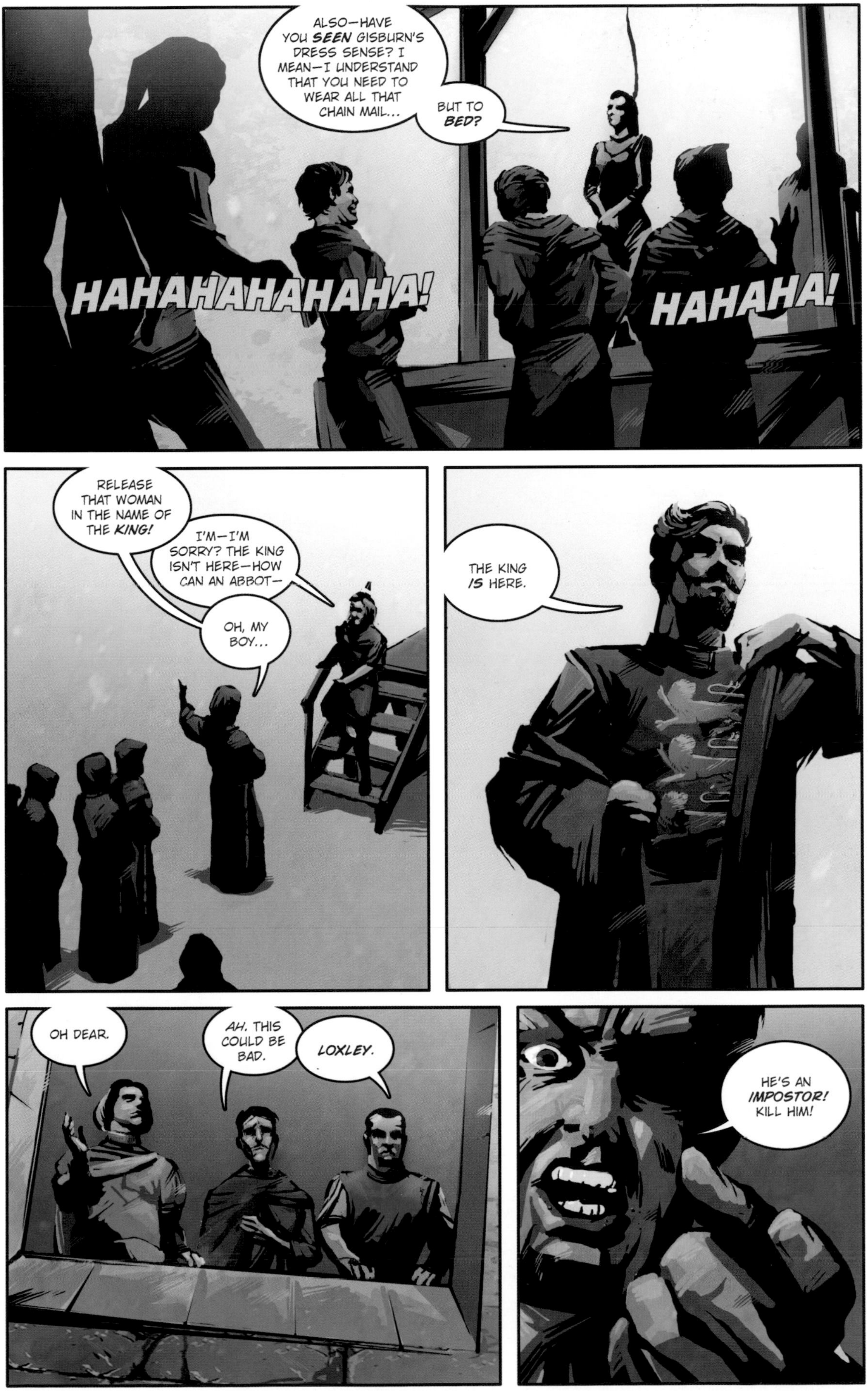
ALSO—HAVE YOU SEEN GISBURN'S DRESS SENSE? I MEAN—I UNDERSTAND THAT YOU NEED TO WEAR ALL THAT CHAIN MAIL...
BUT TO BED?
HAHAHAHAHAHAHA!
HAHAHA!
RELEASE THAT WOMAN IN THE NAME OF THE KING!
I'M—I'M SORRY? THE KING ISN'T HERE—HOW CAN AN ABBOT—
OH, MY BOY...
THE KING IS HERE.
OH DEAR.
AH. THIS COULD BE BAD.
LOXLEY.
HE'S AN IMPOSTOR! KILL HIM!

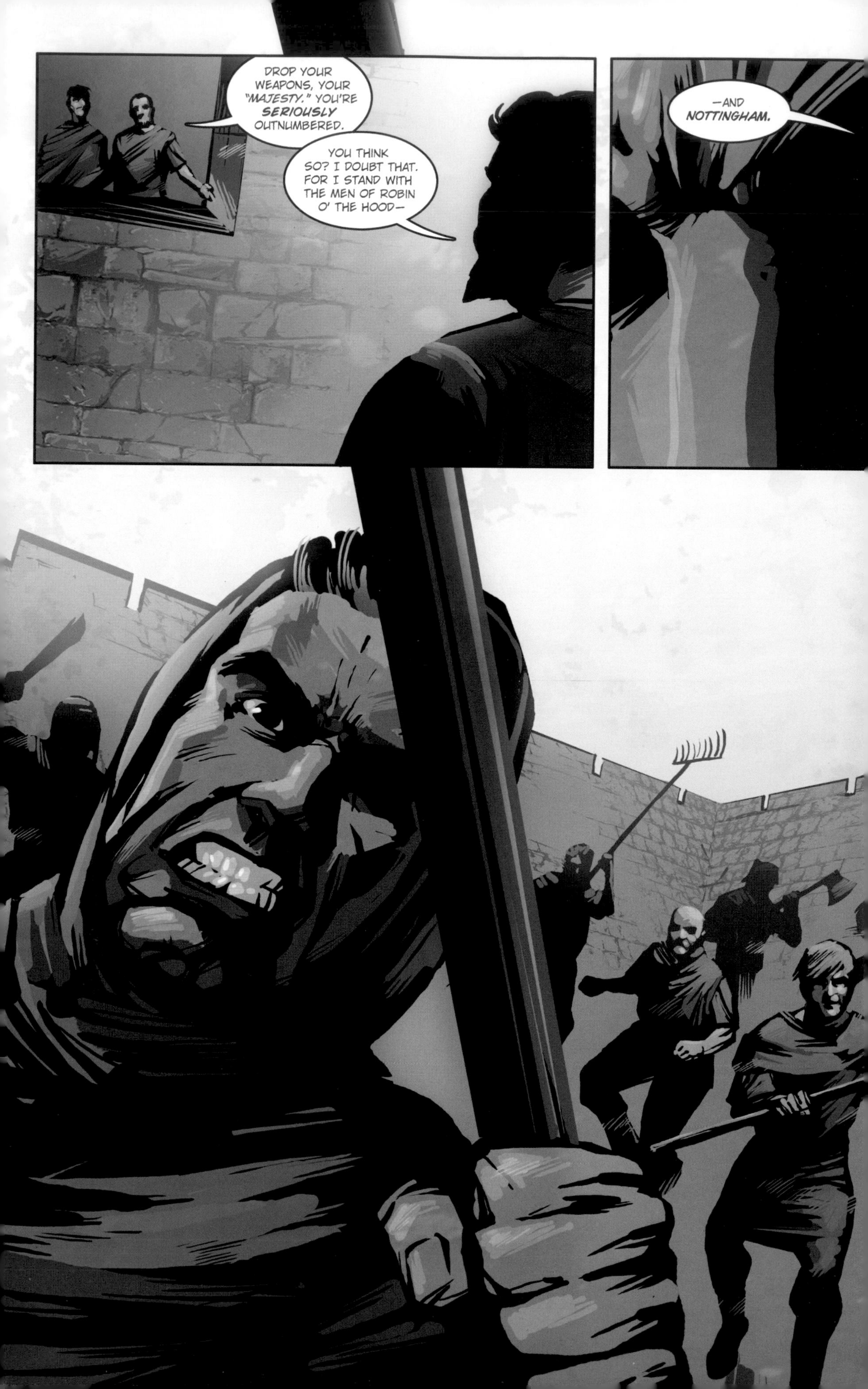
DROP YOUR WEAPONS, YOUR "MAJESTY." YOU'RE SERIOUSLY OUTNUMBERED.
YOU THINK SO? I DOUBT THAT. FOR I STAND WITH THE MEN OF ROBIN O' THE HOOD—
—AND NOTTINGHAM.

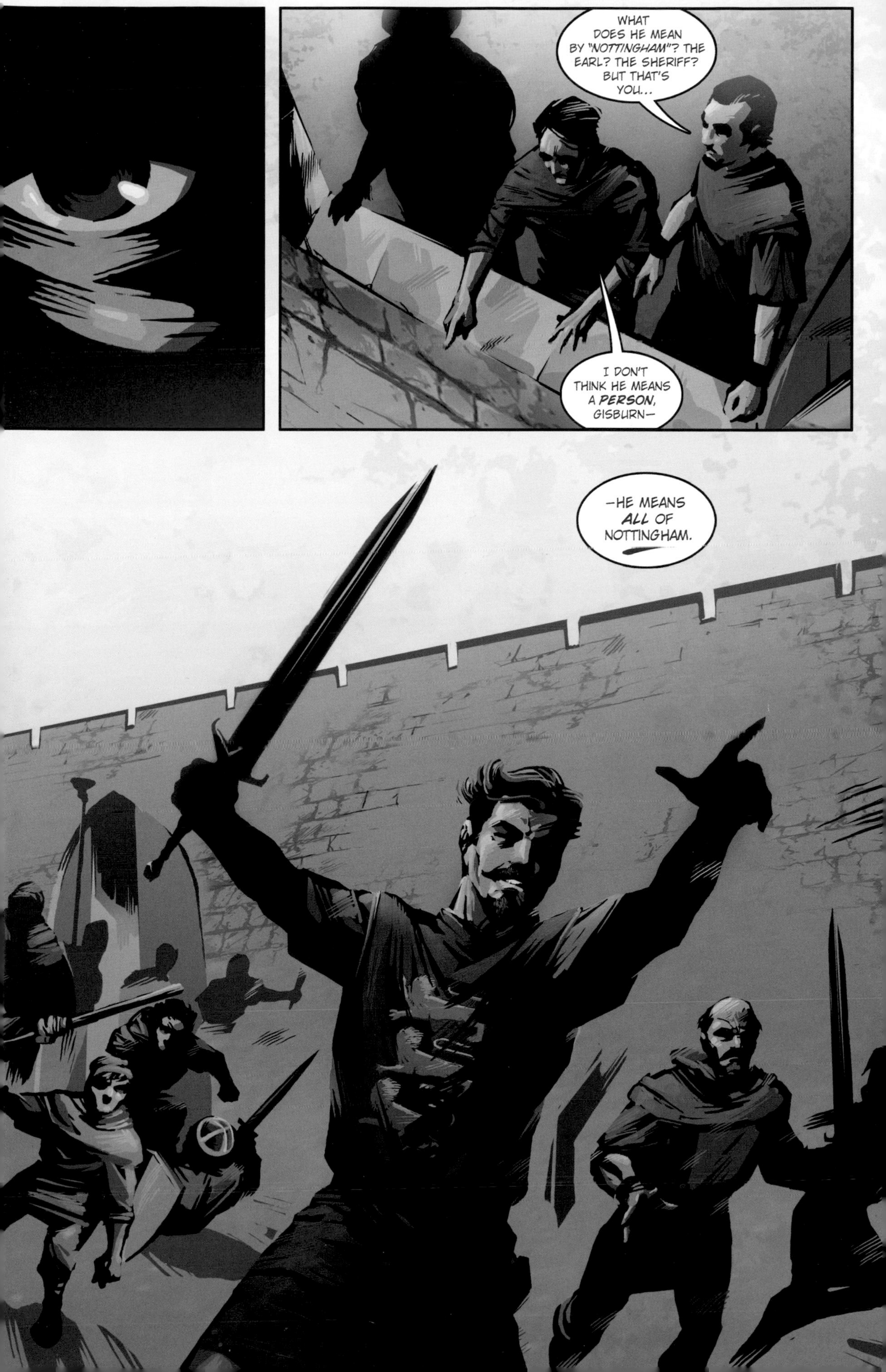
WHAT DOES HE MEAN BY "NOTTINGHAM"? THE EARL? THE SHERIFF? BUT THAT'S YOU...
I DON'T THINK HE MEANS A **PERSON**, GISBURN—
—HE MEANS **ALL** OF NOTTINGHAM.

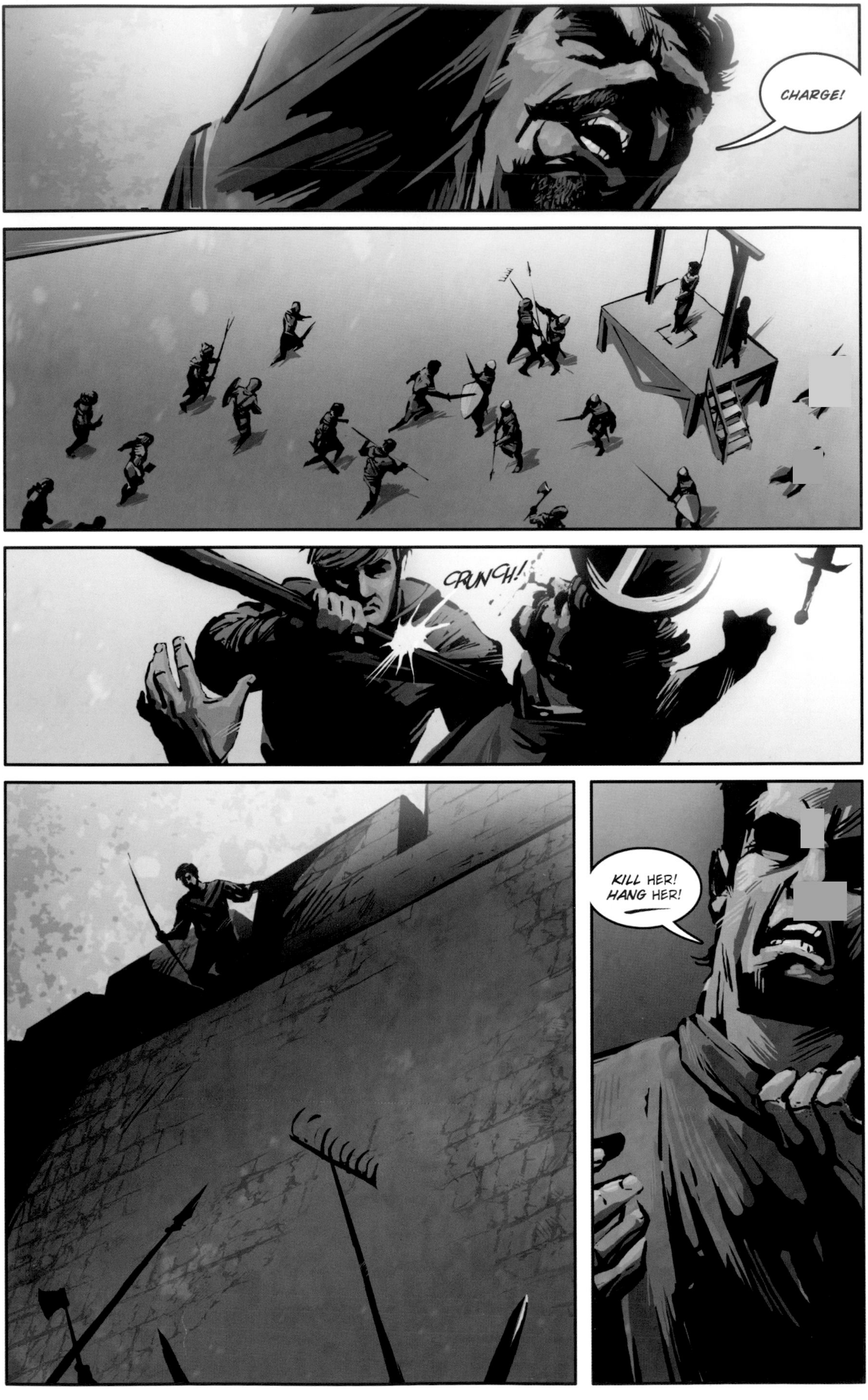
CHARGE!
CRUNCH!
KILL HER! HANG HER!

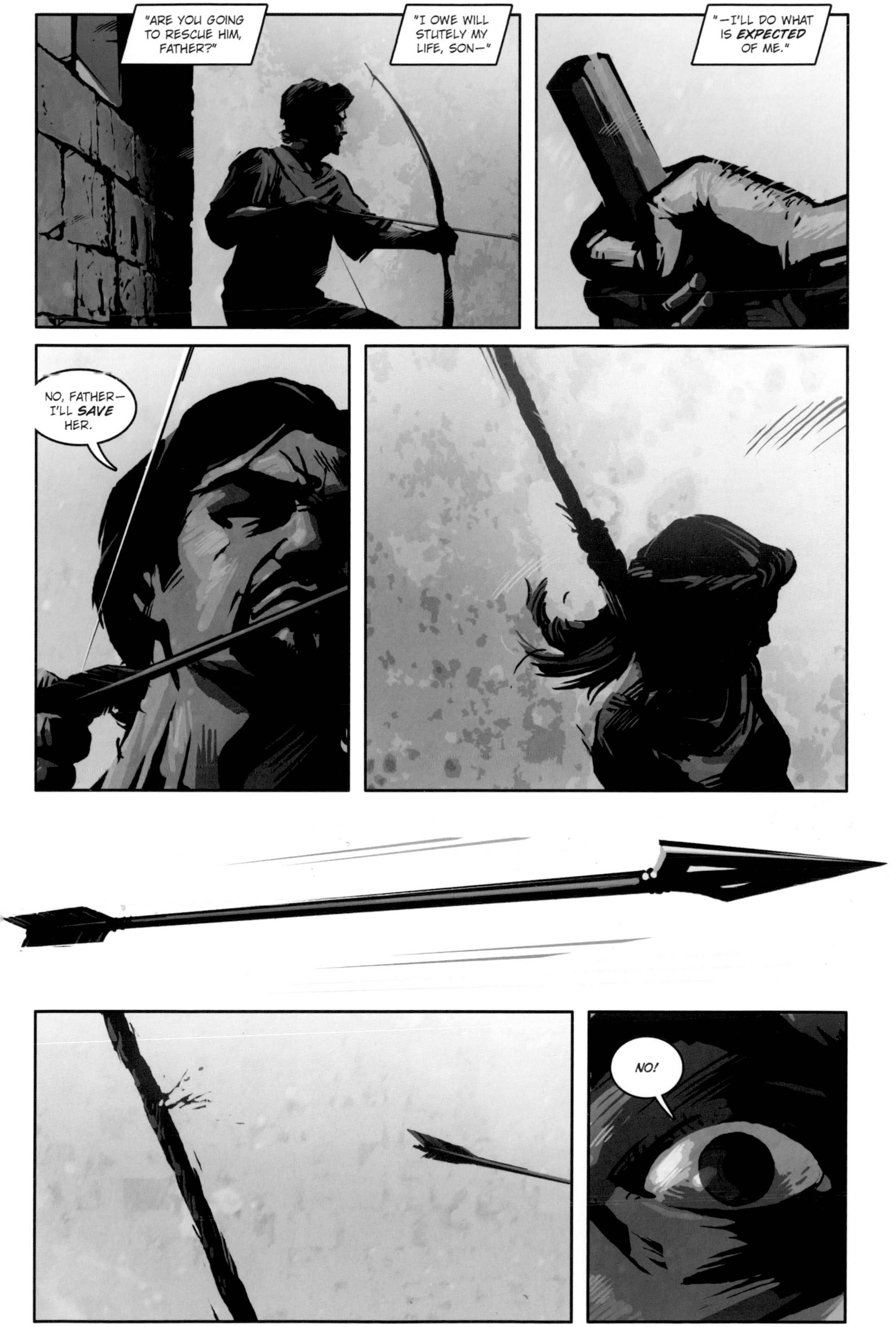
"ARE YOU GOING TO RESCUE HIM, FATHER?"
"I OWE WILL STUTELY MY LIFE, SON—"
"—I'LL DO WHAT IS EXPECTED OF ME."
NO, FATHER— I'LL SAVE HER.
NO!

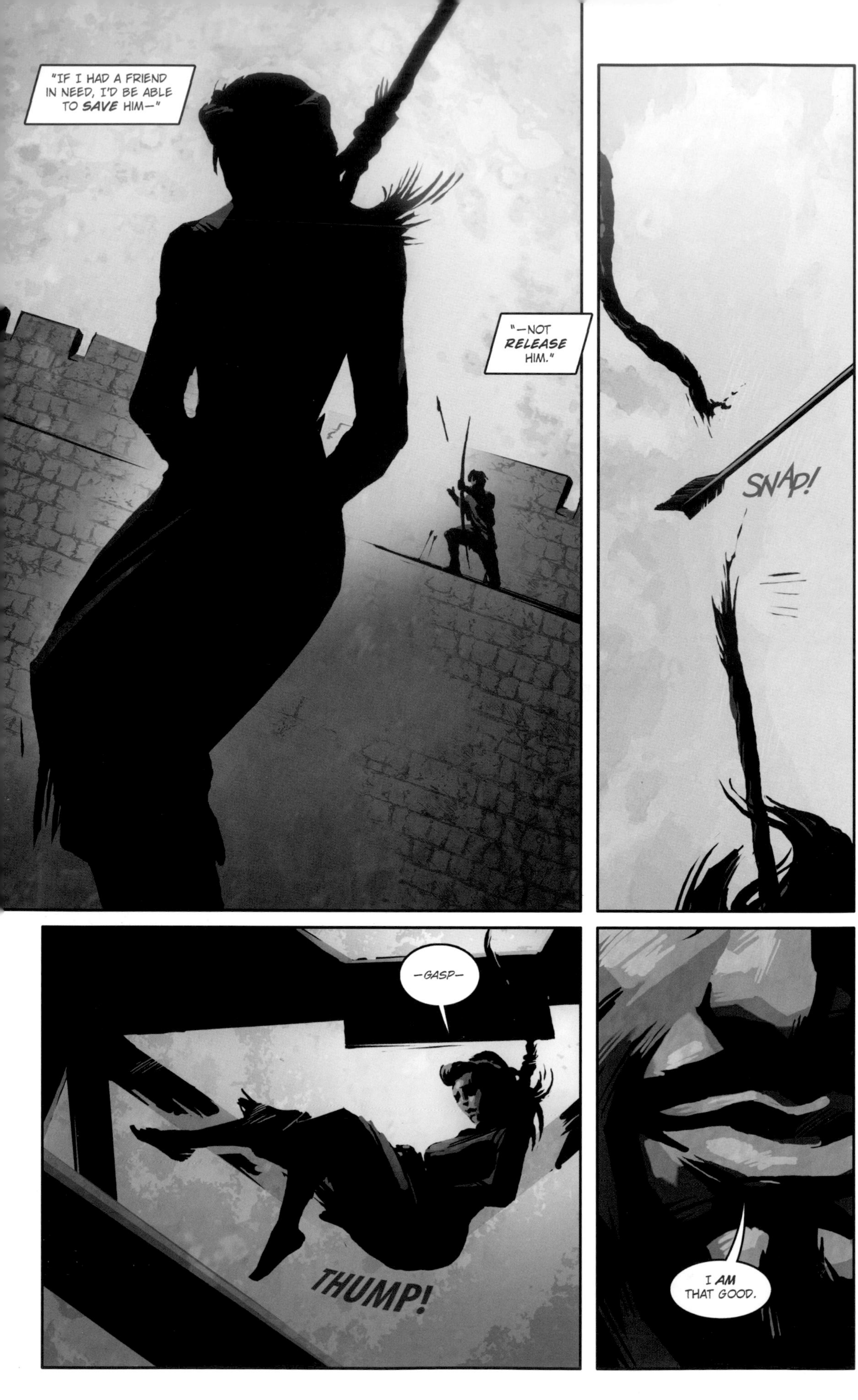
"IF I HAD A FRIEND IN NEED, I'D BE ABLE TO SAVE HIM—"
"—NOT RELEASE HIM."
SNAP!
—GASP—
THUMP!
I AM THAT GOOD.

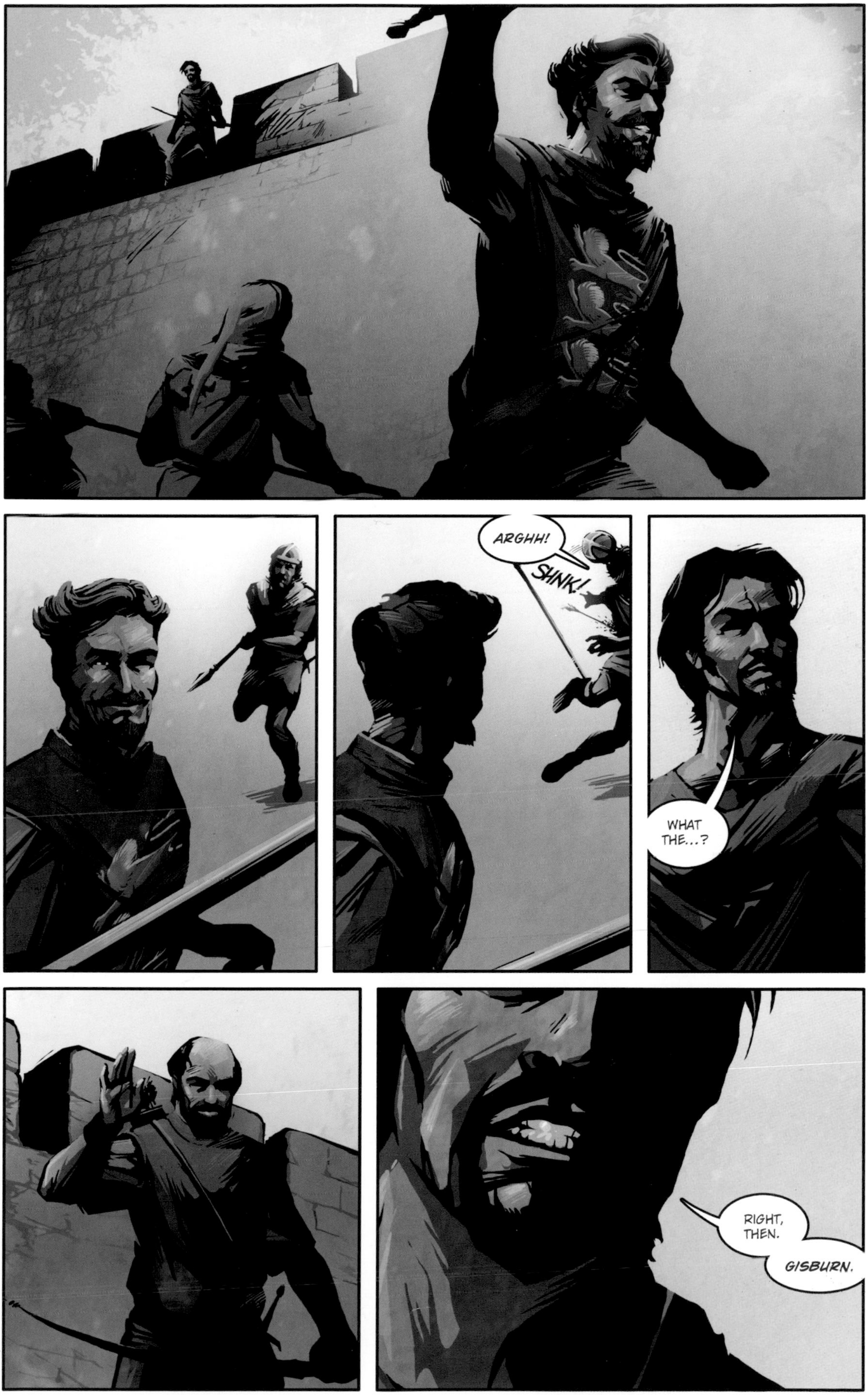
ARGHH!
SHNK!
WHAT THE...?
RIGHT, THEN.
GISBURN.

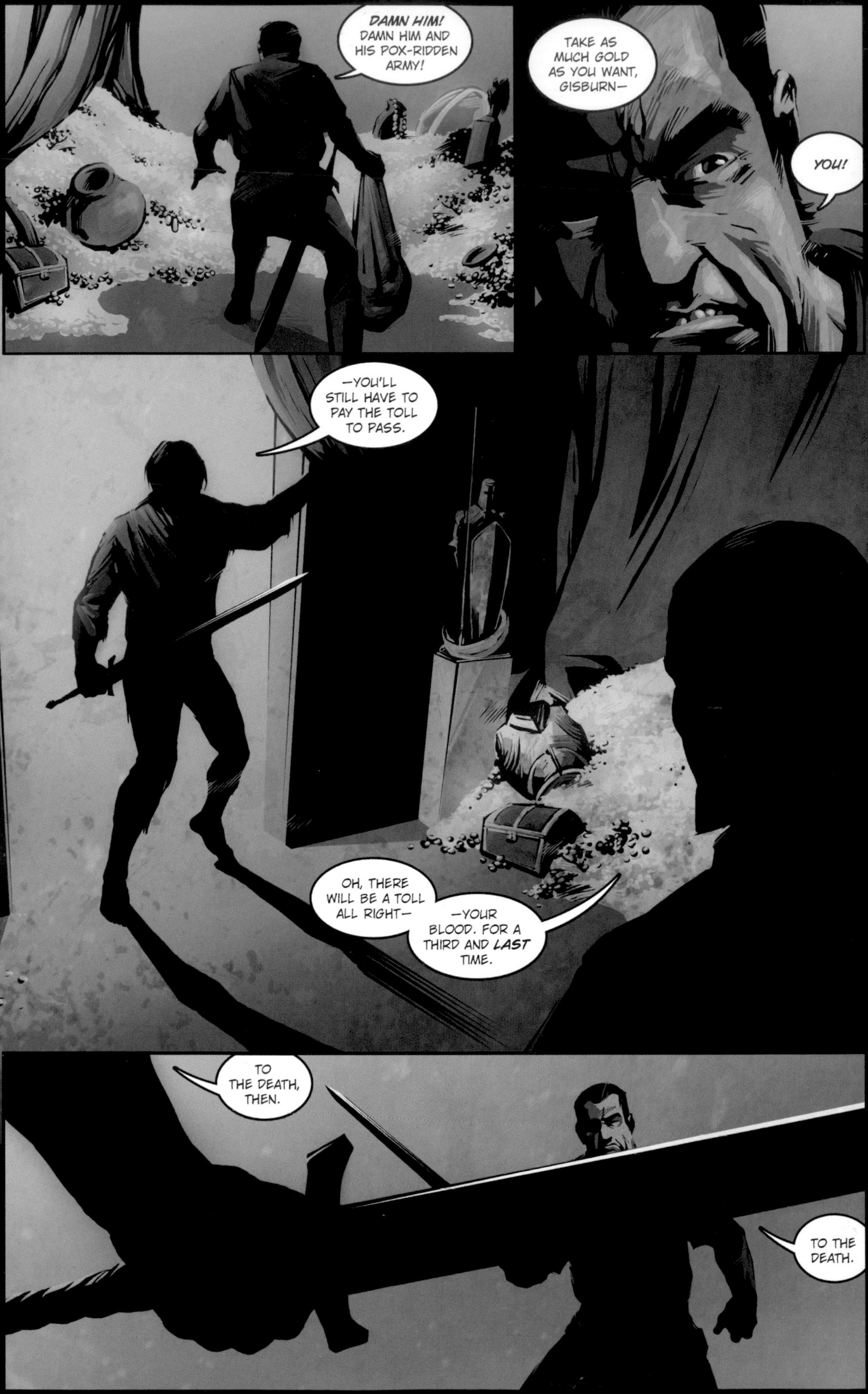
DAMN HIM! DAMN HIM AND HIS POX-RIDDEN ARMY!
TAKE AS MUCH GOLD AS YOU WANT, GISBURN—
YOU!
—YOU'LL STILL HAVE TO PAY THE TOLL TO PASS.
OH, THERE WILL BE A TOLL ALL RIGHT—
—YOUR BLOOD. FOR A THIRD AND LAST TIME.
TO THE DEATH, THEN.
TO THE DEATH.

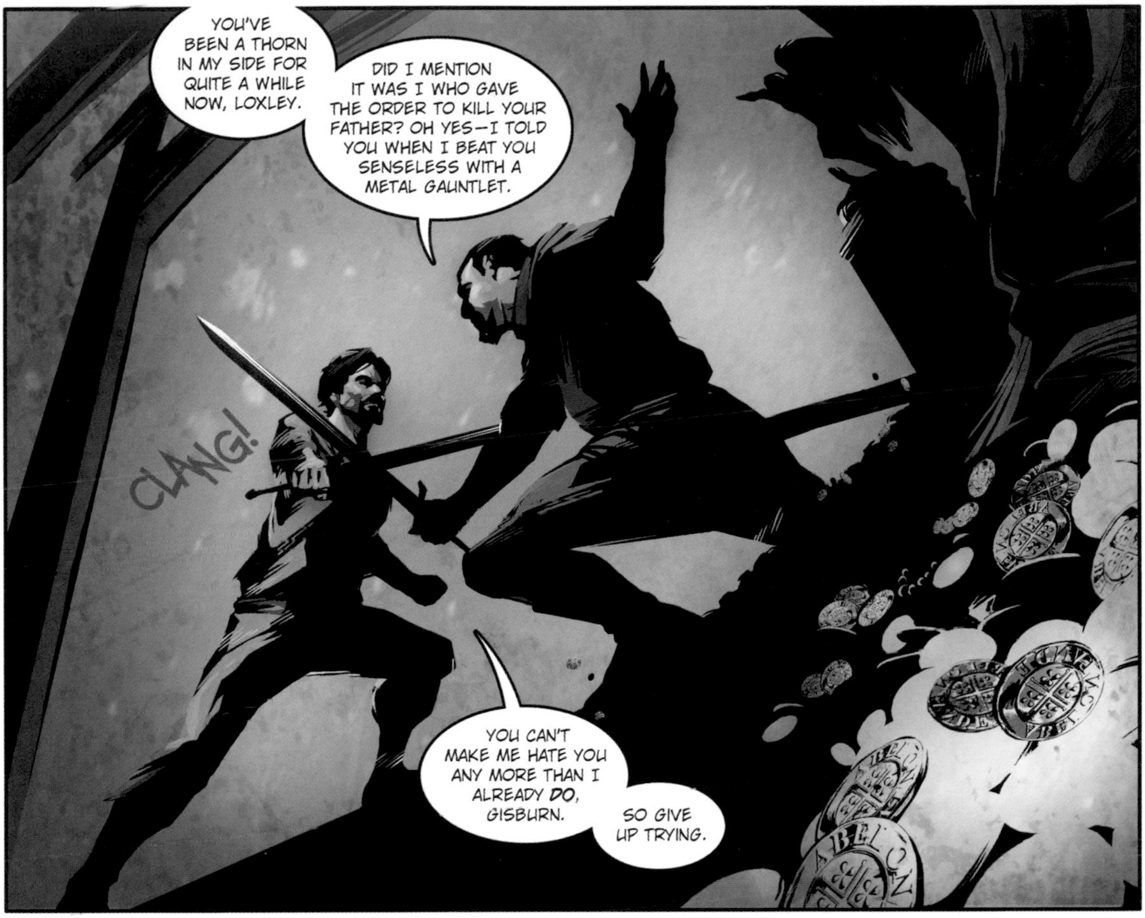
YOU'VE BEEN A THORN IN MY SIDE FOR QUITE A WHILE NOW, LOXLEY.
DID I MENTION IT WAS I WHO GAVE THE ORDER TO KILL YOUR FATHER? OH YES—I TOLD YOU WHEN I BEAT YOU SENSELESS WITH A METAL GAUNTLET.
CLANG!
YOU CAN'T MAKE ME HATE YOU ANY MORE THAN I ALREADY *DO*, GISBURN.
SO GIVE UP TRYING.
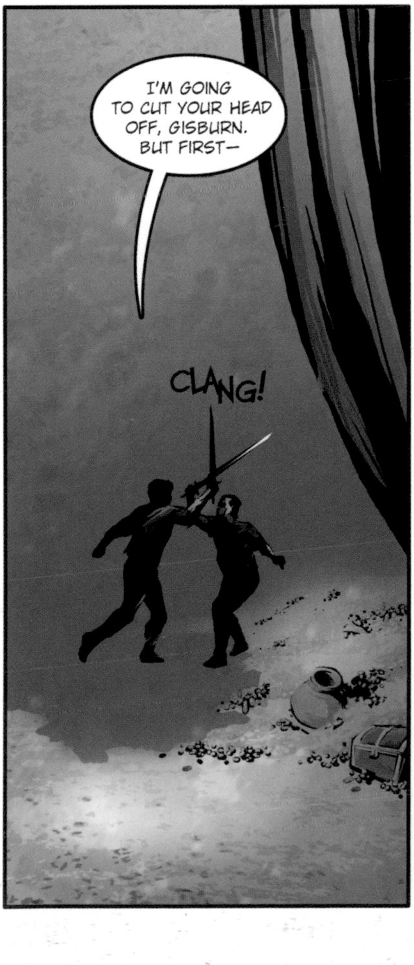
I'M GOING TO CUT YOUR HEAD OFF, GISBURN. BUT FIRST—
CLANG!
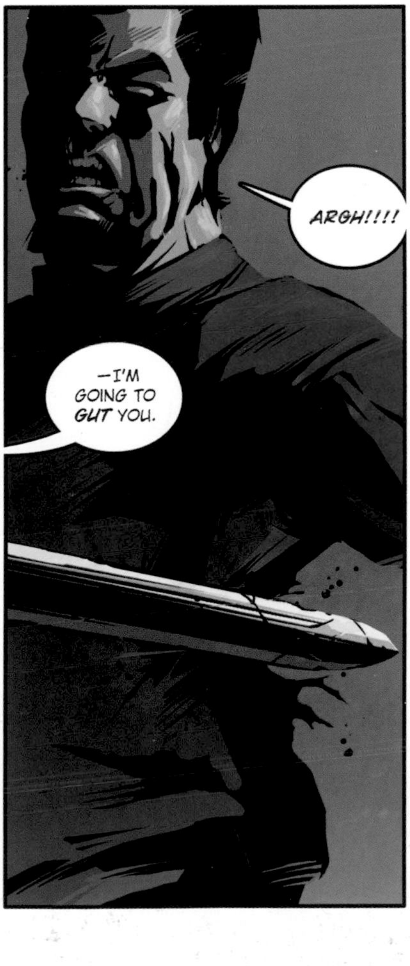
ARGH!!!!
—I'M GOING TO *GUT* YOU.
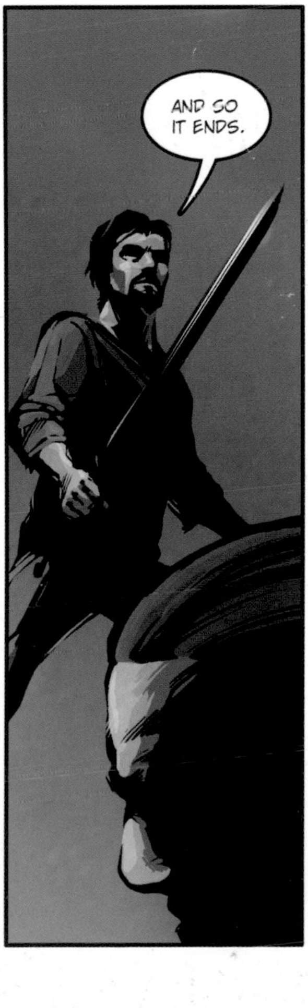
AND SO IT ENDS.

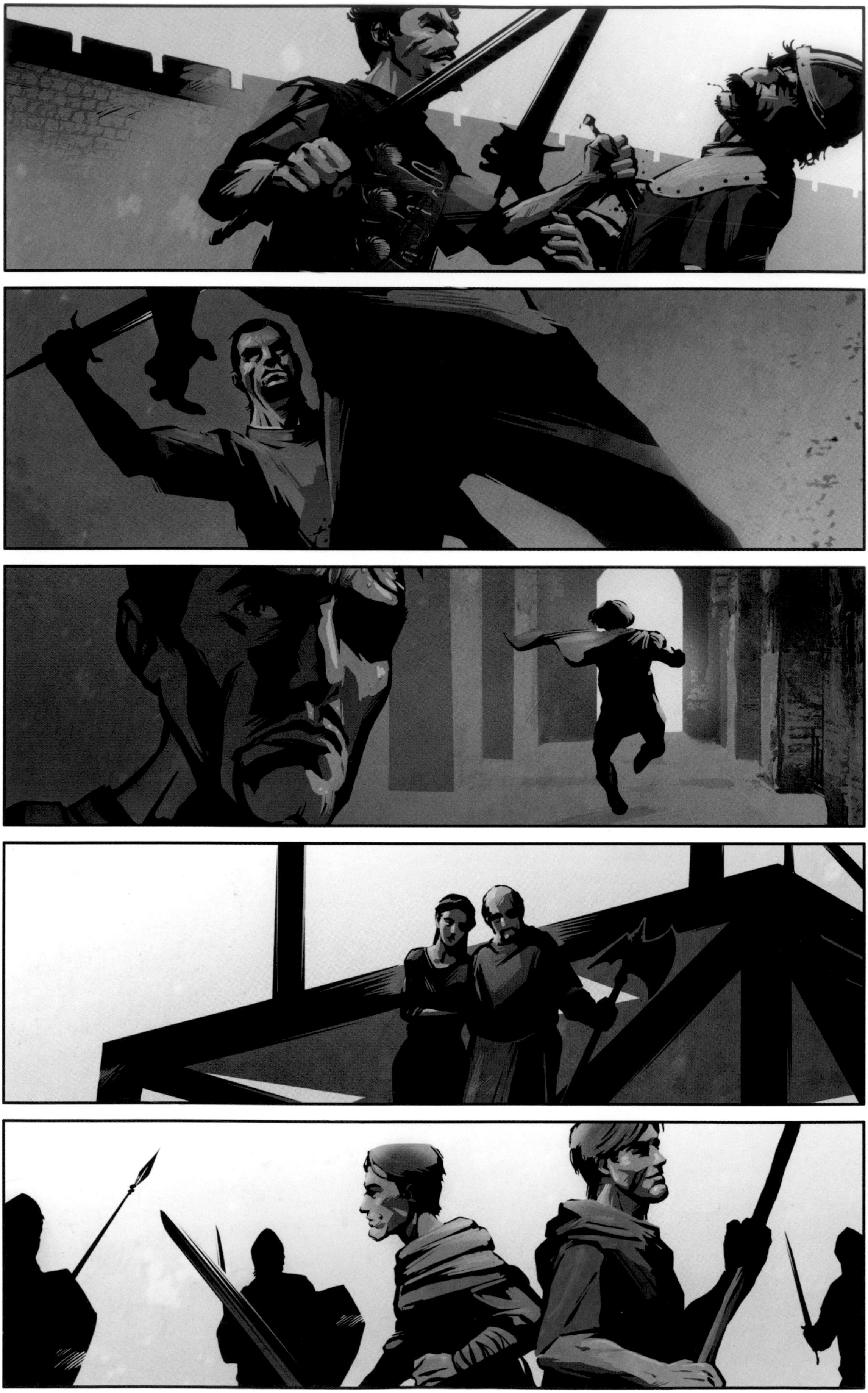

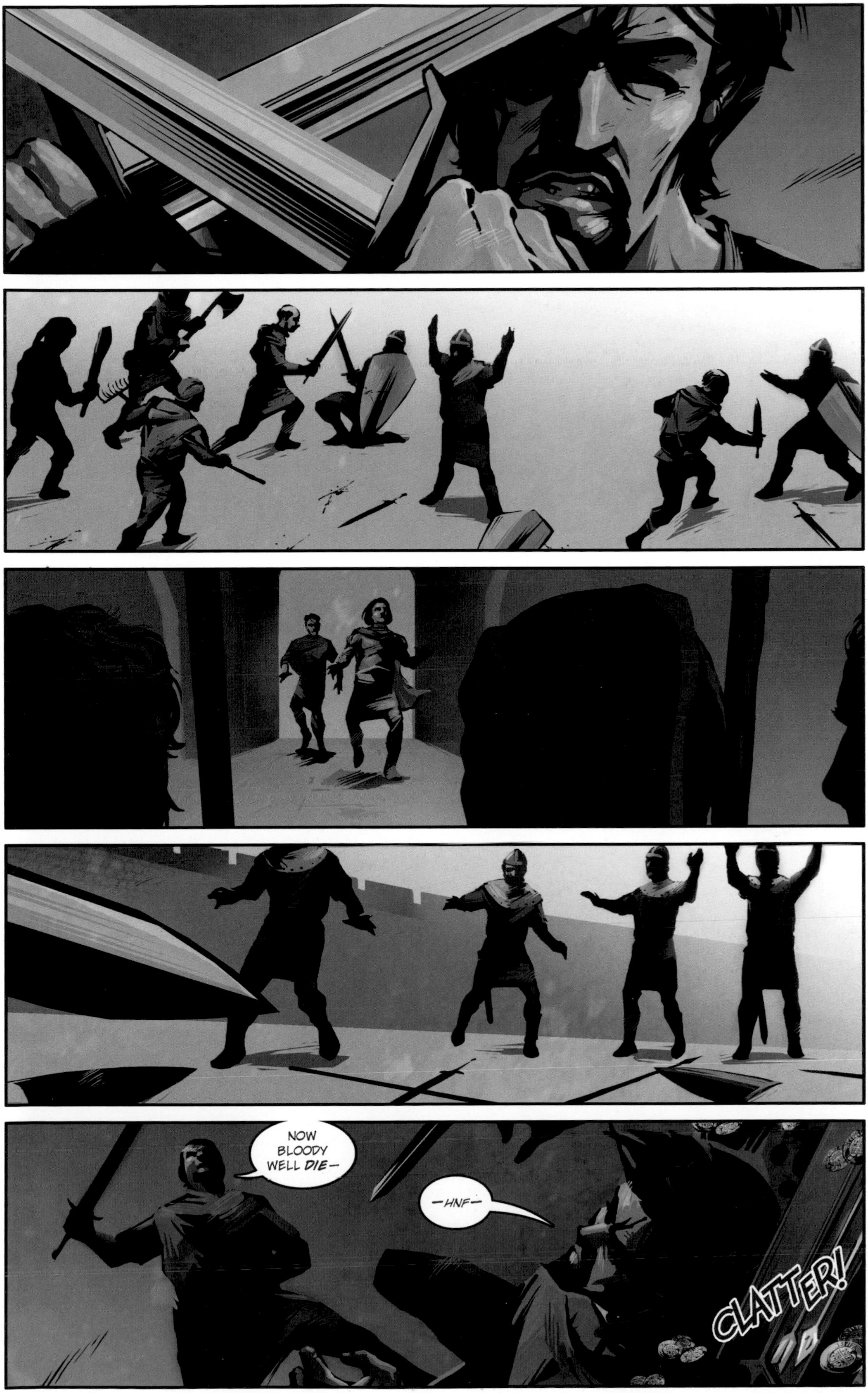
NOW BLOODY WELL DIE—
—HNF—
CLATTER!

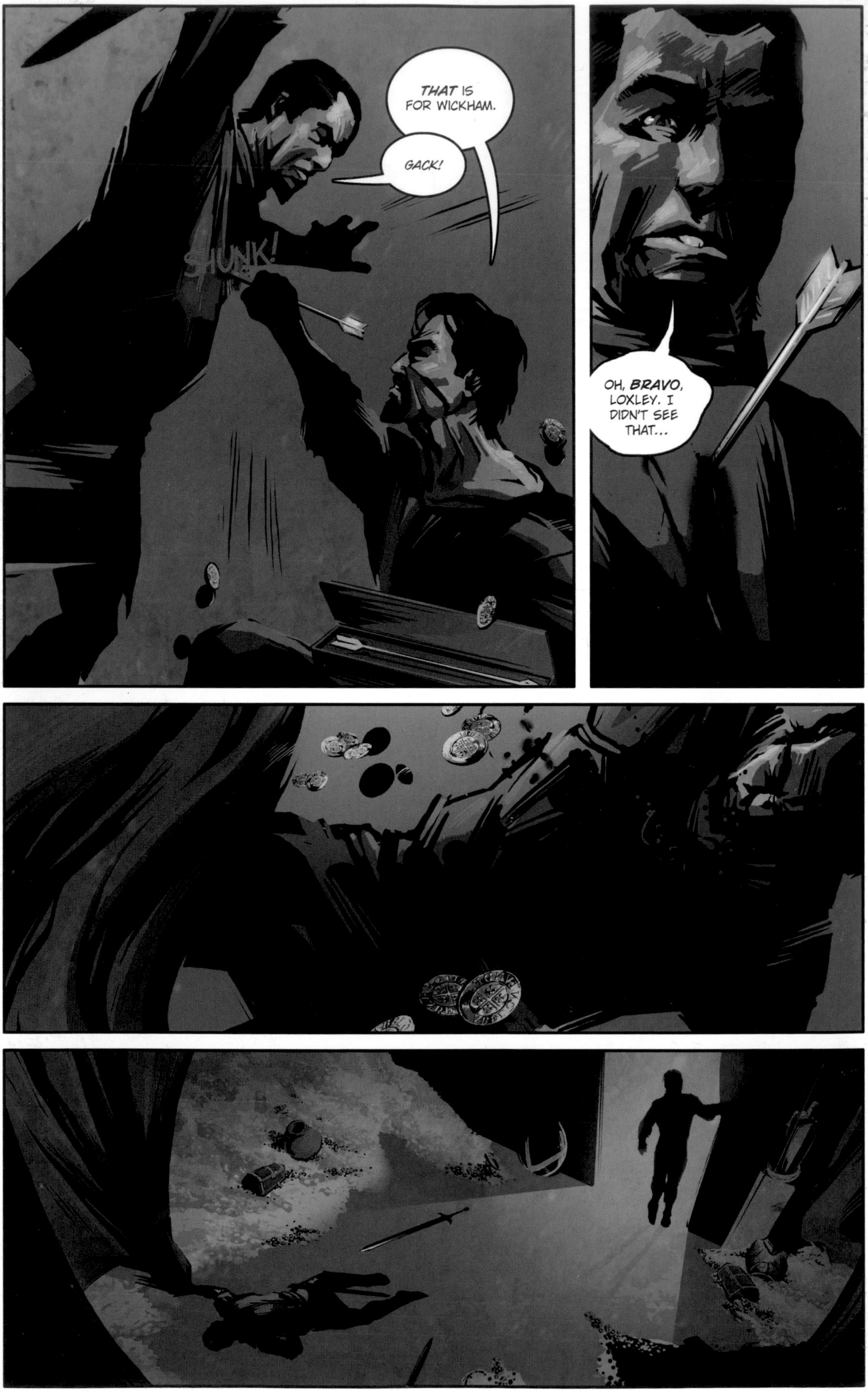

THAT IS FOR WICKHAM.
GACK!
SHUNK!
OH, BRAVO, LOXLEY. I DIDN'T SEE THAT...

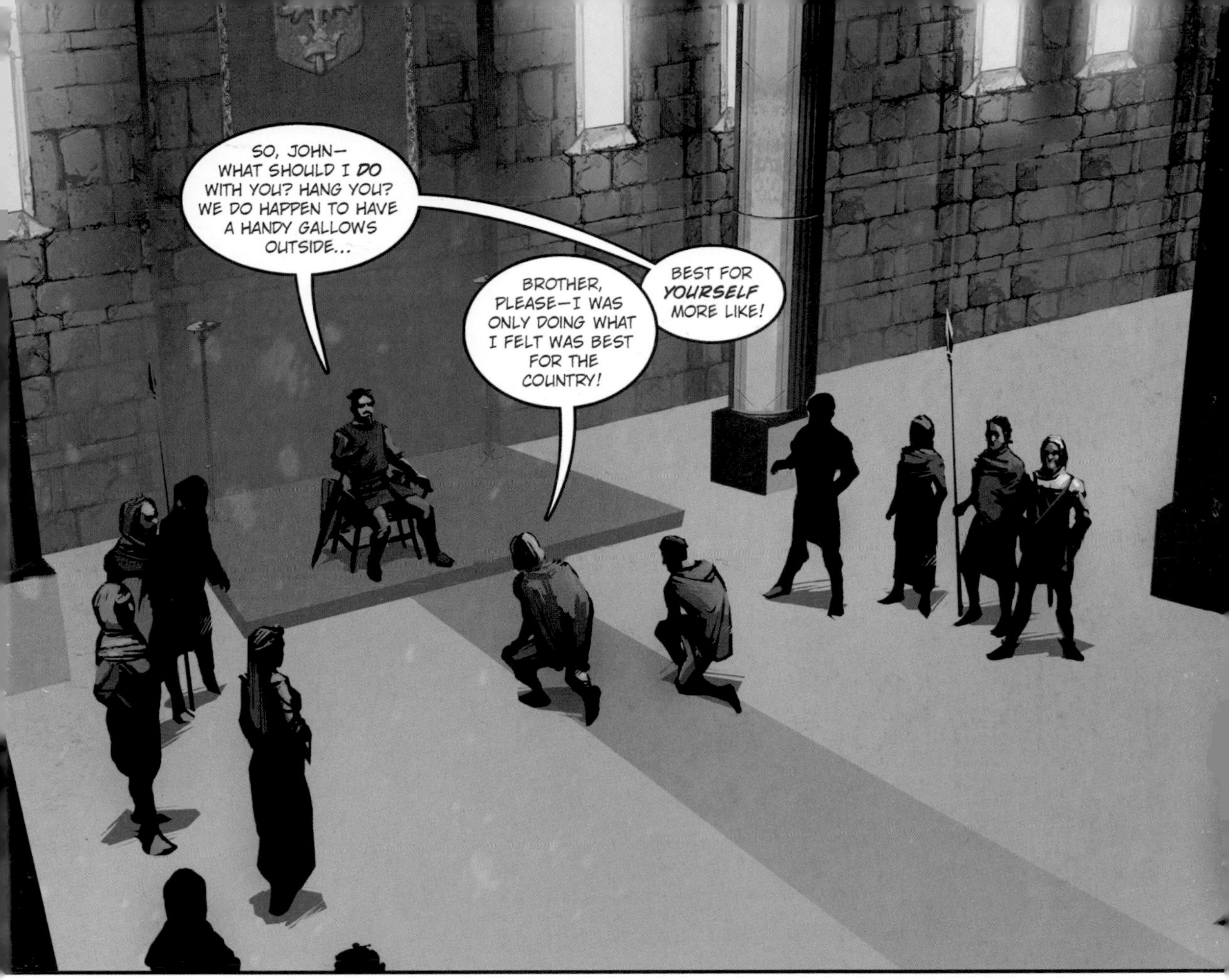
SO, JOHN—
WHAT SHOULD I DO WITH YOU? HANG YOU? WE DO HAPPEN TO HAVE A HANDY GALLOWS OUTSIDE...
BROTHER, PLEASE—I WAS ONLY DOING WHAT I FELT WAS BEST FOR THE COUNTRY!
BEST FOR YOURSELF MORE LIKE!

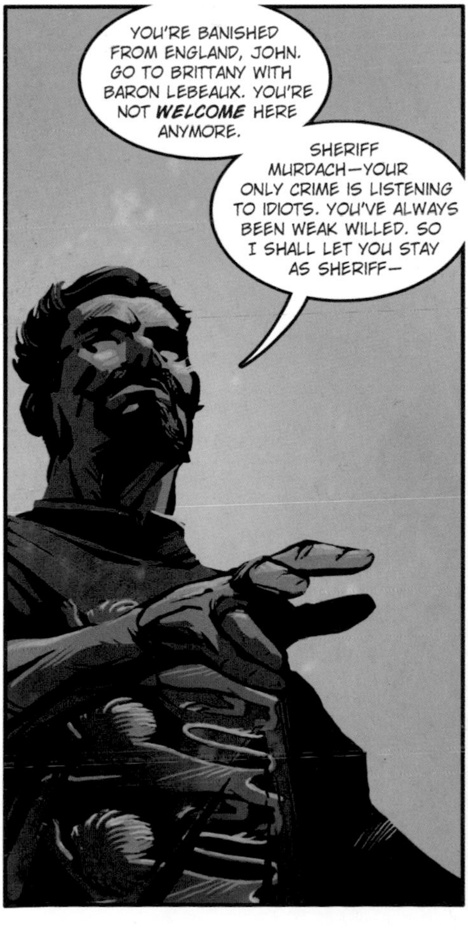
YOU'RE BANISHED FROM ENGLAND, JOHN. GO TO BRITTANY WITH BARON LEBEAUX. YOU'RE NOT WELCOME HERE ANYMORE.
SHERIFF MURDACH—YOUR ONLY CRIME IS LISTENING TO IDIOTS. YOU'VE ALWAYS BEEN WEAK WILLED. SO I SHALL LET YOU STAY AS SHERIFF—

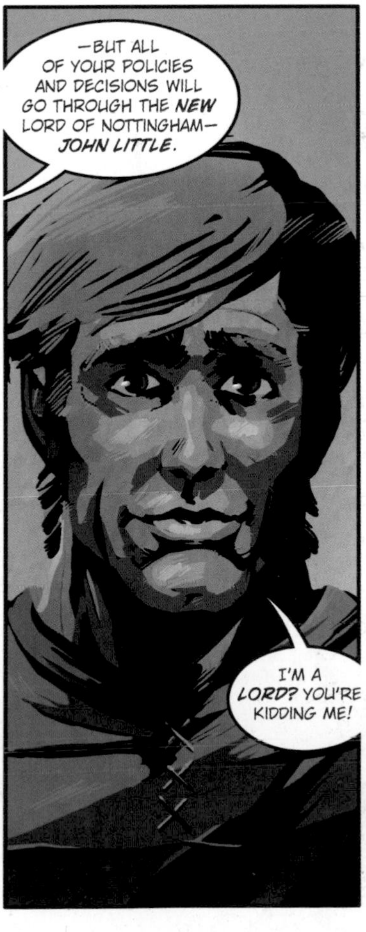
—BUT ALL OF YOUR POLICIES AND DECISIONS WILL GO THROUGH THE NEW LORD OF NOTTINGHAM—JOHN LITTLE.
I'M A LORD? YOU'RE KIDDING ME!

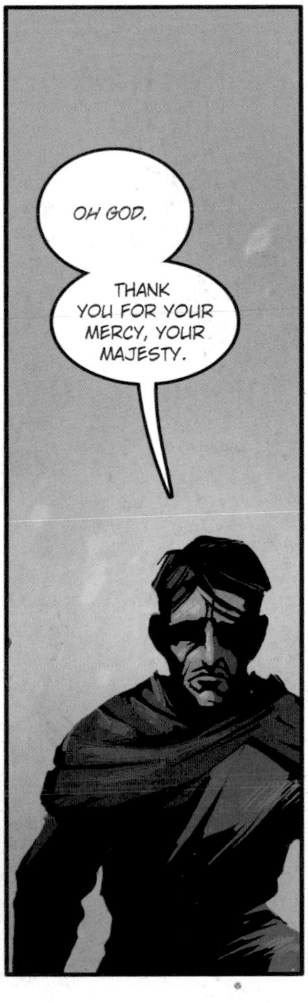
OH GOD.
THANK YOU FOR YOUR MERCY, YOUR MAJESTY.

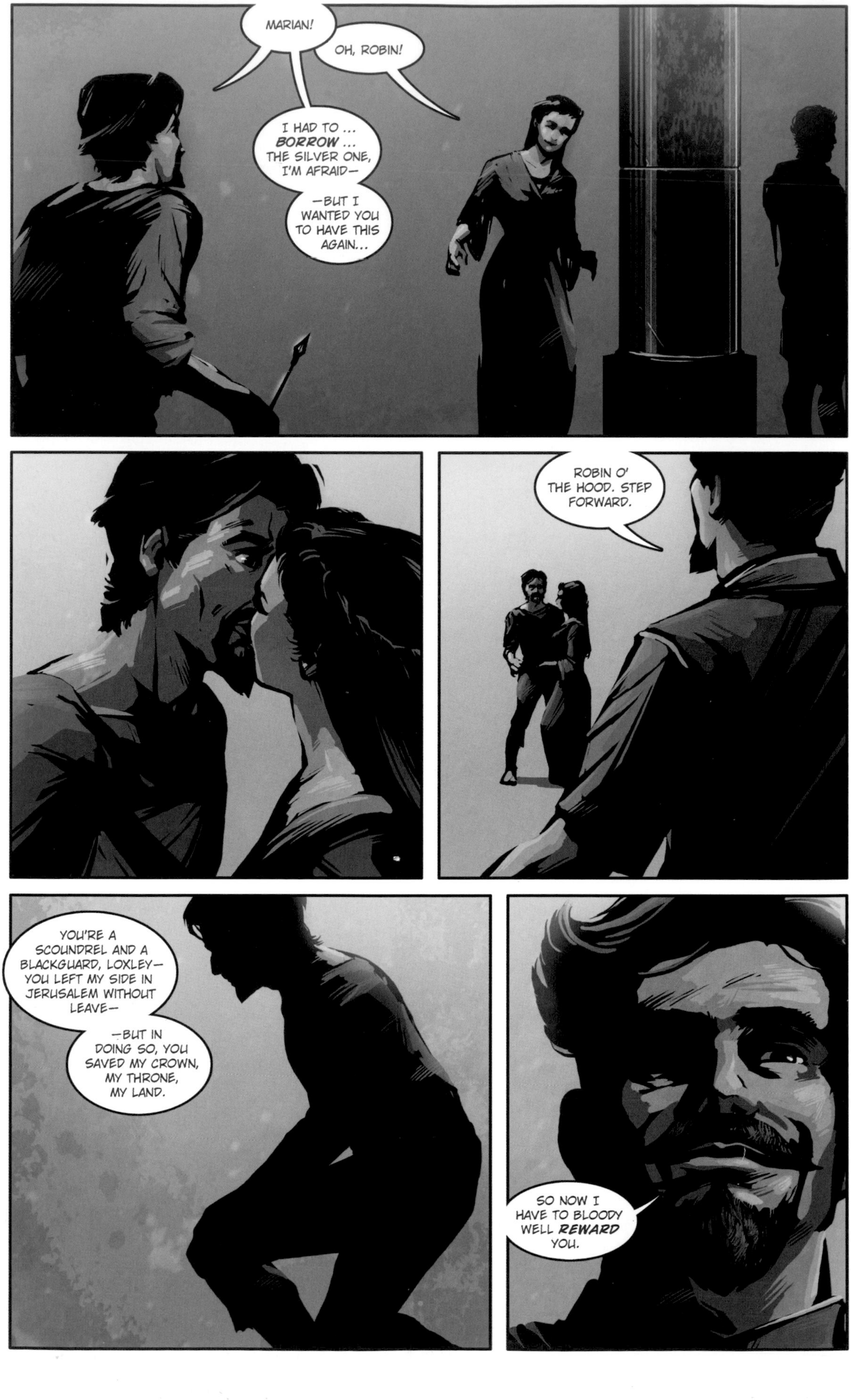
MARIAN!
OH, ROBIN!
I HAD TO ... BORROW ... THE SILVER ONE, I'M AFRAID—
—BUT I WANTED YOU TO HAVE THIS AGAIN...
ROBIN O' THE HOOD. STEP FORWARD.
YOU'RE A SCOUNDREL AND A BLACKGUARD, LOXLEY— YOU LEFT MY SIDE IN JERUSALEM WITHOUT LEAVE—
—BUT IN DOING SO, YOU SAVED MY CROWN, MY THRONE, MY LAND.
SO NOW I HAVE TO BLOODY WELL REWARD YOU.

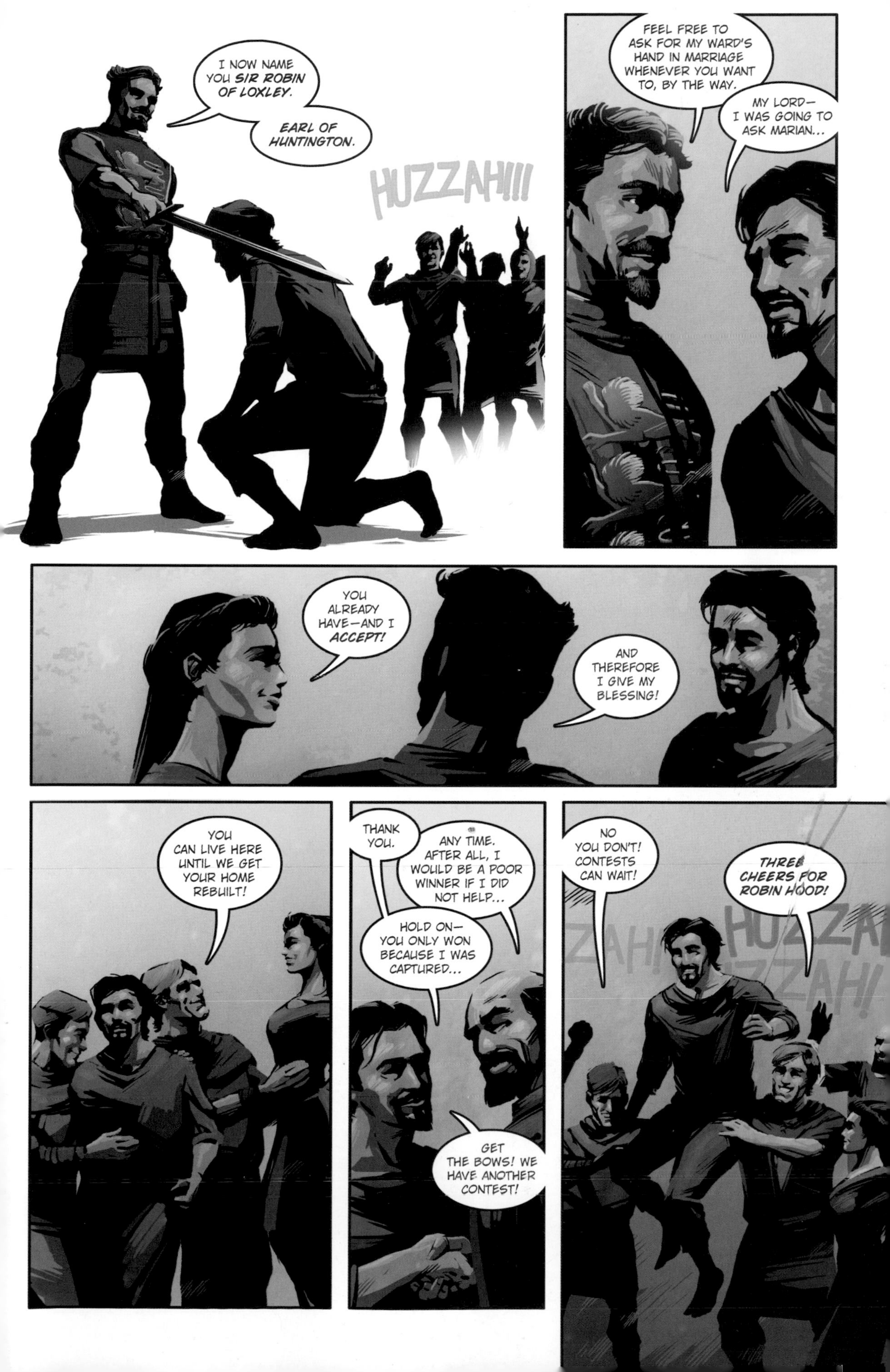
I NOW NAME YOU **SIR ROBIN OF LOXLEY.**
EARL OF HUNTINGTON.
HUZZAH!!!
FEEL FREE TO ASK FOR MY WARD'S HAND IN MARRIAGE WHENEVER YOU WANT TO, BY THE WAY.
MY LORD— I WAS GOING TO ASK MARIAN...
YOU ALREADY HAVE—AND I *ACCEPT!*
AND THEREFORE I GIVE MY BLESSING!
YOU CAN LIVE HERE UNTIL WE GET YOUR HOME REBUILT!
THANK YOU.
ANY TIME. AFTER ALL, I WOULD BE A POOR WINNER IF I DID NOT HELP...
HOLD ON— YOU ONLY WON BECAUSE I WAS CAPTURED...
GET THE BOWS! WE HAVE ANOTHER CONTEST!
NO YOU DON'T! CONTESTS CAN WAIT!
THREE CHEERS FOR ROBIN HOOD!
HUZZAH!

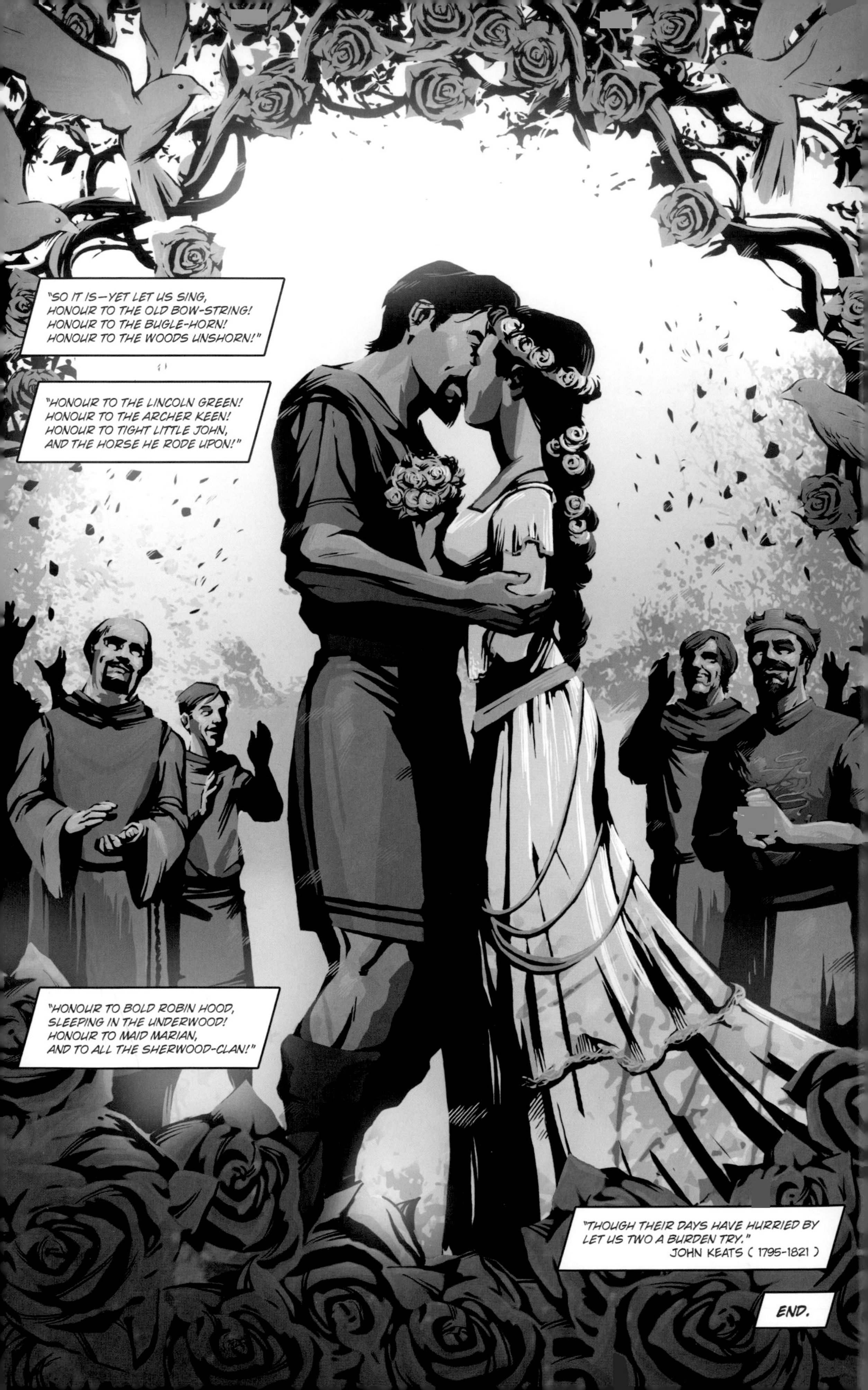
"SO IT IS—YET LET US SING,
HONOUR TO THE OLD BOW-STRING!
HONOUR TO THE BUGLE-HORN!
HONOUR TO THE WOODS UNSHORN!"
"HONOUR TO THE LINCOLN GREEN!
HONOUR TO THE ARCHER KEEN!
HONOUR TO TIGHT LITTLE JOHN,
AND THE HORSE HE RODE UPON!"
"HONOUR TO BOLD ROBIN HOOD,
SLEEPING IN THE UNDERWOOD!
HONOUR TO MAID MARIAN,
AND TO ALL THE SHERWOOD-CLAN!"
"THOUGH THEIR DAYS HAVE HURRIED BY
LET US TWO A BURDEN TRY."
JOHN KEATS (1795-1821)
END.

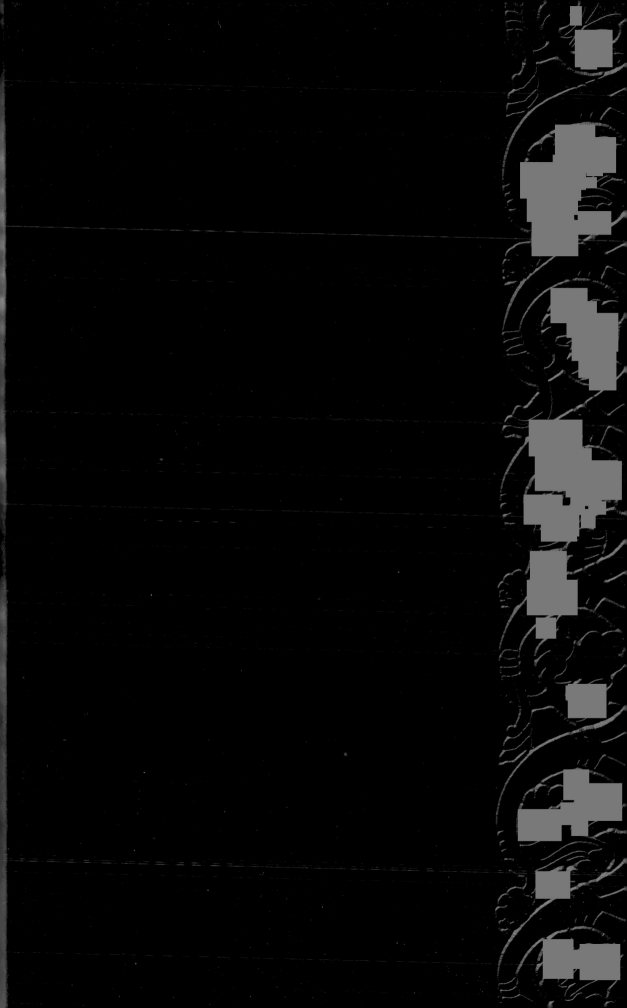

WHO IS ROBIN HOOD?

Who *isn't* Robin Hood? Over nearly 800 years, he's been part of the middle class, a nobleman, a knight, and a peasant. He's been a cutthroat, a rebel, a swashbuckling hero, and an authoritarian busybody. Who is Robin Hood? He's a legend. That means, he's whoever you want him to be. There were several historical Robin or Robert Hoods whose connections to the legend are murky at best.

The earliest surviving Robin Hood ballads are from the last half of the 1400s (the longest of these is *A Gest of Robyn Hode*), and much from those ballads has lasted. Robin's band includes Little John, Will (he of many last names -- Scarlet being the most common), and Much the miller's son. Robin fights the Sheriff of Nottingham. He wins an archery contest. He is pardoned by the king (King Edward in the original ballad; Richard the Lionheart came later). And like most children's book versions of the legend (although few films), he dies at the hands of a wicked prioress.

But that Robin Hood is also different from today's Robin. And while the *Gest*'s final line notes that "Robin did poor men much good," strictly speaking he does not rob from the rich to give to the poor. Also, Robin turns his back on his pardon and the court. He returns to the greenwood to live as an outlaw for another twenty-two years. He does this not because the king did some great wrong, but merely because he is bored and unable to function in normal society. Robin begins and ends the story as an outlaw.

Things changed. Robin Hood settled down and became a bit more respectable.

In 1819, Robin gained new fame as a supporting character (Locksley) in Sir Walter Scott's novel *Ivanhoe*, the most popular book of its day. And a curious thing happened. Robin borrowed the *biography* of the lead character, Sir Wilfred of Ivanhoe. Sir Wilfred was a knight returned from the Crusades, a Saxon who fought against Norman tyranny, and a hero who rescued his lady love from a castle. The original Robin Hood wasn't any of those things, but the TV and film Robin Hood is often *all* of those things.

Modern Robin Hood stories now often begin with him as a nobleman being falsely outlawed and end with his position restored. Being an outlaw is now just a blip— albeit the most interesting one— in Robin's biography. His outlaw career becomes just a temporary reaction to circumstances. But not always. Writers can pick which parts of Robin's long and contradictory biography they want to use.

New elements keep being added. The Robin Hood of 1950s DC Comics fought giant-sized hawks. Those didn't stick around, but the Muslim member of the Merry Men added from the 1980s television show *Robin of Sherwood* has.

It's this sort of change that keeps Robin alive. Robin's not some dusty old tale known to only a dozen academics. He's a *living legend*. The legend survives in every new novel, play, film, TV show, and comic book. Who is Robin Hood? You're holding part of that answer.

Allen W. Wright, October 2008

Allen W. Wright has had a lifelong interest in Robin Hood and in 1997 created a dedicated website www.boldoutlaw.com. He is a renowned expert on the subject of Robin Hood and has been the historical advisor to several major up and coming Robin Hood productions expected over the next couple of years.

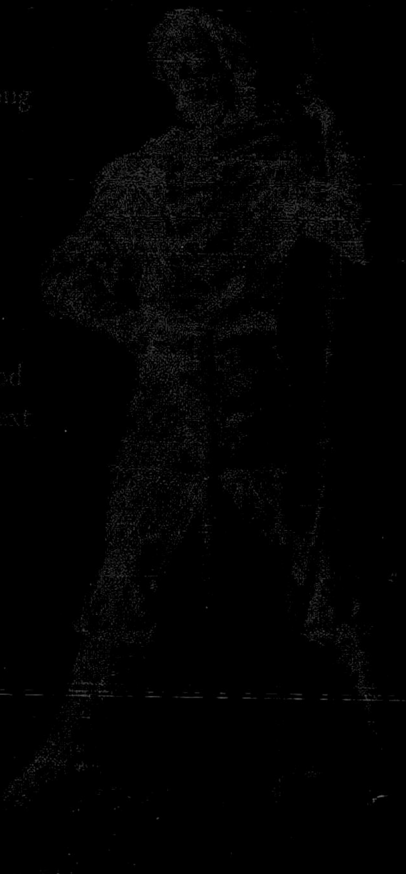

TONY LEE

Tony Lee has been a writer for over twenty years. He started his career mainly in games journalism, but in the early nineties moved into writing for radio, TV, and magazines. Tony spent over ten years working as a feature and scriptwriter, for which he was nominated for and won several awards.

In 2004 Tony turned his attention to comics writing and has since worked for a variety of publishers, including Marvel Comics, IDW Publishing, Markosia, Rebellion, Panini, and Titan. He has contributed to many popular and high-profile properties such as *X-Men*, *Doctor Who*, *Spider-Man*, *Starship Troopers*, *Wallace & Gromit*, and *Shrek*.

In 2008 Tony was nominated in the category for "Best Newcomer Writer" at the prestigious Eagle Awards.

With artist Dan Boultwood, Tony recently created *The Prince of Baghdad*, which has been serialized in the David Fickling / Random House Group's weekly children's comic *The DFC*. And he is the graphic novel adapter of Anthony Horowitz's best-selling *Power of Five* series, published by Walker Books.

SAM HART

Sam Hart is a comic book artist and
magazine illustrator, having worked on
Starship Troopers and *Judge Dredd*, and
for publishers Markosia and DC Comics,
among others. Born in England, he now
lives and teaches comic art in Brazil.

ARTUR FUJITA

Artur Fujita is a Brazilian
illustrator and colorist, of
Japanese descent, who has
worked for major publishers in
Brazil and colored sequential
art for Markosia and Marvel
Comics. He was born and lives
in São Paulo.

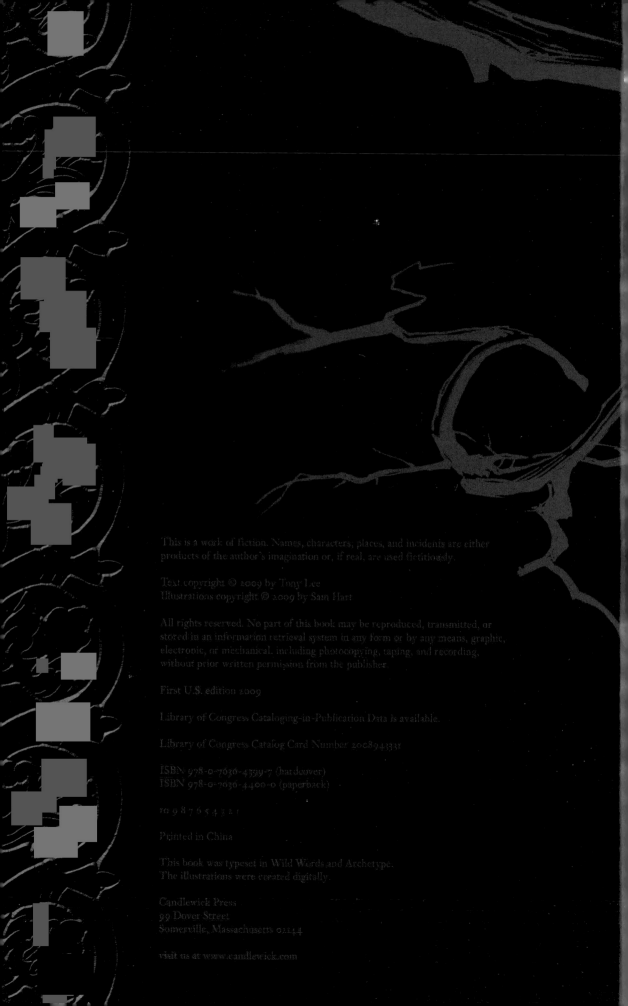

This is a work of fiction. Names, characters, places, and incidents are either
products of the author's imagination or, if real, are used fictitiously.

Text copyright © 2009 by Tony Lee
Illustrations copyright © 2009 by Sam Hart

All rights reserved. No part of this book may be reproduced, transmitted, or
stored in an information retrieval system in any form or by any means, graphic,
electronic, or mechanical, including photocopying, taping, and recording,
without prior written permission from the publisher.

First U.S. edition 2009

Library of Congress Cataloging-in-Publication Data is available.

Library of Congress Catalog Card Number 2008943331

ISBN 978-0-7636-4399-7 (hardcover)
ISBN 978-0-7636-4400-0 (paperback)

10 9 8 7 6 5 4 3 2 1

Printed in China

This book was typeset in Wild Words and Archetype.
The illustrations were created digitally.

Candlewick Press
99 Dover Street
Somerville, Massachusetts 02144

visit us at www.candlewick.com

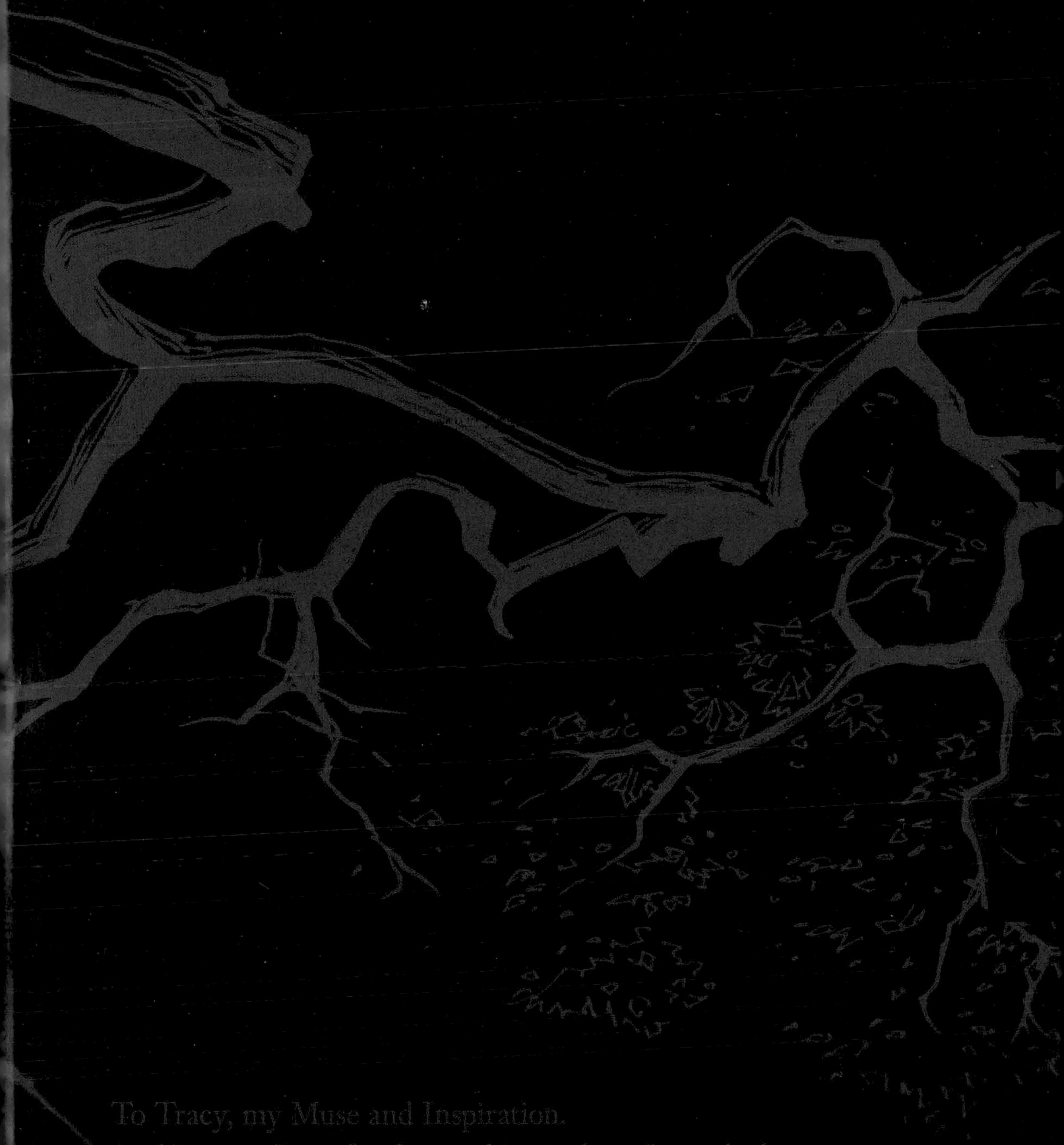

To Tracy, my Muse and Inspiration.
And Doreen Lee, the first and best editor I ever had.
Rest in Peace, Mum. – T.L.

For Mom and Dad. Thanks for having creative lives.
– S.H.

To my family and friends – A.F.

With thanks to Allen W. Wright.

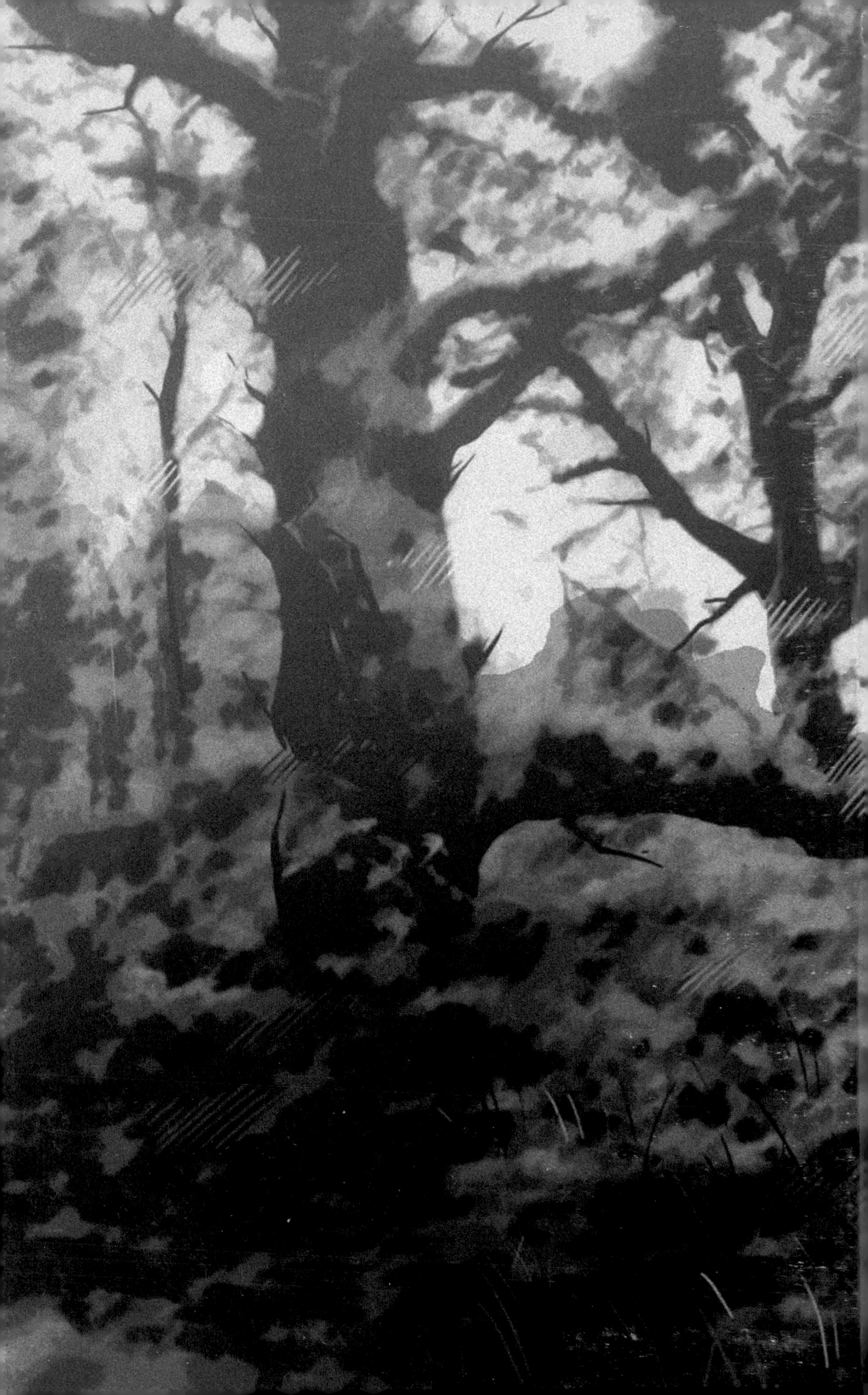